Deadly Bargain

Peter Budetti

This is a work of fiction. All incidents and dialogue, and all characters in the novel, are products of the author's imagination and are not to be construed as real. No one should take offense or be pleased at thinking they are characters in this book because any resemblance to persons living or deceased is entirely coincidental. Nothing in this book is intended to depict actual events or to alter the entirely fictional character of the work.

DEDICATION

*To all the good physicians who believe that
taking care of patients is what matters*

Deadly Bargain

Chapter 1.   Just a stomach ache

"*It's answering,*" whispered Henry Hinkel to the curled-up form of his wife huddled under their bed covers. Hearing a reassuring *click* he blurted into the telephone, "Hello, hello, this is Henry Hinkel, it's my wife, Eleanore. She needs…"

But the automated greeting choked off his plea, ignoring him with programmed indifference:

"*You have reached the offices of Doctors Marlburg and Jefferson. If this is an emergency, hang up immediately and dial 9-1-1. Again, if this is an emergency, hang up immediately and dial 9-1-1. If this is not an emergency, but you believe you are in need of urgent medical care, go to the emergency room at Northeast Suburban Hospital, or to any emergency room or urgent care center of your choosing. If you are not in immediate need of medical care and you are an established patient of Dr. Marlburg or Dr. Jefferson, please call back for an appointment during our office hours, Monday through Friday, 9AM until 4:30PM. If you are not an established patient of Dr. Marlburg or Dr. Jefferson, please note that the practice is accepting very few new patients, and you will need to discuss your request with the office manager during normal office hours. Once again, if this is an emergency, hang up immediately and dial 9-1-1.*"

Henry shook with irritation but suffered through the entire monologue, anticipating an invitation to leave a message after a beep at the end, but heard only a final click, then a dial tone. He threw the telephone handset at its cradle, watching with perverse satisfaction as it bounced onto the bedroom floor.

"Sonofabitch!" he murmured through clenched teeth. "How long have we been seeing Marlburg? What the hell is this now?"

Eleanore stirred at the anger in his voice. "Henry," she said, struggling for the strength to lift her head and speak, "what's wrong? What…what did they say? When will he see me?" The words came slowly, her voice deep and hoarse.

Distracted by the irritating shriek of the off-the-hook signal now blaring from the phone, Henry didn't respond. He bent down, grabbed the handset, then set the phone it in its cradle to end the screeching. He felt trapped, desperate to get help for Eleanore but uncertain how to circumvent the blind loop of their doctor's answering machine. His hands tightened into fists, digging the manicured nails at the end of his small, thick fingers into his soft palms. He could feel his teeth grinding, his normally pale cheeks glowing, his face tightening.

"I got the goddamn answering machine."

"Oh…oh, I'm so…so sorry."

Henry caught himself, realizing that his angry words had increased Eleanore's distress. He strained to bring his voice under control, pursing his lips as he said, "Not you, Honey, I'm not mad at you, I'm the one who should be sorry. It's the damn answering machine, just *'Dial 9-1-1, or go to the ER'* The ER! We must have put two of his kids through Stanford with all the goddamn bills we've paid him over the years, and now we're supposed to go to the damn ER? We're his patients, he's my client, they're our friends, we play golf together – this is the way he treats us?"

Eleanore's response came slowly through shallow breaths. "Please, Henry, don't. It's…it's only a stomach ache, I'll be OK." But the agony in her voice belied her pained assurances.

Henry had just come home from work, never expecting to find his wife suffering in their bed at 6:15 in the evening. Still dressed in his usual dark wool business suit, the slender seventy year-old man looked around their spacious bedroom, a cavernous space with a light spruce cathedral ceiling that soared above them into what had once been the attic. Weekend mornings he and Eleanore would lie in their king-size bed and snuggle under the thick red floral duvet that was now a rumpled mass covering the lump of her body. On the wall above their heads was a memento of happier times, a poster-sized print of an endless field of bright red poppies she had photographed in the fields of Tuscany. Mutt-and-Jeff matching birch dressers stood off to one side, her long, low one with her dressing mirror facing them, his taller, slender one with six drawers standing silently nearby.

The bedroom had her smell, a faint aroma of her skin creams and hairsprays, of the lavender perfume she always used.

Henry removed his suit coat and tie and draped them carefully on the valet stand next to his side of their bed. He dragged the upholstered bench from the foot of the bed up next to where Eleanore lay so he could sit as close as possible to her. Just then his eyes were drawn to the large mirror above her dresser. He shivered, feeling his heart skip several beats at the stark image in the reflection: a shriveled old woman enduring unthinkable misery. The woman he loved, the woman he had been with for more than half his life, lay on her left side in a fetal position, clutching an oversized pillow with both arms, her right knee all but drawn up to her chest. The silhouette of her face, barely visible above the top of the bedcovers, looked far older than her sixty-eight years, her eyes sunken into the creases of pale skin, her long auburn hair splayed in matted clumps across her head and onto the pillow. She lay so still that the reflection might have been a photo of a crime scene with a murder victim sprawled across a bed. The huge bedroom seemed to close in on him as he sat on the bench next to his pained wife.

"It isn't OK, and you're not OK." Again he cringed at the harshness in his words and struggled to sound more like the way he felt — sympathetic, supportive, loving. Softening his voice he said, "You've had stomach aches plenty before, Honey, this is different. You don't look good, you're in real pain."

"It might just be cramps. It…" Her attempt to speak was cut off by several short, reflexive gasps. "*Ah-ah-ah,*" she moaned as her right hand grasped her lower belly.

For much of the previous twenty years Henry might have given in to the urge to tease Eleanore that her long, slow menopause had put an end to her menstrual cramps, but not now, this was no time for humor. "It's not cramps, not any cramps like you ever had, anyway. I think we should go to the ER."

"No…please Henry, no. I don't…want to move. I…"

Her words were cut short by a wave of nausea. Covering her mouth with one hand she gurgled, "*towel….*"

Henry jumped from the bench and hurried into their master bathroom, eyeing the royal blue towels and wash cloths neatly stacked on the stainless steel shelves. In his haste he grabbed a hand towel, not realizing until he had slipped it under her head that it was far too small to absorb a real blast of vomit. Her body wrenched into spasm but produced only a small puddle of drool and greenish puke that pooled harmlessly on the little cloth. He rushed back to the bathroom, threw the stained hand towel into the bathtub and snatched a handful of large bath towels and a stainless steel wastebasket. He returned to his wife's side, set the trash can on the floor next to the bed and tossed the pile of clean towels nearby.

"Sweetheart, you really should get to a doctor. Northeast Suburban isn't that far, we can get there in twenty minutes."

"Please, no, no, Henry. Let me be, please."

Henry was torn between aggravating his wife's agony by forcing her to go the hospital or agreeing to wait out her misery to an uncertain end. Having watched her bear up through three deliveries, one time in labor for over twenty-four hours, he had admired her high tolerance for pain. And he could see that moving her would not be easy. Beyond the agony she would have to endure, he knew she would insist on being presentable before going out in public. No matter the pain she would want to attend to her appearance, put on some real clothes, comb the tangles out of her hair, brush her teeth and gargle away the foul smell of vomit from her breath. All the time resisting his efforts to help.

And if he did manage to get her out of the house, where would he take her? If he could get through to Marlburg she might agree to go to his office, but she would struggle to avoid the Northeast Suburban ER at all costs. The memory of their last trip there was still too troubling to her, however many years ago that had been. Their eldest son, Roger, had been hit by a baseball that afternoon and by ten in the evening was moaning in pain from such a terrible headache that they packed him off to the ER. Eight hours and four thousand dollars later they had a diagnosis: everything was fine, just a headache, no skull fracture, not the potentially fatal subdural hematoma the ER doctor had cautioned them about in fearsome detail. But the relief they felt at learning that their son was not about to die had not overcome the strain of their ordeal, the anguished hours trying to console the restless child amid the blare of incoming ambulances, the horrific sight of countless accident victims and heart attack patients being wheeled wildly past them, the hapless mass of disheveled elderly patients seemingly resigned to a lengthy Purgatory of indifference to their plight. Then the endless paperwork Eleanore had struggled with for months to make sure their insurance would cover at least most of the bills.

No, Henry could not face subjecting her to another experience with that place, especially now that she was in such pain herself.

She shouldn't have to go to the ER anyway, we should be able to get Tony Marlburg to see her, Goddammit, he swore to himself.

Henry Hinkel went back into the bathroom, ran cold water over a royal blue washcloth, wrung it out, then paused, feeling the strain of the moment. He sighed and turned the cold water back on and drenched his face with the washcloth. Then he dried off, rinsed and wrung the washcloth again, and went back to his wife, placing the moist pad gently on her forehead.

Eleanore said nothing, but managed a small smile when she felt the cool washcloth. Henry acquiesced. He would hold off for now just as she wished. They could wait, at least for a few more hours.

But what was he waiting for? For her to die? To scream out in unbearable pain? She didn't want to move, that much he could appreciate, but how much longer could he let her suffer? Henry Hinkel resolved that if she didn't get better soon he would carry her to the ER whether she consented or not.

The hours dragged on. At 10PM she had a bad spell, her body tensing in spasms of pain for several long minutes. He slipped his arms under her to lift her out of the bed, intending to carry her to the ER, but she gasped in pain from the first slight movement.

"Stop, Honey, please stop, don't…don't touch. It's…not that bad, please."

Eleanore's struggle to get even those few words out was so wrenching he relaxed his arms and withdrew them from under her tense body. Desperate to be helpful he retreated to the bathroom for another cool washcloth and stared at the pile of wet washcloths and towels in the bathtub that chronicled their evening. Her retching had slowed, then ceased after he had emptied vomit from the stainless steel wastebasket into the toilet three or four times. But he kept the wastebasket at the bedside, just in case.

Henry wondered what the hell ever happened to doctors who made house calls? If Marlburg had come over last evening on his way home, at least Henry and Eleanore would know what was going on. Now his physician friend just clocks in and clocks out like an assembly line worker, leaving all his compassion at the office. No house calls, no speaking with patients after working hours, just *'Dial*

9-1-1 and go to the goddamn ER.' He agonized over what he would do if Eleanore would not go to the ER. Would they sit around and wonder whether she was dying or just having a rough night? Could she stand it? Could he?

The night crawled onward, minutes seeming to last for hours. Eleanore barely moved, making no sounds other than an occasional series of shallow, labored breaths. She had another bad spell around 2AM. Again Henry prepared to cart her off, but again she pleaded with him to let her stay where she was. At last it was 8AM, time, Henry thought, to try dialing the offices of Doctors Marlburg and Jefferson. But after listening to the first few words of the recording again, he threw the phone down and waited until 9 when the official office hours were supposed to begin. Getting busy signal after busy signal, he punched the redial button on the phone repeatedly until a voice finally answered, a voice so juvenile he briefly thought he had reached a wrong number.

"Medical offices of Doctors Marlburg and Jefferson. This is Jennifer. May I help you?"

"This is Henry Hinkel. My wife, Eleanore, needs to see Dr. Marlburg."

"Is she an established patient of Dr. Marlburg? He is taking very few new patients."

"She's been his patient for over twenty years," he responded, straining to control his impatience at having to convince some child named Jennifer of the urgency of Eleanore's plight. "She needs to see him," he repeated.

"He has an opening at 3:30 next Wednesday, is that convenient?"

"She needs to see him today, right away."

"I'm sorry he's all booked today. *If this is an emergency, you should hang up immediately and dial 9-1-1. If this is not an emergency, but you believe you are in need of urgent medical care,...*"

Henry Hinkel recognized the voice parroting the very words from the office answering machine again, but this time it was a person talking, not a recording. Then he realized that she was reading from a script, she had been told to use exactly those words, and to say the same thing to every caller she was turning away. He cursed to himself that some damn lawyer had probably told Marlburg and Jefferson to do things this way.

"Stop, please," he interrupted her monologue, "I know what you're saying, but we need to get in to see Dr. Marlburg."

The young female voice continued, "*…go to the emergency room at Northeast Suburban Hospital, or to any emergency room or urgent care center of your choosing.*"

Henry Hinkel was shaking, feeling he was at his breaking point, but knew he had to get through this for his wife's sake. No sleep, a wife in agony, now a yapping puppy of a guard dog deaf to his pleas refusing them entry into the doctor's presence. Straining to speak calmly he said, "Please tell Dr. Marlburg that Eleanore Hinkel needs to see him today."

"He's with a patient. I am not supposed to interrupt him when he is with a patient."

"He won't mind. We're not just patients, we're friends, we have been friends and patients for many years." Finally, the thought came: "He'll be more upset if you *don't* interrupt him when he finds out it was me."

There was silence on the line for a few seconds. Then, "I'll check with his nurse. Please hold."

Normally Henry Hinkel loved Mozart, but just now the strains of *Eine kleine Nachtmusik* coming across the phone line grated on him relentlessly for the nearly five minutes he was on hold. When the phone went silent he thought he had been disconnected, that Jennifer had hung up on him. As he started to flush with anger he heard a click and a different voice.

"Mr. Hinkel? This is Dr. Marlburg's nurse, Stephanie Gardiner. How are you?"

"It's not me, it's my wife. Oh, sorry…hello, Mrs. Gardiner. Thanks for coming on the line. Eleanore's had a rough night, she has terrible stomach pains and has been curled up in bed throwing up all night."

"Did you go to the ER?"

"No, she refuses to let me take her there. She only wants to see Tony…Dr. Marlburg."

"How about any intake? Has she had anything to eat or drink?"

"No, she's been nauseated and vomiting, and she won't even take water."

"Fever?"

"She feels a little warm, but she's not burning up. Mostly, it's the pain and nausea and all the retching."

"How long has this been going on?"

"I'm not sure, but at least since before I came home from work yesterday, because I found her in bed like this a little after six. I sat up with her all night, and she isn't getting any better."

"Please hold on, I'll be right back."

More *Eine kleine Nachtmusik*, but this time it was mercifully brief, maybe a minute at most.

"Dr. Marlburg says he can squeeze Mrs. Hinkel in between patients. There might be a lull about 10AM if a couple of follow-up visits go quickly. Can you be here by then?"

"We'll be right over, as soon as I get her dressed." Forcing himself to sound gracious, he added, "Thank you very much, Mrs. Gardiner."

Henry hung up the phone and turned to his wife. "Honey, Tony Marlburg can see you soon. I need to get you up and dressed, we have to get going."

He was moved to tears by the pure anguish on her face as she nodded, released her grasp on the huge pillow, and started to push off the bed covers and twist herself up into a sitting position. But she fell back, crying, *"Ah, ah, Henry, I…I can't."* He put one arm behind her and half-lifted her out of bed, then held her upright as they shuffled together into the bathroom. He helped her out of her nightgown, assisted her with a brief sponge bath, brushed her hair with smooth, gentle strokes, then retrieved the clothes she asked for and eased her into them with a loving, delicate touch.

"Hold on," he said, as he led her to the top of the stairs, "this will be the difficult part." Supporting her with one arm around her waist and one hand grasping tight on the railing, he led her downstairs step by painful step, then out the side door and into their car. He drove slowly, cautiously, dreading any bumps that would send a surge of pain through her, anxious to avoid a sudden stop that would tighten her seatbelt against her belly.

The morning was cold and misty, exacerbating Henry's already dreary mood. To his great relief, Eleanore seemed to tolerate the drive and the short ride in the elevator. He cheered up somewhat as they arrived at Tony Marlburg's office well ahead of the appointed time, joining a short queue of patients at the sign-in desk about 9:45 AM. A young woman greeted the new arrivals from behind a low counter that separated the reception area from the clerical work space and examination rooms. Watching and listening to her speak to patients as though she were selling them popcorn at a movie theater, Henry realized that this was Jennifer. The insufferable voice of the answering-machine and telephone was no longer disembodied, it now had a face and a body.

The young woman had a streak of purple running through her short black hair, and what Henry thought was a piece of glitter stuck to her nose. As he drew closer he realized she had a tiny jewel on a post through her pierced right nostril. He struggled to suppress both his disdain and his anger, to sound pleasant as he said, "Hello. This is Mrs. Eleanore Hinkel. She has an appointment to see Dr. Marlburg at 10."

"Hi," responded the familiar squeaky voice. "Photo I.D. and insurance card, please." After she made a Xerox copy of Eleanore's credentials, Jennifer handed Henry a small clipboard with a stack of forms and a pen attached, saying, "Medical history and consent forms. She should sign wherever it says patient. At the red X's."

"You should have all of those on file already," said Henry, feeling his chest tighten at yet another roadblock.

"More than a year, gotta be updated."

"It's OK, Henry," said Eleanore softly, patting him on his left arm. As Henry turned toward his wife he realized she couldn't remain standing much longer even with his support. He took the clipboard from Jennifer and led Eleanore toward the corner of the bright office where he had spotted two empty seats.

The waiting room was spacious and well-appointed, with eight upholstered arms chairs and two plush couches. Over Jennifer's shoulder Henry could see a panorama of the city through the large picture windows that framed the corner office. As Eleanore dutifully entered her medical information on the forms, Henry let his mind drift from his wife's plight. He thought how buying this office building years ago had proved to be a good investment for Tony Marlburg, an investment Henry had helped arrange.

When Eleanore finished filling out the papers, Henry took the clipboard up to Jennifer. "It's nearly ten," he said. "Will it be long before she can see Tony…Dr. Marlburg?"

"Doctor's running a little behind this morning. We'll call her as soon as he's ready for her."

Henry returned to his seat, took Eleanore's hand, and resigned himself to this phase of their ordeal. At least they weren't in that ER. He marveled at how his wife managed to maintain her dignity, bearing her pain and personal discomfort so gracefully as they waited their turn. Soon they would know what was wrong. But once he heard the scheduled patients grumble that they had been kept waiting well past their appointed times he knew they could be in for a long delay. Minutes dragged into quarter-hours, then half-hours, then an hour and more. As the morning crawled by, Henry wondered how much longer either of them could stand this. Eleanore, semi-upright on the chair next to him, suffering silently under a shawl he had brought from home. He, trying to reassure and comfort her while the suppressed anger seethed inside him.

After nearly two hours they were at last greeted by Nurse Gardiner, a slender middle-aged woman whose gray hair seemed incongruous with her youthful pastel scrubs. In a pleasant voice but without a smile she said, "Hello Mr. and Mrs. Hinkel. Sorry about the wait, we're a bit behind this morning. Follow me, please." She led the couple into the examining room and pulled a screen between Henry and his wife, then helped Eleanore undress and wrap herself with a flimsy pale green medical gown. The nurse's routine professional gesture of blocking Henry's view to maintain Eleanore's privacy struck Henry as somewhat comical, since only a few hours earlier he had been washing and drying that familiar naked body in her sponge bath.

At last Nurse Gardiner pulled back the screen, saying to Eleanore, "Have a seat on the examination table, please." The long black leather table was covered with white paper that crinkled as Eleanore sat down. The nurse took Eleanore's temperature with a gadget Henry had not seen before, one that looked like an otoscope for examining ears, but Nurse Gardiner didn't look into it, just put it into Eleanore's ear for a few seconds until it beeped like a microwave oven. She said, "A little warm, Dear, one hundred one point two," as she recorded the numbers on Eleanore's chart. Then the nurse measured her blood pressure with an automatic machine that also beeped when it was done. "125 over 76," she said, reading the device's numeric screen, "and pulse 88." She watched Eleanore breathe briefly, then noted a respiratory rate of 20 per minute. When she was finished, she smiled and said, "Dr. Marlburg will be with you soon, he's just finishing with a patient now."

But it was nearly another half-hour later, fifteen minutes after noon, when Dr. Anthony Marlburg stepped into the examining room. A bit shorter and paunchier than Henry Hinkel but about the same age, he wore a long white coat and had his professional game face on, firmly establishing a partition between physician and patient. This was business, not a meeting between old friends, not a time to chat about golf or exchange pleasantries. Not even a handshake, just a quick nod of greeting as he walked to the small office sink and began scrubbing his hands. Turning his head in their direction as he washed up, he said, "Hi Eleanore, Henry. Sorry to keep you waiting. Busy morning."

Henry Hinkel was smothering his thoughts. He wanted to ask his friend what kind of doctor he had turned into, what had happened to make him like this, turning cold to patients who were friends, making them beg to see him. But he bit his tongue, swallowed hard, and only replied deferentially, saying "That's OK, Tony, thanks so much for squeezing us in. Eleanore's had kind of a rough night."

Eleanore had drawn her knees up on the table, but now Tony Marlburg walked to her right side and said, "Please, can you extend your legs?" She did so with an effort that brought tears to her eyes. Seeing the strain on her pale face Marlburg said, "You look like you're under the weather, Eleanore. What's up?"

"My stomach hurts, I can't keep anything down."

Henry was surprised by the strength of his wife's words – she was summoning some deep reserve to keep up whatever dignity, whatever self-control, she had left. She was speaking slowly but clearly, not loud but not faltering, as composed as if she were describing a problem with her car to a mechanic.

"When did this start?"

"Yesterday morning."

"It was so sudden, she was fine when I went to work," Henry Hinkel added.

Through her pain, Eleanore spoke apologetically, straining to correct her husband without offending him. "Not really, Honey. Sorry, I didn't tell you, but I felt queasy even then, like I had heartburn. I...I didn't want to worry you."

Henry bit his lip and remained silent as Marlburg returned to his questioning.

"Heartburn? Where was the pain?"

"Here," Eleanore said, making small circles with her hand about midway between the bottom of her sternum and her belly button, "it was here at first."

"Sharp? Dull? How would you describe that pain?"

"At first, dull. Like bad heartburn."

"Now?"

"Sharp, bad, worse than cramps."

"Same place?"

"No, more down here," she responded, pointing to her lower right side.

"You say you've been vomiting. Any diarrhea or other bowel movements?"

"Just vomiting, especially last night."

"Fever? You have a little bit of a temperature now."

"Not much, I took it a couple of times," Henry Hinkel interrupted, remembering how he had to put his reading glasses on and rotate their old-fashioned mercury-bulb thermometer under a bright light to see the thin silver streak and the tiny etched numbers. "Never up to 102."

"Have you tried to eat or drink anything?"

"No, nothing, I just can't."

"She's really just been in bed the whole time, Tony."

"OK, let's have a look."

Tony Marlburg looked Eleanore over quickly, pulling down her lower eyelids to scan the reddened whites of her eyes, then reaching out with both his hands and lightly supporting her hands palms-down on his so that he could glance at her skin and gauge the color of her nail-beds. He helped Eleanore lean forward, opened the back of her gown, and placed a stethoscope on her bare back, as he said, "Now, breathe deeply." He repeated this in each quadrant of her back, then stowed the stethoscope in a large pocket on the front of his white coat and said, "Chest is clear. Now, let's have you lie down, please."

Marlburg supported her back with his left arm and helped her recline, saying in a soothing, professional voice, "Easy does it, there, Eleanore." After easing her head down onto a paper-clad pillow, he said, "Good girl, well done." In a well-practiced gesture he used one hand to raise the gown up to just below her breasts while his other hand pulled a green paper sheet up to cover her groin, leaving only her belly exposed. Retrieving his stethoscope he listened intently to her abdomen, then percussed the area very gently. Her belly was rigid. He asked, "Please relax if you can," but the tension in her muscles did not abate. He stopped tapping and laid his hands flat on her abdomen.

Eleanore was struck by how soft and smooth Marlburg's hands were, as gentle as the touch of a loving parent on a sick child, despite his somewhat curt manner with his two old friends. He felt the different quadrants of her belly, his left hand resting lightly on top of his right hand. As his fingers explored the lower right area, Eleanore recoiled with a gasp.

"That painful, huh?" Marlburg asked mechanically in response to her evident pain. "Sorry."

Marlburg stepped back, walked over to the small sink, squirted a few dabs of antibacterial soap on his hands, and washed thoroughly a second time. Even through her pain the thought crossed Eleanore's mind that it was the endless hand washings that kept his hands so soft.

Turning so that he could address both Eleanore and Henry he said, "You have what we call an acute abdomen – there is a blockage in the intestines that requires surgery. I believe the most likely diagnosis is appendicitis, but there are many other possibilities. And, with women, we always must consider a tubal or ovarian problem."

"What now?" intervened Henry, his voice breaking as the seriousness of his wife's illness began to set in.

"I will order some lab work: a complete blood count to check for signs of infection or bleeding, and an abdominal sonogram and X-rays to see if there's anything that shows up. Mostly, we need to get her to a surgeon. This is clearly something that requires a surgeon to decide on the course of action."

"How do we find a surgeon?"

"I'll take care of that. I have good relationships with several surgeons that I refer patients to. I'll call and see if the one I have in mind is free today."

"Who is that?"

"Dr. McDonald, Dr. Matthew McDonald. I've been sending patients to him ever since I went into practice. If he's available, you'll see why – he's very good with patients, which unfortunately I can't say for all my surgery colleagues. You'll like Dr. McDonald."

Good with patients — we'll see what that means, Henry thought. But all he said was "Thank you so much, Tony."

Almost simultaneously Eleanore said, "Thank you, Dr. Marlburg, thank you."

"You're welcome, that's what I'm here for, after all. Now, let's get going. I'll call Dr. McDonald right away."

Chapter 2.   Acute abdomen

"Thank you so much for seeing us on such short notice, Dr. McDonald. Eleanore has been in a great deal of pain, and it's hard for her to go on much longer like this."

Henry Hinkel was grateful on two counts: not only had the surgeon agreed to see Eleanore immediately, but they had been ushered directly into his examining room after only the briefest of preliminaries at the reception desk. In this office there was a sense of urgency, of evident concern that the patient was getting worse by the minute.

"That is why I am here, Henry. A surgeon must always be available when someone needs his services. Now, Eleanore, let's take a look." Even at their first meeting, McDonald called all patients and family members by their given names, feeling no impropriety, never imagining that his familiar tone might be seen as presumptuous.

To Henry and Eleanore Hinkel, Matthew McDonald embodied the classic image of a distinguished surgeon. The patrician inflection of the man's deep voice conveyed ultimate confidence, a masterful sense of control. Tall, over six-foot-two, and as slender as a competitive skier or runner, he stood much straighter than most men in their late fifties. His impressive body was capped by a striking mane of silver-white hair that billowed into great waves, frozen as perfectly in place as whitecaps caught breaking on the shore in a still photograph. He wore an exceptionally long white coat that further enhanced the larger-than-life impression. The man exuded such poise and confidence the Hinkels knew they were in the care of an extraordinary surgeon just by being in his presence.

McDonald moved gracefully to Eleanore Hinkel's right side, listened briefly to her chest and abdomen with his stethoscope, then started palpating her belly. As his right hand pushed lightly in the area between her belly button and right hip, she recoiled from his touch. Henry Hinkel thought she had reacted even more quickly than when Tony Marlburg had pressed on that same area.

"Now, please, a quick bi-manual exam."

McDonald slipped a latex-free nitrile glove on his right hand, lubricated it with a glob of gel, then inserted one finger into her rectum and gently squeezed down with his left hand on the sensitive area of her abdomen, palpating the contents from above and below to get a three-dimensional feel for the location of her pain. As quickly as he began, he was finished, stepping away from the examining table, removing his glove and tossing it into the trash receptacle near the sink.

"No doubt about it, Eleanore, you have acute appendicitis. Your white blood count and temperature are moderately elevated from the inflammation in your belly. The ultrasound and X-rays show no other problems. You need an operation."

"When, Dr. McDonald? When can you operate?" asked Henry.

"Right away, as soon as we can get into the surgical facility. That's the most important thing about appendicitis, acting quickly."

"What is it, what's going on? I mean, we've heard about appendicitis all our lives, but I don't think I really understand what it is."

"Most people are exactly that way, Henry. No problem, I am happy to explain. You see, the appendix is called '*the appendix*' precisely because that's what it is — an extra piece of intestine that comes off the side of the large intestine. It's a little *cul de sac*, a blind pouch hanging there like an empty little balloon, usually about the size of your little finger. It doesn't go anywhere or do anything useful that we know of. So far, so good?"

Henry Hinkel nodded. Eleanore was doing her best to concentrate through the pain.

"OK. So the appendix is useless because it's too small to help digest any food, but it's also dangerous because things can get trapped inside it. A seed or something gets stuck inside the appendix and inflames the surrounding tissue. Once that happens, the opening to the appendix swells up tight and the blood supply to the appendix gets cut off by the swollen tissue, so the appendix starts to choke off and die."

"So…once it starts to die, it's dangerous?"

"Exactly. If we don't get that thing out, it will start to disintegrate and leak very foul stuff from Eleanore's intestines into her belly. That's what we call a perforated appendix, a ruptured appendix, and that can be quite a problem. We want to avoid that happening."

"Is the operation dangerous? Could she take pain killers or antibiotics or something, and wait instead?"

"Any operation has its risks, but here the risks of not operating are far greater. We need to act quickly."

"OK, that's enough, we get it. Thank you again, Dr. McDonald, thank you so much."

"No problem, Henry. And don't you worry, Eleanore, you'll be fine. I've done hundreds of appendectomies."

***

"She's under, go ahead, McDonald."

The anesthesiologist's voice came from behind the short curtain above Eleanore Hinkel's neck that divided her body into two work areas: head, neck and arms for the anesthesiologist seated at one end, torso to toes for the surgeon standing at her side. Sterile sheets above and below her belly covered her breasts and the lower part of her body, leaving exposed the abdomen that the surgical Physician Assistant, Jorge Edmond, had scrubbed and prepped for the surgery.

"This should be quick," McDonald said to the anesthesiologist, but did not even glance at Jorge Edmond, a big man in surgical scrubs, paper cap and mask who stood directly opposite him.

McDonald made three small incisions through the skin over Eleanore Hinkel's belly. He marveled silently how easy it was to do surgery through a laparoscope. No need to open up her belly, just a few small incisions through which he would thread his miniaturized instruments. In and out in less than an hour, no problem, no big scar. He had no idea how someone had figured out how to bend images around corners in a fiber-optic tube, and he didn't care. It was quick and easy, that was all he needed to know.

McDonald inserted the flexible laparoscope and looked inside Eleanore Hinkel's abdomen. Peering through a binocular eyepiece he had a crystal-clear three-dimensional view of her intestines. As he advanced the tube he pumped in puffs of air to push the tissue away from the lens at the front end of the scope, presenting him with an unobstructed view of her large intestine. Maneuvering the tube past healthy folds of bowel, he came upon the dark, swollen appendix that protruded ominously off of the first section of the large intestine. With the distended tubular mass in clear sight he lassoed the swollen appendix with a loop of suture then pulled the delicate line tight into a surgical knot. He clamped off the trapped finger of tissue and cut the useless, engorged appendage free from the tied-off stump of healthy tissue left behind on the surface of the intestine. He maneuvered the severed appendix into a small specimen bag as though he were landing a tiny hooked fish with a miniature net, then removed the encased tissue in its carrier from Eleanore Hinkel's belly and dropped the sack and its contents into a kidney-shaped stainless steel bowl on the table next to his left arm.

McDonald examined the circular stump of tissue that puckered up and protruded slightly from the wall of the large intestine where he had severed the appendix. The pinpoint central opening of the ring of tissue appeared to be sealed off by the suture, preventing fecal material from seeping into the woman's abdomen from her bowel. Perfect, he thought, a nice, clean separation, leaving only a healthy base of tissue hermetically sealed off. He would be finished in only a few minutes.

But just as he was congratulating himself, he gasped. A trickle of fecal juices was beginning to ooze out of the center of the circular stump of bowel into Eleanore Hinkel's belly, like the first flow of lava dribbling over the lip of a volcano about to erupt. His right hand jerked involuntarily, his whole body twisted as he watched the horror unfolding in front of his eyes. He bent closer, clenched his left hand into a fist, and started pounding on the side of his sterile gown. He mumbled, "Goddamn it! Not again, goddamn it!"

Bent over to watch the surgery through an auxiliary eyepiece on the fiber optic laparoscope, Jorge Edmond had seen the crisis developing inside Eleanore Hinkel. Hearing the surgeon's gasp and curses, Jorge pulled his head back from the eyepiece, ready to help McDonald respond to the catastrophe they had just witnessed. He looked at the surgeon and was startled to see him twist and pummel his gown with his fist. Only a sliver of McDonald's face was exposed between the paper hood covering his hair and the surgical mask over his nose and mouth, but that was enough for Jorge to see the grimace that furrowed the surgeon's exposed forehead and squeezed the corners of his eyes tight. The man had been startled, he had seen his work go awry. And so had Jorge.

"Is something wrong, Dr. McDonald?" Jorge asked politely, suppressing the urge to cry out, *'Dios mío, qué cosa tan terrible!'*

"No! Nothing's wrong," McDonald barked, irritated by the indignity of being challenged by a surgical assistant, especially one with a foreign accent. "Quiet, man, you're distracting me."

McDonald watched in desperation at the stream of deadly liquid flowing into Eleanore Hinkel's belly. He strained to recover his composure as he struggled to snare the short, open stump with the clamp. If he couldn't secure the leaky stump he would have to open her belly and remove a section of her intestine. He grasped the tissue and passed another loop of suture thread over the instrument and pulled it into a second knot over the stump. But to his horror he saw this knot also give way, releasing an ever-increasing flow of fecal material into the woman.

"Hand me an endostapler," he yelled to Jorge.

Always prepared with whatever supplies the surgeon might ask for, Jorge broke the seal on the delicate instrument's sterile wrap and handed it to McDonald. The shaken surgeon took the tool brusquely from Jorge, passed the business end through one of the incisions in Eleanore Hinkel's abdominal wall, and maneuvered it toward the gushing appendiceal stump. He placed a titanium clip on the tissue, hoping against hope this would finally stop the flow. A minute passed, then another, as McDonald watched nervously. At last he was satisfied that the wall of her bowel was sealed tight by the staple.

But the damage had been done. The caustic intestinal juices packed with billions of bacteria from her bowel had been unleashed to attack everything in her abdomen, kill off the healthy tissues, trigger infections and abscesses that would threaten her life. He had to act quickly, do whatever he could to clean up the mess, wash out as much of the toxic liquid as possible.

And he needed cover, he must say something to explain away the horrendous problems that would surely ensue.

"Get me the saline irrigation," he barked. "We need to irrigate the area and begin high-dose antibiotics." McDonald rinsed the area inside Eleanore Hinkel's abdomen with copious amounts of sterile saline solution, then ran several soft rubber tubes through her skin to serve as drains for the expected seepage. As he worked, the lie came automatically to his lips: "The appendix was already ruptured, her belly was contaminated. The tissue was too friable for the knots, so I added the staple to be sure. Too bad she didn't get in sooner to see me."

Jorge knew McDonald was lying. He had seen everything through the observation port: the appendix had been intact when it first came into view, and it was still in one piece when McDonald grasped it with his clamp, then lassoed and severed it. There had been no leakage until the sutures failed. He had heard McDonald gasp and curse, had witnessed the grimace on McDonald's brow, the frustrated pounding with his fist. The surgeon was not telling the truth. The appendix had not been ruptured as McDonald had said. Something had gone wrong, very wrong, and caused the bowel to leak.

Jorge was stunned, wondering what the man was up to. He thought, *Dios mío! That's not true, no. Qué monstruo!* McDonald's lie gnawed at him, filled him with rage. But he said nothing. Then a surge of compassion for Eleanore Hinkel and her family flowed through him. This wasn't right, McDonald had to tell them what had happened. Her life was in danger and they deserved to know the truth.

But what could he do if McDonald lied to the family? Could he, Jorge Edmond, be the one to raise the alarm? Could he, a physician assistant, dare to take on the leading surgeon in Northeast Suburban Hospital? How could Jorge challenge McDonald's story and survive? He knew all too well how vulnerable his position in the hospital's hierarchy was. He felt as though he was suffocating, like someone had bound his chest so tight he could not breathe. Then he had a comforting thought: Dr. Pappelbaugh, the pathologist, would intervene once she saw the intact appendix. She would say something, wouldn't she? That was her job, wasn't it?

Jorge's thoughts were interrupted by McDonald's harsh command: "I'm done here, you close her up. Suture those drains in place and start the triple antibiotics. I'll go talk to her husband."

Matthew McDonald never made eye contact with Jorge Edmond, never called him by his name, just shouted orders and flew out of the room.

While suturing the skin at the end of a procedure, Jorge always said a silent prayer for the patient on the operating table in front of him. This time his prayer was especially long and impassioned, but he had little hope that it would be answered.

21

Chapter 3.   Cybersleuth

Will Manningham's back ached from too many hours in one position staring at his monitor, immersed in his computer algorithms. But it was a good ache, he thought. After a tense and dangerous undercover assignment with the FBI, he was happy to be back on his home turf in the government's top-secret *Anti-Fraud Command Center.* He felt much more comfortable in the spacious facility hidden in a converted warehouse in the suburbs of Baltimore than cramped in the FBI's makeshift workspace in downtown Washington, D.C. Will looked around the large fan-shaped room with satisfaction. Row after row of computer workstations all facing a sixty-foot wide, ultra high-definition screen spanning the entire front wall. Visitors remarked that the modernistic Command Center made them feel like they were in the flight control room of the Johnson Space Center. But here the work was not monitoring spacecraft, it was protecting people and the government from callous criminals who ran healthcare scams that stole billions of dollars and killed or maimed unwary patients.

Will's undercover stint with the FBI had been a brutal time for him and his family. He and his wife, Sally, had been forced into hiding to escape from the Russian mob after Will's computer analysis exposed their phony-cancer scam that had killed his mother with unnecessary chemotherapy. When Will sought to avenge her death the mob murdered his twin brother by mistake in a botched attempt to assassinate him. The FBI gave Will and Sally new identities as Sean and Sara Flaherty but the Russians found out Will was still alive and kidnapped and brutally assaulted Sally to lure him out of hiding. After a harrowing search and a bloody shoot-out at the mob's headquarters in Brooklyn, the FBI rescued Sally from her near-death ordeal. Once Sally was on her way to recovery and the lowlifes working for the Russians were dead or in jail, Will decided it was time for him to bid farewell to the FBI and return to his job with the Centers for Medicare and Medicaid Services, CMS.

Working with the FBI had been a necessity, not a situation Will would have sought. He respected and got along well with the Special Agents, but he had been out of his element with them. The Agents were dedicated public servants who belonged to a different culture than Will. They were armed and trained to kill when necessary. Or die. When one of their fellow Agents was taken down in the mission to rescue Sally they regarded his death as highly regrettable but stoically accepted that dying in the line of duty was a risk they all took willingly. Will preferred a calmer lifestyle behind the scenes, out of the line of fire. He enjoyed developing sophisticated computer models and searching through masses of Big Data with his fellow nerds in the obscurity of the CMS Command Center. Now he was back in his comfort zone, cybersleuthing from the security of his own high-tech quarters.

Will had been mining data for several months on a new project that was beginning to look promising. His preliminary results showed a suspicious pattern that troubled him, and today he believed he was on the verge of a breakthrough. It was time for him to get a better picture of what was going on. Either it was a false alarm and he could drop it once and for all, or he had found something that could mean big trouble. Very big trouble.

Will lifted his hands from the keyboard, spread his arms out, and arched back in his chair to relieve the stiffness that had crept up his spine from his sacrum to his neck. No good. He would make one last entry to command his supercomputer to integrate yet another massive data set into his latest equations, then he'd take a break while the machine did its work. He typed in the final characters of his new algorithm, clicked *"Enter,"* and pushed his chair away from the computer terminal. Gingerly uncoiling his six-foot-three frame, the lanky redhead rose slowly, took a few steps away from his work station, then cautiously inched his gangly body down onto the concrete floor. Lying face-up, he took several deep breaths then began coaxing his back to relax with the stretching moves his physical therapist had taught him: pelvic rotation thirty times, knees bent; relax; repeat; relax. A quiet moment concentrating on his breathing drained his mind of all thought except his mantra. At last he stood, arched backward one more time, and returned to his post.

Will refreshed the screen on his monitor and contemplated the results popping into view. Holding the mouse with his right hand he scrolled the cursor through the lines of data while the fingers of his left hand burrowed through his flaming red hair. One fingernail went directly to the familiar crusty spot on his scalp that he scratched at habitually as he thought. He stared at the monitor and studied the output with increasing excitement. And concern. There it was: he had generated a clear picture of what was going on, and the results were as troubling as he had feared.

The complex numerical tables on the screen were easy for Will to decipher, but he decided it would be useful to transform them into visual formats that would be simpler to explain to other people. He clicked on one column of data and ordered the computer to create graphs and figures that provided a dramatic visual display of the results. Then he repeated the operation on a series of other columns and files. He also entered the data into a geomapping program that generated eye-catching maps showing the distribution of his findings around the country. He kept up the process until he was satisfied that he had reformatted the data to make it easier to present to law enforcement officers who were bright and talented in their own right, but not exactly what anyone would consider computer geeks.

"OK," he said to no one, "time to call in the cavalry." His deep voice echoed off the vacant rows of computer stations and monitors and the gigantic high-resolution screen dominating the front wall. He activated his computer's voice-over-internet protocol, typed a series of keystrokes, and smiled as the familiar voice of FBI Special Agent Adrienne Penscal came through the Command Center's speakers.

"Hello, Will. What's up?"

In the terrible minutes after Will's twin brother had been gunned down, Adrienne Penscal had come up with the plan to mislead the Russians into believing they had succeeded in killing Will, then bringing him and Sally secretly under the mantle of the FBI. Will and Adrienne had worked closely together during the ensuing investigation, becoming close friends as well as colleagues. When they had finished dismantling the Russian scam, she had encouraged him to stay at the FBI. Will had resisted her entreaties and returned to CMS, but he was glad he could call on her at a moment like this.

"Hi, Adrienne. I've found something the FBI just might be interested in."

"Always interested in anything your computers uncover for us. What have you got?"

"Well, it's a bit complicated but the bottom line is that I've identified a whole bunch of unexplained deaths, clusters of excess deaths in several parts of the country."

"That's intriguing. How did you happen to come across something like that?"

"I started exploring trends in the causes of death in this country out of curiosity. It bothered me that our overall life expectancy has reversed course and started dropping recently and I wanted to see if I could find out why that was happening. I started by designing a new algorithm that ties together data on hospital admissions with vital statistics death reports, public death notices, and a wide range of other sources. After a couple of revisions over the past few weeks I spotted an unusual pattern. Nothing to explain the overall decline in life expectancy, just the opposite, these clusters of mysterious deaths. At first I could not find a common thread, so I kept plugging away. Just now I had what might be one of my *eureka* moments: something came into view that I'd like you to see. To me it looks like it's ripe for some hands-on police work."

"If you hook up a display for us to tie into remotely would we see everything you want to show us?"

"Not quite. You would just have access to the first levels of my analyses, the graphs and displays I've created. You wouldn't be able to work with the background files or view the logic behind my algorithms. I know it's a trek for you to travel out here to the Baltimore suburbs from the Hoover Building in D.C. but I think it would be best to show it to you in person if that's possible."

"OK, let's do it. How's this afternoon? If we leave soon we'll avoid the worst of the Beltway traffic."

"Sooner the better for me."

"See you in about an hour and a half. I'll bring Anil, Tom, and Denise."

"Hope the traffic isn't too bad."

***

A little over two hours later Special Agent Adrienne Penscal flashed her credentials at the heavily armed guards providing an incongruously high level of security for what appeared to be no more

25

than a nondescript warehouse in an industrial park outside of Baltimore. Her team followed her down a rat's maze of corridors flanked by endless cubicles until they arrived at a thick, reinforced door. She pressed the buzzer on the video-intercom panel and identified herself. The heavy door swung open and revealed a tall, slender redhead who smiled and said, "Hi Adrienne. Come on in, everyone."

"Hi, Will," Adrienne said, returning Will's smile as she extended her hand for an enthusiastic, firm handshake. An athletic young woman with perfect posture and close-cropped brown hair combed flawlessly in place, she emanated a military look that suited her commanding presence. Dressed in a classic dark blue business suit she was all FBI Agent, a fitting successor to the vintage G-man.

"I'm always surprised when I walk into this old warehouse and find myself in your high-tech Anti-Fraud Command Center," she said. "We were finally given some new resources at the FBI after you abandoned ship, but still nothing as impressive as this." She gestured at her companions. "You know these guys, right?"

"Of course. Hi, everyone. Welcome back."

Special Agents Tom Murphy, Denise Washington, and Anil Maliq nodded affably as they shook hands with Will. Each sported a version of the FBI blue business suit that might have been plucked off the wardrobe racks of an FBI television show, but the Agents themselves did not look like stereotypes from central casting. A huge, bald man who seemed to bulge out of his clothes, Tom Murphy towered over his colleagues like an enormous Michelin Man. Petite, reserved-looking Denise Washington could have passed for a pre-school teacher. Anil Maliq was slender and wiry and stood exactly midway in height between his colleagues. Murphy's physical strength was immediately apparent but Will knew full well not to underestimate either the strength or grit of Washington or Maliq. Washington had taken a bullet but still managed to kill one of the Russian assassins in a gunfight, and Maliq had lifted an attempted rapist off of Sally as effortlessly as if the assailant had been weightless.

"Thanks again for coming over on short notice. How bad was the traffic?"

"Heh-heh," chuckled Tom Murphy, with a genial nonchalance that belied his imposing appearance. "I was angling to pop on the blue light and the screecher but the Boss wouldn't let me."

"Murph gets a bit flustered at anything less than seventy-five miles per hour," said Adrienne Penscal. "OK, Will, what have you got for us?"

Will led them to a workstation with five seats arranged around a pair of monitors. "We can sit here. You can also view the display on the big screen up front if you prefer." He tapped on one of the screens and pointed at a map of the United States. Red dots of various sizes lit up over major cities on both coasts. "See that pattern? Each dot is a cluster of excess deaths, deaths well beyond what we would expect, even after I adjust for the age distribution and other demographics of the populations in those areas. Something funny's going on, no?"

Will clicked the cursor on one of the red dots, then another, and another, about a half-dozen times.

"Let me have a go at it, I want to check something out," said Adrienne. Will slid the mouse over to her and she began clicking on the red dots. With each click, charts and graphs popped up showing death rates in each area compared with the expected rates. Additional clicks revealed tables with the numbers and formulas underlying the graphs and charts.

"Yes," she said after a few minutes, "this is troublesome, very troublesome. Good work, Will. But what makes you think this is something for the FBI? Why us and not the Centers for Disease Control? They've got the epidemiologists who sleuth out epidemics and unexplained local disease outbreaks. Unless there's something criminal or fraudulent going on this would be for the CDC."

"Sure, that was my first thought also, maybe this was some sort of public health problem. So I started looking for patterns that would fit an environmental disaster or suggest some contagious disease spreading out of control. I ran a series of analyses to see if the causes of death were the same in each area. But no luck, there's no consistent pattern. The underlying causes of death are all over the board. Then I tried some new equations and finally discovered a common thread. I called you because my most recent findings made me suspicious that this was more than something for the CDC folks."

"The *eureka moment* you mentioned on the phone?"

Will smiled sheepishly. "Well, maybe that was a bit of excessive hyperbole. But I think that what I found could be important. I'll show you."

Will took back the mouse from Adrienne and opened another file.

"My new analyses suggested that the deaths could be separated into two groups: infections and medical device failures. But even within those two categories, the causes of death are quite varied. And the surprising thing is how mundane the underlying problems are. The infections were not caused by any particularly virulent bugs like some rare bacteria or viruses that were resistant to all treatments. These were infections that should never have been fatal at the rates I was seeing. And the medical devices that failed were pretty much common ones: pacemakers, stents, aortic pumps. All stuff that's been around for a long time, not anything new or experimental."

Adrienne Penscal studied the displays and turned to her colleagues. "Does this look familiar, guys?"

"You bet, Boss," said Tom Murphy.

Anil Maliq added, "Very familiar indeed, yes."

Denise Washington nodded silently with a knowing look.

Adrienne turned back to Will and said, "This may be even more of a *eureka moment* than you realize, Will. You were right, it's definitely FBI, not CDC. You were going on your analytical instincts, but here's something you didn't know: this looks a lot like what we have been seeing in Albania, Romania, and a bunch of other former Soviet satellites. We've been concerned for the past few years that something like this might develop in this country. If it's spreading here now a lot of people could be at risk. We suspect it's originating in Moscow. But we have no idea what's behind it all."

"Glad I called you, for sure. What next?"

"The sooner we get on top of it, the better."

"I was already putting a team together to push hard and see where it leads. We'll make headway a lot quicker if you guys work with us."

"We're in," said Penscal. "I'll assign a group of agents to this immediately. We're not exactly computer geeks like you. Your analytical skills are just what we need to figure out what the threat is and put an end to it."

Will laughed silently at hearing Adrienne confirm his opinion about the distribution of talents within her group: superb police officers, yes; geeks, no.

"That would be great. How soon could they start?"

"How about right now?"

"Perfect. Thanks much, Adrienne."

"The FBI is always delighted to help the Centers for Medicare and Medicaid Services fight international criminals," she replied with a smirk. "And we have a lot of new resources since our Healthcare Fraud Task Force got moved into the Anti-Terrorism Division. Maybe you'd like to leave CMS and come work with us again?"

"Thanks, but no thanks. I'm pleased to hear your team has moved up in the FBI hierarchy, but I'll stay here. At least for now."

"Understood, but don't expect me to give up easily on trying to bring you back into the Agency. In any case, despite the trek and traffic, I love coming out here. I know we're in an industrial park in the suburbs of Baltimore but this place makes me feel like I'm down in Houston monitoring spaceships and astronauts at NASA's Mission Control."

"Well, it looks like we're dealing with an alien incursion but I'm pretty sure these aliens are not creatures from outer space. I think we all know where these invaders come from."

Chapter 4.   Complications

Six nights after Eleanore Hinkel's surgery Dr. Sandy Flowers had just enjoyed the rare luxury of an entire evening of radio silence. But as soon as she got into her car and turned on her BlackBerry it began to vibrate, alerting her to a missed phone call. Even though she wasn't on call that night, seeing the missed call she felt mildly admonished for allowing personal pleasures to interfere with her medical responsibilities. Ever conscious of the demands of being a surgeon with a busy practice she felt as though she always needed to be available. *Thank goodness I didn't have anything to drink tonight, I hate trying to think through a buzz,* she thought as she punched the green telephone icon and watched the BlackBerry dial the return call.

"This is Dr. Meier, hello."

"Hi Nick, Sandy here. You called?"

"Hi Sandy, yes, thanks for calling back so quickly. I know you were out with the girls tonight so I hope you're not too blitzed to help me with something."

"Nah, not a drop, unfortunately. We went bowling – can you believe it? First time in years. Great fun, actually. I broke a hundred in every game. Hot dogs, salty pretzels and Diet Coke, not even a beer. What's up, Doc?"

"I'm covering the surgical service at Northeast Suburban tonight, and I've got one very sick lady here."

"Let me guess – is this one of McDonald's cock-ups?"

"Looks like it. Late 60s, good health, acute appendicitis. Laparoscopic procedure, but he kept her as an inpatient afterward – apparently the appendix was ruptured. She did well in the immediate post-op but then her fever spiked and she started going downhill. McDonald – of course – left on a trip even as she started getting worse. Now high fever, increasingly weak, looks like peritonitis. I'm trying to decide whether she needs to be opened up again and explored, but I wanted to discuss this with you first since this is one of *his* cases."

Hmmm…now maybe I wish I *were* too buzzed to help you. But I'm OK, I'll be right there."

"Thanks, Doc."

"You bet, Doc."

***

As Nick Meier approached her in the hospital hallway, Sandy Flowers found herself admiring his eyes. They were the perfect eyes of a surgeon, she thought, eyes that might have been those of a fighter pilot or an aboriginal hunter, eyes that focused precisely on their target whether it was one millimeter or one mile away. Glancing away from his eyes she noted once again that his hair was exactly the same short length it always seemed to be, perfectly trimmed around his ears and shaved on his neck, never a single hair out of place. Her own hair was short, but not like Meier's 1950's barbershop cut. She wore no makeup, nothing fancy, no jewelry, just small gold studs in her pierced earlobes.

The two surgeons stood next to each other at a small sink just down the hall from Eleanore Hinkel's room. They chatted casually as they scrubbed their hands and lower arms with disinfectant soap, then put on protective gowns.

Sandy Flowers asked, "What's the story on her antibiotics?"

"She's been on triple broad-spectrum therapy since the procedure, but the infection has progressed every day. Now her lab reports show that there are multiple bacteria growing, some of which are resistant to just about every antibiotic."

"How much drainage from the internal areas?"

"A bit at first, but the last 36 hours, not much, according to the nurse's notes. The puncture sites look bad – hot, red, starting to ooze. I'm covering for McDonald while he's on a remote beach somewhere near Cabo on another boondoggle with one of the surgical device manufacturers. In any case, he left word he was not to be reached and wouldn't be back until day after tomorrow at the earliest. I didn't want to take her into surgery without a second opinion, if you get my meaning."

"No need to explain. What's her family situation?"

"Husband is with her 24-7. Nice guy, but he blames himself, says he should have made her come in sooner since she was having so much pain."

"Not his fault, of course, but who knows what the world's most charismatic surgeon might have said to him."

As the two surgeons came into Eleanore Hinkel's hospital room they saw Henry Hinkel sitting in the only chair, a shopworn red leather recliner he had moved as close as possible to his wife, who lay asleep in her hospital bed. When the man stood up his body remained stooped. The few scraggly patches of hair on the sides of his balding head were compressed into random clumps above a face that displayed a scruffy two-day growth of beard. His clothes reflected the abuse they had suffered from being worn continuously for several days, his once starched and crisply pressed white dress shirt with *"HH"* monogrammed on the cuffs now a jumble of wrinkles, his gray slacks criss-crossed with deep creases, the baggy pants hanging loosely from his waist.

Nicholas Meier said, "Good evening, Mr. Hinkel. Let me introduce my colleague, Dr. Sandra Flowers, one of our leading surgeons. She's been going over your wife's case with me, and we would like to examine her if that's OK."

"Good to meet you, Dr. Flowers," Henry Hinkel responded, shuffling toward her and extending his hand. His words came steadily, respectfully, but with little energy, his face friendly but wan, drained. "Of course, whatever you think. Please excuse me, I'll step outside if you don't mind."

"Sure, as you prefer. We'll just be a few minutes."

Sandy Flowers walked to the sink, washed her hands again, then slipped on nitrile gloves. She approached the woman sleeping in the bed and tapped her gently on the shoulder to wake her.

"Hello, Mrs. Hinkel. I'm Dr. Sandy Flowers. Dr. Meier has asked me to consult on your case. I'd like to examine you briefly, if that's OK."

Eleanore Hinkel nodded her assent, straining to force a half-smile but remaining silent. Sandy Flowers examined her quickly, focusing on the swollen red surgical puncture sites and distended belly just long enough to confirm her expectations.

"Thank you, Mrs. Hinkel, that's all for now."

Eleanore Hinkel opened her eyes slightly to look up at the surgeon, but seemed to be staring through her, her gaze off in the distance. She nodded again, then slipped away once more.

Turning to her colleague as she left the bedside, Sandy Flowers said softly but with conviction, "No doubt about it, Nick, she's got a fulminating peritonitis and probably multiple abscesses in all the dependent areas that need to be drained. Let's talk to Mr. Hinkel."

The two surgeons left the room and returned to the washing-up station to repeat their decontamination ritual to avoid spreading any of the deadly germs that now kill tens of thousands of hospital patients every year. Their hands and arms duly cleansed, Drs. Meier and Flowers found Henry Hinkel pacing the corridor. Nick Meier smiled and gestured for him to walk with them to the end of the hallway. As they reached a small waiting area in front of a large glass window, Sandy Flowers said, "Please, Mr. Hinkel, have a seat."

"Mr. Hinkel, your wife has a serious infection," Nicholas Meier began, his unpretentious voice soothing but professional, straightforward. "We call it peritonitis, an infection of the abdomen. The infection comes from bacteria that already live in our intestines and help us digest our food. They don't cause any problems as long as they stay on the inside of our digestive tract, but when they leak into the abdomen, those ordinarily friendly and helpful germs become deadly and cause infections that can be hard to treat. And the digestive juices that leak out into the belly make it worse, since they are caustic and inflame the healthy tissue, making it more vulnerable to infection."

"I know, I know," he said, shaking his head with tangible desperation. His tortured face displayed the self-reproach he was carrying inside. "It's all my fault. I should have made her go to the doctor sooner. She didn't want to move, she was in such pain, but I should have insisted. And then we had a terrible time trying to get through to Tony Marlburg's office. I should have taken her to the emergency room."

"No reason to blame yourself, you did the best you could under the circumstances. Now we have to go forward and take care of the situation she's in."

"Is it serious? Is she going to…to make it?"

"We're going to do everything we can. But I have to tell you that she's in a very precarious condition. If she has abscesses, pools of pus, in her abdomen, the antibiotics cannot get into them to kill the germs, so they can fester until the infection overwhelms her body. We need to go in and drain the infected sites, open up the abscesses. That will give the antibiotics and her body's natural resistance, her immune system, a better chance."

"*Better chance?* What…what does that mean? Is she going to die?"

Sandy Flowers answered the question, choosing her words carefully to give the man a realistic sense of his wife's fragile situation while sounding neither unnecessarily fatalistic nor overly optimistic.

"In all honesty, Mr. Hinkel, I'm afraid this is not a good situation for Mrs. Hinkel. In addition to the infection in her belly, there are signs of infection on her skin where Dr. McDonald inserted the laparoscope. Also she may have infections in her bloodstream as well – septicemia, we call that, blood poisoning. We will do everything we can. We have powerful antibiotics, she's relatively young and strong, she just needs some help to fight this off. But we don't want to mislead you. People who develop peritonitis and septicemia are gravely ill. I'm very sorry to say there's always the possibility she will not make it."

Desolation swept over Henry Hinkel, draining his last reserve of hope. He slumped backward on the chair awkwardly, his head collapsing into his small, thick hands. He rubbed his face repeatedly, sobbing audibly.

Looking down the hallway toward his stricken wife's room he pleaded, "Please, please, forgive me Eleanore. I'm so sorry, it's my fault, I knew this was bad, I should have gotten you to the doctor. I'm so, so sorry. I…"

Sandy Flowers and Nick Meier waited patiently, eager to get on with the surgery but not wanting to press Henry Hinkel to sign the consent forms, not just yet. After a minute or so the man seemed to calm down, still breathing deeply but no longer crying. He raised his head and looked back and forth between the two surgeons. Nicholas Meier walked over to his side, put one hand on his shoulder and said, "Mr. Hinkel, we need to get your wife into surgery as soon as possible."

"Yes, yes, sure, of course. Whatever you think. Please, I'm sorry, I just couldn't…"

"We understand, Mr. Hinkel. We understand."

Nicholas Meier handed Henry Hinkel a clip board with a small stack of papers. "Please sign where the red check marks are, Mr. Hinkel."

Henry Hinkel thumbed through the forms, scribbling his signature without glancing at the paragraphs of legalese. As Hinkel returned the clip board to Nicholas Meier, Sandy Flowers said, "If you'll excuse me just a moment," and walked briskly down the hallway. She returned almost immediately with a nurse who headed directly for Henry Hinkel. "Mrs. Jenkins will stay with you for a few minutes. If you would like to make any phone calls or if you need something, she will help you. We'll be back in a few minutes."

"I'll go back to Eleanore, thanks," he said softly.

Nick Meier and Sandy Flowers walked into the long, narrow doctor's room next to the nursing station and sat at the counter top that served as a desk. The room was little more than an enclosed work station with a blank wall on one side and the work area on the other. Open bookshelves were divided into cubbyholes labeled with the names of different doctors. Many of the cells were crammed with file folders, hospital records, and miscellaneous paperwork awaiting attention from the medical staff. Telephones and obsolete dictating equipment hung from the padded panel between the counter top and the cubbyholes. Two computer monitors and keyboards occupied most of the workspace.

With a somewhat conspiratorial tone Nick Meier said, "We'd better write one hell of a note, we're going to need every bit of documentation we can produce. McDonald's going to be out of his mind when he returns if this lady doesn't make it. He's not the one to acknowledge any problems with his patients, and if she crumps on our watch he'll point the finger at us."

"Exactly what I was thinking. It's not clear if this is McDonald's fault, though. After all, we've all been there ourselves with ruptured appendices. But you're right, if there's the slightest question about her care, McDonald will turn on us in an instant."

"I'm the one who was on call tonight, I'll write the note. You can add your comments as my consultant. We're in total agreement here, right? She needs emergency surgery, needs to be explored and have any abscesses drained and cultured, needs new antibiotics."

"Absolutely, no question about it. Want me in the O.R. with you?"

"You're a saint, but I don't think that's necessary. Mainly I wanted you to evaluate the need to open her up and confirm my opinion. *C.Y.A.*, that's all I need, really. I can do the work myself. But thanks, Sandy."

"Good thing this wasn't a drinking night for me. Usually our girls-nights-out leave me in no shape to drive to the hospital, let alone examine patients."

"You're a better surgeon drunk than you-know-who is sober."

"I'm happy to help – let's leave it at that. Now, I'll write my note and you can start making the arrangements for the operation. This isn't going to be easy."

"No, it isn't, not for her. What do you think her chances are? I make it less than 50-50."

"I've probably had about a dozen or so who got this bad. Only three of them are around to tell the tale. The others are gone, and most of them didn't leave easily. It's not a good way to die."

"Yeah, my experience is about the same," he said slowly, a sudden reserve coming into his voice as he reflected on an old, painful memory. "Very first one…I'll never forget, when I was a medical student, on junior surgery. Teenage boy lying in a bed at the end of the ward. Totally emaciated, couldn't have weighed ninety pounds by the time I saw him, even though he was over six feet tall. Took me the better part of six hours to plow through that boy's paper chart and get ready to present his case to the attending surgeon on rounds the next morning. I was stunned when I found out his story. He was a high school football player, a lineman, weightlifter, had weighed over 250 pounds. Felt a sharp pain in his side the day before the homecoming game and didn't want to say anything out of fear they wouldn't let him play. Rough game, he played both ways, offense and defense. Collapsed in the locker room afterward, ambulance brought him in to the hospital. Macho pride and school spirit are two emotions adolescents just aren't mature enough to overcome, poor kid. Ruptured appendix, bowel contents all over his abdomen. Six surgeries and nearly one year later, there he was, barely hanging on when I arrived. He was semi-comatose by then, couldn't speak, died that month on my rotation. I was pretty shaken – almost made me want to go into Psychiatry instead of surgery."

"Let's hope for a better result this time," she said softly, then added reassuringly, "And good thing you weren't diverted to Psychiatry. You're a gifted surgeon."

"You're pretty good yourself. Thanks again, Sandy."

Chapter 5.   Not-for-Profit

Molly Cavendish could feel the arteries in her head throbbing as she waved the latest *Guidance* from the Centers for Medicare and Medicaid Services in front of her boss.

"Lester, have you seen this CMS bullshit?"

Lester Williamsburg, the President and Chief Executive Officer of Northeast Suburban Hospital, had long ago learned that his Senior Vice President sometimes needed to disgorge the detritus from her mental dumpster on him. He listened patiently to her tirades, knowing that Molly's blood boiled at just about everything that crossed her desk from the government.

"Narrow it down a bit, Molly – which bullshit?"

"This mind-boggling announcement from CMS about their new website to release information on hospitals. They call it *Hospital Compare*. They want us to report all sorts of things to the federal government, like how many patients get bedsores or infections from catheters, or break their hips from a fall, or have complications after surgery. All so the goddamn website can post it all in public. *Puhh*," she spat derisively, her head pounding more with each word.

"This is a bad joke," she sneered. " *Hospital Compare*', catchy name, yeah, that will play well with the public, but it's useless crap, just more work for us. Bullshit, that's what this is, total bullshit. It's an affront to our profession to pretend that hospitals could be judged like television sets or car repair shops or anything else. It's too goddamn much to bear. But this hospital will not look bad, not for a minute. Not with our data. It won't happen, I won't let it happen. No damn website is going to air out our dirty laundry, not on my watch."

Lester Williamsburg shared Molly Cavendish's contempt for yet another government intrusion into the hospital's affairs, but the ponderously obese man did not have as much energy to expend railing against this particular affront as his more youthful second in command did. So he just sat and let her prattle on until she blew off enough steam for him to end their session. He was content to let his Senior Vice President vent. She had many valuable qualities that he had come to rely on. He particularly admired her Irish politician's savvy for spotting and seizing the right moment to act and her natural gift for running things and manipulating people.

And, he mused, she was good to look at. Now in her late 40s, Molly Cavendish still had the figure and the face that had toyed with the hearts of many young doctors over the years. Long black hair, once nearly to her waist, still hung down over her shoulders, black as ever although it would have been salt-and-pepper if she didn't camouflage the salt every month or so. The map of Ireland on her face, bright blue eyes, wonderfully pink cheeks that framed a smile that could charm the vestments off a bishop – and nearly had done so once at St. Adelaide High School. Tall at five-foot-ten, with a sensuous athletic shape and expansive bust that stretched her sheer white nurse's uniform to open an alluring gap between the buttons on her chest.

Williamsburg had heard tales over the years about Molly Cavendish's many short-term romances. But he knew that her dalliances were as far in the past as the tight white nursing uniforms and the little blue-and-white starched caps. Her life now was filled with the pressure and responsibility of senior management. And the power he had given her. Despite the endless sneering her carousing had provoked, her colleagues grudgingly admitted that Molly Cavendish had not simply slept her way to the top. She may have seduced any man she wanted, but men and women alike recognized that she had not climbed up the corporate ladder with just her body. Even her many detractors acknowledged her brains, her fierce loyalty, her tireless work ethic.

For her part, Molly Cavendish did not at all regret that the doctors in the hospital were no longer candidates for bedroom sports. Power was at least as rewarding as sex had been. She didn't have to take orders any more from guys with an M.D. no matter how dull or wet behind the ears they were. Now they kowtowed to her. Besides, not all of them were good in bed. She chuckled at the memory of one particularly disappointing tryst, a high-expectation encounter with an incredibly muscular intern who had turned out to be better at pumping iron than pumping her.

Lester Williamsburg took full advantage of his good fortune in having spotted and mentored such a talented and devoted ally. He rapidly expanded her job responsibilities until she was his second-in-command. But he withheld the final badge of authority that he knew she craved, the title of Chief Operating Officer. Molly Cavendish had all the authority and responsibility of that position but not the title. Williamsburg believed that he needed to reserve at least one carrot to dangle in front of people to keep them motivated. Williamsburg's controlling management style irritated Molly but she consoled herself that no matter what her title, everyone who worked at Northeast Suburban knew she was the one who really ran things.

Besides, Molly figured, her boss was a human time bomb and she would be his heir apparent when he clocked out. She felt the irony that what Williamsburg had accomplished with the hospital had been at visible cost to his health. Always notably plump, the man had ballooned up to dangerously obese proportions over the years. His tiny eyes had receded further and further into his puffy pink face as his bulk expanded, the pupils barely visible behind the lenses of his John Lennon eyeglasses whose wire-thin temples were now engulfed by folds of flesh on the sides of his face. Feeling more disdain than sympathy, Molly watched as he labored pink-faced and huffing for breath down the hallways of the hospital. Nurses and physicians who lectured their patients every day on the health risks of obesity derided him savagely behind his back but knew that any direct confrontation about his weight was strictly off-limits.

Molly Cavendish came to see that Williamsburg's voracious appetite for food was perfectly matched by his cravings for power and success. He was not simply holding things together at Northeast Suburban, he was taking it to a position of notable prominence and unrivaled financial success. In the years since he took over it had become the preeminent general hospital in an upscale suburban bedroom community in northern Virginia, on the outer limits of commuting distance from Washington, D.C. Williamsburg had capitalized aggressively on the hospital's location and clientele to build its reputation and maximize its cash flow.

One of Williamsburg's first strategies that had paid off handsomely was to manipulate the types of patients who would receive medical care at the hospital so they could focus on the most lucrative ones. The big man had exuded pride telling Molly how he had insulated Northeast Suburban from the ravages of the nearby inner city by influencing the local authorities to gerrymander the hospital's catchment area for ambulance transports. Indigent or uninsured patients, drunks, and gunshot victims from the low-income fringes of D.C. would be carried to other hospitals in the area, anywhere but Northeast Suburban. Shorn of most of its burden of indigent patients, the Emergency Room became a major revenue center as ambulances now brought in a continual stream of well-insured suburbanites who had wrecked their Cadillacs or Mercedes or were having chest pain or strokes, patients who required and could pay for an enormous amount of high-tech, expensive care.

Buoyed by his victory in insulating the hospital from the lower end of the community, Williamsburg cultivated its reputation as the fashionable place for people with money to go for medical care. He remodeled Northeast Suburban, cannibalizing the old homes in the neighborhood to build new facilities. He bought the latest equipment so the hospital could emphasize highly profitable medical specialties such as cardiology and radiology and drop the loss-leaders like general pediatrics or family medicine.

But Williamsburg's greatest accomplishment was his mastery of financial ploys that spewed money into Northeast Suburban like wheat pouring into a grain elevator in western Kansas. He loved to brag to Molly about his many different forms of "creative" billing, turning his private sessions with her into tutorials on how to collect the most money possible from insurance companies and well-heeled patients. And, he reminded her, it was all free money — the hospital was a not-for-profit charity that paid no income tax on its ever-expanding margins. She took it all in, contemplating the day when she would be in charge.

Williamsburg was particularly proud of his scheme for double-dipping on Medicare patients, getting paid twice for a single course of illness. When patients were admitted, the hospital would collect a lump-sum from Medicare, a fixed dollar payment that was the same for any given diagnosis, regardless of how long or short a time they would stay or what medical care services they would receive. But since people with the same diagnosis could be anywhere from hardly sick at all to extremely ill and highly complicated, Northeast Suburban made lots of money off the mild cases and avoided the difficult ones. Williamsburg rewarded doctors who admitted their relatively easy cases to his hospital but treated their really sick ones somewhere else. He completed the scheme to double-dip by buying or building skilled nursing facilities, imaging centers, rehabilitation clinics and outpatient clinics where Medicare would pay again for taking care of the same patients after they were discharged from the hospital.

Williamsburg's scheme worked brilliantly, pumping millions and millions of dollars into Northeast Suburban Hospital and its many subsidiary corporations. With its large operating margins, Northeast Suburban was able to cater to the local carriage trade just as he had envisioned, providing amenities that affluent patients in the fashionable suburbs loved: private rooms, extravagant furnishings, gourmet food, cable TV. Pleasing the aging population of wealthy suburbanites further elevated Williamsburg's status in the hospital world. He came to be viewed as such a mastermind for putting his hospital into a strong fiscal position that he became a hot commodity, commanding a multi-million dollar salary far beyond what any of the local citizens could ever have imagined their neighborhood *'nonprofit'* hospital was paying anyone. Williamsburg told himself repeatedly he deserved every penny, he was doing nothing illegal, he was just playing the system within its own rules, staying one step ahead of the feds and the insurance companies for the benefit of the hospital.

Molly was a good student. She learned that Lester's success was built on one simple maxim: *squeeze out every dime.* She was sure that the day would come when she would push that maxim beyond anything Lester had ever dared. It wouldn't take long to prove how right she was.

Chapter 6.   Bumped Down The Pecking Order

Lester Williamsburg and Molly Cavendish ran the hospital, but there was one person whose looming presence kept them from ruling with absolute authority: Dr. Michael Simkowitz. An icon on the medical staff of Northeast Suburban for well over twenty years, Simkowitz had earned the respect of his colleagues to the point that more than one-third of his patients had been physicians themselves or their family members. In his early 60's now, Simkowitz was gray at the temples and growing slack in his waistline, his once-regular exercise regime having been sacrificed to a panoply of lame excuses. In denial of the inevitable onslaught of aging until recently, he now grudgingly accepted the need for the reading glasses that he frequently misplaced. The numerous other frailties creeping through his body he kept to himself.

Like Molly Cavendish, Michael Simkowitz had moved away from taking care of patients and was now fully occupied with the business of running a hospital. His prominence among the medical staff as the physicians' physician had led first to his becoming Chief of the Medical Staff, and then Vice President for Medical Affairs. But for him the transition from clinician to administrator turned out to be an unexpectedly demeaning change of life. He had been seduced into accepting the appointment by a big title that sounded important, stirring his hopes that he could accomplish great things in that position to improve patient care and cull out the incompetent physicians on the medical staff. But titles were only titles. His stature among the physicians protected him and gave him moral authority, but he found that moral authority empowered him very little. When it came to the major decisions in running Northeast Suburban Hospital his position was a humiliating sinecure, his role reduced to being a foil to Molly Cavendish.

The moment Dr. Michael Simkowitz had felt his professional life tumble into oblivion was etched into his memory as clearly as when he heard Walter Cronkite announce that President Kennedy was dead. The momentous change came at a senior staff meeting in Williamsburg's personal conference room, a pretentious, oversized room that accommodated twelve people in richly textured black leather chairs around a massive oval mahogany table. Each place at the table had crystal water glasses, small plates, delicate silverware, and linen cocktail napkins, all embossed with the same fleur-de-lis pattern as the textured cloth wall panels. A platter of baked goodies still warm from the oven was stacked high in the center of the big table below a massive art-nouveau chandelier decorated with more fleur-de-lis.

Simkowitz looked around the room and realized all the senior leadership of the hospital was present. Something big was about to happen. The massive Williamsburg presided like a Shakespearean king from an oversized chair with an ornate high back and carved armrests. Taking a deep breath, then exhaling in a loud wheeze, he started his prepared remarks, remarks that were to change the course of Mike Simkowitz' life.

"All of you are my – this hospital's – leadership team. Dr. Michael Simkowitz, our outstanding Chief of the Medical Staff, our Vice President for Medical Affairs, has the respect and loyalty of every physician on our staff. We would not function well as a hospital without his tireless efforts to align the interests of our doctors with those of the overall medical center. Dr. Simkowitz is integral to the future of Northeast Suburban."

Simkowitz smelled a rat. What was going on? Lester never praised anyone like that, especially not him. He had to be up to something devious.

"Sylvester Sullivan, *Esquire*, as the hospital's general counsel keeps us honest – that must be a challenge, right, Sy?"

The leadership team chuckled dutifully. Simkowitz was particularly struck by the contrast between the slender, even athletic, fifty-three year old General Counsel, Sylvester Sullivan, and their painfully corpulent boss. Sullivan was the picture of dignity, a perfect Boston Brahmin, a walking anachronism still wearing three-piece suits long after they had ebbed out of style, complete with a starched handkerchief folded to show four points above his jacket breast pocket. Simkowitz would not have been surprised to see him pull a gold pocket watch from his vest.

"Actually, Sy makes sure we keep up with – what's the latest count, Sy, 132,000 pages of federal regulations, right? Sy also fights off the local shysters who would drain our blood and feast on our corpses."

"Don't be so harsh, Lester, even shysters have to eat," replied Sylvester Sullivan.

The senior officers of the hospital responded with reserved laughter, the culinary reference in Williamsburg's presence triggering a general unease.

"Frank Applegate, of course, our Chief Financial Officer, has the most difficult job of all – balancing the books. How he does it with all those different managed care contracts, the pittance Medicaid pays, the mind-boggling way Medicare badgers us, and all the free care we have to give away, I'll never know."

"Don't cash your paycheck this month until I tell you it's OK, Lester," responded Applegate.

"Then there's Molly Cavendish, our steadfast Director of Nursing. Molly is the subject of this morning's meeting. We have big plans for Nurse Cavendish."

The hairs on Mike Simkowitz' neck bristled. Molly Cavendish had been Lester's fair-haired sidekick for years and Simkowitz was sure that she was about to be rewarded. Williamsburg's next words proved him right – and revealed that Cavendish's gain would be at Simkowitz' expense.

"Molly Cavendish is being promoted," Lester Williamsburg said enthusiastically, extending both arms in her direction with such a flourish that tiny bits of pastry crust sprayed out from his fingertips. "She is now Senior Vice President of Northeast Suburban Hospital."

Simkowitz immediately recognized the import of the *'Senior'* in her title. She was the chosen one, she would be Williamsburg's second in command.

Williamsburg added what Mike Simkowitz correctly saw as a hollow assurance: "Of course, all of you in the senior leadership team will continue to report directly to me, as President and Chief Executive Officer. But as Senior Vice President, Molly will now be in charge of *all* patient care services, and a good many of our employees will report to her. We are faced with a number of challenges that require this restructuring. We have opened satellite sites all over the county, and subsidiary corporations that run far more specialized services than ever before. All of this is placing new demands on our staff to maintain our extraordinary level of patient satisfaction. We are under increasing pressure to implement measures that outside forces think are needed to protect patient safety and provide a high level of quality of care. And, of course, these new demands have brought a tidal wave of reporting requirements to government agencies that want to know everything that goes on in this hospital. All of these responsibilities will now be under Senior Vice President Molly Cavendish."

An old-school physician, Simkowitz was appalled at the very thought of an administrator, even one who had been a nurse, taking over responsibility for the quality of care. That was for the doctors, the medical staff, the health professionals who actually delivered medical care to patients. And their chosen leader: Simkowitz. Administrators saw patients as revenue centers, not human beings. Their job was to grab every dollar possible, not improve quality or take care of patients. The perpetually calm Simkowitz was boiling, he knew his blood pressure was out of control and realized his face was probably bright red from his nose to his ears. He tried to smile, to avoid wearing his thoughts on his face, but he couldn't stop thinking about the implications for his own life. Simkowitz understood what was happening before his eyes: Lester Williamsburg was cutting him off at the knees.

Addressing Molly directly, Williamsburg said, "Ms. Cavendish, you are assuming responsibility for assuring compliance with all the patient care regulations this hospital is subject to, and seeing to it that the hospital avoids litigation to the maximum extent consistent with the law. You are expected to prevent problems in the first place. And you are to contain them when they do occur."

Williamsburg added, "Of course, we would never want you to conceal anything important, but you must be thoughtful in releasing any information."

The smirk on his face sent the message loud and clear to Molly: her job would be to protect the hospital – e*ven if it meant covering shit up*.

Waving his arms to the entire group, Williamsburg added, "Senior Vice-President Cavendish will develop and implement a new set of activities and internal hospital procedures to assure quality of care and to enhance our risk management. Federal agencies, the state government, every managed care plan, even employers, not to mention consumer groups – everyone now is scrambling to hold us accountable for what they want to call better quality. So she will have whatever staff and information technology she needs for us to demonstrate that we are in full compliance with all these requirements. I want you all to join me in congratulating her for this well-deserved recognition of her many contributions to Northeast Suburban, and to support her fully in attending to her new responsibilities. This is a fine accomplishment for her, but an even greater moment for this hospital. We are indeed lucky to have someone like her to rely on. I will release a formal announcement this afternoon, and there will be a reception for all the staff in the auditorium after work. For now, let's celebrate – we have arranged a nice little lunch for us in the Board Room."

Williamsburg paused as if searching for more words, unable or unwilling to give up the floor yet not sure what else to say. But Michael Simkowitz could stand no more. He was choking for breath, desperate to get out of the room, to contemplate what had just happened. When Williamsburg stopped talking, Simkowitz stood, begged off from lunch with a vague excuse, and walked directly to the doctors' parking lot. He put the top down on his Mercedes SLK Roadster and just started driving, nowhere in particular. Air, he needed air.

Senior Vice President Molly Cavendish proved to be ruthless in cutting expenditures, reducing staff, negotiating deals. She was determined to show Lester that putting his trust in her was the right choice. She would make Northeast Suburban ever more profitable. Then one day her golden opportunity walked in the door: someone as devious as Molly came to her with a ploy to cut some very costly expenses. She seized on the scheme immediately. Williamsburg had made a career of stretching the rules but had been content to stop just short of the breaking point. Now Molly Cavendish had a bolder strategy that promised ever more handsome rewards. This would be her triumph, she would make her mark. The deadly bargain was joined.

Chapter 7.   Foreign Incursion

Will Manningham wasn't sure whether his old FBI passcard from his previous stint as a temporary FBI analyst would get him into the J. Edgar Hoover Building through the employee entrance since the card bore his undercover name, Sean Flaherty, and the photo showed him in disguise with his red hair dyed jet black and an equally dark beard covering his face. But Adrienne Penscal had assured him that she had reactivated his credentials so he decided to give it a try. Sure enough, he should never have doubted her – as soon as he waved the RFID chip in his ID card within range of the reader he heard a reassuring *ping* and the thick plexiglass gate swung open. Will was pleased. Going through the employee entrance meant that he did not need to be subjected to screening like visiting tourists, who were required to squeeze into a claustrophobic glass capsule while sophisticated sensors tested the fumes from their clothes and body for toxins or explosives. He rode the elevator up to Adrienne's floor and as soon as he exited he noticed a new sign on the wall:

Anti-Terrorism Division
Russia/China Hacking Group
Healthcare Fraud Task Force

Adrienne was waiting for him in her office with her entire team of Special Agents: Maliq, Washington, and Murphy, along with Fred Renford and Frances Trainor. "Hi Will," she said, "welcome to our house."

"Hi Adrienne, hello everyone. Good to be here."

"Hip, hip, hooray, he's back!" cheered Tom Murphy, to which the other blue-suited FBI Agents applauded. The enthusiastic greeting gave Will a comfortable feeling almost like returning home after a long journey. Despite matching Murphy's six-foot-three height, the slender Will once again felt dwarfed by the massive bald man. Fran Trainor's bulky presence and Fred Renford's powerful handshake and muscular physique triggered a similar sense of being overmatched physically. Denise Washington and Anil Maliq as always radiated quiet authority.

"And whatever you did worked fine, Adrienne – I had no trouble coming in through security as Sean Flaherty."

"See how easy it would be for Sean to return to the FBI as a permanent employee?"

Will smiled and said, "No thanks, he's fine coming and going as needed. But that is an impressive new sign you have, the *Russia/China Hacking Group*."

Penscal's face tightened. She glanced at the other Special Agents, then said, "At least for now, maybe."

"Why do you say that? What's up?"

"I'm not at liberty to go into any detail, but I can tell you that our group was given that name when it was formed a while back but things are, let's say, a bit different now. There are some internal discussions going on over identifying…over specifying any particular country. Times change. But enough about that – please bring us all up to speed on what you've been finding."

"I think I get the picture, Adrienne, thanks. OK, as all of you know, I detected some unexpected clusters of deaths here in the States. After you told me that you had seen a similar pattern in the former Soviet satellites, I got files from Europol that were very helpful, along with leads from the European Anti-Fraud Office, OLAF, and information from the European Healthcare Fraud & Corruption Network. Bit by bit, the story emerged. The problems spread from east to west across Europe over about a three-year period before anything showed up here. Some countries were fairly quick to notice and take action, others seem to have taken much longer or still haven't intervened."

Denise Washington asked, "What did the European response accomplish? Any arrests or convictions?"

"No, there have been no solid law enforcement actions as far as I could see. The response seems mainly to have focused on dealing with the medical problems as they arose. Treating people who got sick, trying to save lives."

"Any insight into the causes of the deaths?"

"Nothing that I found. There's a cross-national task force looking into the problem but they have not issued a report. Mostly what I found just referred to the deaths as 'perplexing' or 'unexplained' or something similar."

"How about links to the Russian mob? Anything definite?"

"Europol is convinced that Russia is the source but I couldn't find anything to corroborate their view."

"Yes," said Adrienne, "there's probably more going on behind the scenes. We'll have to go through formal channels to find out whether there's any real action. But corruption is rampant in a number of the Eastern Bloc countries, stimulated and exploited by the Russian mob. There are probably some honest officials who are conducting legitimate inquiries but keeping a low profile, while the rest are looking the other way to avoid any conflicts with the mob and leaving it to the doctors to deal with the fall-out."

"Anyway," said Will, "once I had a good picture of what was happening in Europe, I started searching for a number of specific diagnoses and complications in hospital admissions in the U.S. I tied in the death registries and links to obituaries and on-line death notices across the country, anonymous calls to our 1-800-HHS-TIPS hotline from whistleblowers, Medicare billing records, and the FDA databases on drugs and devices."

"How widespread is the problem? Concentrated in certain areas?"

"As you saw on my map, so far it's mainly on both coasts, heavily in the D.C.-New York-Boston corridor, and, of course, Miami and the rest of South Florida. Also quite a bit in L.A. and the Valley."

"Any new details on what's behind the deaths?"

"Yes, I think I found something with a new approach to my analyses. As I mentioned when you came out to our Command Center, the deaths fall into two categories: infections and medical device failures. I looked hard at the data but got no new hints about the underlying causes of deaths because the infections are caused by many different germs and there's a wide range of medical devices that have failed. So I started looking to see if there was anything in common among the antibiotics that were being used to treat the infections or the medical devices that were involved. I examined lots of big data but I still didn't get anywhere at that point. Then I thought of something entirely different: I factored in stories in the media about the big drug and device companies and looked at their SEC filings and a slew of their marketing materials."

"Very creative, as always. So, what emerged?"

"One interesting thing showed up: a relatively new international pharmaceutical and medical device company called *Marquis-Herrant* has been expanding quickly and now has a major presence in the areas with the clusters of unexplained deaths."

"Corporate angels of death?" quipped Tom Murphy, eliciting a round of soft laughter.

"I hope not, Murph," responded Will, "but who knows? For now, all I'm sure of is that the areas with the excess deaths are the ones where *Marquis-Herrant* has its biggest market share."

Adrienne Penscal asked, "That gives us something to work with. Any thoughts on how we should pursue that lead?"

"I'll keep plugging away on the analytics. Maybe I can identify a connection between *Marquis-Herrant* and the deaths. Statistically speaking, it's hard to believe it's just a coincidence."

"So what does this *Marquis-Herrant* company sell, anyway?"

"That's part of the problem. They distribute a lot of different drugs and medical devices. If they only handled, let's say, insulin, and we had a spike in deaths from diabetes, that would be easy to trace. But they sell all kinds of pharmaceuticals and medical gear, and the deaths aren't limited to a few diagnoses. There are just more total deaths than there should be in those areas."

"Do you have all the support you need? Technical assistance? Programmers? Other data bases?"

"Thanks for asking. I've got the high-tech stuff covered, but there just might be something you can do to speed things along. It's a lot easier to spot things in all the data when we know where to focus our efforts. I'm beginning to think it's time for some old-fashioned police work to help point us in the right direction."

"Point taken," concluded Adrienne Penscal. "We'll expand our law enforcement efforts to help unearth some leads. We don't have nearly enough evidence so far to consider shutting down that *Marquis-Herrant* company or bringing anyone in for questioning, but you've given us a pretty good idea of what we're up against. And what we need. I'll brief Chief Hollingshead. Given the international aspect we should be able to get the go-ahead for secret FISA warrants so we can start wiretapping and conducting other surveillance. Tom, you and Frances can handle that. Anil and Denise, you get over to Treasury and enlist *FinCEN* to check banking and financial records for *Marquis-Herrant* and identify any other suspicious details. Fred, you establish contacts with our Field Offices in the different hotspots in this country and get them to look around. And speak with the European law enforcement agencies Will mentioned and see if you can find out more about what they're doing. In the meantime, Will, let me know if you need access to any other data sources, and keep me up to date on your progress."

"Thanks, Adrienne, that'll be a big help."

"OK, gang, that's it, let's get going. Thanks much, everyone."

Chapter 8.   Impotence

Dr. Michael Simkowitz sat at his desk in Northeast Suburban Hospital, one hand clenched in a fist, the other clutching a mug of bitter coffee from the small coffee maker on the sink-top in his private bathroom. Simkowitz mulled over the irony of his position: he occupied an office suite with the universal symbol of high status in the ranks of corporate leadership, a private toilet, while his actual authority had diminished to near powerlessness. He had a personal place to shit, he thought ruefully, but no one gave a shit what he thought about anything that really mattered.

Weary and tense, he took a long sip of coffee and steeled himself for the imminent task at hand: a private meeting with Drs. Sandra Flowers and Nicholas Meier. The two young surgeons were among his favorites in the hospital, but he had a sense of foreboding that they were going to raise concerns about his nemesis, Matthew McDonald. It didn't take long before his premonition was confirmed. Shortly after entering into his office, Sandy Flowers recited the all-too-familiar words that many well-meaning physicians had spoken over the years: "Dr. Simkowitz, we have questions about the performance of Dr. Matthew McDonald. Since you are the Chief of the Medical Staff and Vice-President for Medical Affairs of the hospital, we would like you to intervene in this situation."

"Please, tell me," replied Simkowitz, politely feigning enthusiasm, all the while wondering if complaints about McDonald would ever cease. Nicholas Meier responded, "Thank you, Dr. Simkowitz. Dr. Flowers and I felt it was our obligation to say something, but we weren't sure how to go about it. This has been bothering us and we need to get it out."

Simkowitz nodded, glad to be dealing with these two exemplary members of the medical staff despite the exasperating topic of their meeting. Meier *looked* like a surgeon, Simkowitz thought. He was not all that tall, probably about five-eleven, but he seemed tall to Simkowitz, exuding poise and self-assurance without cockiness. At least that was usually the way Meier came across to him, so Simkowitz had expected that he would be the one to carry the conversation. Instead, Meier sat back in his chair, nervously tracing the outline of his thumbnails over and over with the index fingers on both hands while Sandy Flowers led the discussion.

"Can we speak in confidence, Dr. Simkowitz?"

Flowers was calm, Simkowitz observed, her demeanor perfectly controlled, yet she was not distant, not icy cold. Then he saw her hands. No rings on her fingers, no paint on her manicured fingernails, just the most striking hands he had seen in many years. For one long moment he was spellbound looking at her long, powerful fingers, fingers one might find on the hands of a concert pianist. He would put his life in those hands – she was born to be a surgeon!

Simkowitz had been down this road many times with members of his medical staff. Well-meaning physicians who felt a duty to address a serious problem but were terrified about the risks to their own lives of becoming a whistle-blower, of going public with their concerns. They wanted to purge their own consciences, dump the problem on Simkowitz, and yet stay out of the line of fire. And Simkowitz wanted to help them, to show them that he was willing and able to solve the problem they had brought to him. But the sad truth was that Simkowitz knew they were perfectly right to be cautious about speaking up. If they were to take on Dr. Matthew McDonald openly they could end up never seeing another patient or doing another operation in Northeast Suburban or perhaps anywhere else in the state. No one had ever said a peep about McDonald and survived in this hospital.

An especially painful memory of what had happened to someone who had tried to raise red flags about McDonald kept Simkowitz from ever encouraging anyone else to risk coming forward. Stephanie Sorano had been an outstanding doctor, one of the best, yet Molly Cavendish had destroyed Sorano to protect McDonald. And Simkowitz had been powerless to save her.

Simkowitz agonized over his recurring dilemma. He and the two young surgeons were constrained by legal formalities designed to protect the careers of accused doctors until there was compelling proof of the charges against them. That he could understand. But it wasn't just legal niceties that prevented him from effectively pursuing legitimate charges. He could not get past Molly Cavendish without jeopardizing these two promising careers. Cavendish had the power to protect McDonald no matter how strong the evidence against him. Concealing his frustration, Simkowitz gave his customary response, a most unsatisfying caveat that he hated to deliver, but felt he had no alternative.

"Yes and no, I'm afraid. Our conversation today does not need to go anywhere. Whatever information you give me can stay between us. At least for now. I will look carefully at what you tell me, then decide whether anything needs to be done. And, if so, whether I can deal with it off the record, so to speak. But here's the caution: if the evidence requires filing formal charges against Dr. McDonald or anyone else, that physician has the right to face his accusers and defend himself, so your identities would have to come out."

"So, what could you do '*off the record*,' as you say? I don't know whether we are prepared to go public with any accusations."

"There are quite a few things we can do, Dr. Flowers. Let's say the two of you raise a question that McDonald has been operating on normal tissues or organs. We could initiate a special project to evaluate the pathology reports of all of our surgeons – but it would have to be a general inquiry that did not target only Dr. McDonald. If the analysis then showed that he was an outlier, that his results were worse than the other surgeons, then we could talk with him, and perhaps require that he take certain steps to remedy his performance."

Dr. Flowers nodded, her eyelids narrowing slightly. She was not satisfied.

"Would that do any good?"

"Maybe, maybe not," Simkowitz responded, stifling a profound sigh from years of frustration in dealing with McDonald. Simkowitz cautioned himself to strike a balance with the two surgeons, to be realistic and honest about the pitfalls of coming forward yet positive enough to avoid squashing any chance they might be willing to move against the man at some point.

"If we do an assessment of the quality of care on a particular subject, there may or may not be evidence that emerges that points to Dr. McDonald. But he might not be the only physician we find who is doing poorly on whatever aspect of surgery we examine, in which case we would have to think about broad remedies, not ones that were directed solely at McDonald."

"Why beat around the bush? Why not go directly after the problem?"

Simkowitz felt a surge of professional pride in Sandy Flowers – she was all surgeon, she had little tolerance for indirection or hesitation when it came to dealing with illness, or to life in general. Her instinct for action fit the prototypical surgeon's approach: *"When in doubt, cut it out."* He could see that her urge to do something definitive was straining to break through the constraints she and Nicholas Meier had imposed on themselves to avoid going public with their concerns about McDonald, and the limitations Simkowitz was now describing.

"At some point, yes, we could launch an investigation of Dr. McDonald himself. But then things get more complicated. Our procedures are required to have many of the trappings of a criminal investigation, he would have to be given a clear indication of the charges and a fair hearing. *Due process,* it's called, he would have to be given due process, since any investigation and an adverse action against him would be a major threat to his professional activities. Right from the start, actually – we would need a reasonable basis for launching the investigation in the first place, otherwise we might be vulnerable to a charge of having unfairly targeted Dr. McDonald. We have experience on that front..."

Simkowitz bit his lip, hard enough to wince at the pain. He had been on the verge of citing the case of Stephanie Sorano before remembering that he was sworn to secrecy by a non-disclosure clause in her settlement agreement. Catching himself to avoid violating the legal gag order, he said only, "So we need to be careful if we are going to deal directly with McDonald. And that means, in part, letting him know of the charges. And, the identities of the accusers bringing the complaints against him."

Meier at last found his voice, having adapted to the uncomfortable situation. Like Sandy Flowers, his surgeon's instincts prompted him to seek precision, clarity as to what Simkowitz was telling them.

"So we would have to be witnesses, we would have to testify against him openly, is that correct?"

"If you bring the charges, and we decide to pursue the matter, yes."

"OK, let's tell you our story and then we'll decide how to proceed. For now, this is all off the record, OK?"

"As I said, for now, that's the way we can begin, yes."

Leaving the hospital after the unsettling conversation with Sandy Flowers and Nick Meier, Michael Simkowitz pulled his Mercedes Roadster into the driveway of his home, a substantial but unpretentious three-story shingled Colonial on a street with towering old oak and elm trees barely one mile from Northeast Suburban. Entering through the side door that led directly from the carport into the kitchen he called his familiar greeting to his wife, "Hi Julie, don't get your hopes up, it's only me," and headed straight for the dry bar just off their dining room. Pulling down a bottle of *Chivas Regal,* he poured himself about two-and-a-half fingers, then heard his wife acknowledging his presence.

"Hi there, Doctor. Welcome home. And just what are you doing in the bar? Will you be drinking alone tonight?"

The voice that greeted him was soft, but distinctive, with a trace of the West Texas twang that had survived their move to the East Coast. As the woman he had shared so many years with stood and walked over to him he was struck once again that she had fared far better over their time together than he had. Julie had reclaimed her size-five frame quickly after each child was born and maintained it ever since, in contrast to his own waist that now flopped over the old belt in which he had punched new buckle-holes nearly all the way to the tip. Her amber hair color looked stunning next to the simple red-and-gold dress she was wearing. And the color was still natural — he felt a tingle in his groin at the thought that her hair color was a consistent shade of amber everywhere on her body.

"I'm sorry, *Julia Lynne,* would you like something?" he responded, emphasizing her full double name that she rarely used anymore.

"If my dear husband is hitting the hooch before kissing his wife and saying '*Howdy,*' I guess I'd better be drinking as well. Is there any white wine in your bar?"

Simkowitz bent over cautiously to survey the contents of the under-counter refrigerator, being careful not to move quickly or awkwardly enough to throw his fragile back out, and saw a promising collection of wine bottles.

"*Pinot Grigio Friuli Grave* or *Chardonnay?*" he responded, although he was already pulling out a bottle of the *Pinot Grigio* from

Friuli since this oft-repeated repartee always led to the same conclusion.

"The usual, My Dear."

He and Julie walked around the stovetop counter in the kitchen into their family room, a large but comfortable space surrounded on three sides by glass windows and sliding doors that opened to their backyard deck. The room was dominated by a U-shaped leather sectional and an oversized television on a long, low stand. He saw his wife push the record button on the *TiVo* before turning off the television she had been watching.

"*TiVo*, what an invention," he said.

A broad smirk covered her still-youthful face.

"Honey, *TiVo* is not an invention, it's a member of our family. Maybe my favorite member, or at least the one I spend the most time with. Let's sit down and you can tell me, Dearie, why the Scotch? I always know something is up when you come home and head straight to the hard liquor, Dr. Simkowitz."

"At least I come home, Ma'am. Good thing this house is the closest place to the hospital that serves liquor or I might have stopped off in a bar."

"Uh-oh, let me guess. McDonald, again?"

"You know, I should have had more sense. I've been around this fucking hospital for, what, twenty-some years?"

"Hmm, that's a double uh-oh, f-bombs *and* Scotch, this must be serious. And it's twenty-three, Honey, we bought this house twenty-three years ago when you started at Northeast. Back up – give this old girl a kiss, sip some *Chivas*, then unload your latest McDonald saga."

Simkowitz kissed her, feeling a wave of appreciation for the human connection. She responded in kind with a vigorous, wet kiss, then raised her glass of wine and clicked it against his tumbler of Scotch, and they each took a substantial swig of their drinks.

"OK," he said, "I'll try to keep down the f-bombs, but I need the Scotch. So years ago they offer me the grandiose-sounding titles of *Chief of the Medical Staff* and *Vice-President for Medical Affairs of Northeast Suburban Hospital* and I'm fool enough to go along with it. But you know what? As both a hospital administrator and a physician, I'm caught so tightly in the middle of an unending power struggle in that fu...that miserable hospital that I am, in reality, impotent. Professionally impotent, that is."

"Let's hope that's *all* the impotence you're suffering from, Sugar," she said slowly, her sultry drawl stretching the words out provocatively.

He ignored her seductive but as-yet untimely remark, taking another long sip of his Scotch. Simkowitz let the pungent liquid sit in his mouth for a few seconds, then shut his eyes and enjoyed the faintly burning sensation as it flowed down his throat and began lightly anesthetizing the rest of his body.

"Nominally I'm in charge of all the doctors who practice at the hospital, but in reality I can't do squat. I have practically no authority compared with the cabal that runs the place. Mostly, what I really do is organize and then have to sit through endless meetings. I go downtown or to conferences to represent the hospital when some group wants a doctor to speak about *modern hospital care* or some crap like that. I handle mountains of routine paperwork, processing applications for membership on the medical staff, shit like that. I don't even see the important reports that go to the government until they are pretty much in final form."

"I know what goes on in that hospital, Honey – don't you remember my first job, when you were an intern at Northeast?"

"Of course. You were that dang nuisance clerk who spoke like a cowgirl and rummaged through everyone's medical charts to compile the list of delinquent docs who hadn't completed their dictations. Everyone hated you. Except me, I thought you were cute. And when we got married I took a ton of grief from the doctors you nagged at work."

"Well, Doctor, this cowgirl picked her way among the cowchips long enough to see what was going on, and it sounds like things have gone downhill since I left that place to have our first."

"This job, what a mistake, what a trap. What could I have been thinking? I talked myself into believing I could really be an advocate to improve patient care, they'd all have to listen to me. Instead, once I showed my desire to make real changes, they pulled the hospital's *Quality Assurance* programs out from under me and that power-hungry Molly Cavendish took over. She was a bedside nurse when I started at Northeast, she took orders from me. Then Lester goes and makes her the goddamn Senior Vice President, she's in charge of everything, even their so-called Quality Assurance programs. What a farce. Her shenanigans have cost us some of our best doctors, the ones who try to point out our real problems. If I'm professionally impotent, she's a professional slut, she'd turn any tricks they ask her to."

"Uh-oh, *uppity woman*, huh? Doesn't know her place in the big boys' club? Clearly a slut."

"C'mon, Honey, you know that among my many failings, misogyny isn't high on the list. Besides, once I'd been emasculated, why would a eunuch like me care what the sex was of the one who wielded the scalpel?"

"Now you're really making me nervous with your analogies, Mr. Doctor. First *'impotent'* and now *'emasculated'* and *'eunuch.'* Is there something you're trying to tell me?"

"Give your old husband a break, Sweetheart. This is about work, not my diminishing capacity to gratify your insatiable sexual appetite."

"That's better, I was hoping you could pull yourself out a bit. Whoops, sorry, My Dear, that was a purely unintentional analogy. Don't pull anything out, not just yet. I can see this must be a bad one, huh? No wonder the *Chivas* isn't going to keep aging in that bottle."

"I've been stupid, Honey. I let them paint me into a corner, and I'm trapped there. No way out. I haven't really practiced medicine for twelve years, there's no way I could go back to seeing patients, let alone doing surgery, at my age."

"Your age? You're a young man, exactly my age."

"Maybe to you, Honey, but I'm sixty-one years old, I made this move and I'm stuck. I got into this and I don't see how I can get out. But I can't stand to have this crap happening on my watch, it doesn't make it any better just because the problem is out of my control. I still feel like I should be able to *do* something."

He polished off the glass of Scotch, reached over to pick up his wife's empty wineglass and headed back to the dry bar for refills.

"OK, what happened? This must have been a *really* bad one if it's a two-Scotch day."

"Who said anything about two?"

He returned to the sofa, handed his wife her drink, and they clicked their crystal glasses against each other again.

"Take your time with that stuff, Honey, take your time. I want you to be able to function coherently for a while."

"What kills me is that McDonald has just the opposite image, and he knows how to play it. He always makes it on those phony *'Best Doctors'* lists just because he's such a flamboyant personality. Doctors all over the region send him their patients who need surgery. Hell, patients all over the region *ask* to be referred to the famous Dr. McDonald at the prestigious Northeast Suburban Hospital when they need surgery. But no one inside the hospital would choose him as their surgeon, not in a million years. And yet they put his damn photo on the cover of the hospital's annual report last year, the one that gets sent to all the upper-crust donors. He brings in so much money the hospital has concealed his mistakes – buried his mistakes, I should really say. He's in total cahoots with Cavendish and Williamsburg and Sullivan, they thwart every one of my initiatives to improve patient care, especially if my efforts might threaten McDonald in any way. It's bad, Honey, it's as fucked-up as it's ever been, and it's getting worse."

"Hmmm…back with the f-bombs. So what's the evil McDonald's latest transgression?"

"It's bad enough that patients suffer and he gets special treatment – but now it's affecting some of our junior medical staff as well, and that drives me nuts. I'm there to help them develop, to foster their careers, but I see them heading toward self-destruction instead. I've got to do something."

"Back up, Sugar, back up. What happened?"

"Two of our shining up-and-coming stars, Sandra Flowers and Nicholas Meier, came to see me. They've been in the operating room on and off with McDonald, and have followed his patients post-op when they were on call. They alluded to several truly bothersome incidents that they saw first-hand. I think there's a particular incident that made them come to see me, but they didn't say exactly what it was."

"What did they want you to do about it?"

"They want me to fix it, without getting them involved. They're leery of becoming whistleblowers, going public with what they know. I can't argue with their desire to remain anonymous – it could easily destroy their careers if they took on McDonald. He'd try to make it look as though whatever happened was their fault and the hospital would back him to the hilt. Molly Cavendish would dig out stuff from their own patients that would make them look bad the way she did with Stephanie Sorano, remember? How can I tell them to jeopardize their futures when there would be no point, they'd be the only ones who'd suffer?"

"I can't forget Stephanie, that's for sure, Sugar. What a boot in the hindquarters that was. I really liked that gal, and she was such a good doctor. So you think the two of them are just going to look the other way?"

"I don't know. They don't want to ignore it, but they're torn apart over this, that's why they came to me. They still have consciences, they still have a sense of medical ethics. The medical credo, *primum non nocere*, '*First, do no harm*,' that still means something to them. They're in this business to help people, not for the money or prestige. This kind of crap is very painful for them."

"What are their alternatives?"

"The most likely one, the one that has happened several times before, is that I won't be able to take action and one or both of them, Flowers and Meier, will eventually leave, move away, go somewhere else and start all over. Their consciences will trouble them for a while, but over time they'll learn to tolerate the discomfort once they're gone and don't have to see what McDonald does day in and day out. Or they'll give up medicine entirely – just like Stephanie, for Christ's sake."

"You can't help at all? That doesn't sound like my creative, dedicated, even…conniving husband who always wants to do the right thing."

"No kidding. Hence the Scotch, the wine, the obvious plea for advice from my *creative, dedicated, even…conniving* spouse."

"If you can't rope McDonald in and hog-tie him at the knees, can't you figure out a way to at least put a squeeze on him? Some silent pressure you can hold over him, use behind the scenes?"

"I've tried that before and got nowhere. But I won't give up. I'll come up with another plan, I hope. Maybe I can show problems with McDonald's performance that are bad enough to get the unholy trinity to support me at last."

"Cavendish and Williamsburg and Sullivan?"

"Yup. See-no-evil, hear-no-evil, and speak-no-evil, the triumvirate of clueless innocent monkeys. No knowledge, no blame. If I could get enough on McDonald for the three of them to see that their own careers were in jeopardy, that Northeast Suburban itself was at risk, then maybe they'd realize this can't go on. Someday one of the families of the patients he screwed up on is going to figure it out – not just what happened to their departed loved one, but how those three *allowed* it to happen, and how many other loved ones departed in a similar manner, all with the hospital turning a blind eye. Then it'll really be over. If I can just get the goods on McDonald once and for all they'll have to listen. Maybe I'll have to go public myself."

"That's more like it! There's the old spunk — the brave cowboy willing to take on the whole gang of rustlers to save the herd!"

Julie snuggled up next to him on the couch, set their glasses on the coffee table, and gave him a long, passionate kiss, rubbing her breasts against his chest.

"Mmmm. That's quite a rack you've got there, Julia Lynne."

"*Wey'll, ah thank* it's time to check out *yo'* impotency and emasculation, Doctor, Sir," she crooned in a cutesy Southern-belle voice.

"And *ah thank* the evidence is already beginning to emerge, *Ma'am*."

Chapter 9.   Deepening Conundrums

A fecal stench spewed into the operating room from Eleanore Hinkel's abdomen the instant Nicholas Meier's scalpel cut through the skin and subcutaneous tissues. Meier and Jorge Edmond reacted reflexively to the disgusting smell, taking tight breaths through their surgical masks, but their hands remained steady as they worked together in silence, lancing and draining pockets of pus sequestered under folds of intestine and around her internal organs. Proceeding cautiously yet as rapidly as possible given the woman's fragile state, they irrigated the surgical site copiously, daubed the area with gauze pads to absorb the foul seepage, suctioned off the remaining liquid, and positioned drainage tubes connected to collecting bottles.

When they had finished, both men trudged into the changing room, exhausted. Meier sat down next to Jorge on a bench and said, "Quite a mess in that poor woman's belly, huh? That fetid smell is never a good sign, I'm afraid."

"Yes, Dr. Meier, I feel so bad for Mrs. Hinkel. And her husband."

Meier noticed that Jorge spoke even more softly than usual. The aging PA seemed bothered by something.

"Anything wrong, Jorge?"

Jorge so wanted to say something about the botched appendectomy on Eleanore Hinkel, about McDonald's lies afterward, about the problems he had seen with other patients of Matthew McDonald, but he simply shook his head and said, "No, Dr. Meier. Thank you, but it's nothing special. I was just thinking about Mr. and Mrs. Hinkel, that's all. I'm fine."

"OK, Jorge," Meier replied, unconvinced but sensing he should not probe any further. "But I hope you know you can always talk to me if something's bothering you. I'm always willing to listen."

"Yes, Dr. Meier, I do appreciate that, for sure. Thank you very much." Then Jorge turned his head so Meier could not see him grimacing in an agonizing effort at self-control.

A few minutes later, Nicholas Meier walked into Eleanore Hinkel's room. He nodded his head slowly and raised the palm of his right hand toward her husband in a restrained, almost somber, greeting. Meier was struck that the man had aged visibly in the past few days, even in the hours since they had spoken.

"Mr. Hinkel, I'm afraid the situation doesn't look good."

The young surgeon mustered all his reserve to imagine being in the suffering man's position. He intended to be as consoling as possible, yet the stark reality was bleak and he had no choice but to be straightforward. No matter how he couched his words, the prognosis was grim: Eleanore Hinkel was almost certainly dying.

"Her infection goes well beyond the surgical sites. It is widespread in her abdomen, in multiple locations. Behind her liver, around her internal organs, in the folds of her bowels."

"What does that mean? Can you stop the infection now?"

"The lab will culture the material we drained and give us a profile of the bacteria and the antibiotics they are sensitive to — or resistant to, I'm afraid — and we'll treat her accordingly. We have some preliminary results but we won't really know just what we're dealing with for several days. The most important thing is to give her immune system a chance to fight the infection. It's really up to her to fight this off, all we can do is help."

"Dr. Meier, she's got to live, I need her, we've got to do whatever we can. Please."

"I understand. We are doing everything possible. I have also asked Dr. Ribbeno, our new infectious disease specialist, to consult on your wife's case. He will be involved in making the decision about her antibiotics. I will check on Mrs. Hinkel at least twice every day. When Dr. McDonald returns…"

Nicholas Meier had to choose his words carefully — if it were up to him, McDonald would never set foot in the hospital again, let alone in Eleanore Hinkel's room. He knew a confrontation with McDonald was inevitable but for now he needed to focus on saving

Eleanore Hinkel, not girding himself for a blowup with Matthew McDonald.

"When Dr. McDonald returns, he will also be closely involved. And, of course, your Internist, Dr. Anthony Marlburg, is following her with us. He's an excellent physician."

"But can you tell me if she's going to get better? I need to know that she's going to get better, I must know."

"I wish I could be sure, but the most I can tell you is that we are doing everything possible. We have a lot of weapons to fight the infections with and we're going to use all of them. I have every hope that she's going to win this battle."

As long as he talked about *hope*, Nicholas Meier could reassure himself that he was not deceiving Henry Hinkel. Not entirely. As long as a patient was still alive there was always hope, he told himself. But he did not want the man to ask him how reasonable that hope was, knowing that the odds against Eleanore Hinkel surviving were enormous.

Henry Hinkel's voice became even more plaintive as he searched for the strength to let out the concern that had been forming in his mind that day.

"My kids, our kids, they're waiting to hear whether…whether they…whether they need to come to town. What should I tell them?"

Nicholas Meier had anticipated this question. It was often the indirect way family members would approach the terrible subject of whether their loved one was dying. They wanted a black-or-white prognosis, an answer in simple terms, not the usual medical blather about the inherent uncertainty of predicting nature's course. It was the other side of death: what should the living do? The living needed uncomplicated information to make their practical, real-life decisions. Should they interrupt their lives yet? Make airplane reservations? Take time off of work? Was this to be their last chance to say goodbye? Nicholas Meier had expected the question, but deep down he was not fully satisfied with the response he was about to give, because what seemed to be such a simple question had no easy answer. Death was certain, but elusive, appearing on its own timetable, hazardous to predict with anything like precision until the last moments.

"I don't think your wife is in any imminent danger, although we can never be absolutely sure. It's more likely that it will take several days before we know how things are going. I don't think your kids need to act as though it's an emergency, but maybe they could try to get here when it works for them."

"Imminent danger? What do you mean?"

Meier was torn between keeping the man's hopes from disintegrating or saying forthrightly, *"This woman could die, maybe not today, but soon."*

"If we thought the infection was overwhelming her body, if we thought she was not likely to fight any longer, we would let you know. If that happens, then of course you would want your family here right away. I do not think we're at that point, Mr. Hinkel. Not at the moment."

"My son, Jeffrey, he's…he's very close to his mother. He's coming today or tomorrow. Jeffrey won't fly, he drives everywhere, so it's going to take him a while. He lives in New Hampshire. I think he left yesterday, it's a twelve hour trip. I wish he would fly like everyone else, but he just won't, I don't know why. I just hope he doesn't drive straight through."

"That's good, I'm sure he will be a comfort to you…" Nicholas Meier quickly added, "to your wife and to you, of course," then wondered whether the clumsy attempt to correct his omission might only have accentuated the implication that he had already started thinking of Eleanore Hinkel as over the edge, doomed, too far gone to be comforted by the arrival of her son.

If Henry Hinkel had taken the ominous inference from the surgeon's well-intentioned words, it didn't show. The man's desperate desire for his wife to live, for his crushing feeling of guilt to lighten, had pushed his grief to its limits. In his suffering, he was not about to search for a subtly portentous meaning in Nicholas Meier's words. No words short of pronouncing his wife dead could heighten his anguish.

"My other son, our other son, Roger, he's not so emotional. He'll come *if necessary*, he said, whatever that means. He's a good boy, but he's all wrapped up in his job, in making money, we don't see him very often. And our daughter, Sue Anne, she has the three kids and a husband who travels all the time, so she might not be able to get here very soon. She's good with her mother, not like Jeffrey, but she and her mother have been good ever since they made it through Sue Anne's high school days."

Nicholas Meier was doing his best to be attentive, but now he had to get on with caring for his other patients.

"You have a good family, Mr. Hinkel, that's something to be proud of. I'll be back this afternoon after office hours, and they can always find me if they need to. I'll see you later."

"Thank you, Dr. Meier, thank you."

***

Monica Gould had pestered her husband, Ariel, for more than six months to go to their family doctor to check out the expanding bulge in his groin. When he finally gave in, they went to their family doctor, Dr. Zoe Sanderson, who diagnosed an inguinal hernia. Hernias like that were very common, she said, and some people just put up with the inconvenience and wear a truss. But there was a risk that a piece of bowel might get stuck and twisted inside the hernia at some point, and then he would need emergency surgery. Dr. Sanderson recommended that Ariel have the hernia repaired before anything like that happened. She assured them that it was minor surgery, just a small incision and a few little stitches, then no heavy lifting for a while afterward. Sanderson offered to refer them to a specialist who saw quite a few such cases, but Monica Gould said that several of her lady friends had told her that the best surgeon around was Dr. Matthew McDonald. She asked Sanderson whether Dr. McDonald would do this type of surgery. The physician said she didn't know for sure, but she would be happy to make the referral to Dr. McDonald if that was what Monica and Ariel wanted.

Matthew McDonald was quite gracious on the telephone. No, he said, he generally did not do minor procedures such as repairing a hernia, but he would make an exception since he knew the ladies who had recommended him to Monica. After he examined Ariel, McDonald described the operation as quite simple. He would open up the hernia and patch it with some polypropylene mesh, close things up nice and neat, and then the tissues would grow back over the mesh. Ariel would be good as new in just a few days. McDonald told the Goulds that it would be best to do the surgery in the hospital. Yes, Northeast Suburban Hospital. Just an overnight stay, that would be all.

The late Ariel Gould was the last patient that Dr. Zoe Sanderson would ever refer to Dr. Matthew McDonald.

Chapter 10. Bargaining Positions

Dr. Matthew McDonald felt a tingle in his groin as he stared at the shapely blonde in a string bikini sunning her nearly-naked body on the chaise lounge next to his. This was the life, a trip to a luxury resort in Cabo on a big drug and medical device company's dime, a free ride to spend time with a hot woman like this Alexandra Parushnikova. This was the way it should be, he told himself. He deserved this. He earned it.

His eyes fixed unabashedly on the young woman, McDonald was oblivious to the tropical splendor surrounding them at the poolside. Purple bougainvillea, deep red oleander and bright orange hibiscus interspersed among the clusters of cabanas and chaise lounges. Low coconut palms and Hibiscus tiliaceus dotted small faux islands in the massive pool. And bars, bars everywhere, bars on the islands, bars surrounding the pool, bars wherever they looked.

Alexandra Parushnikova and Matthew McDonald were enjoying the bright sun on the first of four days of a gathering all paid for by their thoughtful host, *Marquis-Herrant.* Some seventy prominent surgeons would hear about the company's new surgical devices and pharmaceutical products at brief lectures interspersed generously with free time, boating and deep-sea fishing excursions, receptions, lavish meals, open bars. And for certain participants like McDonald, special deals. Very special deals.

For her part, the woman loved fitting the new prototype of a pharmaceutical representative. The drug and device companies had put all the old detail men out to pasture. No more fifty-something balding white guys, amiable fellows who made their rounds, charming the *'girls'* as they called all the nurses, receptionists and office managers, passing out ball-point pens and note pads with drug company logos along with copious free samples. The problem for the pharmaceutical and device companies was that the old detail men were no longer getting much face time with the physicians to push their hyper-expensive new drugs and medical devices. So the companies recruited a new generation of detail reps who would be welcomed into the inner sanctum of medical offices to see the doctors. Attractive young women or equally good-looking and personable young Black or Hispanic men, many former high-profile high school or college athletes. Innately charming and bright, able to master sufficient pharmacology and medicine to converse with the doctors about the purported advantages of the new drugs and devices.

The new generation of detail reps was talented and personable. But only a handful of carefully selected ones were given special assignments like the one Alexandra Parushnikova was carrying out.

Leaning back in her chaise lounge on the deck surrounding one of the endless swimming pools at the sprawling Cabo resort, Alexandra reflected on how much she enjoyed her situation. Working for the *Marquis-Herrant* drug and medical supply company was pretty much a dream job, far better than she had ever hoped for once she had been denied admittance to the Siberian State Medical University in Tomsk, Russia, despite her honors degree in biology from the prestigious Novosibirsk State University. She was never able to find out why her medical studies had been blocked. Maybe it was those early years she had spent in the U.S. with her grandfather, a diplomat under Gorbachev. All for the best, she told herself once *Marquis-Herrant* had recruited her. This job got her back to the States with a six-figure salary and frequent trips to exotic resorts. And then there were the opportunities to earn bonuses, really big bonuses she could salt away.

As she lay in the blissfully hot Mexican sun she remembered how the *Marquis-Herrant* trainers had glossed over the '*keep it professional*' part of the detail reps' responsibilities for all the new recruits, emphasizing instead the '*get close to your customers*' instructions. But her particular preparation had begun much earlier, during her interview back in Novosibirsk with the recruiter from *Marquis-Herrant*. "Now, Sasha," the recruiter said, adopting a personal tone by using the Russian diminutive for Alexandra, "I need to know if you are willing to be, shall we say, *flexible* in the assignments you will carry out. There are certain special clients who need special treatment."

Sasha quickly got the gist of what the recruiter meant, and it wasn't long before they were speaking openly about the financial terms associated with her expanded responsibilities. Big money, a piece of the action. The company was just starting up and had a grand design to expand rapidly. If all went well Sasha would be earning seven figures before long, and all it would require would be an occasional *"special assignment."* The offer was irresistible. After all, she told herself, having sex with some doctors now and then would not be so different than hooking up with random guys like she had been doing ever since she was seventeen. Besides, this was much more profitable, and she wasn't freezing back in Novosibirsk. She could keep this up for a few years, then get out with a bulging bank account, set for life. Maybe bring her mother, her sisters, to the States.

Yes, it was all good. Well, *almost* all good…some of the special assignments she would be "invited" to perform could be rather unsavory. Like this one. *Bad with the good,* she repeated silently, sipping her huge Margarita as she gazed at Matthew McDonald over the salted rim of a double-bowled glass so large it resembled an upside-down sombrero on a stick. The longer she looked at him the more distasteful this part of the job felt. She loved her job, the resort was beautiful, but being stuck there with this guy meant that she couldn't really enjoy herself despite the elegance. She recited her mantra again, *bad with the good,* resigning herself to the task at hand.

Masking her deep distaste for the arrogant surgeon, she tossed back her long blond hair, clicked her enormous glass against his whiskey tumbler, and said in her practiced professional voice, "Cheers, Dr. McDonald. Here's to research and development. And sales!"

"Sales, of course, my beautiful Sasha, that's what pays for our educational ventures like this. Here's to sales!"

As they clinked glasses, McDonald scanned the woman's voluptuous torso, from the pale breasts bulging over the cups of her scant bikini top to her glistening bikini-waxed groin, tantalizingly smooth above a slender thong with straps so thin they could have been drawn on her skin with a *Sharpie.* What a life, he thought contentedly. This was it, this was why he loved being a successful doctor.

Sasha looked back at McDonald. It was clear that he was in his element in exotic resorts like this, at least when someone else was paying the tab. And the way he stared at her left no doubt what he had in mind. Of course, she would comply, she was on the job, she was there for a reason. It was her responsibility to get on his good side so he would help her put together an agreement with Northeast Suburban to purchase devices and drugs from her company and pave the way for them at other local hospitals. She had some exclusive deals to offer that would be profitable for her and for McDonald. And she had no doubt that he would be interested in what she had to offer. Everything she had to offer.

She reassured herself that at least this guy was in good shape, it wasn't his body that repulsed her, it was that the man was a real jerk, a classic *pridurok*, even more full of himself than the other surgeons – and that was saying a lot. Then she sucked in a breath and reminded herself that this was a business relationship, all in a day's work – and in her case, a night's work. It was her job to be charming, to make sure he was friendly toward *Marquis-Herrant*, willing to open doors for her.

Matthew McDonald was in his curious world, his own universe. He took a long sip of Bushmills 21-year old Malt, musing that his beautiful companion might not be that much older than the Irish whiskey. He looked into the two bright eyes gazing at him as she took a mouthful of Margarita from the immense glass and decided the young pharmaceutical rep was in the chorus of his admirers – after all, who wasn't enthralled with him? Setting his glass down, he raised one thin black eyebrow in a menacing *Rhett Butler* caricature, and said confidently, "I promise you, Sasha, tonight you will be satisfied beyond your wildest dreams. I am magnificently endowed and I have mastered many ways to bring pleasure to a woman."

A salt-laced projectile of lime juice, triple sec, and tequila spurted through Sasha's gaping lips as she gagged and coughed, spraying a long stream of greenish glop across both chaise lounges. Her giant Margarita glass flew from her grasp and shattered with a loud *ping* on the tile. Puddles of thick slime collected on the pool deck amid the shards of glass. She coughed again, sputtered, and grabbed her beach towel to wipe her lips and tongue, barely noticing the mess she had just made. She had thought she was prepared for the inevitable, but McDonald's come-on was so bizarre it had startled her.

Picking herself up from the contaminated chaise lounge with as much dignity as she could muster she said, "Excuse me, I've got to go to the ladies' room." She slipped her feet into her Balenciaga sandals, stepped carefully around the glass rubble and walked toward the large indoor bar, her small travel wallet with her passport in one hand, the beach towel still held to her lips in the other.

An unlikely couple lying on two nearby chaise lounges watched the Margarita incident unfold with particular interest. Unlikely because one was an enormous bald man whose scalp and face were swathed in such copious white sunscreen he looked like he had lathered up for a total-head shave, while the other was a svelte, athletic woman with short brown hair who was half the man's size. Struggling to keep from laughing out loud at the spectacle he had just witnessed, the big man whispered to the woman, "She's out of here. Maybe you should follow her." His companion said assuredly, "She'll be back, just wait."

In the rest room Alexandra Parushnikova buried her face under a faucet, splashing the water vigorously to wash equal measures of Margarita and disgust off her face. She stared at herself in the mirror. *Sasha, what the hell are you doing?* she asked her reflection, not sure whether she was questioning her unprofessional reaction to McDonald's crude advances or the very life she had chosen. She glanced at her passport. She could gather her belongings and head straight to the airport, get away from this asshole. But she was trapped. If she walked out on him she would get fired, or demoted, or sent back to Novosibirsk or even farther north. She thought of the hardships her grandmother, her *babushka,* had endured under the dire conditions of war and Soviet oppression. This was nothing compared to that, who was she to complain? She dried her face, passed a comb through her hair, and left the bathroom. With perfect poise, she walked quickly past a wandering trumpet quartet in bright Mariachi costumes and returned to her spot on the poolside. An attendant had already removed the broken glass and replaced her slime-coated chaise lounge with a clean one — and a fresh Margarita was waiting for her. Smiling coyly at McDonald as she bent provocatively over the lounge chair she said, "Sorry about the mess. I think the salt made me choke."

"No problem," he said, a lascivious sneer crawling over his face. "We'll have plenty of time for drinks…and who knows what other messes we might make, my lovely Sasha."

Mudak! What an asshole, she thought, continuing to smile.

The woman on the nearby chaise lounge turned to the huge bald man and said softly, "See, Murph, she's back."

"OK, Adrienne, touché. Right as always, Boss."

74

Chapter 11. Our Patient

As Nick Meier stepped back from the operating table and removed his surgical gloves after a routine excision of a fleshy mass from a young woman's back, Jorge Edmond raised his eyebrows and nodded slightly, his smiling face hidden behind a green surgical mask. When he was scrubbed, gowned, gloved, masked, and hooded in green operating room garb exactly like the surgeon, Jorge Edmond felt a surge of pride from being an integral member of an expert team. He was genuinely gratified to be doing this job, even more so to have the good fortune to work around one of the best surgeons in the hospital. Nick Meier not only surpassed most of the others in skill and knowledge but also behaved as a gentleman and, most important, treated Jorge as a fellow professional. Jorge was pleased with himself and full of admiration for Nicholas Meier.

Feeling deep respect for the surgeon he held in high esteem, Jorge let his thoughts wander back to a much earlier conversation in which Meier had asked him if he had ever considered becoming a physician. Although flattered by the question, Jorge understood just how little the surgeon knew about the world he had come from and why he treasured his supporting role. Speaking with the faint hint of a Spanish accent, Jorge had answered cheerfully, "Doctor Meier, that is so good of you to ask, but, please, I am very happy to be doing my job as a surgical assistant. My kids, my grandkids, they can be doctors, God willing, but I am fortunate to be a physician assistant."

"If you don't mind, I would like to know why you feel that way, Jorge."

"I don't mind at all, Doctor Meier. Thank you for asking. You see, nobody in my family ever thought of going to college, they all dropped out of high school just like I did. I never imagined I could get an education. I didn't even do my GED and get to college until I was forty-one years old, and now I'm fifty-two. It took me seven years, first the Associates degree, then the B.S. and surgical training, now I'm almost finished with my Masters. This is good, very good, for me. I am quite content, but thank you, thank you so much for asking."

Jorge had revealed the bare bones of his past but had kept his deeper thoughts to himself. Even someone as well-meaning and friendly as Meier could never appreciate what it was like for him to be doing this job after years of being a day laborer, after seeing his younger brother, Mario, and all those guys he used to hang with die from drugs or gang fights or end up in jail. Jorge could hardly believe that at this point in his life he was a certified health professional, earning a good salary, working indoors with other professionals, using his brain instead of his body, learning more every day. He was deeply appreciative of his hard-won status. He and the surgeon each had their role, two essential parts of a team. Of course the surgeon could do things that he could not do, but Jorge was satisfied knowing that he freed Nicholas Meier up to concentrate on the more difficult or delicate tasks, and the unexpected challenges that always lurked in a surgical operation.

Proud of his position and very good at it, Jorge had no regrets that he was not the one in charge. He was paid well enough that he felt no resentment that his work allowed the surgeons to reap lucrative rewards by billing for many more patients than they could see on their own. He understood that the surgeons he worked with needed him as much as he needed them, now that they were under ever-increasing pressure to increase their productivity, to see as many patients and perform as many revenue-generating procedures as possible. The working relationship was all very efficient – in addition to helping at surgery, the PA could see the returning patients almost as soon as they walked in the door, no waiting, no need for the doctor to be involved. Unless there was a problem, then Jorge would page the surgeon if something needed immediate attention. Most post-operative patients quickly overcame their initial aversion to being treated by a PA once they realized how skilled Jorge was and – especially – how convenient it proved to be. In fact, they loved not having to wait hours for a surgeon who would simply glance at a healing wound for five seconds or take a few quick snips to remove sutures.

All in all, Jorge was satisfied that he had found a good life. The hard streets were a distant memory, thanks be to God. He was in his element taking care of patients, working side-by-side with a gifted surgeon.

In his down-to-earth, slightly laconic Midwestern voice, Meier had responded with genuine sincerity, without a trace of condescension. "That's quite a story, Jorge. Well, I'm certainly glad you got on track. It's great to have you around. You're very talented."

"Thank you again, Doctor Meier, thank you very much."

"Thanks, Jorge. It's a blessing to have you around. I hope I tell you that often enough. When we hired our first surgical PA I didn't know how well it would work out, but it's great for me and for our patients."

Jorge was nearly overcome by Meier's choice of words: *'our patients!'* The words rang through his head, he could feel a lump forming in his throat. Meier had said *'Our* patients,' not *'my* patients.' Nicholas Meier saw him as a full partner. Jorge understood that the doctor could never understand how much that meant to him.

"Thank you, Dr. Meier, that's very comforting to know that you feel that way. I am pleased myself, thanks be to God. It is a real privilege to work with you, Dr. Meier."

"Jorge, I've been meaning to ask you something. The other day when we were attending to Mrs. Hinkel, you seemed bothered by something. I thought you seemed tense or distracted. Was there something I didn't do? Did you notice something about her that I wasn't picking up?"

Jorge felt the terror of the bind he was in, trapped between his yearning to right a great wrong and his instinct for self-preservation. He lowered his head, his eyes shifting back and forth from side to side, his teeth clenched involuntarily, while he tried to decide what to do, what to say. He rocked slowly on his heels several times, then steadied himself, looked up, and caught the surgeon's eyes.

"I don't know, Dr. Meier, maybe there was something I was thinking. She's so sick, and I was in surgery with her when Dr. McDonald took out her appendix. It just bothers me to think about that, maybe. I was so hoping she would be fine, and now she's just lying there, wasting away. For sure I don't remember anything I thought *you* missed, not you, Dr. Meier. You don't miss anything, Dr. Meier."

Jorge Edmond was not voicing some hollow compliment. The surgeon was a man he genuinely admired. He was trying to deal with the nagging concern that Meier would know that Jorge was suppressing a deadly secret, that he would find him out and expose him, embarrassing Jorge and, worse, destroying their professional bond.

"Thanks, but I miss a lot more than you might think. OK, if anything comes to you, you know you can tell me. I want to know anything that might help our patients."

This time the phrase, '*our patients,*' cut into Jorge from a different angle, shaking him to his core. Meier's treasured acceptance of Jorge as his teammate, his colleague, the simple words that had been so precious a minute earlier now carried a painful, discomforting meaning that made Jorge tremble inside. Yes, Eleanore Hinkel was *his* patient too, but now that was exactly the problem that was tearing at him – he was letting *his patient* down, not telling the surgeon what he knew. Yet, what good would it do for him to speak up? Whatever he did, it wouldn't help her, not really, she would be in the same horrendous condition no matter what he said at this point. What was done, was done. And he didn't really have any proof, nothing that would convince a surgeon like Meier who needed something concrete, something definite. Even though McDonald had far too many problems with his patients, more problems over just a few months than Nicholas Meier would ever have, if Jorge did speak up it would be his word, the word of an aging former street hoodlum, a lowly immigrant physician assistant, against that of the most prominent surgeon in the hospital.

Then Jorge thought of a way he might raise the subject that was tormenting him. He could speak indirectly, in his accustomed style of phrasing suggestions to the surgeons as questions.

"Dr. Meier, excuse me. I did not see the pathology report on Mrs. Hinkel in her medical record. Did Dr. Pappelbaugh find anything unusual?"

This was dangerous, Jorge knew, but he had to do something to assuage his guilt, had to let someone know that there was more to this poor woman's situation than they thought.

Nicholas Meier hesitated, thinking, trying to recall what he had seen in Eleanore Hinkel's medical record.

"I don't know for sure, but now that I think of it, I scrolled through her chart last night and I don't recall seeing Dr.

Pappelbaugh's report on her appendix yet. I wouldn't be all that surprised if it's not there, since Pathology's has been backed up on routine stuff lately but it should be there by now. I'll track it down and see if there's anything I missed."

Jorge Edmond said nothing in reply, simply nodding his head to the surgeon and turning away again so Meier could not see the worry he knew was written all over his face.

Chapter 12. The Hinkel Family

As he drove his vintage *Jeep Wagoneer Limited* on his mission to his mother's bedside, Jeffrey Hinkel reminisced about the home he was leaving behind on the shores of Lake Winnipesaukee in the remote woods of central New Hampshire. He loved the bold seasons with their predictable cycles, the hillsides lighting up golden in the fall, the blankets of snow enveloping the frozen lake in winter, the first whiff of honeysuckle in spring, the warmth of summer that always arrived suddenly. He envisioned the vast birch forests that had covered the lake islands before the invasion of pines, then saw images of the lonely birch tree clusters that remained, their scaling white bark and shades of yellow leaves that hypnotized him with their beauty. He smiled at the thought of the treasured group of photos lined up like an extended triptych on the wall over his fireplace. The sequential prints were his artistic pride and joy: four long, narrow pictures of a cluster of three white birch trees taken from the identical location in the peak splendor of each season. It had taken him several years to snap the perfect shots: the spotty black-on-white birch trunks barren and buried in winter snow, sprouting leaves in spring, glowing dark green in summer, then turning bright yellow and red in autumn.

Alone in his old Jeep, just as he was almost always alone in his small, solid cabin, he sighed, thinking how much he loved the solitude, the calm of his secluded home. And yet, he reminded himself, he needed the influx of summer vacationers from Memorial Day to Labor Day who arrived with their thick wallets that kept his shop thriving and provided him with a modest living. He was proud that people came from Boston, New York, all over the Northeast to *Jeffrey's Curios and Antiques* for items he located by scouring farmhouses and estate sales for traditional American furniture and memorabilia. He would buy them at a good price, then sell them for markups of ten or twenty times what he had paid. For the summer crowd they were still amazing bargains, a fraction of what the pieces would have commanded in the galleries back home in the big cities. Even after all these years he sometimes could not believe how willing the tourists were to spend money, not just to pay his price with no attempt to bargain him down, but even shipping costs that often exceeded what the farmer or estate agent had settled for when he acquired it. *Win-win,* he mused. *What I pay the seller makes them happy, what my buyers pay me makes me happy.*

As the miles rolled by, his mind drifted to his parents, how he had gotten his business sense from his father, Henry, but it was inheriting his mother's intuition about the value of old furniture and jewelry and artwork that made his livelihood possible. Eleanore would come to visit twice each year, leaving Henry back home so she and Jeffrey could have their semiannual mother-son outings together. After the crush of summer, during the treasured hiatus between Labor Day and the first big snow, the two of them would scavenge for antiques for weeks at a time. The following spring they would combine their antique hunt with a wildflower and blooming-garden tour.

The other woman in Jeffrey's life was the 1987 classic *Jeep Wagoneer Limited* carrying him to his mother as she lay dreadfully ill in a hospital somewhere near Washington, D.C. He put the horror of the spectacle awaiting him out of his mind with proud thoughts of his precious Jeep. The Jeep was his girlfriend, a relic from the days when Jeeps were still Jeeps, a sturdy, stately companion that he lavished attention on all winter, keeping her in perfect working order. He was delighted that now he could care for her better since he could get parts for her on-line, making his maintenance and repairs far easier than back when he had to beg auto parts stores to find suppliers or search through mountainous mail-order catalogues himself. Time seemed to rush by when he was working on her. He had nothing but disdain for the new Jeeps, unworthy successors to his Wagoneer with her plush leather seats, her push-button AM/FM radio, and best of all, her distinctive real-wood paneling and dashboard. He felt a surge of pride that the powerful old girl had no problem towing his six-foot by twelve-foot trailer up the steepest mountains loaded with furniture he and Eleanore had discovered.

As he pulled the Jeep into the visitor's lot at the hospital he choked at the thought that he and his mother might never again have one of their cherished outings. He shuffled past the information desk, following signs toward the post-op surgical wing just as his father had instructed him on the phone.

"Hello, Mother, it's your Jeffrey," he said as he entered the hospital room, his voice tremulous, nearly inaudible despite his having rehearsed that opening line all the way down from New Hampshire. He thought he had prepared himself for what his mother would undoubtedly look like in her hospital bed, but the ghastly image he now saw sent a devastating shock through the young man. Her hair was matted down in scraggly clumps, her face gunmetal gray, her arms sheathed with transparent skin that revealed webs of blue veins. *And that awful gown —what was Dad thinking, letting her lie there in that horrible gown?*

"Hi, Mother, I love you," he whispered as he bent over and kissed her on a dry, cool cheek, his lips feeling the bones of her face under the thin layer of flesh. These were not the soft, warm cheeks he had kissed so often.

"Jeffrey. Hello, Dear." The words came slowly, softly. "I'm…I'm afraid I don't look very good, do I, Sweetheart?"

"You look wonderful to me, Mother," he lied, struggling to control his voice. "I drove down in the Wagoneer so she can take us for a ride as soon as you get out of here."

"You are a sweetheart, Jeffrey. I can't…can't wait to…"

She slipped away into a sudden sleep, her body too weak to deal with the surge of excitement from seeing her favorite child.

"Hi Jeffrey, thanks for coming down," came a familiar but somehow changed voice from behind him.

Henry Hinkel looked Jeffrey over, feeling pride in his son's trim athletic appearance. Taller than his father at six-foot-two, Jeffrey was wearing a pair of expensive blue jeans so perfectly pressed the creases were still crisp after the long drive down from New Hampshire. An equally pristine blue-and-green checkered lumberjack shirt showed off his muscular torso. His hair was cut short but not as short as Jeffrey would have preferred – for his mother's sake he kept it just long enough to display a hint of the curls she so prized.

"It means so much to your mother to have you here. She's been asking for you."

"Hi Pops. I just pulled in. How much longer do you think she's going to be in the hospital?"

Henry Hinkel shuddered at the question, afraid to search his soul deeply enough to find the answer he didn't even want to think, let alone say out loud to his wife's best buddy, her special child. He thought kindly of his son and his attachment to his mother, how Jeffrey would never be the same if something happened to her. Seeing the fear on his son's face at what he might say, Henry chose his words carefully.

"We're not sure, Son. You know your mother, she never complains, she never wants anyone to fuss over her." *Except you, Jeffrey,* he thought, but did not say. "She didn't tell me she was sick, then she wouldn't let me take her to the Emergency Room."

Hearing his own words, Henry Hinkel realized that his profound sense of guilt was making him sound defensive, as though he had to explain to Jeffrey that his mother's illness wasn't his fault. Jeffrey was the one person who could not, would not, ever forgive him if he had let anything so awful happen to Eleanore. But he couldn't stop trying to explain away his palpable sense of guilt. "She was sick for a day before she would let me take her to the doctor."

Jeffrey stared at his father, not quite knowing where the man was going with this story. He sensed that his father somehow felt responsible for his mother lying there in this horrid state. Then an even more chilling thought crossed his mind: was his father blaming his mother, saying this was all *her* own fault? That would be unforgiveable. He held his peace, let his father go on.

"So I finally got her to agree to see Dr. Marlburg – you remember Tony Marlburg? She thought the pain and throwing up was from the stomach flu, that's why she wouldn't go to the hospital sooner. But Tony knew right away she had appendicitis and needed surgery, and he arranged for the best surgeon in the hospital to examine her almost immediately. The surgeon, that's Dr. McDonald, he said the operation went perfectly well, but her appendix had already ruptured before he got to it. Now she has an infection everywhere in her belly, and they're trying to fight it off with antibiotics."

Jeffrey turned and looked at his mother. Thin as she was, he could see a bulge under the sheets in the area of her belly. He shuddered suddenly at the sight of the drainage tubes dripping slowly into the collection bottles on the floor, the image inexplicably evoking the memory of a cow he had seen once suffering with *bloat* at his neighbor's farm. The poor beast's abdomen was distended from the pressure of the foaming clover she had ingested. He could see again the dairy farmer trying to save the animal by puncturing her belly with a sharp poker to let out the gas, to no avail. Of course he knew this was crazy, his mother was not a ruminating farm animal with bloat, but her dreadful condition triggered the old horror in him. He could not suppress the feeling that his mother was going to die, just like that cow had died. He desperately wanted to believe that she couldn't die, that she was in a good hospital, where they were taking good care of her, that this wasn't like that cow on an isolated farm with no vet around. But the image would not go away.

Tears had been rolling steadily down his face, but now Jeffrey started sobbing audibly, uncontrollably, hysterically. He pounded his knees with his fists, threw his head up and down in giant spasms of grief.

"Mother, Mother, Mother!"

"Jeffrey. Please, Jeffrey..."

Henry Hinkel instinctively tried to comfort his son by putting one hand on Jeffrey's shoulder, but the gesture backfired. Jeffrey twisted and smashed his powerful shoulder up into his father's arm to shove it away. The man was paralyzed by his son's convulsive outburst, hurt by the rejection more than by the impact. He backed up against the wall of the hospital room, leaning against the air conditioning unit for support, and stood watching his wife and their son in their separate agonies. Now Henry was crying, not like Jeffrey and not just for his family, but also from the burden of the guilt, the feeling that he had somehow created this horrific scene, his years of fathering and husbanding were all for naught. His life had come down to this catastrophe, all because he had not lived up to his responsibility to get medical care for his wife when she needed it.

***

Later, sitting alone with his wife, holding her hand, Henry Hinkel had the sensation he was touching a skeleton, feeling only bones encased in a thin layer of papery dry skin. Those hands had been so familiar to him but now they were foreign. They gave off no warmth, had no substance. The desiccated flesh no longer connected him with her. He held her hand gingerly, not with the tenderness of a lover but as one might handle a delicate crystal figurine, fearing that this strange hand was so fragile he might break the bones if he squeezed with the affection he still felt. The back of her hand, like much of the arm from her wrist to above her elbow, was streaked black-and-blue and burnt orange from countless needles puncturing the skin for blood tests and intravenous fluid lines. Looking up from the hand to her face, he could hardly recognize the human shroud he was seeing. Her cheeks were drawn in over her facial bones, the skin dark, her eyes closed or staring without seeing. She was there, but she was not there. Or, what was there was not his wife, not as he had known her for their lifetime together. She now looked like the living dead, like a victim of starvation.

Henry realized that he could no longer pretend that things would get better, that his Eleanore would get up out of the bed and go home with him. As he stared at the hollow shell of his wife, he had the sensation that a spirit had flown out of his own body. She was gone from him, his Eleanore was already gone from his life. She was breathing but she was not with him any more.

"Henry! Good morning, Henry."

The voice startled him back into consciousness. A handsome, well-tanned man had come into the room and was standing in front of him. The face was familiar but it took him a moment to remember: he was the surgeon who had taken out Eleanore's appendix. Henry Hinkel had not seen much of Dr. Matthew McDonald since that first operation – the surgeon had apparently gone off to a medical meeting of some sort, and Dr. Nicholas Meier seemed to have been in charge. And that other doctor, Ribbeno, was around all the time. Then McDonald returned, but Henry Hinkel rarely saw him. But here he was – no mistaking the jaunty presence.

"Oh, Dr. McDonald. Hello, Dr. McDonald."

"How's our girl today, Henry?" he asked, walking over to Eleanore's bedside and pulling back her bedcovers far enough to palpate her belly, lightly touching the oozing, red surgical wound sites.

"I don't know, I don't think she's changed much."

"It's a rough go. She's fighting some bad germs. I can tell you she's getting the best medical care. Our new guy, Dr. Ribbeno, is a world-class infectious disease expert. Did you know he has two doctorates?"

Now McDonald was examining the rubber tubes that drained small amounts of murky fluid from Eleanore Hinkel's innards into the collection bottles.

"Yes, that's what I heard. I know everyone is doing their best, Dr. McDonald."

A torrent of guilt washed over Henry Hinkel. None of this would have happened if she had gotten to Dr. McDonald sooner. His shame ran so deep he sought to reassure McDonald that the doctor had done his best.

"You couldn't undo what had already occurred, Dr. McDonald. If only I had brought her to you in time."

Another person being confronted with the suffering two human beings were enduring because of his own failed handiwork might well have felt a pang of remorse, might have been moved to assuage their distress. But not Matthew McDonald. He did not flinch, did not feel regret at this woman's plight or her husband's unwarranted sense of guilt. There was nothing to apologize to Henry Hinkel for.

"Unfortunately, that is so, Henry. Even the best surgeon can only do so much."

"I know, I know. Thank you again, Dr. McDonald, for trying to help her."

Matthew McDonald accepted the man's misplaced gratitude without embarrassment.

"That's why I'm here, I only wish things were going a bit better. I'll be back again."

As quickly as he had entered the room, McDonald was gone. He headed for the doctors' room, entered his personal identification codes and called up Eleanore Hinkel's electronic medical record on one of the surgical ward's computers. He typed, *"Continues to decline, prognosis grim."* Then he entered the billing code for *"Brief Visit, Inpatient, Follow-up,"* and hit *"finish."* The software program entered his electronic proxy signature at the end of his terse note and on the billing record, assuring that he would be paid for his bedside visit.

McDonald closed the record and signed off. He had done his best, he told himself smugly.

***

"Roger?"

Henry Hinkel was uncomfortable having a conversation with his elder son by the common phone at one end of the hospital hallway, but he could not call from the phone in Eleanore's room. He could not say what he had to with her lying there.

"Hello, Dad. How's Mother?"

"Roger, you'd better come, soon. She's ... she's very bad."

"It's hard, Dad, I'm in the middle of a major deal in San Angelo, two banks merging."

Henry Hinkel stiffened, trying to find the words to let his oldest child know that his mother was about to die. He hesitated, not sure whether even that news would move Roger to come to his mother's bedside, to say good-bye.

"There might not be another chance, Roger. If you want to see her, this is the time. This could be it for your mother."

"Will she know me? Will she even recognize me? I mean, if she doesn't recognize people, what difference will it make if I'm there?"

"I don't know, I just don't know."

He could picture the disdainful look on his son's hardened face and wanted to say, *"You bull-headed, self-serving heartless bastard, what about all she did for you? Get your selfish ass out here and pay tribute to your mother for Christ's sake,"* but it was not in him, and certainly not what Eleanore would have wanted him to say.

He felt the muscles in his neck tighten as he said, slowly, "You decide, Roger, it's up to you."

"Sue Anne and Jeffrey, they're there, right?"

"Yes. Jeffrey came down from New Hampshire and has been at her side religiously. Sue Anne left the kids with Philip's parents in Michigan, they're on vacation and took the kids with them for a couple of weeks."

"Well, if they're both there, and you..."

Henry Hinkel was about to explode, about to release the words of raw anger steaming in his mind, but caught himself again. For Eleanore's sake, he had to avoid poisoning the relationship with his distant child any further. He had tried, he had given his elder son one last chance to express his feelings for his mother, now his part was done. Henry realized that Roger *was* expressing what feelings he felt for his mother, there just wasn't much there. Somehow very little sentiment had developed inside this son when it came to family or other human connections. No wife, no kids, no long-lasting relationships. Another wave of guilt swept through Henry Hinkel, not the one torturing him over his wife's deterioration but a new one, an inchoate fear that he was somehow responsible for his son's seeming lack of human bonds, of emotion. How had it happened that Roger was so cold, so different than his brother and sister? What had he missed with this son? What had he done wrong?

"OK, Roger, you do what you can. I think it would mean a lot to your mother, but you do what you can, it's up to you."

"I'll get back to you, Dad. Thanks for calling."

Henry was struck by his son's lack of reaction to such bad news. Roger had said nothing someone might have expected from Eleanore's flesh and blood, not *"Give Mom a kiss for me,"* or *"Say hello to Sue Anne and Jeffrey,"* let alone *"I love you, Dad."* Something was missing from this boy's makeup. He wondered if Roger would even show up for his mother's funeral when the time came. The three children were so different. Jeffrey had gotten a double dose of emotion. Sue Anne loved her mother intensely but the two of them had struggled to get along throughout her prolonged adolescence. Roger got no warmth, nobody meant anything to him. Nobody. Right from birth it seemed, Roger was the serious, motivated one, Jeffrey the sensitive, affectionate son who always wanted to please his parents, Sue Anne the charmer, the performer, the social creature. He and Eleanore had treated them all the same as far as they knew, but there was no changing their basic personalities. By and large, they were good people, each one doing well in their own right, but they never reacted the same way to anything, to good news or bad. Even their political stances were a mystery to Henry Hinkel: Jeffrey was active in the seemingly endless list of progressive causes that made its way to New Hampshire; Roger held highly Libertarian world views but never got personally involved in anything; Sue Anne had more or less mirrored her parents' middle-of-the-road position once she grew out of her adolescent rebellion.

Henry Hinkel gave up trying to understand how his three children could have grown up poles apart from one another. *That's just the way it is,* he told himself.

"OK, Roger. Good-bye."

***

Eleanore Hinkel's funeral was a simple but crowded affair in the largest of three chapels in the Roxburn Family Funeral Parlor. All twenty or so rows of pews were filled, largely with professional colleagues of Henry and social friends of Eleanore. A single, lightly scented votive candle burned on each of the carved wooden shelves that protruded a few inches into the center aisle from the end caps of the pews. Floral decorations filled the front of the room, the largest displays standing prominently on both sides of the closed silver-and-bronze coffin, the rest lined up along the walls.

Michael Simkowitz and Nicholas Meier stood next to one another in the third pew from the rear of the chapel. In deference to the reverence evoked by the soft background music, Nick Meier spoke in a whisper. "Mike, look who's over there, on the right side, just next to the last pillar? I think that's Jorge, isn't it?"

"Yes, I thought I saw Jorge. I wonder why he's here. He looks so upset, like she was a member of his own family or something."

"He was in the O.R. when McDonald took out her appendix, and he kept pretty close tabs on her course in the hospital. Talked to me about her a couple of times. I think it hit him pretty hard. Sometimes I forget he doesn't have all that much experience at medical care, not for his age anyway. He's still getting used to losing patients, maybe."

"Do we ever get used to losing patients?"

"Touché, compadre. Let's hope we don't. Let's also hope we learn from our losses and do better."

The music picked up volume as the service began, drowning out Mike Simkowitz's soft answer.

"Some of us learn better than others."

Chapter 13. Resting in Peace

Jeffrey Hinkel lay in his bed staring out of his bedroom window but barely seeing the floral rainbows covering the New Hampshire hills surrounding his property. For many years the explosion of colors had stirred him with anticipation of the arrival not just of Spring, but also of his mother for the first of their twice-yearly tours. He would spend weeks preparing for Eleanore's visit, beginning his ritual by getting the Wagoneer purring. The machine seemed to enjoy its fresh oil and lubricated joints, happily anticipating their outing as much as Jeffrey did. Then he would sketch out their route in detail, carefully scheduling flower garden and craft shows and other organized events while setting aside plenty of time for spontaneous excursions to discover farmhouse sales and auctions that were only advertised locally in the small villages they would pass through. But this Spring brought no anticipation, only a profound sense of loss. Now his mother would travel with him only in his mind.

Jeffrey couldn't bear the absence of his best friend. His very life cycle had been interrupted. He told himself he should open his store and keep the business going, but he could not find energy to propel him into action. He felt drained of purpose. Yes, he needed the money and loved selling things but it was all just to make space for the new treasures his mother and he would uncover. It wasn't about the money. Now, what should he do? Drive around his circuit by himself? He couldn't do it, not yet, he just missed her so much. The pain of loss that coursed through him made his skin sting like a summertime sunburn, as agonizing as if he had been beaten with a whip on every inch of his flesh.

Dragging himself out of bed, the normally fastidious man pulled on the same clothes he had been wearing for several days, brushed his teeth from compelling habit but avoided shaving, and headed for the Wagoneer. He settled comfortably into the thick leather seats, started the enormous engine, and pulled out onto the main road. But Jeffrey wasn't heading to Manchester to meet his mother at the airport, or out on a buying trip, or even to the store to prepare for customers again. He was going back to the only place he had visited since his mother was taken from him, the place she would lie in forever. He needed to bring Spring to her in her permanent home, he couldn't let her lie there in the ground without the flowers she had so looked forward to seeing. Not store-bought flowers but fresh ones, wildflowers and garden flowers the two of them would have seen from the road. He contemplated the varieties he would search for, the ones that would get her so excited when they spotted them. Purple lilacs, her favorite, with tiny purple petals that would end up littering the back of his car for months. But so what? She needed her purple lilacs, it was Spring, and the Wagoneer would be deliciously fragrant from the lilacs and his mother's lavender perfume. The lilac aroma would smother the somewhat foul odor of the Red Trillium so long as he covered the Trillium with wax paper for the trip. And he would gather clusters of little bulbous white Bearberrys, those she would love.

It's not the same without her, he sobbed, *but I've got to bring her the flowers, I need to stay in touch with her.*

Jeffrey spent the first day driving slowly on two-lane country roads that passed through countless small towns and fields lush with wildflowers. He stopped often to think about nothing, simply to collect bundles and bundles of perfect flowers. He felt no hunger, just a crushing emptiness, and ate only two bananas and an apple he picked up at a country gas station. As the Wagoneer turned into the road leading to his mother's grave the next afternoon, Jeffrey winced reflexively at the sign that marked the way:

Heavenly Gardens

Cemetery, Mausoleum, Crematorium & Columbarium

A Roxburn-Oliphant Property

Jeffrey shook his head at the sight of the neon flame flickering from side to side above the garish sign. He had never been happy with the burial plots his father had bought for himself and Eleanore when the cemetery complex had opened more than twenty years earlier. Jeffrey had always thought the very idea of a *new cemetery* was an oxymoron. The cemeteries he loved were old places that

91

exuded a sense of history, of lives that had been led, of triumph and loss. Thousands of headstones, crosses, statuettes, family crypts with embossed brass doors. Family plots going back over many generations. Headstones with both spouses' names and birth years, some with only one year of death carved in the granite, a blank space next to the other awaiting the certain arrival of the spouse left behind.

Jeffrey was struck with how undeveloped the *Heavenly Gardens* cemetery still appeared more than two decades after it had opened. A few saplings planted when the cemetery was developed were growing into tree adolescence but the occupied gravesites were still few, in small isolated clusters. Even the plots that were filled did not create a sense of being in a cemetery because this modern cemetery allowed no vertical headstones, only flat grave markers that huge lawnmowers could pass over efficiently. Jeffrey could either scatter the flowers he had assembled so carefully on the gravesite to await destruction by the mower blades or place them in the retractable brass vase he could raise temporarily out of the flat headstone.

Paved pathways radiated out in every direction, winding across low rolling hills of manicured grass. To Jeffrey the acreage was more like a would-be suburban subdivision that couldn't attract developers than a decent burial ground. Or even worse, he thought, a golf course where no one played. He chided himself for not having taken his mother with him to rest in New Hampshire in a real cemetery with people who died two hundred years before the Revolutionary War. But he had kept such thoughts to himself. His father would not have appreciated having to put up with Jeffrey whining about the aesthetics of the cemetery as he was burying his beloved wife.

Jeffrey parked the Wagoneer next to the wooden garbage can holder he used as a landmark to find his mother's gravesite in the barren landscape of this cemetery with no headstones, and started walking the hundred or so yards to her resting place. As he came over a small rise he saw the familiar grouping of four stone benches around a matching birdbath in the area adjacent to his mother's grave. But he was disappointed to see another person nearby, a stranger's presence threatening the privacy he had so anticipated. How could he talk to his mother with someone close enough to hear him? Maybe the other visitor would be finished soon. As Jeffrey came closer, his hopes rose somewhat as he saw that the interloper was a middle-aged Hispanic man and, despite himself, gave in to the stereotype of assuming the fellow was doing some gardening chore and would be going away soon. Or Jeffrey could even ask him to leave. But the man did not have any tools, and he was not wearing work clothes suitable for grounds maintenance. Jeffrey realized the man was standing over Eleanore Hinkel's grave, then was startled to see him suddenly kneel and drop his face into his hands, clearly distraught.

Jeffrey stopped about ten yards away and tried to take in what he was seeing. He focused on the ground-level stone marker to be sure it was his mother's gravesite: it was hers, no doubt about it. After thirty seconds or so Jeffrey could not watch any longer. He approached the man, calling ahead, "Excuse me, excuse me. Are you in the right place?"

Jeffrey saw the man's shoulders drop. One hand began wiping his face with bold energetic passes as though trying to scrape off a caked-on coating. The unknown trespasser turned and looked at Jeffrey, then to Jeffrey's utter amazement said, "I am so sorry, Mr. Hinkel, I am so sorry. Please forgive me. I did not intend to intrude on your visit to your mother's grave, I just wanted to say a few prayers for her."

Jeffrey stepped back a couple of paces, too stunned to respond. Who the hell was this? How did he know his name? How dare he get familiar with him, with Mother, like this? Then a faint hint of recognition passed through Jeffrey: the unwelcome man was not a complete stranger. Jeffrey had seen him somewhere, in some other setting.

The man got to his feet and stepped off of the grave but did not approach Jeffrey. He simply stood at a short distance, his hands folded together, making no move to shake hands.

"Mr. Hinkel," the man said softly, apologetically, his latent Spanish accent emerging perceptibly under the strained circumstances, "please, forgive me. My name is Jorge Edmond. I am a physician assistant, and I helped the doctors care for your mother in the hospital. She was such a lovely lady. I felt so bad for her and for your father and you, you were so dedicated to her. Please, I just came to pay my respects."

Jeffrey rocked from foot to foot, not losing his balance but unnerved by so unexpected an encounter. He had been sure his visit would be solitary, he would be alone with Eleanore, he could chat with her as if she were sitting next to him. And now there was another person. He had nothing against this man, especially now that he was reminded of his connection with his mother, but it was still an intrusion he could not fully accept. The long-awaited moment to be shared only with his mother was now shattered. He was not ready to be gracious, to forgive the loss of his personal time with his mother, but he realized it would be unseemly to be angry with someone for having their own feelings for her.

Finally, he managed, "Hello, Dr. Edmond – oh, excuse me, I'm sorry, it's not *Doctor,* is it?"

Jeffrey did not intend any slight, the words had simply come out of his mouth before his brain could filter them, but he immediately regretted having asked the question as a trace of indignation passed over the man's face. Jeffrey now felt doubly awkward, his botched salutation compounding his embarrassment at having mistaken Jorge for a gardener. Hoping to make amends and stifle his own discomfort, Jeffrey approached the man and extended his hand.

"Of course, Mr. Edmond, thank you for coming to see my mother. Yes, she was very special to me – she *is* very special to me. I come here as often as I can. Usually on Sundays, that was her favorite day."

Jorge Edmond took Jeffrey's free hand, noticing the bundle of flowers he carried in the other.

"Those are beautiful flowers. Your mother would love those flowers, I am sure."

Jeffrey shook Jorge's hand, instantly sensing it was the hand of a laborer, not of a doctor or doctor's helper. But the man had certainly been in the hospital, Jeffrey did remember him. Who was he? What was he doing at Eleanore's grave?

"She did love flowers. Every Spring we would collect flowers together, we had such a good time."

His voice broke. He let loose from Jorge's hand and reached up to wipe his eyes.

Feeling guilty for having caused Jeffrey's outburst of raw sorrow, Jorge could not find words of comfort. Nor did he feel free to hug him or even pat his shoulders. He had intruded into this man's space, he should not have come here. He had just made things worse. Why couldn't he just let this poor lady lie in peace? He stood silent, waiting for Jeffrey to gather his emotions. Finally, Jorge said, "I have worked with flowers most of my life. Flowers, plants of all kinds."

Distracted and relieved by the sound of Jorge's voice, Jeffrey responded, "So you keep a garden yourself? What types of flowers do you grow?"

Jorge was embarrassed, but knew he had to reply, it was he who had raised the subject.

"No, Mr. Hinkel, I live in an apartment building, I do not have a garden. Before I became a physician assistant, I did yardwork, lawn maintenance, you know, that kind of work. Odd jobs. That was how I made a living. It was good for me, I enjoyed seeing the plants grow, the flowers bloom. But I do not have my own garden yet, maybe someday."

Now it was Jeffrey who felt embarrassed – those hands should have told him, what had he been thinking? He smiled at Jorge and nodded his head slightly to show he had appreciated his openness, his willingness to reveal his workaday past, but said nothing. Then he went about his business, scattering loose purple petals over the grave, popping the brass vase up from its silo and arranging the stems of the longest flowers in the container, laying the others on the ground, on top of the petals. The result was a colorful rectangle clearly defining the gravesite, making it stand out amid the sprawling lawn of the bare cemetery.

Jorge sensed he should leave and give Jeffrey time to be alone with his mother. "Mr. Hinkel, I must be going now. I am so sorry I disturbed you. I did not know you would be here today. I am so sorry, please forgive me."

"It's OK, Mr. Edmond…Jorge. I am sure that my mother would appreciate your caring about her enough to come to visit. This place is pretty far outside the city. She would be quite touched that you did her this honor."

Jorge cringed, feeling guilty for misleading Jeffrey. He was not here simply to honor the memory of this woman. No, he had come out of a lingering unrest over his failure to honor Eleanore Hinkel properly by telling someone about how Dr. Matthew McDonald had caused her slow, painful death. He knew she would have died whether he spoke up or not once she had gotten so sick, but her family, this loving son of hers, they deserved to know the truth. And he was disconsolate that the family thought it was Eleanore Hinkel's own fault, or her husband's fault – while the man who was responsible was free, paying no price for what he had done to her. Free and ruining the lives of still more patients and families.

"Mr. Hinkel…" Jorge started to break through the restraints that kept him from telling the man why he had come to his mother's gravesite, but stopped, not knowing what good it would do. Jeffrey was so miserable already that disclosing the horrendous truth would just make the man suffer all the more. But now Jorge knew he could not keep this inside any longer. He must tell someone. It was killing him. He would do something, but not here, not at this woman's grave.

"Yes, Jorge?"

"Mr. Hinkel, seeing you here has been very good for me." As Jorge spoke, his voice wavered, his bilingual fluency failing him as he struggled to find the right words in English, to keep out any Spanish ones. It was difficult – the more emotional the situation, the more he felt comfortable in the language of his parents, even though he had spoken English ever since he first went to kindergarten. "I can see how close you and your mother were – how close you still are, forgive me. My family is everything to me. My mother, my father, they are still with us, thanks be to God, and I can only imagine how you must be feeling. Thank you, thank you so much for letting me be with you here today."

Jeffrey was so taken with the outpouring of sympathy from this near-stranger he was not sure how to respond, but he also wondered just why the man was so emotional about Eleanore. The man takes care of patients all the time, why would he be so wrapped up in his mother's case? He saw that Jorge was distraught but thought that he couldn't possibly be like this with all of his patients, he couldn't survive in his job that way. Why Eleanore?

"On the contrary, thank you for being here. Thank you so much." Jeffrey felt that now he could ask what was going on with Jorge. "Please, I don't mean to pry, but you must have taken care of thousands of patients – do you get so involved in all your cases?"

Jorge felt a wave of panic seizing his chest. He was on shaky ground – if he answered truthfully, he would start down the road he had just decided to avoid. But he could not lie, not again, not to this man. He found enough of the truth to respond honestly, if incompletely.

"No problem, Mr. Hinkel, I understand. You see, I am not so young a man, but I am new to my profession. I have been a physician assistant for only a short time. When I said I had done lawn maintenance, that was the way for most of my life, actually. Odd jobs, no education, until the last few years. So, no, I have not cared for thousands of patients, not yet. But, God willing, I will do so before He calls me away."

Jorge stopped, let his words hang in the air. He told himself to say no more, realizing that if he continued speaking he would lose control and tell Jeffrey everything, and that would not be right. He had to stop now.

Jeffrey Hinkel said, "Ah, yes, I should have realized. I hope you always keep feeling for your patients like you do for my mother."

If I do, I will be in an early grave, thought Jorge, but said only, "I will do my best. Thank you again."

Jorge smiled bashfully at Jeffrey, still sorting out his thoughts, his plans. They shook hands in farewell and Jorge turned and walked toward the bus stop, leaving Jeffrey Hinkel alone near the small patch of color he had grafted onto the endless green terrain. But Jorge walked with a heavy burden, carrying with him all the pain, the self-doubt, the gnawing unrest that had brought him to Eleanore Hinkel's gravesite.

***

Lisa Altuno always seemed to have problems with her periods. They didn't even start until she was almost 16, so far behind the other girls in her school that her parents had taken her to a specialist who had run some tests and assured them that she was normal, just at the later end of the menarche spectrum. Once her periods finally started they were so irregular it was impossible for her to predict when the bloody discharge might suddenly start flowing or whether it would be another couple of months until anything showed up, so she never went anywhere without a bundle of Super Tampax in her purse. Then, when Lisa Altuno started having sex things got worse – her periods would disappear for so many months she kept a supply of pregnancy test kits handy so she would know whether she was late because of her chronic menstrual problem or whether her birth control had failed. Even taking the pill didn't solve things like the doctors had hoped. She continued to have regularly irregular periods, some so scant she wasn't sure they were real, some so heavy she worried about the amount of blood she was losing.

When Lisa Altuno got married she and her husband desperately wanted to start a family, but it took four years before the magic happened. The baby was fine, a healthy girl weighing 8 pounds, 6 ounces. But Lisa Altuno had a massive post-partum hemorrhage. After several days of multiple blood transfusions and continued bleeding, her aging obstetrician, Dr. Shelly Magruder, broke the terrible news to the young couple that Lisa needed to have her uterus removed to save her life. Dr. Magruder explained that she had given up doing major surgery after turning sixty-five, but she called in a general surgeon, Dr. Matthew McDonald, to perform the hysterectomy in Northeast Suburban Hospital. Dr. McDonald was the best there was, Dr. Magruder assured her, Lisa would be in very good hands. The operation seemed to have been a great success. The bleeding stopped, the young mother began nursing the baby, everything seemed fine until her blood pressure fell catastrophically on the third post-operative day.

Lisa Altuno's newborn baby went home without her mother.

Chapter 14. Interesting Figure

During the countless hours he spent at his computer Will Manningham usually positioned his lengthy frame at a medium distance from the monitor, his arms flexed at the elbows, his vulnerable back cushioned by a custom Styrofoam wedge. Sometimes when the work dragged on and on he would lean back in his chair, stretch out his long arms and legs, and assume an all but recumbent position, his chin resting on his chest as he typed. But today his face was nearly against the screen as his fingers flew across the keyboard typing in the new computer program he had just designed.

Day after day he had searched for the missing link between the surge in unexplained deaths and the growth in sales of *Marquis-Herrant* products. An inexplicable trail of death grew in sync with the company's torrid expansion and surging profitability. Will was sure it couldn't be a coincidence, that was statistically impossible. There had to be a connection. And he had to find it. But he had explored all the causes of death, the specific drugs and devices, the demographics of the patients who had died. Nothing. The two trends were locked together like the parallel rails of a train track but Will could not unearth the railroad ties between the rails. He had no way to pinpoint what it was about *Marquis-Herrant* that could have killed the victims.

Then an idea for a new program popped into his head: he should stop examining the *Marquis Herrant* sales patterns, the fatal diagnoses, the characteristics of the deceased, and shift his focus to the people who were involved. The employees of the company, the doctors and nurses who cared for the patients, everyone who touched any part of the as-yet indecipherable clutter of information. Maybe there was a clue there, maybe Tom Murphy was right that corporate angels of death were lurking somewhere.

Adrenaline rushed through Will's body as he transmitted giant clusters of computer code from his brain through his fingers into the keys and onto the screen. He felt as though his mind and his computer were one as he programmed his electronic alter ego to construct an artificial neural network – a sophisticated map that would reveal hidden relationships that only a supercomputer could tease out of massive data. His commands would tell the computer to carry out two tasks: first, identify and gain access to new databases and merge them with the ones he had already explored; then, "learn" from all the data to uncover the veiled linkages that would show who had been involved in the deaths. The artificial neural network would digest staffing patterns and personnel records from the company and the hospital, names of all the workers involved in the inpatient treatments and procedures on the dead patients, whatever information might associate specific people with the events surrounding the deaths.

Armed with banking and financial records for *Marquis-Herrant* provided by *FinCEN* and given direct access by the secret FISA warrants to all the privileged information buried in the hospital's records and the company's servers, Will created new files and links to massive storehouses of data. He wrote instructions directing the computer to sift through and find the relationships he was sure were buried there, like drawing lines among ripe seeds of wheat in a sea of useless chaff. He continued in this near-manic state for nearly four hours, then hit the final keystroke and sagged back in his chair. He had done his part, now it was up to his supercomputer to tell him if this new approach would produce something useful. If it even made sense.

Will rose from his chair and realized he was hungry. He tore open the giant bag of *Fritos* he kept stashed for just such an emergency and stuffed handfuls of chips into his mouth as he wandered around the Command Center. After about fifteen minutes he returned to his computer and sat up straight to watch the output grow on the screen. His eyes flashed back and forth trying in vain to keep up with the rapidly-changing display that resembled a series of inkblots connected to each other by fine lines heading out in many directions. Finally he realized that staring at the monitor like that was silly, he was just making himself dizzy. He lowered his gaze, leaned back, devoured a few more chips, and let the computer chug away until he heard the *ping* that signaled it had completed the task. He grabbed the mouse and scrolled through the results. *"Bingo!"* he yelled, pumping his fist in the air. The monitor displayed just what he had been searching for: the inkblots were now a series of interconnected hubs-and-spokes resembling the route map of a major airline. Instead of parallel lines between the unexplained deaths and *Marquis-Herrant's* rapid growth, he now saw a map of the connections among the deaths and the people and transactions involved.

Will activated the voice-over-internet telephone connection and once again heard Adrienne's familiar voice filling the big room.

"Hi, Will. What's up?"

"Got something, Adrienne. Maybe this time it really is a eureka moment."

"Do you need us to come out there?"

"No, I can come to Hoover and fill you in."

"Good. The team is getting together in two hours for a briefing, so that's perfect timing."

"I'll be there."

***

Adrienne Penscal pursed her lips and squinted as she shook her head and glanced around at Will and her team of Special Agents. "That *Marquis-Herrant* gathering down in Cabo was a boondoggle just as you had predicted, Will. Dozens of surgeons being wined and dined lavishly, supposedly there for educational sessions, but all they really got were marketing pitches. And sunshine, surfing, boat rides, booze, and extravagant meals. Hard to believe that it's all legal, but we're assured it is, as long as the drug companies report the spending to the *OpenPaymentsData* website. In any case, what we saw will be more than enough for Chief Hollingshead to justify the cost of our undercover trip to financial management."

Tom Murphy sniggered, "Some of those surgeons enjoyed other forms of entertainment as well, huh, Boss? Are you going to tell everyone about what else we saw?"

"I was about to get to that, Murph," she said, a clear note of disgust in her voice. "Much as I hate to say this, at least one of the pharmaceutical reps appeared to be there not just to talk about the company's products."

"Looked like she was doing plenty of talking – pillow talking," Murphy chimed in.

"Let me guess," said Will. "Alexandra Parushnikova, right?"

"That's her. How'd you know?"

101

"She's part of what I came over to tell you about. Just today I discovered that she seems to be a central character in all of this. Before I left the Command Center I took a quick look into her background. Interesting figure."

"*Very interesting figure,*" chuckled Tom Murphy in a stage whisper that sent a buzz of laughter around the room. Special Agents Fred Renford, Anil Maliq, Denise Washington and Frances Trainor enjoyed Murphy's sense of humor. Adrienne Penscal, not so much.

"Tell us more about her, Will."

"I had focused on the underlying causes of death to see how they were connected to the rapid expansion of *Marquis-Herrant's* sales in the same areas but I still wasn't getting anywhere. So I decided to shift my perspective and look into the people who were connected in any way with the deaths, and the transactions between *Marquis-Herrant* and the hospitals. Once I had a map of the various relationships I honed in on the links between individuals at *Marquis-Herrant* and the hospitals and doctors in each of the areas with excess deaths. I discovered that the company had young women as their reps in those places. It was relatively simple to uncover details on their backgrounds, education, employment history, everything that could be relevant. The Russian Parushnikova was especially interesting. She took an honors degree in biology from Novosibirsk State University. And she's completely fluent in English – seems she lived in the U.S. with her grandfather who was a diplomat in the Gorbachev era."

"No offense, but you're sounding more and more like an FBI Agent," quipped Tom Murphy.

"I take that as a compliment, Murph. Anyway, after she arrived in the D.C. area, *Marquis-Herrant's* sales began to take off. It took me a while to track down who the purchasers were, but little by little I managed to uncover their distribution routes. At first I was only searching through Big Data that was readily available on-line, stuff like those SEC filings and marketing materials I told you about earlier. But I didn't get very far until we got our secret FISA warrants and I had access to corporate databases. And once *FinCEN* got going they provided me with records of financial transactions that brought the company's operations into focus."

"So where do things stand now? Did you find a connection?"

"Yes, there's a definite correlation: the map of transactions showed that the hospitals with the largest volume of *Marquis-Herrant* purchases are the ones that have experienced the most fatalities. As the new reps move into the local markets and *Marquis-Herrant's* drugs and medical devices find their way into circulation, the number of unexplained deaths rise."

"That's very suggestive. What else?"

"There's one hospital that stands out around here: Northeast Suburban. Since Parushnikova took over the Northeast Suburban account the hospital started buying a large chunk of their drugs and medical devices from *Marquis-Herrant*. It wasn't long before they began to experience a spike in deaths. Deaths during and after hospitalization at Northeast Suburban."

Adrienne Penscal asked, "What were the patients dying from? Did you take a look at their medical records?"

"Yes, sure, I did that right away. Thanks to our FISA warrants I had no HIPAA privacy restrictions to slow me down. The good news is that Northeast Suburban has an electronic medical record system that was easy to hack into."

"You weren't hacking," corrected Adrienne. "You were acting legally under the terms of our warrants."

"Whoops, my bad, Adrienne. Of course. In any case, when Northeast Suburban made the transition to an electronic medical record they purchased an early-generation system without many of the security safeguards in the newer ones, and they haven't upgraded. Their version is so weak that it's possible for unauthorized persons to distort the electronic records after the fact without leaving telltale signs in the computer logs. That *is* hacking, and it's no longer possible with the second- or third-generation electronic records systems."

"OK, sounds like your level of expertise wasn't even necessary to get into their files. What did you learn?"

"Well, that's the bad news. I didn't find anything helpful. In fact, just the opposite. I went through the records of every death over the last three years, before and after the surge in deaths started. Not a single case has a cause of death reported that appears suspicious. In addition, none of the deaths are directly connected with particular drugs or devices from *Marquis-Herrant*. It's a quandary."

"So where do we go from here?" asked Adrienne Penscal.

"I'm not sure. I was hoping that we might come up with something when I presented my new approach to all of you. Anybody have an idea?"

"I have a thought, if I might," said Anil Maliq, his voice quiet but confident.

"Of course, Anil, go ahead."

"Very well. Perhaps some of the information you have uncovered is not reliable."

"You think it's unreliable? In what way?"

"You have discovered inconsistencies between the number of deaths and the causes of those deaths. The number of deaths should be relatively reliable, but the causes are more subjective and are subject to manipulation. The numbers are just a matter of counting and reporting, and hospitals provide information on one-hundred percent of deaths. The total number of deaths can be cross-checked in public health reports, death registries, Social Security notices. So we can be quite confident in your observation that more people have died than would be expected based on usual death rates. But the causes of those deaths depend on medical judgment. And then those conclusions are translated into codes for reporting."

"Are you suggesting that Northeast Suburban is falsifying the causes of death? That they are deliberately reporting causes that would not suggest a connection with any *Marquis-Herrant* products?"

"That would be an explanation for the discrepancies, would it not?"

"Of course it would," said Will Manningham. "What about the lack of any direct link between specific *Marquis-Herrant* products and the deaths?"

"I would suggest a similar explanation. Perhaps those records do not tell the whole story either. It would be a simple matter to conceal the brand names by recording only the type of device or the generic name of the medications involved."

"Good thinking, Anil."

"Thank you," said the slight, composed man in a neutral voice with no trace of self-satisfaction.

Adrienne Penscal asked, "So, Will, any thoughts on how you can check on the validity of the causes of death?"

"Now that I know many of the connections I can take a closer look at the people who were in positions that could have allowed them to skew the reports."

"Do you think that will tell you what you need to know?"

"Maybe, but…"

"But what, Will? Spit it out."

"Of course I'll continue with the computer work, that's what I do and that's what works for me. If the causes of deaths are fictitious, the more sophisticated I make the analytics, the more likely it is I'll uncover inconsistencies or other indications that confirm they have been falsified. We've managed to unravel some complicated scams that way and I'm confident we'd eventually have a breakthrough here as well. But you know…sometimes I think there's only so much we can do with computers."

"I've never heard you say anything like that before. What are you getting at?"

"Artificial intelligence is great, I'm a big believer, of course, but AI can't solve everything. We call it *artificial* intelligence because it's not real intelligence, at least not yet. It's just ones and zeros, positive and negative charges, all meaningless on their own. We human beings tell the machines to sort the data and generate results, which they do faster and in bigger batches than we can. By far. But if we're entering phony data like Anil suggested then, as we say in my world, it's 'garbage in, garbage out.' If the causes of death are fabricated, I'm not sure how long it might take to figure out what's going on. So maybe the computers need some help from us."

"What do you mean, help from us? What kind of help?"

"There are so many alternative solutions buried in the data it can be a very long process to tease out the most significant ones. An infinite number of monkeys hitting keys randomly on typewriters for an infinite period of time might well produce all the plays of Shakespeare. Artificial intelligence could identify the differences among the plays, but it would take human beings to appreciate the contrasting significance of the messages in, say, *Hamlet* compared with *Romeo and Juliet*."

"So it might take forever to tie the deaths to the *Marquis-Herrant* products? We don't have forever."

"No, of course not. But human intelligence could speed things up."

"Are you suggesting an undercover operation? Should we send Sean Flaherty into the hospital?"

"Ha! No, that wouldn't be my first choice. I mean, I – Sean – would do it if that were really necessary but I was thinking more along the lines of trying to enlist someone who's already an insider to come forward and put the pieces together."

"Interesting idea," said Adrienne. "Shake things up a bit at the hospital and see if anyone cracks. Maybe it's time to let someone at Northeast Suburban know that they are the subject of an FBI investigation. I'll run that past Chief Hollingshead."

"If Chief Hollingshead approves some sort of contact with people in the hospital," said Will, "I would like you to hold off taking any action until I do some more work. This discussion has given me another idea. Sean Flaherty would just as soon stay in retirement and I think I can help keep him there."

Chapter 15. Suburban Buses

After leaving Jeffrey Hinkel at Eleanore's gravesite, Jorge Edmond had just come over a small rise when he saw the bus approaching. The big man hustled as fast as he could toward the main road to flag it down. When he reached the road he got within a few feet of the moving bus, but he and the bus were still about fifty feet from the bus stop when Jorge raised his arm and waved to the driver.

The driver's face was close enough to make eye contact with Jorge. The man pursed his lips into a malevolent scowl, waved him off and pointed to the nearby bus stop, mouthing, *"Bus stop."* Jorge wasn't sure but he thought the driver might have added something, possibly an expletive.

Jorge kept running, thinking the driver was just a stickler for obeying rules, that he would pull over at the designated area and wait there to let Jorge catch up and board properly. But then he heard the engine roar as the bus accelerated away. He shook his head and stared in dismay as the bus disappeared down the two-lane road. Jorge examined the small placard on a metal post: the next bus would not arrive for another hour and fifteen minutes. Buses came infrequently on weekends to the suburban bedroom communities surrounding the *Heavenly Gardens* cemetery. Jorge looked in vain for a place to sit, then lowered himself down onto the curb.

As Jorge squatted at the edge of the road an unpleasant but familiar old feeling returned: he felt invisible, just as he had for so many years. He was sure that bus driver would have stopped for a white guy in a suit. He had been disregarded, disrespected, treated like some wandering vagrant or a thug, not like a health professional. He was an old campesino again. Then he scolded himself to stop the whining. It was his own fault after all, he was the one who should have paid attention to the time.

Jorge's mind filled with thoughts of the Hinkels. His eyes filled with tears as the different characters, the haunting moments, the unsettling sensations, came and went in his mind. Eleanore Hinkel on the operating table, her life in Matthew McDonald's hands. The agonizing burden that he was the only one who knew that something had happened that stole that life from her. Her despondent husband Henry sitting at her bedside every time Jorge had come in to check on Eleanore, withering away himself as time passed and his beloved wife disintegrated slowly before his eyes. And now, Jeffrey, bringing flowers to his mother, talking out loud to her burial plot as though he were conversing with a living person. Henry was a nice man who was lost without his wife, Jeffrey was a good son who was lost without his mother. Jorge sighed, overcome with a feeling of helplessness.

At last Jorge saw the next bus coming. Fearing that he was still invisible, he got to his feet and stepped into the road, raising his arm in a friendly wave. But this driver had already seen Jorge – the long vehicle was slowing down and pulling toward the curb. The driver opened the heavy front door and greeted Jorge with a friendly, "Climb aboard, Partner." Jorge was so touched by the camaraderie that he had to choke back the urge to burst out crying. He paid his fare, two-dollars and seventy-five cents for the off-hours ride to the city, and realized he had the entire passenger compartment to himself. There had to be at least 50 empty seats, each richly upholstered in a plush fabric covered with small red and green polka dots. Jorge walked about one-third of the way down the aisle, not so far as to be insulting to the driver but just far enough to make any conversation unlikely.

As the bus rolled down the highway, Jorge settled into his thickly-cushioned seat and stared out the window. Empty land, some in pastures, some plowed, gave way mile by mile to sprawling urbanization as housing developments, strip malls, gas stations appeared. One thought occupied his mind: he had to tell someone about what had happened to Eleanore Hinkel, he must, there was no more thinking about it. But who? Who could he talk to? Dr. Simkowitz? Simkowitz was probably the right one, but Jorge didn't feel that he knew him well enough, he couldn't be sure what would happen if he spoke to Dr. Simkowitz. Then he thought of Dr. Meier. He had always encouraged Jorge to speak up. It had to be Dr. Meier.

With his plan of action set, Jorge felt calm, on track to lifting the weight of Eleanore Hinkel from his shoulders. He pulled himself up out of the seat and walked to the front of the bus, all the way to the seats just behind the glass entry barrier above the front door.

"Howdy Partner," Jorge said with no trace of a Spanish accent, "guess I've got a chartered limo just for myself today."

The driver glanced at Jorge, a broad smile on his face. With obvious pride in his vehicle he said, "Just for you, sir, Suburban Express. You have the luxury of a *Prevost LeMirage XL – 45* motor coach all to yourself, rest room and all. Sit back and enjoy the ride."

Chapter 16. Jorge Opens Up

Nicholas Meier stepped into Sandy Flowers' outer office, a pristine, modern space that conveyed a highly professional ambiance. Her diplomas and licenses were mounted on the wall, a floor-to-ceiling oak bookshelf was filled with perfectly aligned copies of the *New England Journal of Medicine, JAMA,* and *Annals of Surgery,* two large leather chairs faced a simple glass-top table that served as a desk, with no papers or other clutter whatsoever. He passed through the prototypical medical office and down a short hallway with several examining rooms on either side, then knocked on the door at the far end.

"Hi, Nick, come on in," came her reply.

He entered her private working retreat, a small room with papers and journals piled everywhere, on the old oak roll-top desk, on the floor, on two would-be end tables, on the seats of every chair except the one Sandy was sitting in. In this office the bookshelves were jammed with seemingly random stacks of papers, some in file folders, some with rubber bands around them, every square inch filled.

"Hi Sandy. Busy day?" Meier asked, noticing that his friend and colleague looked out of sorts.

"Sort of, yeah. Two surgeries this morning, then an old friend came in as a patient. I had looked forward to seeing her but, truth is, the experience took a bit out of me. I was shocked at how fat – sorry, but there's no other way to say it – she had become, morbidly obese, killing herself with food, literally. She came to see me because she needs gastric bypass surgery or banding. I hadn't realized how hard her deterioration hit me personally until after she had left. She was a good friend, we practically grew up together. She used to be trim and athletic, a cheerleader and gymnast, and now she had ballooned up horribly. I could hardly believe it."

"Ouch. Well, maybe this isn't a good time for something else that's not so easy."

"It's OK, go ahead. That was personal, lots of memories. As long as it's not another one like that."

"Nope, not personal, not in that sense. It's McDonald again, though. You up for this now or do you want to wait until tomorrow?"

"Might as well get on with it now that you're here and you've opened it up. Anything to get my mind off of my unfortunate friend. What is it?"

"Thanks. Actually, it *would* be better to talk now, I've got someone waiting on us: Jorge. He came to me and said he needed to tell me something. I asked what about, and he said 'Dr. McDonald.' So I asked if it was serious, and he said, 'It's terrible, Dr. Meier.' Then he started to talk but I stopped him and said I wanted to get you involved. Jorge said that would be fine. Can I bring him in?"

"Ah, here we go again. Sure, bring him in, but you're going to have to buy me a drink later."

"Deal. I'm not on call. Cheap price to pay."

Gesturing to the papers piled on the two small guest chairs, Nick Meier asked, "May I?" The question was symbolic, a prompt for Sandy Flowers to make room for her two guests. He knew that the room that looked like a hoarder's attic was actually organized with surgical precision and she wouldn't want him to touch anything.

"Ah, no, hold off, you'll screw up my system. You get Jorge. I'll move things around – I know exactly where every scrap of paper is. Don't touch anything, I'll clear off the seats and that way I'll remember where things are."

Nick stepped out, picking his way carefully among the piles on the floor. Sandy thumbed quickly through each stack of paper on the two chairs before selecting a new home for them on the floor, sorting them in a way that would have been obscure to anyone else but registered a pattern in her brain, a spatial recall system that would allow her to hone in on any item in case she needed it some time in the future.

She had just cleared the chairs when Nick Meier came back in, followed by Jorge. They stepped carefully, slipping their feet one by one into the few open spots on the floor among the array of papers, manuscripts, and journals.

"Hi Jorge. Have a seat, both of you, please."

Jorge had no hat, but he felt as though he were holding his dilapidated old straw sun hat in his hands, assuming the submissive posture he had been accustomed to for so many years.

"Thank you, Dr. Flowers," he said, waiting for Nicholas Meier to select one of the chairs.

Nick Meier in turn was extending the same excessive courtesy to Jorge, so they stood for a few seconds making *"You first"* gestures at each other until Sandy said, "OK, Alphonse, you sit there, and you, Gaston, sit in that one. *Sit!*" The reference to the legendary comic characters was lost on both men, but the authority in Sandy Flowers' voice made them both sit as quickly as two obedient cocker spaniels.

"Now," she said, in a businesslike but welcoming voice with no trace of impatience, "what brings you here?"

Nick Meier was about to explain when Jorge unexpectedly began talking. His voice was calm, and though he was characteristically deferential, his determination was evident as he spoke.

"Thank you so much for meeting with me, Dr. Flowers, and you, Dr. Meier. I have something I need to bring to the attention of the medical staff leadership. I know I should have done this long ago, but I was afraid to come forward. Now I can no longer keep this in."

Almost in synchrony, Nick Meier and Sandy Flowers made supportive comments, Meier saying, "It's OK, Jorge, go ahead," and Flowers saying simply, "Yes, sure."

"I came to you, Dr. Meier, because I have always thought I could speak directly to you. And you, Dr. Flowers, you have also treated me well, as a professional, so I am glad you are also willing to hear me out."

This time both surgeons nodded without speaking, a signal to Jorge to get on with the conversation.

"What I have to say, what I want to tell you, is about Mrs. Hinkel, the lady with appendicitis – peritonitis, sepsis – who died. Dr. McDonald's patient. I was in the operating room, so I have been very interested in her case."

Sandy Flowers leaned forward, her head resting on her left arm, her eyes fixed on Jorge.

"Tell us, what's on your mind?"

Jorge Edmond took a deep breath, more to prepare for a long speech than to calm himself. He was too intent on his mission, on redressing the horrendous wrong that had befallen Eleanore Hinkel, Jeffrey Hinkel, Henry Hinkel, the whole family that was suffering, too focused on them to be nervous. He spoke thoughtfully, deliberately but without hesitation, in the professional speech patterns he had developed in PA school, with no trace of the accent that emerged when he was anxious.

"I will tell you what I saw – and also what I sensed, Dr. Flowers, and Dr. Meier. As you know, when I am assisting at laparoscopic surgery I watch through the little lens on the side of the viewer whenever I get a chance. So, I could see what was going on inside Mrs. Hinkel's abdomen. The surgery seemed to be going well, Dr. McDonald hadn't said much, he was working away as usual. Then I could see the appendix clearly. Dr. Meier, Dr. Flowers, that appendix was inflamed, there is no question about that, but it was intact, it was not ruptured, it had not perforated. I am sure of that."

"What makes you so sure, since you could only see the surgical site through the little monocular eyepiece and you had to look away from time to time to assist Dr. McDonald in the surgery?"

Sandy Flowers delivered her question in a neutral tone, conveying no skepticism yet making it clear she needed every possible detail to form her own impression of what had taken place. She was the cautious surgeon, probing, moving carefully into the unexpected, ready to act but only when she knew what she was seeing. Or hearing.

"I know what I saw, Dr. Flowers. I have seen many normal appendices, many inflamed ones, and a number of perforated appendices. Dr. McDonald clamped the appendix, looped it with the suture, and removed it. The tissue of the appendix was not dangerously friable, it did not shred as he manipulated it and cut it free, it remained intact. The wall of the cecum also looked quite healthy. Everything looked just fine at first. Then all of a sudden, the stump started to leak, it spurted liquid from the intestine into her abdomen. The suture, the closure, had failed. I stepped back from the scope and saw everything change with Dr. McDonald, all at one moment. His body jerked, his eyes opened so widely, he muttered some words under his breath. He knew something had gone wrong, but he wouldn't say anything except he started yelling at me to give him some instruments. He tried another suture, which also failed, then he sealed off the leak with an endostaple. The intestinal wall was healthy, the stump closed nicely once the staple was in place. Then Dr. McDonald told me to give him a saline irrigation tube to rinse out her abdomen. After a few minutes he calmed down and said her appendix had already been perforated, that she had come in too late for the surgery. I was…well, Doctors, I was stunned. What he was saying was not true. There was no leak until after he had removed the appendix. I knew he was covering up what had really happened."

Sandy Flowers persisted in her deliberate, inquisitive way. What Jorge had just said could be the key to taking action against McDonald – if it were true. More important, if they could prove it was true. She would not let her personal feelings about Matthew McDonald draw her into accepting Jorge's version without more information, something tangible she could rely on.

"Tell us again, just what you saw, please."

"Yes, Dr. Flowers. Up until that moment everything had been normal. As I said, Dr. McDonald had already removed the appendix when this happened. And I saw the appendix clearly, it did not disintegrate when he touched it with the instruments, that's not what happened."

Then Jorge realized that he had another point to make, one that would make immediate sense to the two surgeons.

"Also, Dr. Flowers, if the appendix had already perforated, which it had not, Dr. McDonald would have proceeded differently right from the moment he saw he was dealing with a ruptured appendix, no?"

"I would expect so, yes. Once he had a clear view of the cecum and the surrounding tissues, he would have seen the perforated appendix and taken measures to deal with it right away."

"But he said nothing like that and he did nothing that would have been required for a perforated appendix. He was nearly finished, then it all changed, it started leaking, and he reacted so suddenly he knew something had gone wrong."

"What happened after that?"

Sandy Flowers was in full interrogation mode now, intent on extracting every detail. She was also running alternative scenarios through her mind, trying to reconstruct what might have happened that would cause a surgeon to react as McDonald apparently had done.

"He put the appendix into a specimen bag before he removed it from Mrs. Hinkel. I carried it to Pathology in the bag."

"The path report should have readily distinguished between a ruptured appendix and an intact one. What does it say?"

Nick Meier jumped in.

"Jorge, you and I looked for that report on her chart, and I seem to recall that it was not there at that point. Did you ever see a pathology report on the appendix?"

"Yes, Dr. Meier, I checked back several times, and finally the report was there. But it said nothing."

Sandy Flowers sat forward in her chair and said excitedly, "Nothing? What do you mean, nothing?"

"It said the appendix was inflamed and was removed. Extensive internal tissue lysis. But no mention of whether it was intact or had ruptured."

"Let's take a look," Nick Meier said, excitedly. Stepping to the side of Sandy Flowers' desk he said, "Sandy, may I?"

"Of course. Go ahead." She pushed her chair back and stood to make room for her colleague

As comfortable at a computer terminal as in an operating room, Nick Meier moved quickly. He went through the security steps to log into Eleanore Hinkel's medical record, but was refused access. Then he tried to enter into the files of reports in the pathology department, again to no avail. He knew that some of the internal hospital documents were archived electronically, so he tried several different times to enter the sites where different reports on her case should have been stored. When those efforts also failed, he tried looking for minutes of the infection control committee, the data analytics and reporting group, the *Morbidity and Mortality* reviews. But each attempt led to the same dead end once he tried to focus in on Eleanore Hinkel: a short *ping* and the words *Access denied.*

"I can't get into files that deal with her case. I tried my own user name and password because I operated on her that one time, so I should have access. Then I tried going through the surgical review committee pathway, which always works. We're supposed to get into any record once we identify ourselves appropriately. Nothing. Very strange."

He stood up and returned to his chair.

Sandy Flowers had a dark, apprehensive look on her face as she sat down at her desk. Something was wrong if Eleanore Hinkel's records were being sequestered – or had been destroyed entirely.

"Tell us again, Jorge, is there anything else? Do you remember anything else taking place? Did you speak with anyone else about this?"

"No, Dr. Flowers. In truth, I have been unable to speak about this at all before now."

"Tell us more about the situation with Eleanore Hinkel. What did Dr. McDonald do?"

"He told me to start triple antibiotic therapy immediately after the irrigation was completed. He placed the drains, told me to close. I sutured the drains in place and closed her surgical entry sites. He didn't say anything else that I remember, he just left. He saw her about once each day until he went on his trip."

Turning to her colleague, Sandy said, "How about you, Nick? When you went back in to drain her abscesses, did you see anything that would tell us what had happened?"

"Not really. It was a mess, of course. I found multiple abscesses, there were pockets of pus, adhesions forming everywhere. I opened and suctioned what I could, irrigated a bit, put in my drains and took my cultures, and that was that. And her surgical sites where McDonald had inserted the laparoscope and the other instruments were clearly infected. She was in bad shape, I wanted to get in and out as quickly as possible. Jorge was with me, he saw what I saw."

Flowers glanced at Jorge, who said, "Yes, Dr. Flowers. It was as Dr. Meier described."

"So you have nothing definite yourself, Nick." Turning to Jorge, she said, "And what you've told us, Jorge, is highly suggestive since it involves Dr. McDonald, but it amounts to your word against his. The only thing going for us is that all the records on her case seem to be in limbo, the paper ones buried somewhere, the electronic ones blocked off from normal access."

"What can we do, Dr. Flowers?" Jorge Edmond's voice was steady, he was not pleading, he had the determination of a soldier on a mission awaiting an order for the next course of action. "I cannot let this be, if you understand what I am saying."

Nicholas Meier answered, "Jorge, this is a very tough situation. I don't want to speak for Dr. Flowers, but I share your concern and I suspect she does also." Seeing Sandy Flowers nodding slowly in agreement, he continued, "We have had our own questions about Dr. McDonald's performance for some time, and we took them to the Chief of the Medical Staff, Dr. Michael Simkowitz. But this may go well beyond Dr. McDonald if Mrs. Hinkel's records are being concealed."

Jorge stirred at this news.

"What happened? Did Dr. Simkowitz do something about Dr. McDonald?"

"Personally, he was quite sympathetic, but he explained how difficult it is to bring charges against a member of the medical staff and win the case. He made it clear that this was because of the legal protections that we all enjoy. The law is intended to keep good doctors from being wrongly accused just because they are not liked by other physicians or they are an economic threat to other doctors…"

"Or made targets because they are the wrong sex, or color, or ethnic background," interjected Sandy Flowers. As soon as the words were out of her mouth she paused, realizing that she might have embarrassed Jorge unintentionally by mentioning that minorities were potential victims of wrongful charges.

"Yes, of course, any kind of real discrimination," Nicholas Meier stepped back in, sensing his colleague's hesitation. "So it is quite legitimate to afford everyone some protection against false accusations, which has certainly happened many times over and can ruin someone's career. But when it comes to certain doctors – and McDonald fits into this group – the system bends over backwards to protect them even when they should no longer be practicing medicine."

"But, Dr. Meier, please – how can that be? Why would the hospital do that? We are professionals, we have ethics."

"Unfortunately, there's a very short answer: money. Some doctors bring in so many patients, they are what we call *'rainmakers,'* they generate a lot of revenue for the hospital. Then there's reputation – there's a feeling that if certain prominent doctors are revealed to be incompetent the public will think the same about all the doctors in the hospital. And if the place became known as a death trap…"

Again Sandy Flowers interrupted. "And, the sad truth is that it is so easy to cover up terrible problems that it has become simple to get away with, so it keeps happening."

"I don't want to discourage you too much, Jorge, but there's something else you should understand as well."

Nicholas Meier was determined to let Jorge know he was on his side and wanted to help, but he could not let Jorge think that this would be easy. Jorge had to know the risks he would face.

"Unfortunately, things can be even worse than we have said so far. Sometimes the person who brings the accusations ends up being the one who is penalized. One way for people in power to avoid dealing with problems like this is to make a scapegoat out of the accuser." Meier paused, not sure whether Jorge would know what *'scapegoat'* meant, and even more unsure how to clarify what he had said without insulting the man. He continued, "So that person, the one who tried to do what is right and ethical, becomes the one whose career suffers. It's not a pretty picture. We even have an ironic expression for this: *'No good deed goes unpunished.'*"

Nicholas Meier's words fell hard on Jorge Edmond. He was stunned, devastated by these revelations, these contradictions of so much that he held dear. He stared at the two surgeons as blankly as though they had just told him he had an incurable illness. When at last he spoke, his voice carried a new hesitancy, but he was not entirely deterred.

"Dr. Flowers, Dr. Meier, pardon me. Are you telling me I cannot do anything about Dr. McDonald, that no one will listen? That they will turn on me instead?"

"We are telling you that is a risk, yes."

Nick Meier hated having to bring Jorge down this way, but he knew how important it was for him to understand what he might be getting into.

"Dr. Simkowitz raised this issue with me and Dr. Flowers when we mentioned our questions about Dr. McDonald. He cautioned us about the possible perverse consequences for us, for our careers, if the tables turned against us instead of Dr. McDonald. We might be forced to leave the hospital or even get pushed out of practicing medicine entirely. Dr. Simkowitz was very clear about what might happen."

Jorge sat silent for a few moments. If that was the way things were, why should he be the one to take the risk? Nothing good would happen, only bad. He would be thrown out of the hospital, disgraced, forced to go back to his old life. Then he thought of Jeffrey Hinkel, the flowers on the lonesome gravesite, the stories about his travels with his mother, the sight of him talking through the earth to her body. He remembered the way Henry Hinkel had looked, sitting helplessly week after painful week as his companion withered away. What about them? What about all the other families who suffered at Dr. McDonald's hands? He knew what he had to do, too many lives had been disrupted and several had been lost. He was the only one who could try to make it right. And what did he have to lose, anyway? If this new life meant that he could not do what he knew was right and honorable, what difference did it make if he were to go back to digging ditches? When Jorge spoke again, the confidence had returned to his voice.

"I must do what I can. If it is God's will that I end up losing my profession, that I must go back to working with my hands in some garden somewhere, at least I will comfort myself knowing that I have done the right thing. Maybe I cannot prove that Dr. McDonald did something wrong, but Mrs. Hinkel is dead, and her husband and her son are in misery, so I cannot rest until I know that I have tried to do right by her and by them. I must do this."

Nick Meier felt a lump in his throat. Jorge's new career, his new life, meant everything to the man yet he was willing to risk it all to do right by the Hinkel family. Feeling quite moved by the man's courage, Meier realized he could never let Jorge take this on alone. Especially not if there were a higher level of involvement here. If the hospital hierarchy was going along with some kind of cover-up, they'd cut Jorge to shreds for speaking up. And if things were as bad as Jorge had described, he would also need to get the hell out of this hospital.

"I will stand by you, Jorge, I will do whatever I can to help. If they go after you, they will have to take me on as well. McDonald should not be treated any differently than the rest of us. And if siding with you means that I lose my job and have to take up a shovel and dig dirt next to you, well, that'll just have to be the way it goes."

With no elaboration or evident emotion, Sandy Flowers said simply, "Me too."

Jorge looked at the two surgeons, nodded his head slowly and said, "Thank you. Thank you both." They all stood and shook hands, then Sandy Flowers led Jorge through the obstacle course of her inner office into the outer room and opened the door for him. Jorge nodded again, then turned and left.

Sandy Flowers returned to her inner office and looked at her colleague. "OK, Nick, how about getting that drink you owe me?"

Chapter 17. Another Informal Chat

As another frustrating day came to a close, Dr. Michael Simkowitz left his office and trudged down the hallway toward the exit to the parking lot, his weary mind contemplating little more than the first tumbler of Chivas waiting for him at home. But before he could leave the building he saw Sandy Flowers coming toward him and brightened, expecting their usual pleasant repartee. She held up one palm to signal him to stop and, to his surprise, began talking without the amiable greeting he had anticipated.

"Dr. Simkowitz, Dr. Meier and I need to follow up with you on that subject we had discussed once before."

Just hearing Sandy Flowers call him "*Doctor*," and refer to her friend Nick Meier in the same formal way, told Simkowitz that this was serious. He sensed that this was to be an entirely different meeting than the last time the two surgeons had come to his office to talk about Matthew McDonald.

"Of course, Dr. Flowers," he responded in kind. "You know my door is always open."

"Thank you. And we will have a third person with us, Jorge Edmond."

"Ah, sure, the surgical PA. I've heard good things about Mr. Edmond. Does this involve him?"

"In a way, yes, it does. And you're right, Jorge is an excellent PA, there is no problem with him. It's what he has to say."

"About someone else?"

"I believe you know the subject all too well, yes. Let's not get ahead of ourselves, Jorge can speak for himself."

"Is this something I should have Molly Cavendish or Sy Sullivan hear?" Simkowitz spoke carefully, testing whether he understood the situation accurately, in which case Cavendish and Sullivan would be the last two people Flowers would want to attend.

Phrasing her answer as precisely as Simkowitz had framed his question, Sandy Flowers said, "Actually, no, not at this point. We want to get your feedback first. There will be time to involve others if you determine that is appropriate after you hear Mr. Edmond's story."

Like secret agents in a room they knew was bugged, the two physicians nodded at each other without making a sound, clear that they both grasped the meaning of their circumspect exchange: *This is about McDonald, keep it between us.*

"That works for me. Did you check with my office for a time?"

"I took the liberty, yes. We're on for tomorrow at 6 PM. I'm sorry it's so late in the day, but getting a time when all four of us can be there was a bit complicated."

Simkowitz had a vague memory that he might have made some sort of promise to his wife for the next evening, that maybe he was due home at six and would have to cancel plans with Julie if he were to meet with the surgeons and PA then. He tried to recall if he and Julie were supposed to have dinner out? Could it possibly be their anniversary? Her birthday? No, it was not anything that important, his memory wasn't so pathetic he could forget an anniversary or birthday. What was it? Then it came to him: Julie would be out with her lady friends tomorrow night. He had made her a promise, but it was just that he would get on by himself for the evening. Perfect timing.

"Tomorrow at six will be fine, Sandy. I'll be in my office at six."

By habit he had slipped back into the informal style he was comfortable with, the way he had always spoken with Dr. Sandra Flowers.

"OK, Mike, we'll be at your office at six."

***

The four people gathering in the conference room off of Michael Simkowitz' office had much in common when they were in their workplace, but outside of the hospital no one would have suspected any connection among them. On the job whatever family ties or personal lives each individual might have in the outside world were masked, subsumed by their professional roles in Northeast

122

Suburban Hospital. Their individual identities were further obscured when, as now, they donned the white coats that pigeon-holed them into the hierarchy of their respective functions in the hospital: knee-length coats signified a doctor, hip length a PA, waist-length a medical student. Even Michael Simkowitz, long absent from patient care, took his white coat down from the hook behind his office door and slipped it on for meetings such as this. Whether he went into uniform to generate a sense of camaraderie with the medical staff or to blunt the impact of his increasingly regrettable transformation from physician to bureaucrat for his own self-esteem, not even Simkowitz himself knew. What he did know was that when he donned the long white coat with the old nametag that read, "Michael Simkowitz, M.D., Staff Physician," for one pleasant moment he had the sense of regaining his real identity, a comfortable sensation that made him feel whole.

And yet, even as he enjoyed feeling like himself again, Michael Simkowitz felt his age as he looked at the two youthful surgeons and the somewhat older but notably robust physician assistant. He was acutely conscious of the paunch around his belly that expanded inexorably as his exercise regime became less frequent than his encounters with the *Chivas* in his dry bar. But the disconnect between him and the other three professionals encompassed far more than age or physical decline, it was palpable, an existential gap he could not bridge no matter how much he tried. The white coat could only work its magic for an instant, then he felt like an imposter – the three of them cared for patients, he pushed papers and endured meetings. Meetings like this.

Jorge Edmond was closest to his age but Simkowitz could not identify at all with the tall, muscular Hispanic former day laborer who hadn't even had bootstraps to pull himself up with yet managed to become a physician assistant late in life. Having grown up in a thoroughly middle-class family with a clear path through college and medical school ever since he could remember, Simkowitz felt no connection whatsoever with Jorge Edmond, however much he liked and respected what he knew of him. Nicholas Meier, on the other hand, had triggered the feeling of a certain bond with Simkowitz on their first meeting. Meier had reminded him of one of his closest friends from his surgical residency, another intense young man with penetrating eyes like Meier, always perfectly groomed and looking like he was ready to taxi a fighter jet down a runway. But that fanciful connection with Meier could not surmount the difference in their ages or the reality that Meier's surgical skills were improving continuously while his were dissipating. And Simkowitz could not identify at all with Sandy Flowers. She was in a different league entirely than Simkowitz, a league that had not existed in his earlier world. There had been exactly twelve women in Simkowitz' medical school class out of one hundred twenty students. A firm quota, ten percent female. And an impenetrable ceiling that kept all women except surgical nurses out of the surgery suites in those days. Simkowitz admired Sandy Flowers greatly, but had no foundation for bonding with her, she was so unlike the all-male surgeons he had known. Yet that did not keep him from recognizing that she was clearly born for her profession, so precise, so confident.

In short, Michael Simkowitz felt old. His was a different generation and world than those of his three colleagues. Even worse than old, he felt useless. These members of his medical staff were about to rely on him to deal with a problem he probably could not solve, a problem that pained and plagued him, but one that he had not been able to resolve for all the years he had wanted to. He held the three in high regard because they were so good at what they were doing, and reminisced that he had been good once, a damn good surgeon. How had he ended up in this dead-end job, all the trappings of power but no authority even to deal with a blight on the medical staff – *Hell*, he thought, *blight on the entire medical profession* – as serious as McDonald? Simkowitz told himself to focus on what the three might have to say. Perhaps they would give him the ammunition he needed to take down McDonald at last.

Simkowitz needed to clear his head. He poured himself yet another cup of coffee and asked his visitors, "Anyone else for six o'clock coffee? High-test, I must warn you, not decaf."

The three visitors shook their heads, only Jorge Edmond saying clearly, "No, thank you, Dr. Simkowitz."

"Please, have a seat."

Simkowitz' meeting room was plain vanilla, a semi-formal setting with bare walls of light wood paneling that did not distract attention from the business at hand. The room had no windows, was lit only by fluorescent bulbs recessed into canisters in the acoustic tile drop ceiling. The net effect was of being in a safe place to speak in private, an isolation chamber away from the thousands of activities going on outside the walls of the meeting room. Simkowitz and the others each took one of the Spartan wooden chairs and drew up to the matching round conference table.

Sandy Flowers began.

"Dr. Simkowitz, Mr. Edmond has a serious matter he wishes to bring to your attention."

Jorge Edmond was about to speak, but Simkowitz cut him short, saying, "Excuse the interruption, but let's establish some ground rules first. I need to know whether you are initiating a formal inquiry or whether this is merely an informal discussion. I say this because you need to understand that as soon as this constitutes a formal process that could lead to an adverse personnel action I need to take a number of steps to comply with certain legal requirements. In particular, I must notify the person being accused once a formal investigation has been opened. On the other hand, if this is only an informal discussion I could do some background work without initiating the legally-required procedures. So, what is your preference, Mr. Edmond?"

His voice was cautionary but conspiratorial, the tone intended to generate a tacit agreement that they would act as though this were an informal discussion – tacit, because pointing the conversation overtly toward McDonald might compromise any subsequent formal action against him.

Jorge had anticipated Simkowitz' cautionary statement, since Sandy Flowers and Nick Meier had let him know that Simkowitz might want to begin this way to avoid legal niceties that would inhibit his investigation. But Jorge had no choice, it was time to tell the story no matter what the consequences.

"It will be fine with me if this is an informal discussion, Dr. Simkowitz. You can decide whether to take any further action after you hear my story."

They did their homework, Simkowitz thought, proud of his junior colleagues. He was impressed that they understood that the less said the better, for starters anyway. He knew that McDonald would unleash all of the lawyers he could buy as soon as he attacked him openly. He had to be prepared. One step at a time.

"Excellent, Mr. Edmond, please proceed."

Although he had replayed his experience in the operating room hundreds of times in his head, Jorge Edmond realized this was only the second time he would describe it to another person. He took his time telling how McDonald had punctured Eleanore Hinkel's belly in three places to insert the laparoscope and other instruments, how it had seemed that the surgery was going well, then how the appendiceal stump had started leaking after the inflamed but intact appendix had been removed. Then her long, slow, downhill course, infections emerging from multiple sites in her body, her final passing.

When Jorge Edmond paused after describing Eleanore Hinkel's tortuous decline and demise, Michael Simkowitz was disappointed. He leaned back in his chair to think, the fingertips of each hand lightly touching their mirror images, his eyes looking somewhere above the heads of the three people at the conference table. What Jorge had related wasn't much. He had hoped Jorge would have something more definitive. How could he take on McDonald with this? With just Jorge's word? Finally, he looked directly at Jorge and asked, "Is that all?"

"No, Dr. Simkowitz. That's all that happened in the operating room. But after Mrs. Hinkel passed…"

"You were at her funeral, as I remember, is that correct?"

Once again Michael Simkowitz had uncharacteristically interrupted Jorge, blurting out the question as the striking image of Jorge standing off to one side at the funeral appeared in his memory. He immediately caught himself and apologized, saying, "I'm sorry, Mr. Edmond, please continue."

"That's OK, Dr. Simkowitz. Yes, I did attend the funeral. I felt so bad for her and her family, and I was trying to decide what to do about the things I had seen."

"Go on, please."

"Yes, after Mrs. Hinkel passed, I realized that I had not seen a pathology report on her appendix. Dr. Meier and I reviewed her chart and it was not present. There was no report for some time after she had passed. Later I did find a report from Dr. Pappelbaugh, but it was very brief. It did not say anything about whether the appendix was intact or had ruptured, just that it was severely inflamed and tissue lysis had set in."

Nick Meier made eye contact with Jorge, who nodded back. Meier picked up the thread.

"When Jorge told us his story about what he had observed and McDonald's behavior during surgery, Sandy and I tried to view the path report and all of the files related to her case. We couldn't gain access to anything on Mrs. Hinkel's case. I should be authorized to see everything since I had operated on her to drain abscesses, and

I even tried my surgical review committee password, which should let me into any surgical case file. Nothing. *'Access denied,'* every time."

"That's when we decided to bring this to you, Mike," added Sandy Flowers. "Between Jorge's description of the situation in the O.R. and the restricted access to the woman's records, we thought you needed to know about this."

Simkowitz perked up at this additional information. Maybe they had something after all.

"As all of you know all too well, the computer systems are unreliable, that could have been a simple glitch. Let's see what happens when I try. I have unlimited access to all records."

A tell-tale series of rejection beeps from his computer soon confirmed for everyone in the room that Dr. Michael Simkowitz, Chief of the Medical Staff and Vice President for Medical Affairs, had also been denied access to the electronic files.

Simkowitz stifled a litany of obscenities, uttering out loud only a pained, *"Mmmpfff."* His stomach churned. This had Molly Cavendish's fingerprints all over it. She must be covering up for McDonald and who knows what else. Now it was clear that Jorge had put him on to something significant – otherwise the records would not be restricted, not from him. This could be the moment he had been hoping for, at last.

Suppressing a powerful urge to pick up the computer, haul it down the corridor and fling it at Molly Cavendish, Simkowitz said calmly but with clear import, "This is most unusual. I have what is supposed to be unrestricted access to all of the computer systems. I've never been blocked from even one record before. Never."

"What now, Mike?"

"This has been a most intriguing conversation. As of this moment there is no formal investigation since I have nothing to base one on. We will have to see if anything else turns up."

His words were dismissive, signaling the end of the meeting, but his tone was clearly conspiratorial, the oral equivalent of a wink and a nod. No investigation, no formal notice to Matthew McDonald or Molly Cavendish or anyone else, no paperwork, no files opened.

"Thank you all for bringing this matter to my attention. I will let you know if there are any further developments."

Jorge Edmond stood up, unsure of what had just transpired, but with a great sense of relief. He was pleased that, as he had hoped, Simkowitz was a good man, that he was not going to let this drop. He knew he had to be patient. "Thank you for listening to me, Dr. Simkowitz."

"I am the one who must thank you, Jorge," Simkowitz said, stifling an unexpected surge of emotion toward the man who was risking so much. "I know this was not easy for you, and I appreciate your being willing to speak up. Please know that I will…" Simkowitz caught himself. He should not say anything that could later be interpreted as his having opened a covert investigation, that could scotch the whole thing. "…I will think seriously about what you have said. It was most helpful."

"Thank you again, Dr. Simkowitz." Jorge Edmond's voice was on the verge of cracking.

Simkowitz stood and extended his hand to Jorge Edmond, then was surprised that the man's thick, powerful hand was moist and clammy. Simkowitz felt a deep pang of sympathy for Jorge, realizing that the poor guy was as vulnerable as any human being could be. He fully understood that for someone who was just a PA, it had taken a lot of guts to come to his office and do this. Jorge had to be careful. McDonald and Cavendish would eat him alive if they knew. If Jorge was right but Simkowitz could not bring McDonald and Cavendish to account, the two of them would get off free and Jorge would be the only one to suffer reprisals.

"I will keep your statement entirely confidential. No one outside of this room needs to know anything at this point. You have nothing to be concerned about. In fact, you should be pleased, you have done your duty."

Simkowitz turned to include the two surgeons in his final words.

"You are all to be commended for coming forward in this situation. I only wish everyone in this hospital would do the same."

Once the trio exited his office, Michael Simkowitz sat back down at the computer and opened a new document. He typed, "Memo to File. Met with Jorge Edmond and Drs. Meier and Flowers about a matter concerning the case of Eleanore Hinkel. Information not sufficient for further action. No investigation warranted."

Simkowitz smiled to himself. He knew how to cover his ass. Those bastards weren't the only ones who knew how to play this game. They'd never be able to divert attention from the charges against them by accusing him of conducting a covert investigation and not giving McDonald due process.

When Simkowitz finished his obfuscating memo, he hung his white coat on its hook and headed home, then had a moment of disappointment at the realization that Julie would not be there to share his evening with. OK, at least his good buddy, Chivas, he'd be waiting for him with a hearty welcome.

***

Jonathan Peters had an embarrassing personal problem: his scrotum was slowly cannibalizing his penis. He had first noticed some swelling of his right testicle when he was a teenager, but kept the fact to himself in an act of adolescent denial. In his thirties he had to acknowledge that both sides of his scrotum were filling up and the entire sack was protruding uncomfortably, occasionally getting caught in his zipper. So he swallowed his pride and went to see his doctor who made a crass joke about getting too big for his britches, then said he could diagnose the problem with a simple test right there in his office. The doctor turned off the lights in the examining room and pressed his pocket flashlight against each testicle. Two clear gelatinous cysts, one attached to each testicle, lit up like a pair of giant fireflies encased in tiny plastic bags. 'Bilateral spermatoceles' the doctor said, not cancer, nothing to worry about. No, the doctor assured him, this was completely different than the elephantiasis that created the gargantuan scrotums Jonathan had seen naked natives struggling with in old *National Geographic* photo essays. Those were caused by tropical parasites that blocked the lymph drainage. Unless the spermatoceles started bothering him with some significant symptoms, the doctor said, there was nothing to be done.

So Jonathan had lived with his private problem until he was fifty-two years old. He was never in pain or suffered any symptoms at all. And, mercifully, had no problem having sexual relations – his receding penis would rise to the challenge when needed, filling with enough blood and recapturing sufficient skin from the neighboring scrotum to emerge from its fleshy tent and perform admirably when excited. For many years, the only thing that bothered him was just the persistent consciousness that he had an embarrassing, ever-expanding, lump in his crotch that was not the enormous penis men and women alike fantasized it must be when they saw the impressive bulge in his bathing suit. But in his early fifties his scrotum had grown so large it had taken over all the loose skin in the surrounding area, penis and all, and he could no longer pee over the bulge without wetting himself. His doctor referred him to "the best surgeon in town," Dr. Matthew McDonald, who assured him that excising the cysts was minor surgery that would require no more than one night in the hospital.

After the surgery, Jonathan Peters never needed to worry about urinating on himself ever again. Not because the operation fixed his problem, which, according to Matthew McDonald, it had indeed done, but because Jonathan Peters never urinated again. A catheter drained his bladder during his last few weeks of life in Northeast Suburban Hospital.

Chapter 18. The Human Factor

Will Manningham glanced at the bedroom clock after what seemed like barely fifteen minutes since he had climbed into bed at 1:23 AM – he knew the exact time because the 1-2-3 sequence on the digital display had caught his mathematical eye just before he switched off his bedside light and pulled the sheets over his head. Now the clock continued the series, reading 4:56 AM. *I'm going nuts,* he thought. *Even the damn clock is teasing me.* Desperate for more sleep he shut his eyes, only to see the swirling kaleidoscope of numbers, patterns, fragments of computer code, unfinished algorithms, that had plagued him through three-and-a-half hours of broken sleep. His brain was supercharged but going nowhere. He could sense that he must be close to finding something, but what? What final piece of the puzzle was just below the surface, taunting him relentlessly?

He shook his head in frustration. The semi-autonomous fingernail instinctively found its way through his dense red hair to scratch the familiar spot on his scalp that somehow seemed to help him think. But nothing came into focus. He began to think that maybe there was no pattern, just random recycling of all the bits of information he had been assembling. Maybe there was no connection between *Marquis-Herrant* and all the dead patients. *No, that's impossible, can't be a coincidence. Keep looking,* his analytical mind insisted.

As his lanky body twisted and turned under the sheets he felt his wife Sally's hand burrowing through his hair, grasping his finger to stop the repetitive scratching. Her long black hair fell across his face as she drew her mouth close to his ear and whispered, "Honey, are you OK?"

He pressed his head up against her hand and exhaled a prolonged *'puhhh'* through pursed lips. "Yes…no, not really. It's my old problem – I'm so far into the forest that the trees, the branches, the leaves – hell, the bugs on the leaves – they're all churning around in my head but I can't get the picture."

"It'll all come together, it always does. You overload your brain with so much material it just takes it a while to make the connections."

"Maybe, but in the meantime people are…dammit, people are *dying*. And I can't get ahead of the curve, I can only track what happens after it's too late. There has to be a key, something that will allow me to decipher this mess."

"A Rosetta Stone, right?"

"Yup, another Rosetta Stone. But the archeologists haven't dug this one up yet."

Sally pulled back her hand, tossed her hair back with a quick shake of her head, and slid up in the bed until she was sitting upright against the headboard. She straightened her red hearts-and-cupids pajama top, stuffed two pillows behind her back, and said, "OK, since we're both awake now, do you want to talk about it? If we talk, Honey, maybe it'll help you focus."

Will was quick to accept Sally's offer. Her insights had often proved valuable when the two of them had been undercover as Sean and Sara Flaherty. She had a way of cutting to the chase, while he often over-complicated things by coming up with endless variations on possible scenarios. And she was brave and creative in her approach to dealing with their enemies. Maybe too brave and creative, Will thought, remembering how she had volunteered to work as a mole for the FBI in the Russian mob's organization, a gamble that had nearly gotten her killed.

"Well, if you really want to talk at five o'clock in the morning in bed, sure, we can talk."

"Doesn't seem like you're up for anything else," she said, a coy smile animating her crisp, angular features.

Will smiled weakly back at his wife and sighed. "Yeah, I'm afraid that's all I've got. For now, anyway. Sorry. But I would really appreciate it if you would hear me out."

"So go ahead, tell me what's going on. Start at the beginning."

"OK, here's the deal. I was scanning Medicare billing records for unusual stuff like I always do when I came across clusters of suspicious deaths in several spots around the country. At first I thought it might be some sort of public health problem, you know, an outbreak of some deadly virus or toxic contamination like lead in the drinking water in Flint, Michigan. But the causes of death were all over the map, not like any epidemic I'd ever heard of. And then I discovered that the deaths fell into two groups: infections and medical device failures."

"Uh-oh, that sounds troublesome."

"That's exactly what I thought. So I showed the results to Adrienne and she agreed that there was something worth pursuing even though we couldn't identify any particular pattern. Then she told me that there had been similar outbreaks over the last several years spreading across Europe, possibly heading toward this country. She assigned several of her FBI Agents to work with my team. We created algorithms to search through tons of Big Data for connections with what I had found: you know, law enforcement stories, press reports, all the various data sets we're tied into. Public files first, then inside information once the investigation got going. We finally got what looks like a key lead: an emerging international drug and device company called *Marquis-Herrant* has a prominent presence in each of the clusters."

"Wow! What was the company doing to cause all those deaths?"

"That's the $64 million dollar question. We don't know, not yet. But once we started looking at the company more carefully, guess what we found?"

"Since this seems to be driving you nuts, I can only think that there must be a Russian connection."

"Yup, exactly. *Marquis-Herrant* has a bunch of Russian expats working here. They are at the center of each of the clusters. But that's it. We're stuck, no real leads to build a case around, nothing solid."

"Tell me about the Russian expats who work for that company. Scary thugs and vicious murderers as usual?"

"Ha! Not at all. Young women, late twenties, early thirties maybe, stationed in various places around the country. They all have solid credentials: scientific backgrounds, college degrees. Adrienne and Tom Murphy even went undercover and tracked one of them to a fancy resort down in Cabo where *Marquis-Herrant* was entertaining a bunch of US doctors."

"Wow, the FBI paid for a trip like that? You'd never get CMS to foot that bill."

"You got that right. Anyway, so we've identified this cadre of women working for that company. Each of them is assigned to a geographic area that turns out to be at the center of a worrisome number of excess deaths. It's very suspicious that the hotspots with elevated mortality rates are the very places where these *Marquis-Herrant* reps work, but that's as far as it goes. We've got nothing that demonstrates what they are doing that could be causing those deaths. Two overlapping findings, no solid explanation. Lots of connections but it could still be a coincidence – as you know, just because two things are associated statistically doesn't mean one is the cause of the other."

"Yes, I've heard you say that many times. But it sounds like you don't believe it's a coincidence."

"I'm trying hard to stick to the data and avoid jumping to conclusions, but yes, the numbers tell me the likelihood is very low that this is only a series of coincidences."

"And that's it? No leads at all?"

"Only the fact that the reps are Russian expats."

Sally took Will's hand and kissed it, then snuggled up against him. "You suspect that this is coming from the same Russian mob that killed your brother, right, Sweetheart? And that phony doctor who killed your mother?"

Will nodded his head slowly and sighed. "Yes, and kidnapped and nearly killed you when we raided their headquarters in Brooklyn. I can't help thinking that we're dealing with the same criminals who were behind that operation."

"Didn't you catch them? I thought the FBI tracked down all the ones who didn't get killed in the Brooklyn shootout."

"Yes and no. The mob's hired hands are dead. And we arrested the former American officials who were helping the Russians infiltrate the government and buy up all kinds of health care companies. They're in jail. But the big kahunas got away from us. We always figured we'd hear from them again, and now I'm afraid we have."

"How did the big guys get away? They were right there when the raid started and…and I got shot."

"Worst day of my life."

"I'm better now, Will, that's all over. Anyway, how did the bosses manage to escape?"

"For a while we didn't have a clue how they escaped or where they had gone. Then the FBI tracked down a private jet that took off shortly after the takedown in Brooklyn. The plane had filed a flight plan for Montreal but diverted to Moscow. Airport security at JFK's Executive Terminal remembered clearing three older guys with US passports and common American names who all spoke with heavy Russian accents. But at the time they had no reason to detain them and their papers seemed to be in order. We didn't even know how many of them to look for until you recovered enough from your injuries in the shootout to tell us. So we're pretty sure the bigshots got back to Russia."

"I'm so sorry for you, Honey. It's hard enough coming up with your computer algorithms and sifting through all that stuff the way you do, but dealing with those old memories must be very painful."

He nodded. As usual, Sally had put her finger on what was agitating him. "Thanks, Honey. You got that right. But maybe this time we'll nail those big bastards."

"Let's hope. Or at least shut down another one of their scams."

"Another scam that's killing people."

"Yes. I didn't want to say it like that, but that's what I was thinking. So what next for you? More data bases, more algorithms, more computer programs?"

"Sure, I can't give up on the analytics. That's what I do, what I've always done. But I can't help feeling that might not be enough."

"What are you getting at?"

"I had a conversation like this with Adrienne recently, about how there are limits to what we can accomplish with our data and algorithms. I told her that all the computers in the world might not be enough to tie things together fast enough for us to understand what's going on anytime soon. Things might come into focus a lot faster if the FBI could give us some clues as to where to direct our attention. That's when she got the team more involved in hands-on police work — like that trip she and Murphy made to Cabo and saw all those doctors with the people from *Marquis-Herrant*."

"So isn't that connection enough?"

"It's provocative, sure, but we don't have anything that tells us exactly what the company and their Russian reps are up to. We need some real proof before we can file charges and take action."

"And you don't think you'll get there with your computer work like you always do?"

"Maybe, but maybe not soon enough. It just feels like we've got lots of pieces of the puzzle but nothing to tie it all together. I'll tell you what would be really helpful: if someone walked in the door and told us how to connect the dots. Then we wouldn't have to have an infinite number of analysts running an infinite number of algorithms until we found the solution."

"Does that happen? I mean, does somebody show up out of the blue and point you in the right direction like that?"

"Sometimes, but usually it's the other way around: a whistleblower starts things off by coming to us with a tip, then we do the analyses to see if their story pans out. Or we discover some suspicious patterns on our own and that's enough to pinpoint the scam. But this time we're stuck. The data tell us there's a problem but we can't get enough evidence to put a case together. We'll probably get there eventually without the benefit of inside information if we keep improving our algorithms, keep sweeping in new sources of data, and chip away with our computers…"

"Chip away with your computer chips?"

"Ha! Yeah, chip away with our computer chips, then chip away some more until it all makes sense. But that can take a while. On the other hand, if an insider comes to us and clues us in to what is going on, we can take a quantum leap forward overnight. Having inside information from a whistleblower can wrap things up a lot quicker than running search after search in the data for the secret."

"Any sign of that happening?"

"Not yet. But I'm working on something. And you know who really wants someone to come forward: Sean Flaherty."

"Aha – I kinda miss old Sean's black hair and beard. So tell me, why would he be interested?"

"Because Plan B is to send Sean into the hospital on an undercover job and he'd really like to avoid that."

"Hmmm…in that case Sara Flaherty might have to dust off her Audrey Hepburn sunglasses and blond wig. And start looking through her wardrobe for her tops with plunging necklines."

"No way. Last time you played that role you almost got killed."

"OK, let's hope it never comes to Plan B. Sara Flaherty is quite comfortable in retirement with Sean."

Chapter 19. Ties that Bind

Molly Cavendish and Fran Pappelbaugh had long been casual acquaintances, which was as close to being friends as either of them permitted. Or desired. Some rare days they might head out for drinks after work, and they had seen a few movies together over the years. Mostly, they chatted on the job and kept their distance. But a powerful bond was to form between Dr. Michela Francesca Pappelbaugh and Senior Vice President Molly Cavendish: they were to be drawn into an intense dialectic from which there would be no escape.

Fran Pappelbaugh was about the same age as Molly Cavendish, but in sharp contrast with the still-attractive Molly, Fran was short and stubby with an unkempt mass of gray hair topping her head. Half-moon eyeglasses perched on the tip of her nose or dangled on a fraying gold cord around her neck. Candy bars in torn wrappers often bulged out of the sagging, overstuffed pockets of her once-white hospital coats that were blotchy with unsavory stains from the autopsy suite and so long they nearly dragged on the floor. The short, squat pathologist moved slowly but steadily, reminiscent of a giant sea turtle crawling cautiously on the shore, the resemblance exaggerated by eyes that bulged slightly through narrow lids.

Yet nature had assured that even sea turtles were endowed with the capacity to mate, and Fran's outward appearance had not cut her off from the pleasures of the flesh. Although relatively chaste compared with Molly Cavendish in their younger years, Michela Francesca Pappelbaugh had had her men. But at this point, having buried her husband many years earlier, she had long felt no need for a new man. Thoughts of sex had settled into her lockbox of embalmed memories, until her life took one of those utterly unanticipated turns that remind human beings of the folly of believing in the predictability of events. She was to experience a resurgence of sexual passion as astonishing as it was unforeseen, bringing her both untold pleasures and, soon thereafter, diabolical consequences.

Fran Pappelbaugh was sitting at the bench in the Pathology Lab, her isolated sanctuary that rarely attracted visitors. Staring intently into her microscope she had not heard the man enter the lab and cross the concrete floor. He stood on the other side of the bench, cleared his throat, and said, "Hi, Fran, hope I didn't startle you."

She raised her head and refocused her eyes from the magnified cells she had been examining through the lenses of the microscope to look at the man standing in front of her. She smiled at her visitor and said, "Not at all, Freddy. What brings you way down here to my lab?"

He smiled back, a pleasant, warm smile, and said, "I thought maybe you'd like to go get a cup of coffee or something."

She and Dr. Freddy Grindel, the hospital's Chief of Infectious Diseases, had been colleagues for many years, but never socialized and only rarely had conversations that touched on any personal matters. His unexpected invitation made her look at him in a new light. She saw that he had a short, compact body that appeared to be in fairly good shape for a man in his 60s. From the low angle of her lab stool she glanced up and marveled with a touch of envy at the tight wattle-free skin of his clean-shaven neck. Then her eyes scanned up his pleasant, rounded face to the long white hair hanging over his forehead. Yes, she would enjoy taking a break with this man.

"Sure," she said, "coffee would be great."

"Have you tried the lattes at the new espresso bar in the private wing?"

"Nope. That sounds like a good idea, let's give it a try. Let me just freshen up a tad — these old white coats get pretty grungy down here."

Fran Pappelbaugh stepped into her office, removed the not-so-white lab coat she had been working in, and exchanged it for the one she rarely wore, the one she held in reserve and referred to as her "cleanest dirty coat."

That first outing to have a casual chat while sipping two overpriced, oversized containers of frou-frou coffee progressed rapidly over the ensuing weeks to a far more intimate relationship. Later she would muse that the speedy advance of their affair had felt so natural it must have been the fulfillment of some premonition, some inchoate expectation that had been forming deep inside of her.

Fran Pappelbaugh and Freddy Grindel became adventurous lovers wandering together blissfully through new territory. The pathologist and the infectious disease specialist had led professionally pristine lives to that point, often railing against the marginal ethics of many of their fellow physicians. Now they found themselves taking perverse pleasure in bouts of wild sex all over the hospital. They mounted each other on the desks in their offices, enjoyed themselves in the cramped quarters of Freddy's bacteriology laboratory among all the dangerous germs that were silently incubating on stacks of Petri dishes, even risked a quick liaison in an unoccupied hospital bed behind a closed but unlocked door of a room on the infectious disease ward, all the more tantalizing by being within earshot of the nursing staff. The two aging lovers often savored rapacious trysts on the floor of Fran's pathology lab out of romantic nostalgia for their first encounter that led to the momentous coffee break.

Freddy's favorite location was a janitor's closet with a small stool that Fran would squat on for an oral quickie, while her most stimulating spot for sex was the stainless steel autopsy table in her dissecting room. She would clean the shiny metal surface with disinfectant and rubbing alcohol, all the time anticipating how she would lie on the cold steel table while he sprayed her all over with water from the hose that she used to wash blood and other bodily fluids from the cadavers into the collecting drains. At first, Freddy did not share Fran's curious delight in having sex among the dead bodies, teasing her that she had become a pathologist because she was a latent necrophiliac. But she would explode with such a burst of sexual energy on the metal table, screaming with delight at his every touch as though the steel transmitted a charge of electricity from his fingers through her, that he soon looked forward to their morbid encounters.

But a cloud was soon to darken their unfettered erotic frenzy. Blinded by a perverse need to tell someone about her torrid late-life romance, Fran made a fatal mistake: she took Molly Cavendish into her confidence. As soon as Fran revealed the lurid details of her affair with Freddy Grindel, Molly knew that she had gotten the leverage she needed to drag the guilty lovers into her corrupt affairs. For two members of the medical staff to engage in illicit sex within the walls of the hospital was such a flagrant violation of their professional and ethical obligations it gave the devious Molly the power to control their lives. She was clever as always, trapping them bit by bit. At first, to test their willingness to remain silent once she revealed her corrupt schemes, she made them privy to minor problems in the hospital she was concealing. Little by little she disclosed a litany of increasingly shady activities until, at last, she ensnared them in a web of deceit more horrific than they could ever have imagined.

Fran and Freddy would have resisted Molly had they been in their right minds, but they went along, knowing that she would retaliate with a vengeance and end their professional lives in disgrace. Then, to their surprise they found an unexpected benefit: sharing Molly's evil secrets brought a wicked delight to their newfound carnal pleasures that proved irresistibly erotic, almost as though they had formed a wildly titillating *ménage a trois* with Cavendish that enhanced their already-exploding sexual energy. The graver the risk from their devious pact with Molly Cavendish became, the more their libidos surged, their bodies teeming with insatiable lust like two adolescents discovering sex for the first time.

But even as the lovers whirled ever downward into the darkest of Molly's dark secrets their illicit pleasures came to an abrupt end.

The fateful night that undid everything had started out the same as many of their long evenings of lovemaking. Freddy had left her a message with his signal: "*SOB.*" That was their droll code for '*Sildenafil on board*,' an alert that he had just ingested 100mg of generic Viagra and they should be going at it full speed within an hour. And they were.

"Hi, Dr. Grindel, ready for some deadly pleasure?" she called to him as he walked into the autopsy room where she lay naked and as still as a cadaver on her dissecting table.

"I'm *coming*," he teased.

Freddy hopped gingerly over the open troughs in the floor, shedding his clothes as he hurried, sprayed her with the hose, then climbed on top of her. His belly was only slightly rounded, his chest more burly than flabby and covered with salt-and-pepper fuzz, his arms slender but muscular. Running her fingers through the long white hair that covered his head she kissed him softly on his nose, his chin, then on his lips. When he started to speak she said, "Shhh," running a finger over his lips, "shhh, my dear."

Soon she was moaning in delight as his chemically stiffened organ slid in and out of her.

"Oh, Doctor, I think you're bringing me back to life," she joked.

She had uttered that revivification quip lightheartedly many times. Now her little joke was to haunt her for the rest of her life. Even as the words came breathlessly from her, their world changed in an instant. Freddy suddenly went limp. Not just his penis, but his entire body became flaccid, motionless. He collapsed on top of her, inside of her. No longer supported by his powerful arms and knees, his body was crushing her. Her protuberant eyes that had been closed in pleasure opened to see that the blissful smile on his face had twisted into a deep purple grimace.

Fran Pappelbaugh immediately realized the awful truth: Freddy was dying.

"*Freddy, Freddy!*" she screamed, distraught but for one last moment still in the role of his lover. Then she reverted to form as a doctor: her sex partner lying on top of her became her patient, a man she needed to resuscitate. With all her strength she pushed him out and off of her, lowered him as gently as she could to the floor, and started compressing his chest rapidly. But she only managed to keep Freddy Grindel alive long enough for him to utter a few, final words. Not, "*I love you, Fran,*" which would have meant so much to her, but only a strained, guttural, "*Tell them. Tell them. Stop it all.*"

Fran Pappelbaugh knew exactly what his desperate words meant.

***

Freddy's death did not release Fran Pappelbaugh from Molly's grip. Now, even as Fran was agonizing over losing Freddy, Molly was about to call in her chits.

"We have a problem to deal with," Molly said, her deep, dry voice conveying a note of seriousness that grabbed Fran's attention immediately.

"I don't like that Grim Reaper tone, it means trouble. Is it what I think?"

"Yes, our recurring problem: McDonald. I need to talk to you about the path specimens from Eleanore Hinkel. You remember her, that woman who died from a festering wound infection, peritonitis, sepsis, the whole ugly array. Her downhill course caught my attention – I think you can understand why."

Fran Pappelbaugh felt the hairs on her neck tingling as though someone had crossed live electric wires around the base of her skull. She looked at her colleague and sensed that the two of them were about to plunge deeper into the unpleasant terrain inhabited by Matthew McDonald.

"Well, whatever it is you want to know about Eleanore Hinkel's path specimens, it's timely – I was just starting to clear up a backlog in the lab reports. You know, I'm still catching up on things since…well, since Freddy died. I just now got around to Eleanore Hinkel. I did manage to review the slides and can tell you that the appendix was clearly inflamed, it needed to come out, absolutely. But I suspect that my delay in filing the report is not what's on your mind, is it?"

"*Ptuh*," Cavendish spat with a dismissive sneer. "No, it isn't. Just the opposite – it's fortunate that you haven't written anything yet. I came to find out if my suspicions are correct about the complications that killed her. I looked through her chart and saw that McDonald's surgical report states that the appendix was already ruptured when he performed the surgery. Is that what you found?"

"That's total bullshit. The appendix that I saw had not ruptured. Until you just told me what McDonald said in his report I would have just read her case out as a routine appendicitis. It's clear to me that the walls of the appendix are intact, the only obvious opening is the crushed anatomic one at the base, where the instrument clamped the tissue before it was removed. No sign of perforation. Whatever caused the peritonitis, it wasn't a ruptured appendix. That's what I would post into her chart."

"No, that's not what you're going to write. I need something that would be, shall we say, a limited but sufficiently accurate reflection of your medical opinion without mentioning that the appendix had not ruptured."

"Ah, crap, Molly. You really want me to fabricate my autopsy report to help McDonald?"

"Maybe to help you as well. If there's a big flap over that woman's death, maybe certain information about your relationship with the late Dr. Grindel would leak out."

Fran saw the evil look on Molly's face and understood the threat: play along or Molly would destroy her career. And Freddy's legacy.

"You won't stop at anything, will you?"

"I do what is necessary to protect this hospital. And if you're smart you'll do the same. Besides, what's one more?"

Fran hesitated for a long moment, then resigned herself to what she had to do. *Fucking Molly, someday I'll get even,* she thought. But all she said was, "OK. I'll do it. If I confine my report to describing the appendix it won't be too difficult – on gross inspection the tissue is not normal to look at. And microscopic exam confirms that the walls of the appendix are loaded with inflammatory cells, with clear signs of infection."

"How much do you need to put in your report?"

"I could quit with a simple description: *'Appendix, surgically removed, multiple areas of inflammatory response, extensive internal tissue lysis…Compatible with acute appendicitis.'* Less I say, the better, right?"

Molly's bright blue eyes turned black as she stared at Fran and coolly delivered her order: "Exactly. Say what you must, correct as far as it goes, nothing *overtly* inaccurate. But no more than necessary."

Molly Cavendish's conspiratorial tone once again reminded Fran that she had been sucked down a whirlpool into turbulent waters from which there was no escape. OK, she would give in again and create a misleading autopsy report on Eleanore Hinkel. But that was just one rotten case and Fran had a lot more on her mind to confront Molly over.

"Look, what about all the other…"

Molly cut Fran off before she could get the words out, before she could give voice to the much larger secret that only the two of them shared now that Freddy Grindel was gone.

"Yes, and your dear Freddy isn't around to handle things anymore. Damn inconsiderate of him to die like he did."

Molly's tone was distant, cool, as though she were talking about some inconsiderate member of the staff who had gone on vacation at an inconvenient moment, not about the lover who had brought unfathomable carnal delights to Fran before dying in the saddle.

"Now it's up to you to take care of things, *Doctor* Pappelbaugh. You know that, don't you?"

"Damn you, Molly. You'll get your phony report on Eleanore Hinkel. But…I hate to ask, but what are you going to do about McDonald?"

"Look, he's been very valuable to this hospital in a lot of ways. And my job isn't to bring down our most productive source of revenue. All kinds of revenue. We need to hold things together, as tough as that may be. OK?"

Fran Pappelbaugh struggled to come to terms with what she was doing, how she was helping Molly cover up the swath that McDonald was cutting through the hospital. And worse.

"I know, I know. I'll leave McDonald to you while I finish drafting one very short pathology report. But you really should take more definitive measures about…about all the other shit, even if you can't touch him."

Molly was pleased. Fran would do what she wanted without sticking her nose in anywhere else. A secret kept silent was a secret kept safer, as though speaking the truth out loud even in private was to broadcast it to the world.

"Good, Fran. No need to stir things up."

All Fran could say in reply was, "Don't mention it." Then the pathologist clenched her teeth and drew her lips back, adding with a snarl, "I mean, really, *don't mention it.*"

Molly returned the look. They were at a standoff.

"Sure, Fran. Nothing to mention."

A self-satisfied smile formed on Molly Cavendish's striking face as Fran Pappelbaugh turned her back and left the room. The grin lingered well after the Pathologist was out of sight, then erupted into a low cackle as she congratulated herself for the way she had manipulated Fran into helping her dodge a bullet. Two bullets. She had managed to save McDonald again and she had silenced any discussion of other problems plaguing the hospital. Getting leverage over Fran and Freddy had paid off handsomely. What would this hospital do without Molly Cavendish?

Chapter 20. Sons and Brothers

Jeffrey Hinkel had not expected to see Jorge Edmond again, not soon anyway. Maybe never. But there he was, coming toward the gravesite, carrying himself upright, nothing apologetic in his walk, no hat-in-hand bearing in his stride. No wave or other sign of recognition from Jorge either, not from the distance. When he got closer, Jorge raised his right hand in greeting, then extended it to Jeffrey.

"Hello, Mr. Hinkel."

Jeffrey returned the welcome, extending his hand to Jorge somewhat grudgingly, miffed that his most private moment had yet again been interrupted by the man.

"Hello, Mr. Edmond. I'm surprised to see you again. Do you come here often?"

"No, but I've been here a few Sundays. I have been hoping to find you here."

Jeffrey was not a suspicious person. His brother, Roger, seemed to have inherited the skeptical gene in the Hinkel family. And yet, encountering Jorge like this was inexplicable to Jeffrey. He didn't feel threatened by the former day laborer with the thick hands, but he knew there was more to the man and his relationship to Jeffrey's mother than he had learned the first time they met. Why would Jorge want to see him? The two of them had nothing in common except Jeffrey's dead mother, and she was his mother, not Jorge's. What did this guy want?

"Me? Why would you want to find me, Mr. Edmond?"

Jorge looked Jeffrey directly in the eyes. His bearing was calm, assured. As Jorge nodded his head and pursed his lips Jeffrey realized he was about to learn just what was behind this unexpected encounter.

"I have to speak with you about your mother, about what happened in the hospital. It was not as you were told. She should not have died."

The words smashed into the grieving son's belly like the sucker punch that killed Harry Houdini. Doubling over, Jeffrey nearly fell to the ground before Jorge's strong arms caught him. Jorge helped him walk to one of the stone benches a few yards away. Jeffrey sat bent forward, palms down on the bench, gasping for air. He looked up at Jorge but said nothing.

"I am very sorry, Mr. Hinkel, I did not mean to startle you like that. Please, please forgive me."

"What...what are you saying about Mother? What do you mean she should not have died? *Tell me!*"

"Please, maybe this is not the right place. I just knew I might be able to find you here, and I did not want to try to call you on the telephone. But we could go somewhere else, maybe?"

"It's OK, I'll be alright. Now, tell me."

For the third time, Jorge unleashed the burden he had been carrying. This time he knew there would be no going back, this was it. But it was the step he had to take, the only one that would make him feel that he was on the way to paying his debt to Mrs. Hinkel and her family, to all the patients of Dr. Matthew McDonald who had died at Northeast Suburban before their time.

Jorge Edmond could not know he was opening a Pandora's Box that would have repercussions far beyond the Hinkel family.

***

"Hi Roger. Yes, this is Jeffrey, your brother. I need to speak with you, please call me back when you have time. I'm at my place in New Hampshire. It's actually important. Very important, Roger."

Jeffrey Hinkel felt awkward leaving his name and mentioning their relationship on Roger's voice mail. But the two spoke so rarely these days, and Jeffrey knew that his businessman brother always had so many different activities filling his mind, that he feared Roger might absentmindedly overlook a casual call or skip so quickly through his messages he might not recognize his own brother's voice. Or, his brother might simply ignore his call. He couldn't allow Roger to blow him off, not now, not when he really needed him.

Jeffrey and Roger Hinkel had gone about separate lives since childhood, having nearly no contact with each other, not even exchanging occasional letters or holiday cards. Now Jeffrey reflected on how strange it was that after all those years he needed Roger, needed his worldly savvy, his aggressive attitude. For the first time he could remember, Jeffrey was thankful for having a brother like Roger, felt fortunate that there was at least one hard-boiled tough guy in the family. During the entire drive back to New Hampshire from *Heavenly Gardens* after suffering through Jorge's horrifying description of his mother's death, Jeffrey had fretted over calling his brother. Curiously, thinking about Roger's reaction to his forthcoming call had taken his mind off of the reason he would be calling in the first place. He had obsessed over what he should say, how he should tell his brother why he was needed. Now, having placed the call and gotten only the automated outgoing message, Jeffrey hoped he had made it clear how important the situation was. How long should he wait for Roger to call back before trying again? Would Roger even take him seriously?

Silent hours passed. Jeffrey at last became convinced that his brother was not going to return his call, not that night anyway. After all, Roger really was a strong-willed jerk, what should he expect? Jeffrey hadn't called him on the phone in years and now Roger hadn't called back right away even though his own brother had said it was important. He couldn't help wondering what was the matter with him. Maybe Roger would call the next day.

Jeffrey waited until just before midnight, then went to bed. He had been asleep for about two hours when the noise at his bedside awoke him. At first he thought it was an alarm, maybe the carbon monoxide detector he had installed after hearing that a family in Meredith had died the previous winter from the deadly fumes seeping from their wood stove. He slapped at the lamp on the nightstand, and when the light came on he realized the noise wasn't an alarm, it was his cordless telephone with the squeaky ring he hated, the bargain phone he had paid $9.87 for at a *Tuesday Morning* in a small New Hampshire strip mall. He reached first for his eyeglasses, as though he couldn't speak on the phone without seeing clearly, then picked up the receiver. He couldn't imagine who would be calling at two in the morning. Thinking this had better not be a crank call, he steeled himself to answer.

"Hello?"

"What the hell took you so long to answer the phone? I almost hung up."

"Nice talking to you, too, Roger. Why are you calling at this time of night?"

"You said it was important, Jeffrey. Besides, it's only eleven o'clock."

"There, maybe, not in New Hampshire. Where's there?"

"La Jolla. Just got back from Scottsdale. What did you want, Jeffrey?"

"Can't we talk tomorrow? Later today, I guess that would be?"

"I'm heading out of town again. You said it was important. If it's important you'd better tell me now, I don't know when I can call again."

"It's about Mother."

"What about Mother? She's still dead, isn't she?"

The blithe response seared Jeffrey's ear like a hot needle.

"Stop it, that's not funny. Yes, she's still dead, and there are serious questions about how she died."

"What are you talking about? She had a ruptured appendix, complications set in, she got peritonitis, wasted away, and died. Shit happens. You were there practically the whole time, you know how she died."

"Yes, I thought I did. But this Mexican guy, some kind of doctor's aide or something, told me a different story today. Yesterday, I guess, on this Coast anyway. He said that the doctor who did the surgery screwed up."

"What the hell are you talking about? No one said anything about something going wrong. All we heard was that she had an infection and died. Who the hell is the Mexican guy, anyway?"

"He was in the operating room helping, that's his job."

"Like a nurse?"

"I don't know. No, not a nurse. Physician assistant, that's it. Anyway, he was there, says the surgeon is something of a problem, has been for a long time."

Suddenly Roger sounded interested, maybe even concerned.

"Jeffrey, this is serious. You realize what you're saying? Some surgeon killed Mother? You've got to find out what happened, make that hospital tell you what happened."

"Roger, no, not me, I can't handle this, that's why I called you. This is your world, dealing with big problems like this. I can't do this, I'm lucky I can run my little antiques business. Please. I...I almost fainted when the physician assistant guy told me at the cemetery."

"Cemetery? What are you talking about, *cemetery?* He was at the cemetery with you?"

"I'm sorry. Yes. I drove down to visit Mother's gravesite, to talk with her..."

"You talk to her? She's dead, Jeffrey."

"Shut up, let me talk. I know she's dead."

Jeffrey's voice was no longer tentative. Now he was wide awake, and Roger wasn't going to make fun of him for still loving their mother, for missing her so much he had to talk to her. If he felt closer to her at the cemetery, it was none of Roger's business.

"This guy, Jorge, he came to the gravesite once before when I was there and apparently he came back several times looking for me until he found me there again. He wanted to tell me all about this in person. I think it has really been bothering him, he seemed very upset."

"He'd better be upset if he had anything to do with killing Mother."

For once Jeffrey was pleased to hear anger in his brother's voice. His brother had taken up the cause, had gotten wrapped up in what happened to their mother. *He's on it,* Jeffrey thought. At long last he was glad to have Roger in the family.

"Can you come out here and look into this, Roger? I can drive back down and meet you somewhere, I don't mind the drive."

"I've got a trip back East next Tuesday anyway. I was going to return here Wednesday night, but I'll plan on staying over."

"What do you think we should do? You're the lawyer, you know about this stuff."

"Hardly. This is way out of my wheelhouse."

"Not as far as mine. You don't have any idea?"

"Not really. But...you know, I just had a thought – I've got a law school classmate who I think still lives around there who does this kind of work. Real hard ass, used to be a doctor until something happened. I don't remember the whole story. I haven't been in touch with her for years but I'll track her down and see if we can meet with her. I'll call you back."

"Not at two in the morning, please."

Roger paused briefly, then in an unexpectedly soft, almost contrite voice, said, "I'm sorry, Jeffrey. I just didn't realize the time difference."

Jeffrey was stunned. Roger actually sounded apologetic! He couldn't remember Roger ever apologizing, to anybody for anything in their entire life. Their mother had to die for Roger to say 'I'm sorry!' A wave of – what was it, Jeffrey had to think for a second – of *Brotherly Love* passed over Jeffrey, moving him almost to tears.

"It's…it's OK, Roger. Forget it. Better to get on with it. Thanks for calling me back."

"OK, get back to sleep. We'll be in touch. Good night."

Chapter 21. Fall and Rise of Stephanie Sorano

Dr. Stephanie Sorano was at the peak of her career, enjoying every moment of being a physician, a surgeon, a leader of professional women. Whatever she wanted to do, she could pull it off. Impeccable credentials that no male surgeon in town could challenge and few could equal: undergraduate degree *summa cum laude* from Vanderbilt, medical degree from Columbia University College of Physicians and Surgeons, residency and Chief Residency at the Brigham and Women's Hospital. And the skill and knowledge to go with her surgical pedigree. That was why she was elected president of the Northern Counties Woman's Surgical Society, their delegate to the national association of women in surgery. Many members of the association also called on her as an informal source of support from time to time to discuss personal and career issues as well – even into the twenty-first century, it wasn't entirely a piece of cake becoming or surviving as a woman surgeon.

But not everyone admired Stephanie Sorano the way her surgery peers did. Like a hawk circling overhead waiting for the moment to strike an unsuspecting prey, Molly Cavendish had long had Sorano in her sights. The talented surgeon was an aggravating nuisance, a barrier to Molly carrying out what she saw as the only work that mattered: raising Northeast Suburban Hospital's bottom line and keeping its reputation unscathed, however many problems might be festering under the surface. To Molly Cavendish, Sorano was a meddler, always trying to tell her how to do her job, interfering with her tightly-knit system of doing things the Cavendish way. And despite Molly Cavendish's own disdain for the pervasive male dominance she had endured in her career, having to contend with another strong woman grated at her even more. Stephanie Sorano had to be dealt with.

Once Molly set her mind to destroying her adversary, victory had proved all too easy. Stephanie Sorano had pushed Molly Cavendish hard on a number of fronts, but when she filed charges of incompetence against Matthew McDonald, Cavendish retaliated with a vengeance.

Rather than investigate McDonald, Molly Cavendish turned on his accuser. Cavendish knew that random events spared no doctor. No matter how remarkable their overall performance had been, every physician had complications that were hard to explain and could be portrayed in a damaging light. Just pick and choose isolated incidents when patients had unexpected complications and package them together to make a defenseless case against someone, no matter how blameless the doctor involved. Ignore hundreds of brilliant cases of lives saved that could well have been lost, ignore mitigating circumstances, and assemble a litany of unavoidable but inexplicable bad outcomes, and a supposedly fair hearing would become a kangaroo court.

Molly Cavendish scrutinized the medical records on every patient Stephanie Sorano had admitted to the hospital over her four-and-a-half years on the medical staff, selecting a handful of cases that she was able to misinterpret to trump up charges against Sorano. She confronted Stephanie Sorano with the contrived package of one-sided allegations. She enumerated all the patients she alleged Sorano had mistreated and offered her a Hobson's choice: leave the hospital or stay put and face a full-scale mock trial before a jury of doctors hand-picked by Cavendish. The farce would expose Sorano to public humiliation and could have only one verdict.

Stephanie Sorano's first instinct was to engage the battle and contest the outrageous charges. She would rally support among her colleagues and quash Molly Cavendish once and for all. She was a fighter, not a quitter. That was how she had made her mark in surgery, never backing down from a challenge. It would go against every fiber of her being to give in. But she was also a realist. After her initial outrage began to subside she realized that Molly Cavendish had her trapped in a no-win situation. If she were to engage the charges publicly she would risk being disgraced among her peers. Once the word got out, the trumped-up charges would sully her reputation forever. The very colleagues she had looked to for support would feel betrayed, angry that she had deceived them into trusting and admiring her. However false, the shadow of suspicion would follow her wherever she went.

A sense of impending doom overwhelmed Stephanie Sorano, suffocating her with a despondency she had never known. Her innate combativeness vanished. She had been riding so high that when Molly Cavendish pushed her she fell from too great a height, landing with such force that her powerful will to survive shattered, her lifelong drive to overcome obstacles abandoned her. Then her deep dejection gave way to a profound anger that magnified her suffering. She became disgusted with the profession she had worked so hard to master. She saw only hypocrisy and self-righteous arrogance everywhere around her. She had believed so strongly in the high ideals of her medical calling but now felt an overwhelming sense that her chosen field was corrupt, dominated by amoral people like Molly Cavendish. Matthew McDonald was the one who was placed on a pedestal, idolized, defended at all costs, not her.

Crushed, feeling hopeless for the first time in her life, Stephanie Sorano gave up on all she had accomplished, all she had ever wanted to do in life. Depressed and desperate she could see no option but to walk away, her head held high but her heart broken. Yet she was not dead, not entirely. Through the pain she told herself she would get even, of that much she was sure. Somehow, someday, her time would come.

***

Roger Hinkel reflected on how he had met Stephanie Sorano all those years ago when he had just started law school. He was fascinated by her photo in the face book distributed to all the incoming first-year law students, a picture of a woman with a pleasant, full face, razor-sharp eyes, and lips that parted slightly into an intriguing smile. Reading the caption below the photo, he saw that she had graduated from college two years after him and then gone on to medical school. He figured she had to be in her mid-to-late thirties like he was. Relieved to find a prospective compatriot among the sea of twenty-one year old students just out of college who looked like grade school kids to him, he was delighted when he found himself next to her in a registration line. Suppressing his inherent awkwardness at dealing with other people, he caught her eyes, forced a smile, and asked her whether their new classmates looked as young to her as they did to him. When she responded with a knowing chuckle and a friendly, "You bet," he suggested they get some coffee

153

and explore the George Washington University campus. They bought a couple of cups and sat to relax and chat on a wrought iron bench sporting a plaque memorializing the long-departed Class of 1966. A gigantic bronze head of the Father of Our Country loomed over their shoulders.

"So, you're a doctor. What brings you to law school? Isn't that a bit schizy? Don't all you doctors hate lawyers?"

"Not me. At this point in my life I actually have more issues with doctors than with lawyers. Some of them, anyway. And hospital administrators. I just can't take any more of that stuff."

"Sounds like there's a story there."

"Yeah, there's story all right. But you've been around the block also, young man – what's your story?"

"I'll tell you mine if you'll tell me yours."

Stephanie Sorano took a long sip of coffee through the thin slats in the cup's plastic cover. After staring at Roger noncommittally for few seconds, she broke into a smile that made him all the more interested in learning about her.

"Deal. I grew up wanting to be doctor, never thought of anything else. I went to medical school, became a surgeon, a pretty good one, actually. At least that's what my patients and colleagues told me. It was great, just as I had hoped."

She took another sip from the cup.

"So, what happened. You were happy, so what are you doing here? Why law school?"

"I had a thriving practice, got very involved in medical staff work at my hospital. Too involved, as it turned out. There was a particular surgeon who had complications of all sorts with his patients. I found myself patching up his cases. I initiated charges against him internally, through hospital channels. I thought the hospital leadership would deal with it. Turns out he's the hospital's biggest money-maker. The rainmaker. Of course, I was an idiot for not realizing their cash flow was far more important to them than how they generated it."

"So, what happened?"

"Me, they turned on me. That's what happened. They killed the messenger. I went after the big kahuna, and I was massacred. So now I'm a law student, an ex-doctor."

"You played with fire and got burned?

Her smile twisted into an ironic grin.

"In spades. They accused me of all sorts of things and leaked the charges to my fellow doctors. Rumors went around about mistakes I had supposedly made with my patients and covered up. At first everyone was very supportive, but little by little I was shunned by doctors who I had thought were my friends as well as my colleagues. When the leadership threatened to bring a formal professional review action against me I had to resign to end the investigation before they threw me off the medical staff and disgraced me forever."

"So you gave up medicine? Doing what you loved?"

Roger Hinkel was absorbed by Stephanie Sorano now, her intensity, her conviction, her unrestrained candor with someone she had just met. She seemed so confident in her own story, displaying no fear that he might quietly think, *"Methinks she doth protest too much; where there's smoke, there's fire."* Either no fear of a skeptical reaction on his part, or she just didn't care what he thought. In either case she was tough, and he immediately laughed to himself that she was so tough she'd be a great lawyer.

At that moment he realized it wasn't just her fiery personality he was attracted to. Still sitting next to her on the bench with George Washington staring into the distance over their heads, he glanced down and saw that her skirt had slid up well above her knees, far enough for him to see several inches of the pale white skin of her lower thighs. He was done for. Trying to avoid staring at her legs, he elevated his gaze to her face, only to realize how captivating her smile was, two rows of perfect teeth behind glistening lips that begged to be kissed.

"I haven't given medicine up entirely, not yet."

He came back to his senses abruptly as she responded to his question. Her straightforward, determined tone of voice did not change – either she hadn't noticed his momentary lapse of focus, or she didn't let it affect her. Or perhaps she was interested in him!

"Can't give it up. I'm still in debt from med school and have all my usual bills as well as this incredible law school tuition. And these law books cost twice as much as my medical books did! So I work part-time in a couple of clinics. I'll do some *locum tenens* covering practices for docs taking vacations during the summer, enough to keep going until I'm earning a living as a lawyer. Then I will give it up, you bet. I'll have to give it up."

Intrigued by the finality of this comment he managed to suppress his more prurient interests and asked, "Why, why give it up entirely? What do you mean, you'll *have to*?"

"I'm going over to the dark side as far as the medical profession is concerned. It's not just that I'm going to law school, that's bad enough in the eyes of most doctors, but I'm going to be a trial lawyer, a plaintiff's attorney specializing in medical cases. Personal injury and malpractice cases against doctors and hospitals, nothing else, and never on the defense side. I'll be *persona non grata* in the medical community the day after I pass the Bar."

He took a sip from his coffee cup and used the downward movement of his head to sneak another long glance at the six inches of thigh that had now appeared below her hem line. Whether she noticed this time or not, he was brought back to reality again by her voice.

"OK, your turn, unload. What's an old…old guy like you doing in a place like this?"

She unwrapped a blueberry muffin she had bought along with her coffee and took a tantalizing bite with those perfect teeth, those appealing lips.

He lapsed again into fantasy. How exciting it would be to slosh around in her mouth like that blueberry muffin. But for now he had to tell his own story, it was his turn.

"You were about to say '*old fart*,' I'll venture. Me, not nearly as interesting as you, Doc. I'm just a businessman who wants another edge. I have an undergraduate degree in business, and I've been in and out of various large corporations ever since college. The money's been good but I wanted my own show, I wanted to build something for myself, make or break. Thought about getting an MBA, but then I had this idea about doing law instead. I'd do both the law and business degrees but I don't think I have the brains for that. But a lot of businesses can't keep up with the legal side of things. They know how to buy and sell things and raise capital but they are often at the mercy of their lawyers. I decided that if I am going out on my own I'm going to know the legal side as well as the business side. So here I am."

Stephanie Sorano swallowed the last bite of blueberry muffin and smiled at him. A small crumb of muffin lingered on her lower lip, mesmerizing him. The tiny imperfection made her smile even more alluring, sending a wave of desire tingling up from his groin, across his body.

But his budding arousal suddenly wilted as quickly as it had appeared. Something began gnawing at him, sending a wave of caution over his burgeoning entrancement with this independent, strong, extremely attractive woman. What was it? What was clouding his mind, distracting his thoughts? A vague recollection of some sort was emerging from his distant memory, a sense of prior knowledge, of *déjà vu*. His heart skipped a beat as the anxiety grew stronger: he had the distinct impression that Stephanie Sorano looked familiar. Did he know her from somewhere?

He struggled to sound casual, to avoid destroying the mood. It was like the moment in a bad dream when the bottom starts to fall out of a blissful reverie, when things begin twisting and turning the wrong way but you have no power to stop things from crumbling except to end it all by waking up.

"Look, this is going to sound like a bad pickup line, but seriously, did we meet somewhere before? You didn't tell me where you went to college – did you go to Penn by any chance?"

"You're right, it would be a really bad pickup line," she chuckled. "Nope. Brown. But my brother Stephan went to Penn – is that where you went?"

"Yes. Wait a minute – Stephan Sorano? That's your brother? Stephan? Sure, I knew Stephan Sorano, we were in a group together, like a fraternity, except not with all the Greek and wild stuff, more like an honor society. Stephan's your brother?"

"Uh huh. Twin brother, actually. Wow, what a coincidence! What's that, zero degrees of separation? Stephan and I anguished over whether to go to college together but I just didn't want to live in Philadelphia and he hated Providence. So we split up, which was fine. We had always been so close and yet so competitive, so it was just as well we didn't keep it up during college. But we both went into medicine. He's a cardiologist outside of Denver. He understands why I'm doing what I'm doing but he's not happy about it, he hates lawyers as much as any doctor does. But he also knows how vicious things can get in hospitals so he isn't switching sides against his twin sister."

Roger Hinkel's attraction to Stephanie Sorano exploded like the Hindenburg, sending his libido careening to the ground in tatters. He recoiled, no longer seeing a beautiful woman sitting next to him but only a feminized version of his old college friend. A male-female chimera. Worse, he had not just been seeing the hybrid image, he had been drawn to it, stimulated by his male friend's alter ego. She was a near-perfect likeness of her brother but it was all wrong, it was like seeing Stephan with long hair and lipstick. Stephan and he had used the same showers, for god's sake, he had seen his…his entire body a hundred times. Roger shuddered. He was put off to the point of being slightly nauseated. If he tried to kiss her now, he could never get her brother's face, his body, out of his mind. What if they had gone further before he found out she was Stephan's twin? Even the thought of sex with the spitting image of his old friend made him quiver.

Once he saw her brother's manly face when he looked at her, Roger Hinkel never again wanted to find out whether Stephanie Sorano might have shared his amorous interests. But the end of their truncated romance turned out to be the beginning of a solid friendship. They became each other's best buddy throughout law school. Nothing more developed. And Roger Hinkel was determined never to let himself be vulnerable again like this. Never.

Now, years later, he needed her. Professionally.

Chapter 22. Last Piece

Will Manningham was determined to delve further into what was going on at Northeast Suburban Hospital. He took a deep breath and booted up his computer, hopeful that his latest brainchild would end the nagging frustration he felt at being unable to close the loop between the excess deaths in that hospital and some specific cause. His neural network program had constructed a map of the connections between certain hospitals and *Marquis-Herrant* that had led him to Alexandra Parushnikova and the other Russian detail reps and ultimately to Northeast Suburban. But he had found no smoking gun. The patients who died had different diseases, infections from a variety of germs, medical devices of all sorts. And most perplexing of all, their autopsies led nowhere.

Anil Maliq had to be right, Will thought. His computer analyses might be leading nowhere precisely because some of the information he was putting into his equations had been fabricated to cover up what had really happened. *Garbage in, garbage out.* So he had to change perspective yet again, explore the deaths in Northeast Suburban from another new angle. This time he would look in far more detail at the people involved with the dead patients. Maybe he would uncover Anil's record-forgers. And Tom Murphy's corporate angels of death.

Will decided to learn more about everyone who had been delivering the treatments, carrying out the procedures, administering the drugs. Which doctors had taken care of the patients who died? Which nurses had given them their medications? Which pharmacists had prepared the doses? Who were the orderlies, nurses aides, janitors, maintenance workers, all the staff that had any contact with the patients who died? He set about designing instructions for his computer to search for any correlation between staffing patterns at the hospital and the medical records of every one of the patients who had died since the death rates had started to rise a couple of years earlier.

He worked frantically on the new program for several hours, then, at last, set it into motion. A tortuous forty-five minutes crept by as the computer searched through the personnel files and medical and death records to tease out the connections. When the findings began to come into view they appeared to be no more helpful than all the other information he had amassed. For many of the dead patients nothing suspicious emerged – they had been cared for by a seemingly random assortment of doctors and other hospital personnel and had died from overwhelming injuries, chronic debilitating illnesses, advanced old age. Will was disappointed at first, but then realized he should not be surprised at the wide range of people who had contact with the dead patients and the many different causes of death. After all, this was a hospital, people died there all the time, he couldn't expect that every death would be related to whatever was going on with *Marquis-Herrant*.

Just as Will was beginning to think he had gotten nowhere once again, the computer presented him with something that made his pulse rise. A cluster of patients who had died in Northeast Suburban had one thing in common: they had all undergone surgery performed by Dr. Matthew McDonald. And McDonald's name rang a bell with Will – he was that surgeon Adrienne Penscal and Tom Murphy had spotted in Cabo cavorting with the Russian rep from *Marquis-Herrant*, Alexandra Parushnikova. Here it was, the first direct connection between the dead people and the *Marquis-Herrant* company. Will was sure this had to be what he was searching for.

As the names of the dead and their surgical procedures cascaded across the screen Will began to tremble with anticipation:

> Eleanore Hinkel – appendectomy;
> Lisa Altuno – simple hysterectomy;
> Jonathan Peters – bilateral spermatoceles removed;
> Mandy Bellmont – routine lumpectomy;
> Felix Heinz, post-traumatic splenectomy;
> Ariel Gould – inguinal hernia repair.

The list went on and on.

The next step was to figure out why those patients had died after McDonald had operated on them. Will created a new file with all of McDonald's dead patients and directed the computer to search for clues about what had killed them. But there was nothing. In every case McDonald's post-operative report said that the surgery had gone well. Other entries in their medical records asserted that the patients died from unrelated causes. The message was consistent: *The operation was a success, but the patient died.*

Will wondered just what all those "unrelated causes" were that had led to the deaths of so many patients whose surgery supposedly had gone well. When he saw that Dr. Michela Francesca Pappelbaugh had performed an autopsy on each of them he thought he would find the answer easily. But when he pulled up the autopsy reports he was surprised to see that they were remarkably brief. And uninformative. Pappelbaugh's pathology reports failed to explain why patients with ostensibly non-fatal illnesses had died after low-risk operations. The autopsy reports simply supported the causes of death that had been listed in the medical records and on the death certificates. And none of the autopsies suggested any problems with Mathew McDonald's surgery. Or mentioned any products from *Marquis-Herrant*.

As he read through the results, Will noticed a third name appeared in conjunction with all of the deaths up to a certain point, then stopped abruptly: Dr. Freddy Grindel. The charts showed that Grindel had spent countless hours fighting infections that proved fatal despite his efforts. But then he disappeared from the computer records. Intrigued by Grindel's sudden departure, Will ran a quick search on the internet and found his obituary. No wonder Grindel was no longer involved in caring for patients.

Will was sure he had found the linchpin to understanding what was killing patients at Northeast Suburban and why he had been unable to pin it down sooner: Drs. McDonald, Pappelbaugh and Grindel would be the key to figuring out what was causing the deaths. Grindel would remain silent forever but the other two doctors would be persons of interest to the FBI. McDonald was a direct link between *Marquis-Herrant* and many deaths. And Pappelbaugh had probably covered up for him. Will was pleased. At last his computer programs gave him something to bring to Adrienne Penscal. But even his program was not sophisticated enough to reveal the rather personal connection between Pappelbaugh and the late Grindel that had led them to be involved.

Chapter 23. Engaging Counsel

Roger Hinkel was impressed by the plush quarters of the law firm where Stephanie Sorano practiced. He looked around admiringly as he and Jeffrey walked through the heavy wooden doors with the inset words, "*Vagram & Marin, L.L.P., Attorneys and Counselors at Law.*" His old classmate had indeed succeeded at the law.

The Hinkel brothers approached a reception desk staffed by a youthfully-dressed but visibly aging man sitting behind a name plate that read "*Tommy Lester.*"

"Well, *hello*, gentlemen!" Tommy said with an almost adolescent vitality and a subtle but distinct flirtatiousness that was plainly directed at Jeffrey. "You must be the *Hinkel* brothers?"

"Yes, we're here to see Dr. Sorano," responded Roger, annoyed at the marginally disrespectful tone of Tommy's voice and the playfully seductive way he looked at his brother.

Turning to Roger, Tommy adopted a mockingly formal tone that was equally inappropriate, saying, "Of *course*. The doctor will see you right away, *Mr.* Hinkel. And you, Mr. Hinkel. Follow me, *please.*"

Tommy led the brothers down a long corridor of glass walls formed by the internal windows of a series of meeting rooms. Two of the large rooms had their shades lowered but the others displayed impressive conference tables and a stunning view of the city through their outside windows. At the end of the hall Tommy turned to his left and stopped in front of a door with a small plaque that read, "*Stephanie Sorano, M.D., J.D. Partner.*" "Here you are, gentlemen," he said as he opened the door and gestured for the Hinkel brothers to enter.

As Roger and Jeffrey stepped into the office they saw a woman seated at a desk that was backlit by sunlight streaming through floor-to-ceiling windows with a panoramic view of the city.

She looked up and smiled, catching Roger's eye. He said, "Hello, Stephanie," rather tentatively, realizing suddenly that he felt awkward. She was his friend, she had been his close companion, his fleeting love interest, but it had been over a decade since he had seen her and now they were about to establish a new and different relationship. Now he would be dependent on her, he would be her client, not just her friend. Unsure how to approach her, he hesitated in the doorway. Should he hug her? Kiss her? *Kiss his lawyer?* Shake hands like he was greeting an old buddy?

Stephanie Sorano quickly resolved Roger's dilemma.

"Hello, Roger," she said enthusiastically, standing up and walking around her desk to give him an energetic embrace. She turned her face to solicit a kiss on the cheek, a friendly kiss, not one on the lips, then released him after a few seconds.

Somehow she had both changed and remained the same, Roger realized. Her body was that of a much younger woman, her skin a rich tan and drawn tight over her facial bones and the muscles of her forearms. As he hugged her, he could sense that she was in good shape, her firm, full breasts pressing against his chest, the muscles of her back powerful against his palms. Her smile still displayed the flawless teeth and the alluring lips, bringing back the memory of that day on the wrought-iron bench when he had been so attracted to her until the intruding image of her brother had repulsed him. And yet there was a discordant note: the warm glow that she had radiated during their years in law school was missing. He no longer sensed the feminine softness that had complemented her powerful drive to succeed. She felt and looked harder somehow, her athletic body still eye-catching but now conveying a severity that had not been there before.

As she stepped back he was struck by another change: she didn't look at all like Stephan anymore. At least not the way he remembered her twin brother. She had been through a lot, had made her way up in the law firm, but she had paid a price. The thought came to him that perhaps it was all for the best that they hadn't ended up together, that he and this toughened woman might have clawed each other to bits.

Roger struggled to be gracious.

"You're looking good, Stephanie, you make me feel old."

"Hey, you're not so bad, yourself, Roger. I probably have more time to get to the gym than you do. Are you still on the road a lot?"

"Still on the road, yes. Deals don't stay in one place, unfortunately. I'm sorry to say I haven't seen the inside of a gym since law school. Stephanie, this is my brother, Jeffrey."

Stephanie Sorano turned to the lean, nervous man next to her old friend. She thought she could recognize some features that they had in common but guessed that this one must have favored his mother, while Roger looked more like their father.

She smiled and offered her hand, "Hello, Jeffrey. OK if I call you Jeffrey?"

As they shook hands, Jeffrey Hinkel felt another grasp stronger than his, although this hand was slender and smooth, not beefy and calloused like Jorge's.

"Sure, of course. And should I call you Stephanie, Dr. Sorano?" The question sounded so awkward, they both laughed.

"In this office you're a client, not a patient, so you can call me anything you're comfortable with. Stephanie is fine by me. Have a seat, both of you."

Like a hostess ushering guests into her dining room, she lifted her arm and turned an open palm toward an oblong mahogany table in front of the windows. The table was surrounded by six matching chairs, two on each side and one on either end. Roger sat facing the windows while Jeffrey walked around the table to have the light at his back, leaving two seats on each side between him and his brother. Stephanie took a legal pad from her desk and positioned herself at the end of the table on Roger's immediate right, but pulled the extra chair between her and Jeffrey back a few feet from the table, more or less equalizing the distance between her and each of the brothers.

"Stephanie," Roger Hinkel began, "as I told you on the phone, this is about our mother."

"Yes, I was so sorry to hear that she had passed. She was still a young woman – people in their sixties seem younger all the time, don't they?"

"Exactly, a young woman, very much alive," responded Jeffrey. "We spent a lot of time together every year."

Jeffrey was about to burst into tears at the memory of his semi-annual travels with his mother, the two of them riding joyfully around the bucolic New England countryside in his Wagoneer.

Unable to bear the thought that his mother's body was decaying in the grave, he thought of her as intact but inanimate, resting forever in one grassy spot of ground. "She was the most important thing in my life, and that doctor killed her, he killed her."

Roger cut his brother off. "We're not sure what happened, but we have reason to be concerned that whatever caused her death, we haven't gotten the full story."

"I think you are aware that lawyers like me wouldn't be needed if members of the medical profession were honest about their mistakes. Or if they at least policed their most corrupt and incompetent elements themselves like the public has every right to expect them to do."

The glistening teeth that could grace her captivating smile barely parted as she spoke. Her face showed sympathy for the brothers and their mother, but her voice revealed the depth of her anger at her foregone profession, her bitter frustration from years of exposing the veiled inadequacies of so many rotten physicians.

"Tell me all about it. Take your time, by the way, I cleared my calendar."

Roger Hinkel felt a storm of conflicting emotions. He had thought he knew Stephanie Sorano so well, but now he wasn't sure just who this person was that he was dealing with. In a way she was still beautiful, he would notice a woman like her anywhere, but up close the loveliness was gone, the warmth had vanished, the compassion was lacking. Those beautiful teeth, those lips that he had so wanted to kiss, that body, now they seemed to be coated with a gloss, an overlay, of…of what? *Harshness? Ruthlessness?* She was all business now, yet he sensed that she truly cared about the Hinkels, about their tragedy. He thought, *I'm glad we're on the same side.*

"Thanks, Stephanie. It's Jeffrey's story to tell. He was with her and Dad for much of her stay in the hospital."

"Northeast Suburban, right?"

"Yes, sure."

"My favorite place, as you'll remember, Roger."

"Couldn't forget."

"Sorry, go ahead, Roger. Or Jeffrey. It's your time."

Roger Hinkel continued, gesturing toward his brother, but doing the speaking.

"Jeffrey met someone in the hospital who came to him later with the story that brought us here. We want you to tell us what we should do. Jeffrey, please tell Stephanie what you told me."

As was his way, Jeffrey Hinkel had rehearsed his opening line, but still had great difficulty getting the first words out. Finally, instead of the chronicle of his mother's suffering and slow death that he had meant to begin with, his voice quaked as he blurted out, "He told me that they killed Mother."

"Who, who, Jeffrey? Who told you, and who killed your mother?"

"I'm sorry, that wasn't what I was going to say, but it's what I've been thinking. It's all I've been thinking since he told me."

"OK, let's start again, at the beginning. Back up, please, so I have the full picture. When did you first know that your mother was ill?"

"Dad called from the hospital. He said Mother had been in a lot of pain but had resisted his efforts to bring her to the emergency room. By the time they got to the doctor, she needed immediate surgery."

"Who did the surgery?"

"McDonald, Dr. Matthew McDonald."

"McDonald! That incubus!"

"*Incubus!* Wow, pretty harsh, Stephanie. Are you accusing him of demonic behavior, Counselor?"

"Not exactly," she said with a wry grin. "But in some ways he's just as bad as those creatures. But let's not get ahead of ourselves, it's your story, not mine. We can chat about the notorious Dr. McDonald later. Please, Jeffrey, go ahead, I'm sorry for interrupting you."

Just as Jeffrey Hinkel was about to resume his story, she interrupted again.

"Sorry, just one more thing. Where's your father? Why isn't he here?"

Jeffrey bit his lip and turned toward Roger, who answered for both of them.

"When Jeffrey and I talked it over we decided we would meet with you first before we said anything to Dad. He's…he's having a tough time without Mother, as you can guess."

"I'm sure he misses her very much, yes."

"That's for sure, but there's even more to it. It's hard for me to understand, but he feels guilty that he didn't make her go to the emergency room even though she didn't want to go. We don't think Dad is to blame in any way. We know how stubborn Mother could be, how strongly she probably resisted. So we thought we shouldn't add to his pain until we looked into this a bit and knew where we stood. I told Jeffrey this was way outside of my area of the law, but I knew someone who was an expert, so we agreed to meet with you and get some advice on how to proceed before dragging Dad into this."

"You have a sister, too, right? What about her?"

"Good memory, Stephanie. Yes, Sue Anne. She wants us to deal with everything. She says she has her hands full with her kids, her husband. I think losing Mother took a lot out of her also, and she needs time to adapt to things."

"That's fine. I understand. Now, please, continue. I'll keep quiet for a while, I promise."

At last the agonizing story of his mother's suffering and death came streaming out of Jeffrey Hinkel. He described the weeks of watching her waste away, the tubes draining the purulent secretions out of her belly, the day when she no longer awoke and they knew that she would never escape from her coma. He spoke in elaborate detail about his trips back and forth from New Hampshire, first to the hospital, then to the cemetery. His anguish was evident at every mention of his mother's distress.

Stephanie Sorano paid close attention, but could not figure out how this sad story had led them to her office until Jeffrey finally got to the strange encounters with the large Mexican man at his mother's gravesite. Her sympathy for the Hinkel family grew into intense anger as Jeffrey related how Jorge Edmond had revealed McDonald's lies about the catastrophe that had led to his mother's death.

"That's McDonald," she replied with ferocity. "That bastard! Pardon my French, gentlemen, but he should have been barred from performing surgery years ago. If Jorge Edmond will tell me that same story, if he'll swear to it under oath, that's enough for us to get started. We will find out what happened in that hospital, I promise we will."

Roger Hinkel sensed that Stephanie Sorano's reaction was well beyond a dispassionate lawyerly interest in a promising case. This was personal with her – she hated McDonald. Ever savvy at spotting an opportunity to gain an edge in any transaction, he realized that her personal investment would be to their benefit. He was sure that she was too smart to let her emotions cloud her judgment, but she'd never let up until they knew the truth. Stephanie Sorano was everything he had always thought she would be, and more. He complimented himself on his good fortune for knowing her, on having thought to approach her after all these years with a difficult situation. Reestablishing ties with her was a good move on his part. For one brief moment he let himself muse over what his life with Stephanie Sorano might have been like. Maybe the image of her brother wouldn't have been all that bad after all, maybe he would have gotten over it, who's to say? And maybe they wouldn't have clawed each other to bits…at least not in a bad way.

Then he returned to the matter at hand. Whatever might have been between him and Stephanie Sorano was long gone. But they were in very good hands, that much he was sure of.

Chapter 24. Jorge's Liberation

As Jorge Edmond entered Stephanie Sorano's plush offices he felt as if he had been transported to an alien planet. To him and his boyhood *compañeros* the law had meant uniformed police, crowded courtrooms, wasted weeks in the Youth Guidance Center. And the lawyers had been either well-meaning types clocking their first years out of law school in the Public Defender's Office or burned-out old guys with bad teeth and foul breath. None of those lawyers had ever put more than five minutes into learning his situation.

Jorge wore his Sunday-go-to-meeting clothes: a dark brown three-button suit tightly woven from a wool blend, and a narrow gunmetal tie over a white dress shirt he had ironed that morning. The dress-up clothes gave him a curiously ambivalent feeling. The white-collar business outfit lessened his awkward feeling of being so far out of his element. And yet the suit and tie also made him a bit uncomfortable since the only outfits he had been used to wearing were workmen's clothes or, more recently, surgical scrubs or white coats. He was still on unknown ground when Stephanie Sorano greeted him with a friendly smile and outstretched hand.

"Mr. Edmond, welcome. I am Stephanie Sorano."

Jorge extended his hand to her and said, "Thank you…" He stopped, not sure what more to say. In Spanish he would have said *Abogada,* but he knew that one did not address lawyers by their profession in English. Besides, he had seen the *M.D., J.D.,* on the nameplate outside her door and felt that he, the physician assistant, should refer to her as *Doctor.*

Stephanie Sorano sensed his hesitation and quickly said, "Stephanie, just Stephanie will be fine, or you can call me Ms. Sorano. Either way."

As she ushered him into her office, Jorge saw that there were two other men already present, one he knew, the other a stranger, although somehow vaguely familiar.

"Hello, Jorge," said Jeffrey Hinkel, shaking the big man's hand, then gesturing toward the other man. "This is my brother, Roger."

Jeffrey Hinkel's greeting was polite, but not warm. Jorge immediately sensed that he was struggling with his own discomfort in this setting.

"Hello, Mr. Hinkel," Jorge said to Jeffrey. Then, turning toward the brother, he added, "I am pleased to meet you, Mr. Hinkel."

Under less strained circumstances the repeated name might have triggered some laughter, but the Hinkel brothers and Stephanie Sorano let it pass in silence.

"Please, everyone take a seat. Would you like something to drink, Mr. Edmond? Some coffee or a soda? Water?"

Too accustomed to his role as a physician assistant to address her as *Stephanie* or even *Ms. Sorano,* Jorge said, "No, thank you, nothing, please, Dr. Sorano."

She did not correct him, understanding that he was not going to call her anything but Doctor. And it was of no consequence to her what he called her. All she cared about hearing from him was his story.

"If you have questions or would like to take a break at any time, please, just ask. Mr. Edmond, I believe you know we are here in the matter of Eleanore Hinkel, the mother of these gentlemen?"

"Yes, sure, Dr. Sorano."

"I am serving as their lawyer. They have retained me to look into the circumstances surrounding her death. Their father, Mr. Henry Hinkel, is aware of the situation and, as the executor of his wife's estate, has agreed that we should proceed for now, but he does not wish to participate actively at this point. Mr. Jeffrey Hinkel has described his understanding of your version of events. Now I would like to hear them from you first-hand."

"Yes, sure, that is what I am here for, Dr. Sorano. I understand."

"Would you have any objection to my turning on the video recorder while you speak? It's a big help in making sure I get things straight."

Jorge had not noticed the small black microphone console in the middle of the table or the glass eye peering down at him from high on the wall. Now, hearing that his words, his gestures, his face, were all to be recorded, made him even more conscious of how big a step he was taking. He was about to open up a new phase of his life. A phase that was irreversible and not at all guaranteed to have a good result. Everyone would know that he was the one pointing a finger at Dr. McDonald. His accusations would reach powerful people in the hospital where he made his living. Who knew what those people would do to him? He felt as though he was about to jump out of an airplane and wasn't sure whether he had a parachute on his back. But there was no going back.

"OK," he said, his voice strong with determination. "That would be fine with me, Dr. Sorano. Go ahead, I am prepared."

Stephanie Sorano pushed a recessed button on the tabletop device, causing two red lights on the front panel to blink momentarily, then stay illuminated. Jorge glanced up and saw another red light on the camera as she said, "This is in the matter of Mrs. Eleanore Hinkel. Present are Mr. Roger Hinkel and Mr. Jeffrey Hinkel, the sons of Mrs. Hinkel, who, together with their father, Henry Hinkel, have retained me, Stephanie Sorano, and the Vagram & Marin law firm, to explore the circumstances surrounding Mrs. Hinkel's recent death. With us is Mr. Jorge Edmond. Mr. Edmond, please state your full name, address, profession, and date of birth."

Responding "Jorge Manuel Edmond Rey," Jorge felt his usual ill ease when reciting his full name, which he rarely did in English-speaking company. But he complied with the formality, saying his name in the original sequence of the words. He felt even more awkward as he pronounced the Anglicized "Edmond" in place of "Edmondo," the surname his family had carried for generations before having changed it in the U.S. But the lawyer had asked for his full legal name, and that was it. *Edmond*, not *Edmondo*, not any more.

When Jorge said his birthplace was the city of San Salvador in El Salvador, Jeffrey Hinkel cringed, mortified that he had simply assumed all along that Jorge was Mexican.

Jorge followed with his address, then said with some satisfaction but not a trace of conceit, "I am a certified and licensed physician assistant," and ended with his date of birth.

"Mr. Edmond, please tell us in your own words what you believe is of importance with respect to Mrs. Hinkel's illness and death."

Jorge had thought about Matthew McDonald's actions and behavior in the operating room and Eleanore Hinkel's tragic course so many times, had recited the story to Dr. Meier and Dr. Flowers, to Dr. Simkowitz, and at last to Jeffrey Hinkel, that now it all flowed easily. The inflamed but normal appendix; deadly leakage from the stump of the severed appendix; McDonald refusing to acknowledge what had occurred; the gnawing feeling that McDonald was covering something up well beyond the Hinkel case; frustration that no one in authority was doing anything to acknowledge or eradicate the danger; anguish over keeping his suspicions to himself; embarrassment at intruding on Jeffrey Hinkel repeatedly at his mother's gravesite.

As soon as Jorge moved on to his conversation with Drs. Meier and Flowers in the presence of Dr. Michael Simkowitz, Stephanie Sorano abruptly interrupted him.

"Excuse me, Mr. Edmond, did you file a formal complaint with Dr. Simkowitz?"

"I am not sure exactly what a formal complaint would be, Dr. Sorano, but, no, I do not think so. Dr. Simkowitz said he would think about what I had said, but there would be no formal investigation, not right then, anyway. I'm sorry, I wasn't completely clear about what he was saying. I think it had to do with legal rights for Dr. McDonald but I did not completely understand everything. I just wanted to be sure he heard the story. It was not easy for me, telling the doctors what had happened, what was happening."

Stephanie Sorano nodded. She understood precisely what Jorge was telling her. She knew Michael Simkowitz well, still respected his basic good character and dedication to the higher principles of his profession even though he had failed to keep her from being thrown to the wolves. She had come to see Simkowitz as well-meaning but weak. A good man, but one who had fallen into line, had come to tolerate his position as a highly compensated figurehead with no power to deal with matters such as the sinkhole her own career had been thrown into, or the wretched mess surrounding Dr. Matthew McDonald. But she still had enough regard for Mike Simkowitz to sense that he might be planning to do something behind the scenes, that he didn't want to trigger

McDonald's panoply of legal protections by taking visible action too quickly.

"Yes, Mr. Edmond, I believe I understand," she said reassuringly. "Please, go on."

"That is the end, Dr. Sorano. I have not heard anything from Dr. Simkowitz – or from Dr. Meier or Dr. Flowers – since our meeting. It was only a few days after that when I got the call from your office about coming here."

Stephanie Sorano recited her standard perfunctory closing for the recording device, noting the time and case name again, and mentioning that all the participants she had identified at the beginning of the session had remained throughout and that no one else had entered the room.

"Gentlemen," Stephanie Sorano said to the Hinkel brothers once the recorder was shut down, "let us thank Mr. Edmond for coming forward."

Roger nodded in agreement, saying softly but firmly, "Yes, thank you Mr. Edmond."

Jeffrey was deeply moved by the courageous act that he had witnessed. He stepped toward Jorge, unsure whether to hug the big man, finally deciding on an extended two-handed handshake and an impassioned, "Thank you, thank you for this, Jorge. Thank you for caring about my mother…our mother. This means a great deal to all of us."

He might have continued, but Stephanie Sorano interrupted, saying "I expect that you will hear from us again before long, Mr. Edmond. Please keep all of this to yourself for now. If Dr. Simkowitz or the other surgeons try to speak with you, please find out what they want and put them off until you call me. Here is my card. I have written my cell and home phone numbers on the reverse side. Feel free to call any of the numbers, any time, night or day. Is that acceptable?"

"Yes, Dr. Sorano, I will do as you have directed. Thank you. Thank you so very much." Then, the big man who had been so calm coughed slightly and, nearly choking on the words, said, "I would like to say just a few more words, if that is permissible, please."

Stephanie Sorano was not sure what Jorge was getting at but she saw that he was straining to keep back tears and his powerful hands were shaking slightly. She smiled and responded, "Of course, please say whatever is on your mind, Mr. Edmond."

The words came slowly, with long pauses during which he lowered his eyes and swallowed several times to keep his composure.

"I must tell you all how relieved I am that I have spoken with you here. I have been very worried about everything, carrying this around with me these past months. Nothing else seems to be on my mind these days. I have lost a great deal of sleep feeling that I should have done something sooner but I did not have the courage to speak up." Raising his head and looking directly at the Hinkel brothers, he added apologetically, "I feel that I let your mother down. She was my patient and I have not done my duty. I think I will never stop feeling that way. I was too worried about myself, about how I could lose everything if I spoke up. That was not right, I should have done what was right for her. For you." Turning to Stephanie Sorano he said, "But, Dr. Sorano, I feel a great burden has been lifted off of my shoulders, knowing that you are now involved, that you will bring justice to the Hinkel family. Thank you so very much. Thank you all."

"My pleasure, Mr. Edmond."

Little did the others in the room realize the deep significance of her seemingly off-handed response. If Jorge Edmond was providing her with the tools to bring Matthew McDonald down at last, she would indeed derive a great deal of pleasure from his story. She cautioned herself not to get ahead of things, she was close but she didn't have McDonald by the short hairs yet. The experienced lawyer in her cautioned the vengeful doctor to remember that McDonald had slipped away many times already. But it was impossible to resist anticipating the satisfaction she would feel, the transcendent sense of redemption, if she could expose a high-level cover-up at Northeast Suburban that involved McDonald. It would be better than winning a thousand malpractice cases if this went all the way to the top, to Cavendish and Williamsburg.

At that point Jeffrey Hinkel could not contain his emotion any longer. He stepped forward and hugged Jorge, patting him on the back several times, laughing with the tearful laughs of suppressed sobs mixed with joy.

Once Jeffrey let go of him, Stephanie Sorano led Jorge down the glass-walled corridor to the front door of the Vagram & Marin suite. She shook his hand one more time and let him out into the corridor. As he walked toward the elevator she admired the man for being very brave but knew full well that he didn't comprehend what he was really up against. He had no way of understanding how dangerous the peril was that he had just gotten himself into. She quietly swore to do whatever she could to protect him. There was no reason to send him to be slaughtered if it were not going to help her clients. But she would need to come up with something to corroborate his story or Jorge would be the one who got carved up, not McDonald. And she knew exactly where her loyalties were as a lawyer. If she had to take actions on behalf of her clients, the Hinkels, that could help their case but compromise Jorge, then Jorge would just have to suffer the consequences.

Jorge stepped into the elevator, then turned around and saw Stephanie Sorano standing in her doorway, still looking at him. As he waved his thick hand at the woman his thoughts silently mirrored hers. He had put his life, his career, in Stephanie Sorano's hands, but he realized that, in the end, he could not count on her to protect him. She was not his lawyer, she was not there to look after him. She needed him, and he believed she would be fair, but she would have to use him, put him out front. He was on his own.

Jorge was drained, but it was a satisfying exhaustion. He remembered feeling like this after playing a grueling baseball game into extra innings in the hot sun and winning in the bottom of the fourteenth inning. But he knew that this was not a game and he hadn't won anything, not yet. And yet, it felt so good to get this out of his head, out into someone else's world. She was smart, she was honest, she would give it her best, and now he could do his work in peace and wait for her to tell him what to do next. *The lady was now The Man,* he chuckled to himself. As Jorge stepped out of the elevator and headed home he sensed a burst of fresh energy surging through him. The feeling of having been liberated from his burden rushed through his body, stimulated his heart, made him lift his feet just a bit higher as he walked.

This was a good feeling, the feeling of being alive again.

***

Mandy Bellmont had looked forward to a very special wedding, to be celebrated in six weeks on her twenty-ninth birthday. But today she was not thinking about the myriad details of wedding plans that had to be dealt with. She sat frozen at the desk in her doctor's office, staring at the man in horror, still not comprehending what he was telling her. She heard only one word: cancer. Everything else was a blur, just *cancer, cancer, cancer.* She tightened up inside,

175

struggling for breath. Finally her doctor said, "Mandy, Mandy, are you still there?"

She was silent for a few moments, unable to find words to respond. Then, "Yes, Dr. Terrazo, I'm here. You said I have breast cancer."

"Yes, I did, but it's small, Mandy, it should be no problem. All of your tests for metastases are negative. You are looking at very favorable odds, better than 95% long-term survival. Total cure, even. I will arrange an appointment with the surgeon right away. My office will call you once we have set it up. OK?"

"Sure. Thanks."

Four days later Mandy Bellmont was sitting in an examining room listening to the tall, handsome surgeon who assured her that the surgery would be only a minor blip in her life.

"No problem, Mandy, the cancer is limited to one part of your right breast. We caught it very early. I will be able to remove it all with a simple lumpectomy, then you will have a quick course of radiation and you'll be done and off on your honeymoon. Good as new. And the lucky guy will never notice any difference, you'll still have those two big, beautiful breasts after I insert a silicone implant to fill in the empty space."

Matthew McDonald's words were so reassuring that Mandy Bellmont cried with relief. "Thank you, thank you so much, Dr. McDonald."

After the surgery, Dr. Fran Pappelbaugh's pathology report confirmed the diagnosis of localized, early-stage breast cancer. The lump had been fully excised, there was no extension to the surrounding tissue or lymph nodes, no sign of metastases. Mandy Bellmont did get married six weeks later. Not as she had planned, but in a simple bedside ceremony in Northeast Suburban Hospital, where she wasted away until her birthday. She gasped through the wedding vows, barely managing to utter her final words, *"till death do us part."*

Chapter 25. Sweat

Molly Cavendish was in a heightened state of alert – Lester Williamsburg had summoned her for an unscheduled meeting well after they had generally left for the day. That was unusual enough, but what made her most anxious was that whatever the new crisis might be, it was something she didn't already know about. When she walked into Williamsburg's oversized conference room she was surprised to find Mike Simkowitz and Sylvester Sullivan already sitting at the table with her boss. She looked at Williamsburg and got no hint of explanation, but the copious beads of sweat dripping off the ridges of the big man's forehead told her this had to be big trouble. Stifling her impulse to hand Lester a tissue to wipe his brow, she took a seat and looked away as if she had not noticed his obvious distress. She studied Sullivan's face for a clue as to how serious the trouble might be. But Sy was his usual self. Never ruffled, not Sy.

Sylvester Sullivan opened the suitcase-sized leather case he had placed on the table, pulled out several stacks of paper, then looked to Lester Williamsburg for a sign that he was to proceed, ignoring both Molly Cavendish and Mike Simkowitz.

Williamsburg lifted his right arm, waving his hand rapidly in a series of small circles to signal *'Get on with it,'* holding the hand so close to his face that the vigorous gesture spewed sweat around the table. Several disgusting droplets nearly rained into Molly Cavendish's coffee cup, others formed tiny wet spots on the papers in front of Sylvester Sullivan.

"Very well, then, let's get started," said the lawyer. He stood and circled behind Molly, his suit coat open, his shoulders back and chest forward, his thumbs resting in the armholes of his vest so that his fingers spread across his chest. "Molly, I have just informed Lester that the Hinkel family has filed a lawsuit against the hospital that raises numerous charges, all quite serious I must say. The suit is based largely on the testimony of a physician assistant in this hospital, one Jorge Edmond. In short, the Hinkel Family contends that the hospital was negligent in failing to oversee the quality of medical care delivered under our auspices to Mrs. Eleanore Hinkel by Dr. Matthew McDonald, whom they have of course also named as a defendant. That charge is grave enough, but they have added a far more troublesome one: they accuse the hospital of engaging in a conspiracy to cover up negligence by Dr. McDonald and unnamed others by falsifying Mrs. Hinkel's medical records, failing to follow our usual procedures in investigating hospital deaths, failing to report incidents of patient harm and death, and numerous similar allegations. They have filed a request for discovery that would require us to provide them with all documents, reports, records, tissue samples, or other material evidence related to their allegations. This would include all e-mails, meeting diaries, everything in print or electronic form. Accordingly I have issued a formal order to retain and produce any such items – nothing is to be destroyed or withheld that could be pertinent, no emails are to be deleted."

Sylvester Sullivan spoke in a soft, Atticus Finch voice, but his description of the lawsuit seemed to grow in volume as it crossed the massive table to Molly Cavendish, like a distant siren getting louder and louder as it came closer until it blasted directly into her head. Lester Williamsburg suddenly was no longer the sweatiest person in the room. She felt the moisture pooling on her forehead, under her arms, around her breasts, under her waistband, everywhere she had sweat glands. The color drained from her face, her shoulders rose and fell suddenly as her back stiffened then drooped, her eyes darted back and forth with no apparent focus. Struggling to regain a modicum of composure she stammered, "What…what…exactly what did they…did they say?"

Sylvester Sullivan noted the woman's uncharacteristic agitation but ignored her question, instead posing one of his own as he sat opposite her and stared directly into her blurring eyes: "Do you have any knowledge of this situation, Ms. Cavendish? If you know something that is relevant to this case, you must tell us now. We cannot defend this hospital if we do not know just what it is that we are to defend the institution against."

Sullivan's words tore into Molly like a thousand bee stings. Her mind was swirling, replaying scene by scene, word by word, all the answers she could not give. She must think, force herself to think hard. What could the Hinkel family possibly know? No one besides Fran and Freddy could have seen the surgical specimens or the pathology slides. And Freddy was dead. Slowly she told herself to breathe, to relax. There was no need to tell anyone about the pact with Fran and Freddy to cover up McDonald's horrific mistakes.

And then there was everything else. She might be able to deal with the Hinkel mess but she could never contain her far more extensive plot with Fran Pappelbaugh and Freddy Grindel should that come out. No one could know how she had extorted Fran's agreement to play along, to support the hospital's reputation despite her misgivings as things got worse and worse. None of that could ever see the light of day. She had to take it slow. She had to be very careful. But she had to answer.

"Ms. Cavendish? Please, tell us what you know about the circumstances of Mrs. Hinkel's medical care and death."

Now Sylvester Sullivan was more insistent, not raising his voice, simply modifying his tone slightly to convey the seriousness of his inquiry, the importance of her response.

Molly had to say something. She couldn't just continue to sit there silent in front of the three men. But what, what could she say?

"Ms. Cavendish, please."

"I…I had some concerns about Mrs. Hinkel's situation and took…took some steps to…to assure the integrity, the security, of her records."

She caught herself, remembering Sullivan's own advice never to say too much, never to volunteer anything. She would wait for Sy's reaction, wait and see what direction he would go in with his questions.

But the veteran lawyer was stone silent, an immobile Sphinx staring resolutely at Molly, content to await her next words. A skilled professional in getting information out of reticent witnesses, he would have waited out anyone sitting in her chair – but in this case he was also taking a most unprofessional pleasure in seeing Molly squirm.

Michael Simkowitz was also enjoying watching Molly Cavendish squirm for a change. He had always seen her as a tough piece of work, but now she seemed to be coming apart at the seams like an old car whose bumpers and wheels were clanging as though they might fall off any second. Something was going on with his old adversary, she must know something that she was struggling to keep to herself. He chuckled in silent amusement.

Sullivan and Simkowitz may have been content to wait for Molly's response but the silence heightened Lester Williamsburg's agitation. He could feel the pressure rising in his chest, his breath getting labored. Already disconcerted at hearing that the hospital faced a serious lawsuit, Williamsburg now found himself straining to come to grips with the unthinkable possibility that his most trusted assistant, his protégé, his frequent co-conspirator in nefarious plots, might have gone off on her own and done something that aggravated the Hinkel mess. Was there a catastrophic debacle lurking, something that would bring them all down? Had he been turning a blind eye to some scheme Molly was involved in? His heart skipped several beats at the thought that if his loyal henchwoman fell, he was sure to follow. Leaning forward so his elbows rested on the table to support his bulk, he felt larger and larger beads of sweat coalescing into currents streaming down his face. Utterly helpless to suppress his anxiety any longer he started shaking, pounding his fist on the table and yelling, "Molly, goddamn it, what the hell did you do? What's going on, *for Chrissake?*"

Molly Cavendish's mind was racing, but she would not rush to answer. She must be careful, not get Fran Pappelbaugh implicated, not admit to anything out of the ordinary, never give Simkowitz an opening or trigger Sullivan's legal machinations. And stick to the Hinkel matter, nothing else. Bit by bit a sanitized version of events took shape in her mind. The countless times she had wormed her way through tricky situations were now paying off, restoring her confidence. She took a deep breath and found her voice.

"I took care to sequester Eleanore Hinkel's records, lab work and tissue samples. The computer systems are behind a firewall – no one can get access to them without my personal security codes. They have not been tampered with in any way. I secured the hard copy records in the old bank vault in the lowest basement. You know, the vault that we use for safekeeping our most sensitive materials that we absolutely have to protect from being stolen or lost. Nothing has been lost or destroyed or tampered with in any way, it is all safe and sound."

Molly knew she was on thin ice saying that Eleanore Hinkel's materials had been preserved, since she had ordered Fran Pappelbaugh to destroy all of the woman's specimens and Fran always obeyed orders. But she had to get some breathing room right now, she could deal with that problem later.

Knowing his sidekick's great skill at surreptitious behavior, the very characteristic that he had exploited for his own purposes, Williamsburg was not mollified. Fearing that she was holding back, possibly setting him up in some way that he did not understand, he cried out, "*Why? Why* did you think we might be in trouble? Why did you pack that stuff away in the vault?"

Sylvester Sullivan chose to remain a perversely amused spectator for the moment, happy to let his two unsavory colleagues joust like a couple of old boxers fending off each other's jabs while looking for an opening for their knockout punch.

But Molly was on a roll, she was back on her game. Her quick, evasive mind all at once delivered the devious answer that would deflect the wrath of her accusers, two magical words that would shift attention from her motives to a target they would all understand: "Matthew McDonald."

Her words hit Lester Williamsburg sharply in the deep fold of flesh between his recessed eyes. He sat back, drained. Nodding his head in resignation, he knew Molly Cavendish had played a trump card. He could believe anything about McDonald. McDonald was incorrigible, rampaging around the hospital so recklessly he could undermine the reputation Williamsburg had worked so hard to create. Williamsburg muttered an unintelligible expletive, then out of total exhaustion said to no one in particular, "That *bastard*. Goddamn it, it's always McDonald."

Molly Cavendish took Williamsburg's curse as affirmation of her strategy. She had drawn attention away from herself to McDonald.

But Sylvester Sullivan quickly shattered her moment of triumph. Ever the defense lawyer worried about his client's exposure he continued his interrogation with another laser shot.

"Molly, does anyone else in the hospital – or, for that matter, outside of these walls – know anything about this? *Anyone? Anything at all?*"

Molly Cavendish lowered her glance from Sullivan's face, her eyes now darting swiftly from side to side as she considered how to respond to this new, highly troubling, question. Sullivan had sprung another trap. She forced her mind to focus. She must be direct, utter words that were truthful as far as they went, but reveal only as much of the truth as necessary. She had to keep their attention on McDonald, make them appreciate that he was the one at the center of this, not her. They had to see that Matthew McDonald was the threat, she was the loyal one, she was protecting Northeast Suburban Hospital from him.

Finally she looked up, turned first to the stately lawyer, then to the quivering corpulent mass of flesh that was her boss, and said, calmly, reassuringly, "Not really, no details. With McDonald involved, I decided that any post-op death might come back to haunt us. After all, he's so visible, people have such high expectations from his reputation, who knew what might happen, what bad publicity this might attract? So I put everything into a lock box. The only person I spoke with was Dr. Pappelbaugh. I did have to ask her to carry everything to the vault since she controls the area. She knows all about McDonald, she's seen his catastrophes on her autopsy table and under her microscope many times over. But that was all, I never mentioned this to anyone else."

Having spoken Fran's name, she resolved to get to her before they did, to warn her about what she had revealed. She did not believe she had thrown Fran under the bus as yet, and in any case, Molly was confident that Fran was no dummy, she would know how to handle herself.

"No one?" The intensity of the question came through the lawyer's composed demeanor. Keeping his gaze locked on Molly, watching carefully for a telltale clue from her body language, he gestured toward Mike Simkowitz. "How about Dr. Michael Simkowitz?"

"Not a word. Mike knows nothing about this, I said nothing to him." Catching Mike Simkowitz' eyes for the first time in the entire meeting, she said, "No reason to have gotten you involved, Mike."

Mike Simkowitz barely managed to contain his fury, to keep from screaming out the expletives surging through his head. Molly hadn't been protecting him, that was pure bullshit. She was keeping him out of the loop again, that's what she was up to.

Suddenly Simkowitz' surging anger at Molly was displaced by a more troubling realization: *this was his doing, he had let Jorge down.* Jorge had been so brave, he had tried to get help internally, had gone to Nick Meier and Sandy Flowers and then they had all come to him. And Simkowitz had all but promised he would do something. But he had obsessed over sticking within the rules, not risking anything, and the result was: nothing. He had convinced himself that his cautious approach was needed to protect Nick and Sandy and Jorge from reprisals – but to what end? And at what cost? Jorge must have given up on him and gone to the Hinkels. Jorge was the only one with the courage to do something, and what would become of him now that he had come forward and was squarely in Cavendish's sights?

Sylvester Sullivan, too, was taken aback by Molly's response, stunned to hear that she had kept Mike Simkowitz in the dark on a matter of such importance. Despite his many years of experience dealing with difficult legal matters and handling tough adversaries calmly, this was too much even for him to take. For the first time his voice betrayed emotion.

"*No reason?* Ms. Cavendish, Dr. Simkowitz is Chief of the Medical Staff and Vice-President for Medical Affairs. How could Dr. Simkowitz *not* be involved in a matter such as this?"

Sullivan intended no irony in his questions, never imagining that his words burned into Michael Simkowitz like iodine on an open wound. He spoke without malice, the outrage in his question coming solely from what he perceived as an intolerable breach of propriety by Molly Cavendish. What concerned him as the hospital lawyer was that she had committed a serious violation of the hospital's formal structure, its required procedures. Not that Sullivan was naïve about Simkowitz' diminished role in the hospital – after all, he was the one who had drafted the very documents that reorganized responsibilities away from the chief physician. But despite the executive restructuring he himself had put into place, the lawyer still regarded someone with Simkowitz' designated slot on the hospital's organization chart as representing a key member of the hierarchy. Dr. Michael Simkowitz was still a senior officer of the corporation, holding a position with legal fiduciary duties spelled out in the bylaws of the hospital and the medical staff. But Sullivan did not know the extent to which Molly Cavendish and Lester Williamsburg had effectively gutted their medical colleague's power, turning him into a figurehead. Nor did he realize that the two of them had cut Simkowitz off from vital information.

Again Molly Cavendish found ready cover, deftly twisting the truth into a plausible justification for her actions. Giving Simkowitz a *we-both-know-how-you-hate-McDonald* grin she said, "Mike, I know that you have had your…difficulties…with Matthew McDonald for years.

I was concerned that you could not have resisted tearing into the Hinkel matter, hoping to nail McDonald somehow." Looking back at Sy Sullivan, she added, "And he's not the only one who would jump on McDonald's case. I didn't want anyone else rummaging through the Hinkel files looking for something to use against McDonald. I can understand why people detest the guy, but I knew we had to avoid attracting attention to his problems. Publicizing trouble with McDonald would not have been good for this hospital. All anyone else knows is that Eleanore Hinkel died from overwhelming infections following surgery for a perforated appendix. That is all they know and all they need to know."

"And is that what the records and tissue samples that you have sequestered establish conclusively?"

In his civil but inexorably probing manner, Sylvester Sullivan had cut to the chase. His legal instincts told him that Molly Cavendish was holding back something that he would need to know if he were to defend this lawsuit.

Sullivan's demand for a definite answer to a question she had not anticipated unleashed another flash flood of sweat that burst through Molly Cavendish's restored self-control, drenching her body from her scalp to the soles of her feet. Now there would be no evading the truth, everything would come out. Struggling to contain her panic she told herself over and over to keep calm, to let the story out little by little, never admit to any wrongdoing. Would they find out how she had pressured Fran to craft a misleading pathology report? Maybe they didn't need to know everything. Maybe…

"Ms. Cavendish?"

"I…I cannot tell you for sure. I do know that the medical record is entirely supportive of that description. It clearly demonstrates that she suffered from peritonitis and systemic infections and that heroic efforts were made to save her life. She had the best possible medical care, all fully documented. Many expert consultations, a second surgery to drain abscesses, the most advanced antibiotics. There is nothing in her medical record that will point toward any problems with her medical care."

Sullivan was unrelenting. "What *exactly* do the pathology reports and her lab results say?"

"I don't remember the precise words, but I do know they are consistent with the rest of her chart."

"But you do not know what the tissue samples and cultures reveal about her diagnosis?"

"I am not a pathologist, I cannot tell you."

Rising from his chair and circling the table a second time, Sylvester Sullivan was all Brahmin lawyer once again.

"We need access to everything, Ms Cavendish: medical records, lab reports, everything. We will also need Eleanore Hinkel's actual pathology specimens, all the tissues that were removed from her body. I want you to prepare an inventory of all the materials you have any knowledge of. You must be specific about their location, and provide all the relevant pass codes or other means of access. *Nothing* is to be held back."

Sullivan's firm demands hit Lester Williamsburg as hard as they did Molly Cavendish. Williamsburg was unsettled, unable to come to grips with seeing his right-hand person, his anointed sidekick, on the defensive like this. Williamsburg now saw that the trusted aide he had groomed to stand by him at all costs, to handle all the sensitive matters that could threaten the hospital, might have done too well the job he had trained her to do. The creature he had created might have become a monster out of control, threatening his treasured dominion. He had made Molly Cavendish who she was and now she might bring him down. It was too much to bear.

Williamsburg gasped for air as a burning sensation in his chest spread out from his heart to his arms, his shoulders, his belly. Suddenly a deep guttural *"EHHHHHH"* exploded from his mouth, a howl like a walrus choking on an immense fish.

Seeing the acute distress on Lester's face through the eyes of the nurse she had once been, Molly stood up and moved over to tend to him. As she reached down to loosen his tie Williamsburg brushed her back with one arm, a hostile signal to leave him alone, to get away from him.

Ever the physician, Mike Simkowitz leaned toward his agonized boss and said, "Lester, are you OK? Should I call someone?"

This time the response was louder, still incoherent, a piercing *"AAAHHHHHHGG,"* synchronized with another, more powerful wave of his arm, the sound and gesture dismissive of the doctor as well as the nurse.

Molly Cavendish had tried to come to Lester Williamsburg's aid out of deeply ingrained habit, but in truth she could have cared less if the man had collapsed in a paroxysm of pain and died right there. So what if his poor overtaxed heart were finally to give up after years of struggling to pump blood through the miles and miles of blood vessels that kept expanding to feed his massive body? She had no sympathy for Williamsburg whatsoever, indeed she was filled with contempt, not compassion. A delightfully evil thought crossed her mind: she should page Dr. Matthew McDonald urgently and then watch Williamsburg keel over dead the instant he saw McDonald walk into the room to attend to him. But she resisted the temptation and sat still, remaining silent.

The only non-clinician among the three observers to Williamsburg's distress, Sylvester Sullivan was the one who made the correct diagnosis: the grunts were not signs of a heart attack but of intense gas pain. At that moment the portly man proved the calm, savvy lawyer correct, letting loose a belch as loud as a tugboat whistle, filling the air with the stench of half-digested cheese Danish. The pressure in his belly gone, Lester relaxed visibly in his chair.

Sullivan decided it was time to call the meeting to an end.

"I believe that is enough for today. Ms. Cavendish, those materials are to be in my office first thing tomorrow morning."

Tomorrow. Tomorrow is good, thought Molly. That would give her time to think, time to speak with Fran.

"No problem, Sy. I'll take care of it right away."

***

After several long hours of mulling over how she might satisfy the orders from Sylvester Sullivan yet keep from divulging the extent of the nightmare in Northeast Suburban, Molly Cavendish plotted a way out. Eleanore Hinkel's medical record posed no problem. As far as anyone could tell, everything was in order in the record. And one medical record was not the key to the much larger Pandora's box she was managing to contain. And as for producing the tissue samples that Fran had by now destroyed, that was Fran Pappelbaugh's problem. Fran was the one whose ass was on the line, Molly Cavendish had seen to that. If it came to it, Fran would be the one who would pay the price for falsifying the pathology report and trashing the specimens. And if somehow this inquiry eventually uncovered their deeper, more horrendous secret, it was also Fran Pappelbaugh, Fran and her dead lover, Freddy Grindel, who would suffer. They were the ones with unclean hands. Pappelbaugh's career and Grindel's legacy would go down the toilet. Molly Cavendish would deny any knowledge of the evil that would be blamed on the pathologist and the infectious disease doctor – and no one could prove otherwise.

A smug grin crossed Molly Cavendish's face. She was safe. She would survive, she would come out on top again.

Chapter 26. Executioner

Fran Pappelbaugh lay face down under her thick comforter with one curled-up furry ball of a cat on her back and another stretched out by her side purring like a white-noise sleep machine. Both creatures went flying off the bed when the bedside phone rang and she yelled, "*Sonofabitch*, who the hell is that this time of night?" Her anger was reflexive. She still could not restrain the knee-jerk resentment at being awakened suddenly and forced into duty that had plagued her during her years on call taking care of live patients, a suffocating feeling of being a slave to duty that had led her to go into pathology in the first place. There was no night call required for patients waiting on her autopsy table. But angry or not, she was awake now, she had to answer the phone to shut it up.

"*Goddamn it,* shut up,*"* she yelled at the two cats who were howling indignantly over the disruption of their last sleep of the day.

"Fran Pappelbaugh," was all she could muster by way of greeting.

"Fran, this is Molly."

Molly Cavendish gave no apology for waking her colleague, her sometime friend. Time was short.

"I need to speak with you."

"What the hell have you been drinking, Molly? What the hell do you mean calling now? It's after midnight, for Christ's sake."

"It's about Eleanore Hinkel. We've been sued and I have to turn everything over to our lawyer tomorrow morning. *Tomorrow morning!* You need to replace all those pathology tissues and slides that you destroyed and get me a clean set of samples from someone else that will support our version of what happened to her."

"You're out of your mind – I told you we've got everything under control."

"You won't be in such great shape yourself if they don't see what they're expecting."

Molly Cavendish let her words linger in the air until their message sunk in, until Fran Pappelbaugh realized the fragile position she was in.

"You asshole, this is your fault. You asked me to file my reports the way you wanted them. And you ordered me to destroy tissue samples from a patient and now you want substitutes? Goddamn it, this is your work, you're the one who should pay if anything comes of this."

"It isn't my name on those pathology reports, is it? And I'm not the pathologist who trashed stuff from a patient."

Fran Pappelbaugh quickly understood that the limits of their friendship had just been breached, if friendship were really what they had ever shared. Molly Cavendish would hang her out to dry as the villain in this mess and no one could prove otherwise. Pappelbaugh's mind was in turmoil, burning with anger at Molly Cavendish and with disgust at herself, her unrest further aggravated by the way Molly reveled in their dirty work. Fran was deeply disturbed by what they were doing, by what she was doing, by what her sometime friend had manipulated her into doing. And now the guilt for having betrayed her profession, for having allowed herself to descend into a seedy world she could never have imagined, was no longer buffered by the great pleasure of illicit sex with Freddy. She cursed Molly and cursed herself for going along. Fran felt the sting of having committed an indefensible violation of her professional responsibilities, but ethics, morality, professionalism – none of that meant anything to Cavendish. And on top of her loathing for Molly Cavendish she cringed at the painful irony that McDonald was the one who was benefitting from their perfidy. She was risking everything just to save that asshole McDonald. What was she thinking?

Feeling violated to her core, trapped by the filthy situation she had allowed herself to be enveloped in, Fran Pappelbaugh could not tolerate another moment speaking with Cavendish, could not bear to hear another word out of the woman's mouth. "I'll take care of every goddamn thing," she said dismissively. "You'll have a clean set of everything in the morning. Go to bed."

As Pappelbaugh hung up the phone she murmured, "Screw you, you pompous bitch. I've gone far enough, my hands are as dirty as they're going to get. No more." With this last surge of emotion, a thought she had long suppressed burst through her self-control, sweeping aside her professional dignity and restraint: she would have the last laugh someday seeing Molly Cavendish be stone-cold dead on her autopsy table.

***

Ten-thirty the next morning Molly Cavendish was ebullient as she greeted Sylvester Sullivan, Lester Williamsburg and Michael Simkowitz. Pushing a stack of papers toward Sullivan she said, "Here you are, Sy. This is everything you asked for: a copy of Eleanore Hinkel's entire medical record and the logs from the security system that show our electronic files have not been manipulated improperly. You can see the identity of every person who ever gained access to her record, what they entered into the computer and when." Taking liberties with the security of their outdated electronic record system she added, "Nothing could have been changed after the fact."

Then, oozing with smug satisfaction, Molly slid several small wood boxes holding the bogus materials Fran Pappelbaugh had delivered to her earlier that morning. "And here are Eleanore Hinkel's tissue samples, pathology slides and lab results. Fran Pappelbaugh assures me these will prove beyond any doubt that the patient died from an overwhelming infection after successful surgery. Poor woman."

Then she bared her teeth in a malicious smile, saying, "That unfortunate family. How they suffered from her unlucky course and death. I simply cannot imagine what Jorge Edmond was thinking, making such outrageous accusations. We'll have to deal with him sternly for starting all this unnecessary trouble and aggravating that poor family's agony. We will have to let him go entirely. We can't have physician assistants who make up stories that get us sued."

Lester Williamsburg and Sylvester Sullivan looked pleased, gratified that this annoyance apparently would prove to be no real threat to their empire.

"That's excellent, Molly," said the lawyer. "This will blow over easily. Once the family's experts review the documentary evidence they'll drop the case. No trial, no settlement, no negative publicity. Just one maverick physician assistant to fire. And terminating Mr. Edmond will be no problem, even if he is a minority. He violated a number of rules. He most probably stands to lose his license and in any case will never get another job."

190

"Yes, good work, Molly," Williamsburg chimed in, his tiny, recessed eyes glowing with pride. "You have once again showed that your systems are beyond reproach. This is very gratifying, indeed."

Michael Simkowitz seethed with anger, unable to believe what he was seeing and hearing. It was impossible, it had to be bullshit. Last night Molly was sweating bullets like she was about to be caught with her pants down, and now she was strutting like a damn show horse? What the hell had she done overnight? Jorge was telling the truth, Simkowitz was sure. And now Molly was going to make Jorge the scapegoat. She would deliberately ruin the man's career when he was the only one with any guts, any sense of ethics. He could not let her get away with this. But what did she have up her sleeve that she didn't have last night? What?

Then the bottom fell out for Michael Simkowitz. What he heard next was even more distressing than learning that Molly Cavendish was out to destroy an honorable man. What Mike Simkowitz was about to hear would put a tragic, indelible stain on his life forever.

"Dr. Simkowitz," Lester Williamsburg said casually, as if he were offering Mike Simkowitz one of the cheese Danish the massive CEO at that very moment was reaching for from the pink pastry box in the center of the table. "Dr. Simkowitz, as Chief of the Medical Staff and Vice-President for Medical Affairs you are responsible for everyone with clinical privileges, whether a physician, nurse practitioner or, in this case, a physician assistant. As such, you have the duty to deal with Mr. Edmond."

Pointing at Mike Simkowitz with the cheese Danish in his stubby hand, Williamsburg adopted a more serious tone, making a ludicrous attempt at emphasis with an accusatory pastry that would have seemed comical under other circumstances.

"Mr. Edmond seems to be unable to live up to his professional responsibilities. We cannot have a trusted member of this hospital's staff fabricating stories about one of our most valuable surgeons. His irresponsible accusations have challenged the very heart of this institution, our dedication to the highest quality medical care. He cannot go unpunished. I trust you will do your job."

"He should be suspended immediately, right Sy?" Molly Cavendish chimed in.

Molly Cavendish was tasting blood, not Danish. She could not resist the opportunity to hand Dr. Michael Simkowitz a spike and order him to drive it through the heart of an innocent, to exacerbate his humiliating professional impotence by forcing him to do her dirty work.

Hopelessly misled by the fantasy fabricated by Molly Cavendish that Jorge Edmond was making baseless allegations, Sylvester Sullivan added his official *imprimatur* to the death sentence they were ordering Simkowitz to execute.

"Yes, under the rules of the medical staff of this hospital, Dr. Simkowitz is responsible for initiating disciplinary procedures. There are certainly grounds for immediate suspension of Mr. Edmond from all clinical activities. That would be appropriate, given the evidence before us. Mr. Edmond must cease his activities and leave the hospital immediately. Dr. Simkowitz, you must make sure we go through proper procedures to discipline him. He will have the right to defend himself in due course. We will afford him a hearing on the merits within a reasonable time, say, a couple of months."

Mike Simkowitz saw that Williamsburg and Cavendish were now like hyenas going in for the kill. Those two were heartless, they would relish saving themselves at Jorge's expense. But his anger shrank as a pall of guilt spread over him — *he was the one who had let this happen*. He had done nothing after Jorge and Nick Meier and Sandy Flowers had come to him. They had relied on him and he had hesitated. Caution had coagulated into inaction, deadly inaction. He had insisted on abiding by the rules, and now those rules were being invoked against Jorge. Against him as well. How could he have been so stupid?

The room was closing in on him, the air refusing to fill his lungs. He had to get out of there, had to end this and get away. He needed to think, to figure out how to save Jorge. How to save himself.

Turning to Molly Cavendish he said ruefully, "No one needs to tell me how to do my job." Turning to the CEO, who had just taken another bite of cheese Danish, he added, "Are we done, Lester?"

Williamsburg responded with a garbled "Mmmhh" that was nearly inaudible as Mike Simkowitz pushed his chair away from the table and headed for the door.

***

Felix Heinz was excited as his Ford pickup truck rounded the last curve before his home one dark winter night. He was looking forward to enjoying a pleasant evening with his wife, Sarah, and their four-year-old triplets, Hannah, Anna, and Sam. The three kids had told him they had a surprise for their father when he got home, something they had been working on all day. Lost in reverie thinking about his family, Felix did not notice the lone deer that suddenly appeared in his headlights until he was nearly on top of the animal. Felix swerved the steering wheel reflexively, missing the deer and sending the pickup careening wildly across the lawn of a neighboring house. The truck slipped between two huge oak trees and slowed as the tires dug into the lawn before crashing into a stone retaining wall just hard enough to explode the air bag from the steering column into his chest and belly.

Felix Heinz was stunned but alive and conscious as the ambulance carried him to Northeast Suburban Hospital. Some combination of the air bag, the steering wheel and the safety belt had shattered several ribs and he had internal bleeding, said the physician who examined him in the emergency room. Felix would require immediate surgery, but not to worry, the ER doctor said. Dr. Matthew McDonald was on call and would take good care of him. After the surgery, the confident surgeon told the young couple how lucky Felix had been. His spleen had been punctured and had to be removed and he had suffered major internal bleeding. But McDonald assured them that he had sealed everything up tight with some new surgical staples that worked beautifully. Felix would be fine now, he assured them. The operation had gone exactly as expected and people don't really need a spleen to live long and perfectly healthy lives. Felix and Sarah Heinz were profusely grateful to the distinguished-looking surgeon who had saved Felix from bleeding to death.

But the deer outlived Felix Heinz. Hannah, Anna, and Sam watched helplessly with Sarah as their father and husband deteriorated in Northeast Suburban Hospital for five weeks before succumbing.

Chapter 27. The Insider

Will Manningham greeted Adrienne Penscal and her team of Special Agents, then spoke directly to Anil Maliq. "I have to thank you again, Anil, for opening my eyes to the possibility that the death certificates and public reports had been falsified. I believe you were right, absolutely right."

Anil Maliq said, "You are most welcome, Will. That is quite generous of you."

Will nodded back at Maliq, then began speaking. The Agents listened in stony silence as he recited the names and what should have been the nonfatal diagnoses of Eleanore Hinkel, Lisa Altuno, Jonathan Peters, Mandy Bellmont, and Felix Heinz. Although battle-hardened from their years in law enforcement, the Special Agents were visibly moved as Will described how these patients had died, how many others met the same fate, and how the real reasons for their deaths had been covered up. He told them about Mathew McDonald's reports claiming that the patients had died from unrelated causes after successful surgery. About the autopsies Dr. Michela Francesca Pappelbaugh had performed that exonerated McDonald and never mentioned *Marquis-Herrant*. About another doctor, Freddy Grindel, who cared for the hopeless patients until he passed away suddenly.

When Will finished, Adrienne Penscal said, "Good work, Will. What you've uncovered is highly suspicious. But at this point, as troubling as those deaths are, it's all circumstantial. Dr. McDonald operated on those patients, yes, but we have no hard evidence that what he did was responsible for their deaths. Actually, just the opposite, since Dr. Pappelbaugh conducted autopsies on them and did not raise any questions with McDonald's performance. She may have fabricated her reports, but we cannot prove that she did. In short, we have no way to confirm that the deaths were caused by anything other than what is shown in the medical records."

"I suppose you're right," said Will. "But at least we have enough to get a search warrant, don't we? There's got to be hard evidence of what really happened in that hospital. And we could get our own pathologist to collect forensic evidence from the bodies of the patients who died."

"No, unfortunately I don't think we have enough for a warrant to search the hospital. FISA warrants for surveillance when a foreign influence is involved are one thing, but judges are particularly strict on warrants to pry into medical records, let alone to seize surgical specimens. And exhuming any of the bodies is out of the question without a lot more to go on."

"So we're stuck?"

"Not entirely. We know about McDonald carousing with Alexandra Parushnikova, which suggests a connection between him and the *Marquis-Herrant* company. After our earlier conversation I followed up with Chief Hollingshead and he approved your idea of enlisting an insider to help us make sense of all of this. At the time I told him we would put off taking any action until you had done the additional analyses that you said you were designing. Now that you've identified the extent of the problem and the individuals involved I think it's time to move forward. I'll take your new findings to him and let him know we're ready to go into action."

"Good," said Will. "I've gone as far with the analytics as I can without the kind of specific guidance we might get from an insider. A whistleblower. It's time to add in the human factor."

"It seems to me we have only one realistic target: Dr. Pappelbaugh," said Adrienne. "Dr. Grindel is dead and I have no expectation that our Dr. McDonald would be likely to cooperate. Unless someone has strong feelings about another way to proceed, I suggest that Denise and I have a conversation with Dr. Pappelbaugh and see whether she might be willing to play ball. You have given us strong indications that she has engaged in unethical and probably criminal activities. She should understand that she could face serious professional and legal consequences. Maybe we can convince her that things are likely to go much better for her if she works with us."

"Yes" said Will, "if she'll cooperate she should be able to help clean up the mess in Northeast Suburban. But I'm really hoping she'll give us information that will go far beyond just this one hospital. After all, we're facing a much bigger problem with unexplained deaths across the country. And *Marquis-Herrant* appears to be involved in every area. With any luck, if she can help us understand what's going on here that will be the key to deciphering the links everywhere."

"And leading us to the Russians," said Adrienne.

"And leading us to the Russians," agreed Will.

***

Nestled in her overstuffed recliner under a thick red afghan, Fran Pappelbaugh longed to be able to relax like the two cats purring on her lap as she scratched their heads and kneaded their bellies. Since Freddy died, her two cats had provided all the companionship she wanted and were as independent as she was. But while the cats were oblivious to worldly cares, the pathologist was profoundly troubled. She had gotten a call from an FBI Agent who would be coming by to speak with her the following morning. The looming encounter was weighing heavily on her. Would she lie? Could she? Pensive, unsure of what to do, Fran Pappelbaugh turned to her closest friends for advice: her cats. She had long grown accustomed to sharing her problems with them and believed she could read feline wisdom in their reactions.

While the cats purred softly in her lap she told them all about the nightmare that was haunting her. Molly Cavendish. Matthew McDonald. Freddy Grindel. Scores of dead patients. The FBI coming to talk. At the end of her long monologue she sought their counsel: "So, what do you think about all of that, Mr. Slickers? Punkie? Huh?"

A jet-black cat with a single spray of white across his face awakened from his pleasurable coma, stopped purring, and turned his head to look directly into her eyes. Reaching for her tumbler of whiskey she gazed back for a long moment and sensed that he was answering her question. "What's that, Mr. Slickers? You think we've all had enough of this, right?"

The cat pushed his head insistently against her fingers, spurring them back into action once she had taken a swig of her drink and returned the glass to the end table. When she restarted the scratching he shut his eyes and twisted in her lap to expose even more of his belly and resumed purring.

"You're right, Mr. Slickers, that's what I need to do. Let it go, put all of this crap behind me. How about you, Punkie? What's your opinion?"

An immense head emerged from a mass of honey-orange fur as the second cat heard the sound of her name. The big, fuzzy creature also stared intently at her mistress, her eyes as wide as when she smelled leftover salmon in her bowl. Fran knew the cat was responding to her plight.

"You too, huh? You also think I've had enough, don't you? You're right, both of you. But what should I do about it? How can I get out of it now, I'm in so deep?"

The cat put one huge, soft paw onto the back of Fran's hand, not as if she were making any demands to be petted as Mr. Slickers had done, simply in what for all the world seemed an act of reassurance. The gesture touched Fran to her core, filling her with a sense of gratitude for the loving loyalty of her precious companions. She swallowed to clear the lump in her throat. A single tear rolled down her face. She massaged the cat's head and buried her fingers under the animal's front legs, and was immediately rewarded with a second round of vigorous, noisy purring that streamed through her and made her sigh with relief.

"You guys, you're right, it's time to put an end to all of this. You must know what Freddy told me to do. Maybe you're in touch with him, huh? Is that it? OK, you tell Freddy I'm going to make things right."

Fran Pappelbaugh knew exactly what she would do next. She had to carry out Freddy's dying wish: *'Tell them. Tell them. Stop it all.'*

***

Denise Washington parked the boxy Ford sedan from the FBI motor pool directly in front of a large Victorian house in Northwest D.C. Fran Pappelbaugh lived in one of the units formed when the elegant old mansion had been subdivided into four condominiums. Washington, a slight African-American woman not much over five feet tall, placed a finger over the reading glasses that hung on a strap around her neck to keep them from swinging freely as she climbed out of the car. She had her game face on, her penetrating, insightful eyes and resolute determination evident to her companion, Adrienne Penscal, as they conferred one last time on the sidewalk. Both Special Agents wore their customary dark blue business suits.

"OK, Denise, ready for this?"

"Sure. How did she sound on the phone when you told her that the FBI wanted to speak with her?"

"A bit strange, actually. Her voice was flat, no emotion, no sign of being surprised. It was as if she had expected us to call and was resigned to whatever might happen."

"Did she say anything or ask any questions?"

"She only wanted to know if I was allergic to cats. I said, no, I liked cats. And I mentioned that you would be with me and I was pretty sure you had no problem with them either. Didn't you used to have a cat?"

"Yes," said Denise, "a beautiful, affectionate Ragdoll. I loved that big guy but I got him before I became an Agent. When he passed away I decided not to get another cat because I was tired of him shedding all over my dark outfits."

The two agents walked up to the entryway and scanned the keypad next to the front door. There were four buttons, one labeled "F. Pappelbaugh," which Adrienne pushed once. From the speaker next to the keypad they heard, "Yes?"

"Dr. Pappelbaugh, this is Adrienne Penscal. We spoke on the phone. I've also got Denise Washington with me."

The only reply was a buzzing sound indicating that the front door had been unlatched. Penscal opened the door and the two Agents walked into a large hallway. They stood on a well-worn tile floor below an elaborate old chandelier. The walls displayed a half-dozen photos of the District of Columbia from the late 1800s and early 1900s. Adrienne said, "Number 4, second floor." They mounted a dark oak circular staircase and saw a short, chubby woman standing in an open doorway.

"Dr. Pappelbaugh?" said Adrienne as they walked toward the woman. "I'm Special Agent Adrienne Penscal and this is Special Agent Denise Washington. Thank you for agreeing to speak with us."

"Come in, please," she said in a throaty monotone. She walked slowly as she led them into the apartment. Two large furry masses jumped off the couch and disappeared down a hallway as Adrienne and Denise approached. Pappelbaugh swept at the seat cushions with one hand and said, "Doesn't look too bad, I've been brushing them all morning."

"Not to worry," said Denise Washington as she took a seat. "I had a cat for many years. Cleaning off a little fur is a small price to pay for the companionship."

"Yes," agreed Fran Pappelbaugh. "They do a lot for us." She returned to her recliner but kept the backrest upright. Adrienne

Penscal settled in next to Denise Washington on the couch, ignoring the strands of cat fur she sat on.

"Thank you for speaking with us Dr. Pappelbaugh," said Adrienne Penscal. "We are…"

"You can skip the preliminaries," said Pappelbaugh, cutting Penscal off brusquely. "I think I know what you're here for. There's a lot of terrible stuff going on in that hospital and I'm right in the middle of it. What we've been doing…"

This time it was Adrienne Penscal who interrupted Pappelbaugh. "In that case, Dr. Pappelbaugh, I must tell you that you have the right to remain silent and whatever you say will be taken down and may be used against you in a court of law. You are entitled to a lawyer and if you cannot afford one, an attorney will be provided for you. Is that clear?"

"Yes, sure. I want to talk and I don't want an attorney. I'm desperate to get all of this off my chest." Noticing that Denise Washington was writing on a small notepad she said, "I guess I do want to know if I'm under arrest or whatever?"

"No, not at this point. But your name has come to light in an ongoing investigation into potentially criminal activity at Northeast Suburban."

"OK," she said. "What would you like to know?"

"Whatever you have to tell us, Dr. Pappelbaugh. Why don't you just say what's on your mind in your own words?"

"OK. Can I get you anything? Coffee? Tea? Anything?"

"No, thank you. We're fine."

For nearly two hours the Special Agents listened as Fran Pappelbaugh related chapter and verse of the corrupt acts she had participated in. She had considered whether she could tell the story without revealing her affair with Freddy Grindel but realized that was impossible since she wanted to explain how Molly Cavendish had blackmailed her and Freddy into going along with her schemes. She did withhold the most lurid details of their trysts, telling the Agents just enough about the various ways she and Freddy had violated hospital rules to give them a clear picture of why they were vulnerable to Cavendish's threats to expose them. She broke down crying only once, when she was describing how Freddy had worked himself into a frenzy trying to save the patients, essentially working himself to death. She did not mention her central role in triggering the final frenzy that led to his death *in flagrante delicto*.

"OK," Fran said at last, "that's about it. What next?"

"We will need you to come into headquarters and make a formal statement," said Adrienne Penscal. "But before you do, we have another matter to discuss with you. We have been conducting an investigation into the excessive deaths in Northeast Suburban and other locations. What you have told us is entirely consistent with what we have learned so far, and it goes a long way toward explaining some things that concern us. With all due respect, however, at this point all we have is your version of what is going on. Do you have any hard evidence to support your allegations?"

Fran Pappelbaugh took a deep breath, squinted, and rolled her eyes up in thought. This was it, the moment of truth had arrived. Time to put up or shut up. "Yes," she said resolutely. "In fact, I have quite a bit."

"May we take a look at those materials, please?"

"I'm happy to turn everything over to you, but I don't have it here. It's all in a highly secure location in the hospital."

"Relevant materials that are lawfully in your possession would be useful, of course. But to be clear, since we do not have grounds for a search warrant, we cannot tell you what to do with whatever it is that you possess or have access to. That is entirely your decision."

"OK, that's clear. I started this and I'm going to finish the job and do it right. Now, let's get going to your offices for that statement."

Chapter 28. Thrown Under The Bus

Dr. Michael Simkowitz sat immobile in the dark, staring into the blackness of his office. His mind and body were numb with the realization of how hard he had fallen, how far he had wandered off the course he had set for his life. All that work to get through medical school, struggling to comprehend basic science classes like biochemistry that had never seemed relevant to the work of a physician. All those years of surgical residency that had consumed his life in gigantic clumps of time that seemed to move glacially from hour to hour back then but now felt like they had slipped by fast-forward in a blur. His early life was an ethereal shadow that had passed into vague memories. All that…for what? To get to the point where he had utterly failed a very good man who had painstakingly chipped away at the bonds of a hard life until he had risen to a position of respect? And now he had to cut the legs out from under that man?

The surgeon, the man who became a physician to save lives, now felt like a hangman about to slip the noose over the head of an innocent man. But there was no way out. It was his duty now to deliver the crushing edict to Jorge Edmond and execute the judgment. If he refused on principle and resigned from the hospital rather than obey there would be no public outcry to bring down the hospital's junta, no uproar like the one that followed Nixon's *Saturday Night Massacre*. No, they would find another flunky, a Bob Bork in the ranks of the medical staff to take his job and carry out the order, someone who had no idea they were dealing with a fabricated crime, enforcing a callously unjust sentence. The only way Simkowitz could see to be able to clear Jorge was to carry out his heinous task so that he could remain on the job until he could find a way to counter the evil that had engulfed him. Then he would leave this place forever.

But not yet. First he had to atone for his failures, he had to repair the damage to Jorge that he might have prevented.

Michael Simkowitz steeled himself for what was sure to be the most difficult moment of his life. What he was about to do to Jorge weighed on him more than the fear of losing a patient had when he was working as a doctor. At least then he had been on the side of the angels, trying to do something worthwhile even when he had failed. But this…this was the devil's work, this was the final depredation of his professional life. And worst of all, he had done this to himself, he had painted himself into a corner from which there was no escape other than knocking another person down and walking across his body. If he did not carry out his odious assignment he would be cast out himself, he would lose any opportunity to salvage things, to rid the hospital of its corrupt leadership and McDonald.

When the dreaded knock on his door came, Simkowitz did not stay at his desk and call out, "Come in," as was his custom. He would not have invited someone into a dark office in any case, but even if the room had been brightly lit he would have felt the need to exercise a degree of respect for the person he was about to destroy. He stood, flipped on the lights, and walked to the door to greet his caller personally.

"Hello, Jorge," he said, at first looking at his visitor over his reading glasses, then removing them quickly to look the man directly in the eyes. As Simkowitz said, "Please come in and be seated," the formal tone of his own voice surprised him.

"Hello, Dr. Simkowitz," Jorge responded, but when they shook hands Jorge Edmond immediately sensed tension between them. Simkowitz had never treated him with such reserve. He sat on the edge of a chair facing Simkowitz's desk.

"Is something wrong, Dr. Simkowitz?"

Simkowitz knew he had to move quickly, his surgical instincts compelling immediate action, like clamping a severed artery that was rapidly exsanguinating the life from a patient. He could feel the muscles in his chest tighten as he spoke.

"Yes, Jorge, there is. I have been ordered to suspend your hospital privileges immediately, pending the investigation of the charges you are bringing against Dr. McDonald. You will have the opportunity to defend yourself in a formal hearing, but in the meantime you cannot work in the hospital. I want you to realize I do not agree with this decision, not at all, but I have no choice since the leadership of the hospital has determined that this is in the best interests of patient safety. I assure you I will do everything I can to find out the truth of your allegations and if you are proved correct, as I have no doubt we will, your privileges will be reinstated with no further actions against you."

Jorge went numb, stone cold. He heard nothing after the terrible words, "…suspend your hospital privileges…" He stared blankly at Simkowitz, not in anger but in desolation. His life had just ended as surely as if his very soul had departed from his body and left behind an empty shell to breathe and move about aimlessly. But he wasn't moving, he was barely breathing.

Simkowitz paused, realizing he was no longer connecting with Jorge. He spoke with deep concern for the man, but now he was speaking with what seemed no more than the vacant carcass of the big, powerful man, a form with no more life than the abandoned skin of a molted snake. He said softly, "Jorge, did you hear what I said? I will do what I can to help you."

After a long silence Jorge replied so faintly that Simkowitz could barely hear the words. "Yes, I understand." To Simkowitz' dismay, Jorge rose from the chair, nodded slightly, and without reaching to shake hands or make eye contact, turned and headed for the door of Simkowitz' office.

"Jorge. *Jorge…*" Simkowitz called after him, but Jorge was gone before he could rise from his desk and chase after him. Stunned, depleted, Simkowitz collapsed back into his chair, staring at the door that closed behind Jorge Edmond.

Jorge headed out of the hospital, past the visitor's desk and the security station, through the gigantic revolving doors, over the cobblestone circular driveway, and toward the street. He was moving away from the life he loved, the life he had worked so hard to create. But he had nowhere to go. He could not be alone at home, could not face telling his extended family that he was disgraced, could not return to the old crowd he had grown away from. Dazed, drained, he wandered aimlessly down the sidewalk, oblivious to the crowds, to the passing traffic on the road next to him, walking like a blind man with no white cane, no seeing-eye dog. His mind was jumbled with thoughts about what had just happened, what he should do, where he should go.

The agonizing realization that he had lost everything reverberated in his head. One minute he had been an accomplished health professional, the next he was an ex-handyman wandering the street. He had no job, no one to turn to. Dr. Meier and Dr. Flowers could do no more for him. Dr. Simkowitz had abandoned him. The sense of loss was total. He was nobody. He was disgraced, he was just an old campesino again. He would be disregarded, disrespected, invisible to people.

Jorge's body was on a crowded sidewalk but his mind was somewhere else, floating in his desolation. He moved as though he were sleepwalking, not noticing when his elbow knocked into an elderly woman wheeling a wire cart loaded with groceries. He had no idea that the impact made her lose her grip, tipping the cart over and sending the contents sprawling on the sidewalk. He did not react to the incensed passersby yelling at him, spewing nasty slurs at the big man who seemed to ignore what he had done to the woman. Outraged bystanders continued their catcalls even as they helped her recover her groceries.

Suddenly the cries of anger turned to shouts of warning, then to shrieks of terror as the crowd saw Jorge wander into the street, evidently oblivious to the city bus racing to beat the stoplight. The huge vehicle hit him at full speed. Jorge Edmond did not feel the impact, had no pain, only a wave of profound relief as his body flew limply through the air, then struck the pavement head first, his skull shattering with a wet, cracking sound. The horrified onlookers recoiled, screamed for help, dialed 9-1-1 frantically on their cell phones. He did not hear the ER crew running out of the hospital howling, "Oh my God, it's Jorge, it's Jorge," or the wailing siren of the ambulance that responded a few minutes later. He was in a peaceful, quiet place.

Chapter 29. Molly Sweats Again

In the cab with Sylvester Sullivan sitting next to her, Molly Cavendish had felt fine about the deposition she was about to give. She was confident that she could match Stephanie Sorano tit-for-tat in any exchange. She would remain calm in the knowledge that there was nothing Sorano or anyone else could prove that was false in the story she would tell now that Fran Pappelbaugh had destroyed the damning evidence. But as soon as she walked into the deposition room she started sweating, unnerved by the studio atmosphere, the large videocamera, the recording equipment, the mass of black cables running everywhere. And the sight of a dozen strangers in dark suits staring at her.

Goddamn it, she cursed under her breath. Sullivan had assured her she was well prepared, but he had never said it would be like this. She had been comfortable in his office rehearsing answers to the questions he thought would come up, but this was different, this was like being hogtied and splayed on a 60 Minutes interview.

When she held up her right hand and swore out loud that she would "tell the truth, the whole truth and *nothing but the truth*," her own words cut through her like a laser. Sweat surged across her body, wetting her exposed and private parts alike. Her armpits went pasty, her waistband began to itch. She struggled to compose herself, to regain her footing and fend off this assault. She must be calm, get control of herself, just tell her story. They had nothing on her, nothing. She forced in a deep breath, held it for several seconds, released it slowly. Again. She couldn't be seen losing it on the video, her distress captured permanently for all to see. No, she couldn't let that happen, that wasn't her, she was always the one in charge. Smile, she told herself, smile.

Stephanie Sorano took it all in, expressionless but gratified at seeing her old antagonist struggle to contain her emotions. She relished seeing the woman quiver who had banished her and suffocated her professional life. This was Stephanie Sorano's territory now, Molly had to play by her rules: the rules of law.

"Ms. Cavendish – you understand that you are under oath?"

The question was unnecessary but not vengeful, purely tactical. Stephanie Sorano could see the fine but perceptible trembling of Molly's hands increase as she reiterated the obvious. Molly hadn't said a word, yet she was coming apart at the seams. Stephanie Sorano was eager to seize the moment.

"Yes, of course, I just took the oath, didn't I?" Molly's voice cracked with a mix of terror and hatred that exposed her feeling of defenselessness. The risks she was taking reverberated through her head: *'Perjury.' 'Contempt of court.' 'Jail.'*

"Ms. Cavendish, please tell us your full name, date of birth, address, and title at Northeast Suburban Hospital."

The tall, black-haired, shapely woman who had once had her pick of men and now dominated men and women alike in her hospital choked with bitter anger as she recognized that on this unfamiliar turf she was subordinate to her longtime adversary.

"Molly Ann Cavendish, June 1, 1959, 476 E. Birchwood Place. I am the Senior Vice President of Northeast Suburban Hospital."

That was good, she thought, very good, a few more questions and she'd be back in control. She had to keep talking but not volunteer anything she hadn't been asked. That was what Sy had lectured to her repeatedly: *Just answer the question, that's all.*

"Please describe your responsibilities as Senior Vice President."

"I am the chief operational official. I oversee most of the hospital operations."

"So you are the Chief Operating Officer, the COO?"

Stephanie Sorano could not resist needling Molly's long-festering sore spot, but again, however agreeable the taunt felt, it was not simply vengeful, it was also tactical. She expected that the comment would discombobulate Molly even more.

But the ploy backfired: Sorano's goading words made Molly seethe with anger and sent her into fighting mode. A surge of new energy focused her attention on her adversary. She sat up in her chair, tossed back her long black hair with a quick snap of her head, and stared defiantly into Stephanie Sorano's eyes. With a display of confident dignity she said, "No. I am the Senior Vice President."

Sorano immediately realized she had lost that exchange. Worse, she had inadvertently helped Molly get back on track. She told herself to let it go and move on, there was plenty of time to tweak Molly, make her suffer. Any fun at Molly's expense would have to wait. First they needed to get her lies on the record, that's what they were there for.

"Yes, Senior Vice President. And in that capacity, are you responsible for the hospital's Quality Assurance programs?"

"Yes, I am. Among many other responsibilities."

"Please describe the Quality Assurance programs."

"All of them?"

"Whatever you think falls under that heading."

Stephanie Sorano was letting Molly know that there was no short cut to ending the deposition, that it would continue however long it needed to, could even be extended to additional days.

Molly took a deep breath and decided two could play this game. Sorano wanted details, she'd give her details. She'd read every manual in the hospital to her if she had to. In a flat but confident voice she said, "We set a very high standard of quality at Northeast Suburban. Our main objective in our Quality Assurance programs is to assure that untoward events never happen, but should something go wrong, to discover what the problem was and to correct it as quickly and effectively as possible. We believe in the systems approach to quality assurance. We practice Total Quality Management and Continuous Quality Improvement, following the principles of Deming and Juran, the leading gurus of the quality movement. Our Risk Management department is second to none in the country. We..."

Sorano recognized a filibuster when she saw one. It was time to get Molly on track with information that was relevant to the case. She interrupted Molly, saying, "Yes, thank you, Ms. Cavendish. Please just describe your systems for detecting medical errors in the operating room."

"This is a difficult job because at Northeast Suburban we have so few mishaps that our systems have to be very sensitive to detect the rare occasions when something does go wrong. As I said, we have a high standard..."

"Ms. Cavendish, please, just answer the question."

"As I was saying, we have a systems approach to quality improvement. That means we believe that medical care is so complex that errors are systems failures, not simply the result of one person making a mistake."

Molly Cavendish's monologue struck a raw nerve in Stephanie Sorano. Sure, medicine was complex, but assholes like McDonald were the weak links and the hospital's *systems* hadn't done a damn thing about him. And Molly Cavendish had not taken a '*systems approach*' when she singled out Stephanie Sorano to destroy her medical career. Sorano fought to suppress her loathing, saying flatly, "Let's narrow this down a bit, Ms. Cavendish. How would you – the corporate you, the hospital, I'm talking about – how would the hospital know whether a surgeon had properly removed an appendix or had made an error and not reported it?"

"It would be obvious."

"How? Obvious to whom? In what way?"

"Most important, to the surgeon. The surgeon would immediately know and act accordingly. He would modify his procedure to deal with that situation, then he would describe what happened in his operative report, which is in her medical record."

"So the hospital would be dependent on the surgeon's own report to know what the surgeon under question did?"

"Not at all. Anyone in the operating room would see the complication, should it occur, as well."

"We understand that Dr. McDonald did this procedure through a laparoscope without projecting the image onto the monitors or recording it, although he did permit his assistant to observe from time to time through the eyepiece."

"Yes, well, that is certainly his prerogative. In any case it would be the pathologist who examined the specimen who would know whether the appendix was intact or not."

"Are you familiar with the pathologist's report on the Hinkel appendix?"

"You should ask the pathologist about her report."

"I have every intention of doing so, Ms. Cavendish. But right now I am asking you: Are you familiar with the pathologist's report on the Hinkel appendix?"

"I can't recall the words of her report."

"Let me refresh your memory. Here is a certified excerpt from Mrs. Hinkel's medical record. The pathologist's report is on the page that I have indicated. Are you familiar with that report?"

"I need to look this over."

"*Take your time, take your time,*" Sy had instructed her over and over. She shouldn't allow herself to be rushed. She should be responsive, but never let them rush her. "*Think first, speak second.*"

But Molly Cavendish was picking and choosing among the lawyer's instructions, avoiding the basic one she could not obey: "*Tell the truth, always tell the truth.*"

"Of course, Ms. Cavendish. Take your time. We don't want to rush you. When you are ready, please answer – and remember, Ms. Cavendish, you are under oath."

This time the anger, the hatred that suffused through Molly disconcerted her, made her lose focus. But she knew she had to answer. Stalling for time to gather her thoughts, she read through the brief pathology report slowly, tracing the words back and forth several times with her finger. At last she said, "I have seen this report, yes."

"Did you discuss this report with Dr. Pappelbaugh?"

"I may have, I think so."

"Is that 'Yes'?"

"Yes."

"When did you have that discussion with Dr. Pappelbaugh? To be specific, did you discuss what Dr. Pappelbaugh was going to say *before* she prepared that report?"

Molly was terrified that Sorano actually knew she had pressured Pappelbaugh to create a misleading pathology report. If she admitted speaking with Fran ahead of time, wouldn't that be suspicious? But if she denied it and Sorano knew they had spoken, what then? But she had no choice, she could never admit they had scripted the report.

"No, certainly not. Why would I have spoken with her before she prepared her report?"

"I have no doubt that counsel informed you that I am the one who asks the questions – unless you need a clarification. Just to be clear, are you telling us that you had no conversation, no discussion whatsoever with Dr. Pappelbaugh about the content of her report on the Hinkel tissues prior to her preparing that report?"

"That is exactly what I said. Yes."

"OK. How about the tissue samples themselves? Have you had any discussions with Dr. Pappelbaugh about the pathology specimens from the Hinkel case?"

Sylvester Sullivan sensed something was amiss. He knew that the leadership group had discussed what their response would be to the request for documents and materials, and that Molly had spoken with Fran Pappelbaugh about getting the pathological specimens together to hand over to the other side. But that was all privileged information – those discussions had taken place in his presence and dealt with their preparations for this lawsuit, so they were protected by the lawyer-client privilege. He intervened, speaking to the record but intending his words to refresh Molly's knowledge of the limits of what she did or did not have to say in the deposition: "Without implying any answer to that particular inquiry, I would just state for the record that Ms. Cavendish is aware that discussions with counsel that might have occurred in the context of this lawsuit are privileged and not subject to examination here."

"Counsel's remarks are duly noted, but I repeat the question: Ms. Cavendish, have you had any discussions with Dr. Pappelbaugh about the pathology specimens from the Hinkel case? You may of course take counsel's admonition into consideration in answering."

Molly Cavendish was confused. What were they getting at? What could she talk about and what could she conceal? Was it possible that Fran had already told them? She couldn't entirely deny talking to her. Her eyes fluttered several times as she struggled to come up with a response.

"Ms. Cavendish?"

"Yes, I spoke with Dr. Pappelbaugh about the specimens."

"What was the substance of your conversation?"

"I informed her that she needed to collect and prepare all the specimens for us to respond to your request to submit them for independent analysis."

"Was that the entire conversation?"

"Yes."

"What exactly did you say?"

"That was all. I told her we needed everything, to get it all together, to be sure we had all the correct materials."

"And that was the only conversation you had with Dr. Pappelbaugh about the Hinkel case?"

"Yes."

"And that discussion took place *after* Dr. Pappelbaugh had reviewed the Hinkel tissues and slides and written her report?"

Sylvester Sullivan felt the need to assert his presence again.

"That question has been answered, Counsel."

"So, let me summarize, Ms. Cavendish: You had no discussions with Dr. Pappelbaugh about the Hinkel case before she filed her report on the surgical specimens; the only discussion you had with her was about getting the specimens for submission in response to our request; and you have never said anything to her about what was or should be in her report. Is that an accurate summary?"

"Yes, it is." Molly could feel the torrent of sweat gushing under her arms and breasts, surging down from her neck into the small of her back, drenching her bra and accumulating in the waistband of her pants. That's that, she thought, the deed was done – she had just lied under oath.

Nearly the same words ran through Stephanie's head: that's it, she just lied under oath.

"Thank you, Ms. Cavendish. That is all for today."

Hearing that the deposition was coming to a close without going beyond the Hinkel case, Molly Cavendish breathed a sigh of relief. Stephanie Sorano had no clue how insignificant that case was compared with everything else that was going on in Northeast Suburban. Cavendish smiled to herself with smug satisfaction – once again she had triumphed over her nemesis.

Chapter 30. Collecting Evidence

Fran Pappelbaugh spent much of the next day mulling over her plan. She had told the FBI everything but now she needed the hard evidence. With only her word she might be crushed by Molly Cavendish. It was time to play the ace she had been holding up her sleeve: against Molly's orders, Fran had preserved everything and she was the only person who knew what she had and where it was hidden. It was an imposing volume of material: samples of the shoddy sutures, defective devices she had removed at autopsy, counterfeit pharmaceuticals, reams of paper records, backup computer files, the whole lot. As she added it all up she realized that there was far too much for her to retrieve on her own. She decided she would start small, collect a manageable amount of material to turn over to the FBI and prove she was telling the truth. Then, she figured, they would probably have grounds to issue a search warrant and she could show them where to find everything else. But she couldn't risk having Molly discover what she was up to or she might never get her hands on the proof she needed. She would have to work secretly. And quickly.

Fran ran through the catalog in her head of all the things she had sequestered away. How to start? What examples of the materials would be the most useful to make her case? Then it came to her: Eleanore Hinkel's pathology specimens. Fran had prepared phony tissue samples for Molly that appeared to support McDonald's assertion that the woman's appendix had ruptured before surgery and shore up his contention that Jorge lied about it having been intact. Molly had relished splattering egg all over Stephanie Sorano's face with the fake materials. But if Fran were to release the real tissues it would serve two purposes at once: the egg would be on Molly's face when the hospital's defense to the Hinkel lawsuit collapsed, and the

FBI could collect whatever else it needed. That was it, she would retrieve Eleanore Hinkel's real slides and turn them over to the FBI. And she would do it right away, before Molly suspected anything. Tonight, she would get them tonight.

Fran stayed in her office well past 10 PM, an hour not so far out of the ordinary as to attract attention. After all, she was often there well past midnight when she had difficult cases to review. But this night she was on a mission, a mission that required waiting to be sure her staff on the evening shift had left the pathology lab.

The hospital's elegant new buildings and façades dominated the neighborhood, but the pathology lab was housed in an old, dreary crypt secluded several stories below ground that still looked much as it had a full century ago. And the materials she needed were sequestered in a huge safe that had been part of a bank when the original hospital was built in 1898. Faced with abandoning the ancient bank vault once the structural engineers discovered it could not be detonated without damaging the underground supports of the hospital, an earlier generation of administrators had seized upon the idea that it could provide the highest level of security for the hospital's most sensitive documents, laboratory specimens and other important materials.

The only route down into the lowest level of the hospital was through an ancient freight elevator with an old-fashioned metal scissor gate for a door. Hospital security came down to the deepest recesses of the hospital once every hour, and she would only have time to carry out her mission if she was efficient, if everything went well. She had every right to be in her own pathology lab, but if the guard found the open vault and saw her there at this late hour he would probably get suspicious and detain her while he called Molly. So she waited for the guard making his rounds to be far enough away from the vault area that he would not hear the sound of the ancient Otis elevator descending into the depths of the hospital. At what she hoped was the right moment, Pappelbaugh entered the old lift, shut the gate quietly, and began her slow descent.

As the elevator lumbered downward a distant memory from her first year in medical school distracted her momentarily from her stressful mission. Two college friends had come to visit and thought they'd like to see the cadaver she was dissecting. She led them down this same old elevator, through the ancient hallways lit only by bare light bulbs hanging from electric wires strung randomly overhead, and into a narrow basement corridor crowded with large canvas-shrouded objects that cast eerie shadows. Her friends convinced themselves the shrouds concealed mummified cadavers or something else bizarre and begged her not to uncover them so she played along, even though she knew the objects under the dust covers were perfectly tame filing cabinets. They gasped in horror as they walked past shelf after shelf of human brains, hearts, livers, lungs, eyes, kidneys, every bodily organ floating in formaldehyde-filled glass jars. Insensitive to their mounting terror, she took her friends around the dissection room and pulled the plastic sheets off of the dismembered corpses arrayed on steel tables.

Pappelbaugh always thought she had meant well, she was simply showing her buddies what they had wanted to see. So years later she was flabbergasted to learn that her college classmates were forever convinced that she had deliberately terrified them that night in the pathology lab. OK, maybe she had gone too far when she showed them the beautiful young blond woman about their age who had died on her honeymoon and told them how her parents were fighting the decision by her distraught husband of two days to donate her body to be dissected by medical students. So in fairness she could understand why her friends had just about crapped in their pants. But what made Pappelbaugh chuckle as the old freight elevator carried her down was how her classmates had held onto their version of the story all these years despite her repeated denials. They were all over sixty now and they still couldn't stop harping on the way Pappelbaugh had terrified them and left them with nightmares of being trapped in a ghastly medieval catacomb.

The thud of the elevator coming to rest on the bottom of the shaft brought her back to the task at hand. This trip to the basement was far more serious than sneaking around with college friends. And she had to move quickly. She pulled the gate open and walked into the familiar hallway that had changed little since the night her college buddies would never forget. Bare incandescent light bulbs hummed and flickered overhead, providing just enough light for her to find her way around the familiar spaces. She turned to the left, walked past two doors, and stopped in front of a large iron grate whose heavy chain and ancient padlock always reminded her of a dungeon in a horror movie. She unlatched the padlock and passed beyond the grate.

41 minutes left.

Time was slipping away, she had to get this done quickly. She spotted the entrance to the huge walk-in safe where specimens were stored. Pappelbaugh studied the dials to a pair of combination locks on the door and found exactly what she was expecting: one dial set on 27, the other on 3. The two dials had always been left on those settings as a crude way of detecting whether anyone had tried to tamper with the vault. Pappelbaugh rotated the dials through the correct combinations by rote, then swung the thick door open.

So far, so good, she thought.

Once inside the spacious old vault she took out her pocket light and looked around. The vault resembled the basement of a museum. Where once there had been long rows of safe-deposit boxes, now there were oak storage cabinets, some with massive file drawers, others with thin flat drawers, all sporting brass handles and rectangular frames with neatly-typed labels identifying the contents. Floor-to-ceiling shelves held storage containers of various sizes and shapes, meticulously labeled to identify the body organs and human tissues inside. In the back of the room row upon row of similar floor-to-ceiling shelves held sturdy green cardboard file boxes with a curious fan-shaped black ink pattern emblazoned on the front and sides. Others held newer plastic storage containers with electronic storage media of every vintage: floppy disks, CDs, DVDs, external hard drives, flash drives.

Pappelbaugh knew where the microscope slides were stored, but there were thousands to sort through and she had to locate Eleanore Hinkel's tissue slides quickly.

More precious time had expired. Twenty-three minutes until the guard would be in earshot of the elevator.

She passed by the legendary items that had caused the hospital to keep the vault active in the first place: medical records and body parts from high-ranking politicians, movie stars, sports heroes — grisly human keepsakes whose street value was so great it was necessary to hide them to keep souvenir hounds or curiosity seekers from pilfering them. A famous baseball player's brain, an Oscar-winning actress' uterus, a skin biopsy from a First Lady. Pappelbaugh had understood how alluring they would be to the wrong eyes, how irresistible to the wrong hands. She had enjoyed browsing through those objects many times but tonight she could not allow herself to become distracted.

She turned to the filing drawers with the inventory lists. There were so many it took some time before she could match the code numbers and identify the location of the slides she was looking for. She was growing ever more tense, she couldn't risk getting caught down there. After ten long minutes she found the long, flat metal drawer she was seeking, slid it open, and saw the treasure she was hunting: glass pathology slides, multiple sections of the appendix removed from one Eleanore Hinkel. She sighed with relief.

Thirteen minutes left.

Hustling back down the ancient hallway from the vault to the Pathology lab, Pappelbaugh turned on a bright light under a magnifying glass suspended on a flexible arm and sat at one of the microscopes to examine the precious evidence. There it was: the longitudinal- and cross-sectional pieces of tissue showed the fully intact appendix just as she remembered, definitive proof that McDonald was lying. She wished she could go back in time and refuse to falsify that despicable path report.

Stopping to examine the slides had left her with only six minutes.

Pappelbaugh hurriedly left the microscope and returned to the vault. She reopened Eleanore Hinkel's drawer, pulled several additional glass slides out of their grooves, then relocated the remaining slides down a few notches so as not to leave any empty slots that would be an obvious sign that some had gone missing. She cushioned the slides she had removed between the pages of her pocket notebook, pulled open the vault door and stepped back into the dark corridor. Then she caught herself one more time – she had to follow protocol. She had to leave a record that she had taken the slides, and if she was going to use them in the lawsuit or other legal proceedings, she had to be able to identify them with certainty and say that she followed proper procedure for signing them out of the path lab.

Pappelbaugh reentered the storage area and rummaged through the inventory lists again until she found the log-in and sign-out sheets. Time was running out. Her heart was thumping in her chest so hard she thought she would keel over dead any minute. Pappelbaugh turned the log over so she could open it from the back, fill in her information and sign her name on the last sheet of the primitive paper records, and get out as quickly as possible. As she opened the back cover she saw the dozens of entries she had made over the last couple of years, the log that documented all the horrific deaths she had covered up. The sight made her quiver. But she had no time to wallow in guilt, she had to focus on getting out of the basement safely or she would lose everything. For now she had to deal with Eleanore Hinkel's death, not the other dreadful records in the vault.

Pappelbaugh entered the numbers of the items she was removing, the date, and her initials, then put the sheets back in their drawer and headed out for the last time. She shut the massive vault door and, from blessed habit, remembered to return the combination lock dials meticulously to their previous settings, one on 27, the other on 3.

Two minutes before the security guard would come into range of the noise from the elevator mechanism.

She rushed through the iron grate, relocked the massive padlock, and ran back down the main hallway. She felt a wave of relief at finding the elevator sitting at the ready, the scissor gate open just as she had left it. She entered, pulled the gate shut, and pushed the brass button with the raised '*Up*' arrow.

Less than a minute left.

The noise of the old lift clunking upward seemed deafening, she thought it surely could be heard miles away. But all went quiet just as her window of safety expired. Looking through the metal gate she could see that the corridor was empty – no guard, not yet. She pulled the scissor door open just wide enough to exit, closed it as quietly as she could and ran for the exit, shutting the door just as she heard footsteps approaching.

Safe. She was safe and had the evidence she needed. Now for the real fight.

Chapter 31. Whistleblower

Sylvester Sullivan leaned back in his richly upholstered leather desk chair but didn't feel at all comfortable. He was growing increasingly anxious over what he was about to share with Mike Simkowitz. Sullivan heard a single knock on the door to his office, then watched as Simkowitz walked in without waiting for him to reply and sat in the chair facing him. Neither man was smiling.

"Hi Mike. Thanks for dropping by. I hope you were able to clear your calendar."

"I'm fine, Sy. I'm free for as long as we need. What's up? From the sound of your voice on the message you left me there must be something serious going on."

"You can say that again. This is highly confidential, at least for now. I got a phone call yesterday that shook me up. A call from the FBI. First time I've had anything to do with the FBI in all these years. More than a bit unsettling, I can tell you."

"Uh-oh," Simkowitz said, "FBI. I can understand why that would be unsettling."

"They called me in for a meeting with some of their Special Agents and a high-tech investigator from the Medicare Agency, you know, CMS. They told me to keep everything to myself, but when I heard what they were interested in I decided to bring you into the picture. Seems that CMS investigator, I think his name is Will Manningham, ran some fancy computer analyses and identified clusters of excessive deaths in a number of places around the country. So he alerted the FBI and they initiated an investigation that led them right here to Northeast Suburban."

"Did they tell you why they're interested in us?"

"Yes. Manningham's computer work showed that there were too many people dying in this area, but at first they weren't able to connect the deaths with any particular cause. The main lead they uncovered was to a Russian front operation, a rapidly expanding drug and medical supply company called *Marquis-Herrant*. Manningham did more analysis and provided the FBI with the names of hospitals that have been purchasing from *Marquis-Herrant* and have experienced a surge in deaths. It turns out we're at the top of the list."

"Sy," replied Simkowitz, clearly taken aback, "I may not have much control over things anymore, but I do see all the files on people who die in the hospital or shortly afterward. I'm aware that there has been a definite uptick in our mortality rates, but I can tell you that we have not had any deaths that looked suspicious. Not even one in the last few years. I go over death cases carefully, and they all have a sound explanation. In fact, we have a superb autopsy rate and Fran Pappelbaugh has signed them all out without raising any questions. And you know how reliable Fran is. So I've been writing off the increased death rate as just a statistical variation. Up some years, down others, all to be expected. I can't imagine that there's anything there the FBI should be interested in."

"You're right, Mike," said Sullivan, leaning back and hooking his thumbs inside the arm holes of his vest. "We have not reported an unusual number of unexplained fatalities. None at all, just as you said."

"So what's the issue for the FBI?"

"They came up with a whistleblower who supplied the missing links. It seems our perfect record isn't so perfect. The whistleblower told them something about the deaths in our hospital that explained why we look so clean. So they called me to come in today to fill me in. I told them that I would want you to come with me, and they said that would be fine."

Simkowitz sat back and shook his head, trying to take in the news. He felt confused. Their perfect record was somehow tainted? How could that be? Then he opened his eyes wide and leaned forward, tapping his forehead as he spoke. "Uh, Sy, that's quite troubling, I'll be very interested in what they have to say. But you know what? Something just came to me that might fit with what you said. Remember that god-awful meeting when I was told to suspend Jorge? Well, at our previous meeting the night before, Molly went nuts when you said she had to produce Eleanore Hinkel's surgical specimens. But by the next morning she was smug as usual, totally sure of herself. And out for blood. I was sure she had to be up to something. If the FBI has uncovered a suspicious trail in our hospital I can't help feeling that it might be related to whatever Molly was up to."

"Maybe we'll find out if you're right. Let's go, you and I have a date with the FBI and we don't want to keep them waiting."

***

Mike Simkowitz and Sy Sullivan froze in their tracks when they entered the FBI offices and found Fran Pappelbaugh sitting in the waiting room.

Sy Sullivan's greeting was friendly but his voice sounded perplexed. "Hi Fran. Good to see you but...tell me, why are you here?"

"I'm in pretty deep with the FBI, Sy. They told me you and Mike were coming and asked me to join you."

Mike Simkowitz understood immediately. "I take it you're the one who came to the FBI about whatever it is that's going on in our hospital, right?"

She nodded her head slowly, her gray hair parted sharply and matted down. Simkowitz thought she looked as dejected as a death row prisoner resigned to her fate.

"Yes. I'm the stool pigeon. That's me."

"Not a stool pigeon at all, Fran. You're doing the right thing coming forward as a whistleblower if you believe that people's lives are at risk."

"I know they're at risk...and I helped put them there. I'm as..."

Just then the door to the office opened and a huge bald man wearing a signature FBI dark blue suit emerged. Smiling broadly and extending an enormous hand to each of them, he said, "Greetings. I'm Special Agent Tom Murphy. Please come in."

Simkowitz and Sullivan stood still, waiting for Fran Pappelbaugh to lead the way. She rose slowly, then shuffled past them into the office. Once inside, Simkowitz was surprised to find that the FBI Agent in charge was not the imposing Murphy but a lithe, athletic, thirty-something woman with close-cropped brown hair combed flawlessly in place. Attractive and engaging but self-contained, somewhat distant with a military-style manner, she wore no makeup or jewelry to accompany her FBI-uniform blue business suit. She extended her hand as the two men and the woman entered.

"Welcome. I'm Special Agent Adrienne Penscal." Pointing to a woman nearly as large as Tom Murphy, who also wore a dark blue suit, and to a tall, lanky redheaded man in casual business attire, she said, "You met Special Agent Murphy. These are two of my other colleagues, Special Agent Frances Trainor and Will Manningham, a cyber analyst from CMS."

"Special Agent Frances Trainor," said the ponderous woman, nodding so vigorously the mass of black curls covering her head jiggled freely with each movement.

"Will Manningham," said the redhead.

Handshakes all around.

Special Agent Penscal said, "Please, have a seat." She gestured toward a round conference table that was already so crowded that the generously-endowed Murphy moved his seat back to make room for the others.

"Mr. Sullivan," began Special Agent Adrienne Penscal, "thank you for coming in on short notice. We appreciate your suggesting that Dr. Simkowitz join you, and we are pleased that he was able to attend as well. If you've been talking with Dr. Pappelbaugh you know that we are already familiar with her. She has been most helpful."

"Thank you for inviting us, Special Agent Penscal. Dr. Simkowitz and I are both eager to hear what Dr. Pappelbaugh has to say."

"Certainly," said Special Agent Penscal. "I will ask her to repeat everything she has told us. But first, Dr. Simkowitz and Mr. Sullivan, I need each of you to acknowledge that you are here of your own accord and that you understand that you are not suspected of any crimes at this point and are entirely free to leave at any time. Should you become a suspect we will inform you and advise you of your rights. Is that clear?"

"Yes," they said in unison.

"OK, fine. Please proceed, Dr. Pappelbaugh."

Fran Pappelbaugh sat silent for a long minute, shuffling her water glass from hand to hand on the table. She sighed. "Mike, Sy, this is tough. You know me, I've never done *anything* like this before. I don't know how I got to this point. It's hard to believe and even harder to talk about."

Simkowitz and Sullivan nodded at her. Feeling sympathy for his dejected long-time colleague yet anxious over what she might be about to tell them, Simkowitz managed to say, "It's OK, Fran, take your time." Sullivan remained silent.

She stopped playing with the glass and said, "Thanks. I have to do this, and I have to do it right. I'm in this up to my armpits. Deeper, actually."

Fran spoke softly, as if telling the awful story quietly might somehow mitigate her culpability.

"Let's start with Eleanore Hinkel. Molly ordered me to create a misleading if technically accurate path report on the real appendix, and I went along. Then I provided phony tissue samples for the lawsuit."

Simkowitz choked back the anger that displaced any feeling of sympathy, thinking, *And you destroyed Jorge.* He said, "I suspected as much. I knew something had happened because Molly was about to have a meltdown when Sy said we would have to turn over the Hinkel woman's tissues and slides, but by the next morning she was her usual cocksure self. What happened to the real materials?"

"Molly ordered me to destroy everything and eliminate any trace of the real Eleanore Hinkel."

"So it's all gone?"

"No. I kept everything."

"You did?" Simkowitz' eyes widened with excitement. "Can we get our hands on it?"

"Yes, I sequestered it all in the old bank vault under the hospital."

"But Molly thinks you destroyed the slides and tissue samples?"

"Yes. I told her I had carried out her order."

"So why didn't you?"

"Sad to say, I was about to do it when I caught myself. I can't say I came to my senses, but at least I stopped. Destroying tissue samples was…well, it was just too much. I had written an ambiguous post-op pathology report, I had given Molly the fake samples, I was letting McDonald off the hook. Those were all terrible things that I had already done. But somehow I just couldn't bring myself to trash those slides and tissue samples. I couldn't take that last step. In some ways that seemed worse than everything else I had done. I'm not sure why, it just did. Maybe because those were pathology specimens and I'm a goddamn pathologist, that's my life's work. I don't know. I wasn't being a saint, though, it wasn't a real act of contrition. When I put the stuff in the vault I was simply leaving everything hidden where I figured it would sit in obscurity until…until, I don't know, until I got around to telling the truth, I guess. Just knowing the specimens were there I felt better. I sure as hell hated the idea of trashing that stuff, that's all I know for sure."

Suppressing his profound disappointment with Fran Pappelbaugh, Simkowitz said, "Well, at least you kept everything. If those materials show that Eleanore Hinkel did not have a ruptured appendix, that will bring down McDonald once and for all."

Sy Sullivan added, "Yes, and will surely resolve the Hinkel's lawsuit in their favor."

Turning to the others Simkowitz said, "I understand the FBI has uncovered other problems. What's that all about?"

"Yes," said Adrienne Penscal, "Eleanore Hinkel does not represent the extent of the problem by any means. Mr. Manningham ran extensive computer analyses and identified clusters of excessive deaths in your hospital."

"Deaths that I understand we never reported as being suspicious, right?"

"That's right, Mike," said Fran Pappelbaugh. "That's what Mr. Manningham and the FBI uncovered. Cavendish concealed everything, and I helped her. Freddy and I, we helped her. We covered them all up, we covered them up from everyone. You and everyone else, Mike."

Simkowitz stared at Fran, not out of surprise, his capacity for surprise having been exhausted several minutes earlier, but out of pure wonder.

Fran Pappelbaugh looked at Simkowitz and said, "We've never talked about my…my relationship with Freddy Grindel, Mike, but I'm sure you know all about it."

Simkowitz nodded. Sy Sullivan shut his eyes and shook his head slightly in dismay at being reminded of the scandalous behavior of two of the hospital's leading physicians.

"When Molly found out about me and Freddy, she blackmailed us, dragged us into something much worse than what I did with Eleanore Hinkel. It was her doing, but I went along. I have no one to blame but myself."

Simkowitz stared quizzically at Fran.

"Worse? How much worse could it be? We know what McDonald did, how Eleanore Hinkel died. Now we understand that you helped Molly cover it all up. What more could we possibly need to know?"

The frumpy pathologist was quiet, pensive. Once again she began shuffling the empty glass back and forth between her hands on the table. For a long moment the only sound in the room was the *tick-tick-tick* of the glass bouncing rhythmically off of her rings like the timer on a bomb. Then she stopped moving the glass, held it tight with the fingers of one hand and clawed at the tabletop with the stubby fingernails of her other hand. She looked up at Mike Simkowitz and Sy Sullivan and said gravely, "Listen up, my friends. What I have to tell you is not just about an unnecessary death from appendicitis, as bad as that is. Yes, that bastard McDonald lied about what caused Eleanore Hinkel's peritonitis and he should fry in Hell for that. But her peritonitis was...it was not just something McDonald messed up. The suture material that McDonald used was shoddy. It fails frequently, just like it did in Eleanore Hinkel's belly. Eleanore Hinkel is far from being the only post-op surgical patient who died unnecessarily. And that's not all, there's a lot more, and it's all bad. Very bad."

Mike Simkowitz was stunned by the words coming from his longtime colleague who had always seemed beyond reproach. What had she just said? *Shoddy suture material* in Northeast Suburban Hospital? How was that possible? And what could be even worse?

He leaned forward suddenly, not able to fully comprehend what she had just said. "What...what are you saying? What shoddy suture material? What the hell are you talking about? If that happened in the hospital, I would know..." His voice tailed off as he grasped the extent to which he had been kept in the dark. "I *should* know, anyway," he said, contemptuously, his voice rising as he bellowed, "Cavendish! It's Cavendish, right?"

"Yes, of course, it's her doing. We've had a growing string of patients with serious complications, deaths from what should have been relatively simple surgery or other routine medical problems. The hospital has a deadly crisis inside its walls, my friends." Her voice thickened in her throat. She paused, took a few sips from the water glass, and continued, "I can name all of them by heart. I covered up their deaths. And..."

Now her voice failed her completely. She put her face into her hands and wept violently.

Mike Simkowitz reached over to comfort her but she gently pushed his hand away. Finally she uttered, "Freddy…Freddy Grindel…and I helped. We helped Molly. She couldn't have done it without us, without me, the hospital's pathologist who examined the tissue samples and did the autopsies and wrote the bogus reports, and Freddy, the infectious disease specialist who took over all the cases that went south when the counterfeit antibiotics couldn't kill the germs festering in those patients. Dear Freddy, he worked desperately to save those patients without letting anyone else know what the problems really were. We put the patients in intensive care, we thought we could buy time by doing everything possible – short of telling the truth, of course. It was so difficult for poor Freddy to try to save them without their doctors or the nurses at their bedside or anyone else involved with the cases knowing what they were really dealing with. We worked night and day to get the situation under control but we couldn't do it by ourselves. I think that's what killed Freddy. Molly was covering it all up, and we went along. We're as dirty as Molly, that's the truth."

She stopped talking, her throat choking up as she thought of her lover Freddy's dying words: *"Tell them. Tell them. Stop it all."*

Simkowitz sat back in his chair, stunned. Even the self-contained lawyer Sullivan shook his head in disbelief.

Fran swallowed a mouthful of water, took a deep breath, then started reciting the litany of victims. As her throaty voice enumerated the victims she counted the names and diagnoses on her fingers: "Your lady, Eleanore Hinkel, her appendectomy should have been routine; young Lisa Altuno had a baby and needed an uncomplicated hysterectomy; poor Jonathan Peters, he had bilateral spermatoceles that posed no threat whatsoever to his life; Mandy Bellmont had early cancer and underwent a straightforward lumpectomy then died in the hospital on her wedding day; Felix Heinz, post-traumatic splenectomy after his truck crashed; Ariel Gould had an inguinal hernia like millions of men. They're dead, they're all dead."

"My god, Fran," said Mike Simkowitz. "None of them should have died."

"Exactly. And there are more, I could go on for ten or twenty minutes."

"This is horrendous. How…how could this happen? What was going on?"

"Brace yourself, Mike – it all started with McDonald. He's on the take from some goddamn medical supply and drug company. He gave Molly the idea of buying the damn sutures that failed in Eleanore Hinkel's case and lots of other devices and drugs that don't work. They're counterfeit, manufactured in countries where they don't care about U.S. standards. It's all part of a big international black market in counterfeit drugs and medical supplies. McDonald is tied into them somehow, he gets kickbacks and boondoggles, and they send us shit."

"Why? Why on earth would we buy stuff like that?"

"McDonald connected Molly with some company that operates out of Russia. When she found out they would charge us only a fraction of what legitimate supplies cost she went nuts, thought she could save lots of money. Then she manipulated the records, created two sets of books so the bills we sent to insurance companies looked like we were paying normal prices, and our profits went through the roof. But we're getting crap, all kinds of crap. Freddy and I fought her like hell but she was determined to stick to her deadly bargain, no matter what."

Simkowitz felt his face pulsating with anger. He shivered at the thought that if he had still been operating, he might have had patients die at his hands without ever knowing what was going on.

Fran Pappelbaugh continued, "Besides the sutures, I'm talking about pacemakers that stopped working and killed people, surgical staples that came loose, blood glucose strips that were totally unreliable, defective spinal implants and aortic pumps, polypropylene mesh that was not sterile, breast implants that leaked and triggered infections. Antibiotics that couldn't kill the germs they're supposed to target. The situation with the sutures got so bad I finally pressured Molly to stop buying them, but it was too late for a lot of patients like poor Mrs. Hinkel."

"All those deaths and this was never noticed? How is that possible?"

"I made it possible. I performed their autopsies and filed ambiguous reports. I gave them all death certificates with misleading causes of death. So not one of them got reported as an avoidable death, not a single one. We boasted about having zero hospital-acquired fatal illnesses and Molly wouldn't let anything smear that image. She got me to cover everything up. Freddy did what he could to treat the infections, but it was hopeless."

Sy Sullivan stared at Fran in disbelief, then said, "Can we prove what you're telling us? I mean really prove it, you know, in court?"

"Yes. I've already turned over samples of the real tissues from Eleanore Hinkel to the FBI."

Adrienne Penscal nodded in agreement.

Sullivan continued, "What about all the other cases?"

"It's all there. I have documentation of the lethal infections and device failures. All the evidence you'll need. Molly told me to destroy everything, but I didn't. Freddy and I, we kept it all."

"Where? Where do you have it?"

"Same place I stored Eleanore Hinkel's materials: in the old bank vault under the hospital."

"This is way beyond anything I could have imagined even Cavendish was capable of. This is callous disregard for human life. This is horrendous, it's like … like mass murder."

"I know, believe me, I know exactly what it amounts to. It's my job to know. This was all Molly's scheme, but the only one that the fingers will point at is me. There's nothing that could prove that anyone but me – and poor Freddy, of course – knew about this, nothing."

"What about McDonald?"

"OK, McDonald. Maybe there's enough to show McDonald's role. But for sure, not Molly. She covered her ass as always. She put all the arrangements in place so they'd look legitimate, so it would appear that the hospital was buying from approved suppliers. Freddy and I were the ones who were supposed to identify any problems. We told her countless times, we screamed about every patient who died or got hurt, but she would never let us put anything in writing. Nothing. When we open up our storehouse of the stuff we preserved in the vault it'll look like we were the ones who covered this up, not Molly. She'll claim she was never told anything about problems with the phony materials she was buying. We have nothing on her, she'll walk away."

She paused, but was not finished. With tears rolling down her fleshy cheeks she said, "Mike, Sy, I'm sorry, I'm so very sorry. I cannot describe how much I regret what I've done. I let you down, I let the hospital down, my profession, all those patients, I let everyone down. I deserve whatever punishment comes my way. I don't ask or expect you to forgive me, what I did was unforgiveable."

Neither man said a word but she could read the reproach on their faces.

"I know, I know. Freddy and I should have done something to stop it. Maybe we would have if Freddy hadn't died when he did. But we didn't. Molly was blackmailing us and we…we lost it, we were just idiotic. Sex makes people do crazy things, even at our age."

In a soft voice that belied her seemingly stern look, Special Agent Penscal said, "Thank you for coming forward, Dr. Pappelbaugh. We realize how difficult this must be for you, and we greatly appreciate your cooperation. Now, Dr. Simkowitz and Mr. Sullivan, I asked you here as a courtesy so you would hear directly from Dr. Pappelbaugh what she had revealed to us. I also want to give you a heads-up on our next steps. With Dr. Pappelbaugh's testimony and the materials from Eleanore Hinkel's autopsy that she provided we have obtained a search warrant and will be heading to the hospital at the conclusion of this meeting. Do you wish to ask any questions or have anything to add?"

Mike Simkowitz and Sy Sullivan exchanged glances, then Simkowitz spoke.

"Yes, thank you, Special Agent Penscal. I do have a reaction, a very strong reaction. Mr. Sullivan can speak for himself on this, but from my perspective we should proceed in a manner that will allow you to pursue Molly Cavendish. I am concerned that if you act precipitously she will never be held responsible. She is a nefarious, self-serving character who has gotten away with all kinds of bad things over the years. She has carried out personal vendettas that ruined careers. Her actions recently led to one of our staff becoming so distraught that he lost his bearings and had a tragic accident. I take Dr. Pappelbaugh at her word with respect to Ms. Cavendish's being at the center of this atrocity. But as she said, Cavendish is an expert at covering her tracks, keeping her fingerprints off of her despicable actions."

"I agree with Dr. Simkowitz about Ms. Cavendish," chimed in Sy Sullivan. "Unless she confesses, it will be very difficult to hold her accountable. The only people who have been privy to Ms. Cavendish's actions are Drs. Pappelbaugh and McDonald. And the late Dr. Grindel. I fear that if you execute the warrant without any evidence to corroborate Dr. Pappelbaugh's allegations, it will just be her word against Dr. Pappelbaugh's, or Dr. McDonald's. And I can assure you that Lester Williamsburg, the President and Chief

Executive Officer of Northeast Suburban Hospital, will take Ms. Cavendish's side, as he always has done. He will support her if he thinks he can get away with doing so."

"We are of course always interested in identifying and bringing down the mastermind behind criminal activities. Do you have a suggestion as to how we might gather evidence on Ms. Cavendish?" asked Special Agent Penscal.

"I have a thought," Simkowitz said with a self-deprecating smile. "It may be just a cockamamie scheme but since you asked, here goes: How about the FBI gets Dr. Pappelbaugh to wear a wire and confront Molly Cavendish?"

"Just like on television?"

"Just like on television."

Sullivan and Simkowitz again exchanged glances, then Sy Sullivan said, "I do not think that's such a cockamamie idea. I agree with Dr. Simkowitz and suggest you seriously consider planting a wire on Dr. Pappelbaugh and have her confront Ms. Cavendish."

"Very interesting proposal, gentlemen," Special Agent Penscal said. She thought for a few seconds, then added, "Mr. Manningham has documented extensive purchases by Northeast Suburban Hospital of drugs and medical devices from the *Marquis-Herrant* company. He has also traced numerous connections between Dr. McDonald and *Marquis-Herrant*, and Dr. McDonald's involvement in many of the suspicious deaths. His findings are entirely consistent with Dr. Pappelbaugh's description. But as you suggest, we have turned up no evidence linking Ms. Cavendish to any of this." Turning to Fran Pappelbaugh, she said, "Dr. Pappelbaugh, would you be willing to do as Mr. Sullivan and Dr. Simkowitz propose? Would you agree to have a conversation with Ms. Cavendish that would be recorded?"

"I'd *love* it, Special Agent Penscal!" she said, slamming her fist on the table with a sudden display of energy, her sea-turtle bug eyes popping open wider than Mike Simkowitz had ever seen.

"In that case, we will discuss this internally and let you know what our decision is."

Will Manningham chimed in. "Adrienne, I do have a thought that might affect your decision. We haven't discussed this here, but we know that the unexpected deaths connected with *Marquis-Herrant* are by no means limited to this one hospital. It sounds as though Ms.

Cavendish handled the business end of the deals. She may have information that would be helpful in our broader inquiry."

"Good thinking, Will. If we can turn her she might be quite useful in the broader inquiry. OK, if no one has anything else to add, please accept our thanks. In any case we will be in touch shortly."

Will Manningham breathed a sigh of relief. It seemed there would be no undercover mission for Sean Flaherty. He and Sara Flaherty could stay retired for now.

Chapter 32. Listening to Molly

"We're on, Mike." The palpable excitement in Fran Pappelbaugh's voice across the phone line gave Simkowitz a nervous thrill.

"Wow, that was fast. What's the plan?"

"They want to do it *tonight!* I need to get Molly to invite me into her office. The FBI agents will come over and set everything up."

"Nervous?"

"Not a bit! I just hope this works."

At seven o'clock that evening Fran Pappelbaugh, Sy Sullivan, Mike Simkowitz, the three FBI agents, Will Manningham, and an FBI technician gathered in Sullivan's large conference room. The technician inserted a device into one of the breast pockets of Pappelbaugh's dingy-white lab coat that looked like a ball-point pen but concealed a tiny microphone and transmitter. Then the tech added a similar-looking fake pen that held a voice-activated recorder with a capacity of up to four hours. "Dr. Pappelbaugh," said the technician, "please step into the inner room and carry on a normal conversation with Special Agent Trainor so I can test the transmission." The two women left the conference room, closed the door, and began speaking. Every word of their conversation came across with perfect clarity through a wireless speaker on the conference table.

The test a clear success, Tom Murphy fetched Pappelbaugh and Trainor back into the conference room. "OK," said Special Agent Penscal, "let's do this. Dr. Pappelbaugh, Ms. Cavendish is expecting you in her office, right?"

"Yes, at seven-thirty. I sure hope this works." She laughed when she heard her own voice echoing through the speaker.

"The electronics will," said Penscal. "Getting her to say something incriminating is up to you."

Fran Pappelbaugh took a deep breath, then smiled at Special Agent Penscal and said, "Yup, I hope I'm as good as those fancy devices." She gritted her teeth, stood up straight, and exited Sullivan's conference room for her meeting with Molly Cavendish with a look of grim determination on her face.

Now that they were actually about to carry out their plan, Sy Sullivan felt pressure building up in his chest, his breathing constricted like someone was tightening a corset around his ribcage. He was out of his element playing cops and robbers, frightened like a little boy. And his chest wasn't the only part of his body that was feeling pressure from the tense situation. Mike Simkowitz heard the normally staid lawyer curse under his breath, "I've got to pee. Damn my overgrown prostate."

"You don't have time, they're about to start," said Simkowitz.

"Not entirely under my control at my age. OK, I'll try to hold it for now."

The speaker broadcast the sound of Fran Pappelbaugh knocking on the door to Molly Cavendish's office and the gruff response, "Yeah?"

"It's Fran," came Pappelbaugh's voice, then the sounds of the door opening, footsteps, door closing, chairs moving.

"What is it you want, Fran,?" said Molly in her imperious style, not bothering to get up from her desk.

"Hi Molly. Mind if I have a seat?"

"Go ahead."

"We've got to talk."

"So, talk. Spit it out, I haven't got all night."

Fran cautioned herself to be patient. "I appreciate your letting me come here."

"Fine. Get on with it."

"It's the Hinkel matter."

"What about it?"

"As you know, I went along with your suggestion on her pathology report. I didn't mention the fact that her appendix was intact, that McDonald had lied."

"The report was in your words. You wrote that report, not me."

Fran strained to avoid letting her rage show. It wasn't going to be easy to trap Molly.

"You were pretty clear about what you wanted me to do. Sure, I went along, I agreed to say as little as possible. And you were happy with the result."

"What's your point?" Molly Cavendish asked, feeling her skin tingle. "Is something wrong?"

"The slides, the tissue samples, that's what's wrong."

"What about them?"

"The ones you had me put together to turn over to the experts for the Hinkels, those slides and samples."

"Yes?"

"There's a problem."

"What problem?"

"They know that stuff is not from Eleanore Hinkel."

Molly raised her eyes and glared at Fran, her voice sharp, angry. "What the fuck are you talking about? How could they know? What the hell went wrong?"

"Modern science, that's what happened. They're running DNA tests on the materials we sent over, and they're comparing the results with DNA from her sons. They'll be able to prove beyond a shadow of a doubt that they didn't come from Eleanore Hinkel."

Molly Cavendish felt her stomach twisting into a knot.

"DNA? Why the hell would they run DNA? Do they suspect anything? Did you tell them something? I'll burn your sorry ass if you said anything. You're the one who prepared the phony tissues and slides, not me." Molly was screaming now. "What the hell happened?"

"Remember what you told me to do with the real Hinkel slides?"

"Of course — you trashed them, right? You did, didn't you? You swore you would."

In the other office, two dramas were unfolding, one shared by everyone in the room, the other personal to Sy Sullivan. The entire clandestine audience was growing tense as they listened to Molly and Fran jousting back and forth about their horrific actions. Sullivan's bladder was creating a much higher level of tension just for him.

"Goddamn it, Molly, speak faster," Sullivan mouthed *sotto voce* at the speaker as the pangs of urgency increased with every second. Turning to Mike Simkowitz he whispered, "I can't stand this. I'm dying here. I've got to stay and listen, but I'm going to pee my pants if this goes on too long. I can't confront Molly with wet pants, goddamn it."

Simkowitz nodded, putting a finger to his lips and suppressing a smile.

Fran Pappelbaugh felt satisfied. Molly had taken her bait.

"Well, I had second thoughts about that, about destroying Eleanore Hinkel's slides," Fran said somberly.

"What the fuck are you talking about? You know those slides and shit had to go, we couldn't take the risk that someone would find them. They prove that the damn appendix wasn't ruptured, for god's sake."

"I did something that I thought would be just as good as destroying them."

"What? What could be as good as eliminating them forever?"

"I just couldn't bring myself to do what you wanted. I'm a pathologist after all, I needed to keep some shred of my professional dignity. So I stored the specimens in the old vault instead of trashing them. I figured no one would find them there for years and years, until long after we were gone."

Molly's pitch rose to panic levels.

"The vault? The fucking bank vault? You put them there instead of destroying them? Go get them, you stupid shit, before it's too late."

Fran remained calm, savoring her reply. "It *is* too late, Molly. I sent the original slides and tissues to Stephanie Sorano. It's over, done. She can prove that the phony stuff wasn't from Eleanore Hinkel, and that her appendix never ruptured."

Simkowitz felt a surge of smug satisfaction. He looked over at Sullivan and saw that the lawyer was experience no such pleasure. He had gone white, so pale that Simkowitz was afraid Sullivan was about to faint.

Sullivan said, "I've heard enough. Let's get this over with."

The FBI agents and Manningham looked inquiringly at Mike Simkowitz. But to Sullivan's dismay Simkowitz shook his head, saying, "Let's wait just a bit and see what else she has to say."

"Easy for you to wait!" said Sullivan, his bladder begging for relief.

Simkowitz nodded sympathetically but gave no sign he was ready to end things. "This isn't just about Eleanore Hinkel."

Adrienne Penscal agreed. "Yes, that's correct. We should wait."

Sullivan took a deep breath, then exhaled audibly. "OK, just for a minute."

Back in Molly Cavendish's office Fran Pappelbaugh continued as if she had taken a cue from Simkowitz and Penscal.

"What about everything else Freddy and I helped you cover up, all the junk you've been buying for medical devices? All the bootleg pharmaceuticals? What about all of that? That's all sure to come out once Sorano comes after us with proof that the Hinkel slides are phony."

"You're a goddamn idiot if you think anyone can pin those problems on me. You and Freddy have the only fingerprints on that shit. You're the ones who hid the warning signs that those damn devices and miserable drugs were failing. You're the one who handed over the phony specimens. You're the one who changed the lab reports. All my paperwork is in order. I made it look like all the right controls were in place. I kept my name out of all the arrangements with that *Marquis-Herrant* company."

"So…what? You're going to leave me twisting in the wind? I get myself into this because of you and now you're going to leave me with all the responsibility? That whole goddamn phony purchasing scheme was yours. You made me and Freddy cover it all up."

"Yeah, and it was all damn good for this hospital. We made a lot of money for this place buying those devices and drugs on the cheap. How was I supposed to know that some of them were fake and wouldn't work? All I knew was they were bootlegged into this country and dirt cheap."

"You knew damn well, Molly. Freddy and I told you over and over about the terrible problems we were seeing with patients. I think that stress was what killed him."

"Tough shit, it's a hospital, shit happens, people get complications and die. Once that crap started, I couldn't let this hospital look like a septic tank. We had to do something, and you went along with me in the cover up. Both of you. You can't even prove you ever documented any problems. You and Freddy never filed any written reports, you never followed all the procedures I put on the books. I can say I never saw anything."

Fran smiled, confident that Molly had made a full confession, that Sylvester Sullivan, Mike Simkowitz and the FBI agents would have had heard enough and that any second they would burst into the room.

In the other office Sy Sullivan was indeed satisfied with what he had heard. The inner Brahmin recaptured his persona as he pronounced his conclusion in his most elegant lawyerly style: "I believe we can stop now and proceed to confront Ms. Cavendish." He looked at the others and got nods of agreement all around. Adrienne Penscal stood up and said yes, "We're ready." Mike Simkowitz and the other FBI Agents stood and began to head toward the door. But Sullivan held up one finger to the group. "Just give me a quick minute first, please," he said as he headed for his private bathroom.

Fran Pappelbaugh sat silent, wondering why it was taking so long for the final act to begin. Were they on their way? Had she misjudged whether they had indeed heard enough? Did she need to prod more out of Molly? Did something go wrong with the microphone? Just as she was about to stall for more time, she was relieved to hear a loud pounding on the door to Molly's office.

Molly Cavendish reacted with an angry start.

"Who the hell is at the door?" she barked. Then, "Stay where you are, don't answer it," she screamed at Fran, who was rising and heading toward the door.

"I think your days of giving the orders are over, Molly," Fran said defiantly as she pulled the office door open.

"Hi Molly," Mike Simkowitz said with a broad smile, making no effort to contain his sense of triumph. He opened the door wide and led the small parade into the office.

"What the hell is this?" she gasped.

Molly Cavendish asked the question automatically as she rose from her chair, groping for something to say, but she needed no answer. She sensed what was happening as clearly as if a conga line of accusers had paraded into the office chanting *"Na-Na-Na-Na-Na-Na, You're Busted."* Simkowitz' haughty buoyancy irritated her, made her want to spit at the man she had so long trod upon, but her anger toward him withered suddenly when she turned and saw the look on Sy Sullivan's face. The lawyer's eyes were about to pop out of their sockets, his face deep violet, his jaw clenched so tight his teeth might crack any second. This was a new person to her, a man so full of rage and resentment that she stumbled backward to step out of his reach, to try to remove herself from his ominous aura.

"Ms. Cavendish," Sylvester Sullivan said from between his teeth, exerting every ounce of self-control he could muster to speak with the full authority of his position, "we have heard and documented your conversation with Dr. Pappelbaugh. As Vice President and General Counsel of this hospital, I am suspending you immediately from your position as Senior Vice President for your conduct in the case of Eleanore Hinkel. I am turning you over to these agents from the Federal Bureau of Investigation. You must leave these premises straight away and you may not return except to retrieve personal items, which you may do only in the presence of an official of this hospital at a mutually acceptable, pre-arranged time. You will receive written notice of the charges against you with respect to your position in the hospital, and you will have an opportunity to be heard at a later date, at which time you may be represented by counsel if you so choose."

"You...you can't do that, I'm Senior Vice President... I...What about *her*? She's the one, not me," Molly stammered, gesturing toward Fran Pappelbaugh. She struggled to defend herself, to retrieve control, but it was an empty effort. She knew she had been fatally exposed.

"I most certainly can relieve you of your authority, and I just did. What happens with Dr. Pappelbaugh is none of your concern. Your keys and hospital I.D., please, Ms. Cavendish." Then he delivered the *coup de grace,* savoring the words even as he spoke them with the greatest formality: "And your parking lot passcard."

Molly surrendered a janitor's-sized key chain, her photo I.D. and the precious VIP parking lot entry card to the lawyer one after the other. Then her astonishment and anger were suddenly swept under by a tidal wave of anxiety. "FBI? Did you say FBI?"

At that moment a woman in a blue suit stepped forward. "Ms Cavendish, I am FBI Special Agent Adrienne Penscal. You have the right to remain silent. Anything you say can and will be used against you in a court of law. You have the right to speak to an attorney, and to have an attorney present during any questioning. If you cannot afford an attorney, one will be provided. Do you have any questions? If not, please come with us."

"As for having an attorney, Ms. Cavendish," said Sy Sullivan, "I have one final word. Just to be clear, you must realize that I am acting on behalf of the hospital in this matter and I no longer represent you in any way. I strongly recommend that you seek independent legal counsel. Any inquiry you or your counsel would wish to make of the hospital in this matter should be directed to me."

Mike Simkowitz stood silent, savoring the moment, his back slightly arched, his arms folded on his chest in triumph. Fran Pappelbaugh collapsed into her chair, exhausted, knowing she would pay a steep price now that her deadly crimes were out in the open but relieved that she had finally been purged of her secret. Facing the consequences seemed less threatening than continuing to carry the weight of her offenses.

Sylvester Sullivan felt a deep sense of satisfaction at having finally severed his connection with Molly Cavendish. He stepped back and held the office door open, gesturing to Molly and her handlers to leave. Molly Cavendish kept her head down as she shuffled into the hallway in the company of the FBI agents.

Chapter 33. Awaiting Redemption

Lester Williamsburg pleaded with the Board of Directors to let him hang on to his position at Northeast Suburban despite Molly Cavendish's arrest by the FBI, but even his cronies realized they needed to sacrifice him to protect themselves. The big man was given the choice to resign and retire or get fired. The Board then considered what to do with Dr. Michael Simkowitz. A lengthy discussion ensued in which some members of the Board argued that Simkowitz should be held responsible for failing to deal adequately with Matthew McDonald over the years and for not realizing what Molly Cavendish and Fran Pappelbaugh had been doing. In the end the Board decided that Simkowitz had been boxed in by Cavendish and Williamsburg, and that in light of his many years of service to the hospital he should be given the opportunity to demonstrate what he could accomplish in a position of real authority. They voted to appoint him as Acting CEO, to be reviewed after six months.

After all those years of being under Molly's thumb, Simkowitz relished the feeling of real power. His first official action as CEO was to suspend Matthew McDonald while he prepared to revoke McDonald's hospital privileges once and for all. He also suspended Fran Pappelbaugh, who was stoic in accepting a fate she had brought on herself. Then, planning for a future in which doctors like Sandy Flowers and Nick Meier would be the leaders in Northeast Suburban, he restructured the position of Vice President for Medical Affairs to shift power back into the hands of the medical staff. Then he met with Sandy Flowers and asked her to assume that position.

But Simkowitz soon realized he could not take much pleasure in his new job. The grave threat to patients in Northeast Suburban was gnawing at him. More people could die, this time on his watch if he did not quickly purge the hospital of all of the defective medical devices and counterfeit drugs the hospital had in stock. And he would have to identify all the patients who might be walking around with a faulty medical device like a time bomb somewhere in their bodies. Simkowitz had no idea how long it would take to straighten things out or what disruptions it would cause. But it had to be done right away, even if it meant shutting down the hospital for a period of time and sending patients elsewhere.

One patient in particular consumed his thoughts. A darkness had passed into his life that would never disappear: Jorge Edmond lay in Northeast Suburban Hospital in a deep coma. The man was on the brink of death and Michael Simkowitz would forever feel that he had pushed him in front of that city bus.

Simkowitz visited Jorge every day, often coming into his room before going to his new office in the early morning, and always stopping by on his way home. From time to time he would find another visitor at Jorge's bedside: Jeffrey Hinkel. The two men rarely talked, usually just exchanging nods, sighing nearly in unison. What was going through Jeffrey Hinkel's mind he did not know and would not ask.

When he was alone with Jorge, Simkowitz would sit by the bedside and say, "It's over, Jorge, you've been vindicated. One hundred percent. You were very brave to take the risk of coming forward, and we owe you our gratitude. I am very proud of you, Jorge." Sometimes Simkowitz had a vision that Jorge would awaken and respond softly, *"So I can continue my work? Gracias a Dios. And thank you, Dr. Simkowitz, thank you so much, I am so happy. This means everything to me, Dr. Simkowitz, I cannot tell you how grateful I am."* For as long as the fantasy lasted it would fill Simkowitz with an indescribable sense of relief and lift the gloom in his heart like sunshine burning through fog.

But even as the dialogue played itself out over and over in his dreams and in his semi-consciousness, Simkowitz was condemned to wait helplessly to see if the scene would ever come to pass.

Chapter 34. Make Whole Relief

Henry Hinkel led his sons into the meeting room with an energy and air of authority they had not seen since long before their mother got sick. His frame had filled out with a few healthy pounds, the grief had gone out of his face, his dark brown herringbone suit was freshly cleaned and pressed, a stunning burgundy-and-gray striped tie was perfectly knotted over a crisply starched white shirt. Even the patchy strands of hair on his head looked thicker, fluffed up and combed into place. He was ready for whatever was coming.

"Good morning, Dr. Sorano. You said you have good news for us?" Henry Hinkel's steady voice was at once businesslike and gracious.

Roger was impressed with the way his father took control. The head of the family was back, he was himself again, just as he should be. His father's resurgence gave Roger a sense of relief, liberating him from the troubling burden of acting as the head of the family that had been imposed on him. He could let the elder man handle things now, he no longer had to be the point person for this messy affair.

Jeffrey was of two minds. Mostly, he wanted to retreat back into what was left of his life without his mother, to be surrounded by his antiques, to watch his flowers shoot up out of the ground and blossom. But this tragedy had brought a new closeness with his father and brother, a sharing and mutual support that he could not recall having known even in his childhood. Roger was like a different person, no longer so cold, so distant, the way he had been when Jeffrey had called to tell him about their mother's illness. He was like a real brother.

"Yes, under the tragic circumstances that your family has suffered, this is comparatively good news with respect to your legal case," began Stephanie Sorano. "We are dealing with both the hospital and Dr. McDonald's malpractice insurer. Let's start with the hospital. They have made an offer to settle your lawsuit that we need to discuss. Financially, my opinion is that it represents a starting point, a figure that we can work from, but I recognize that there are limits to their resources." She paused, then added with a note of foreboding, "There are other terms as well that you must consider."

"Please go on."

"First, the hospital is willing to pay five hundred thousand dollars to settle their role in the case. They will also reimburse all costs and my fees."

Roger Hinkel interjected, "Where would they get a number like that? We had asked for unspecified compensatory damages and punitive damages for the deliberate cover-up – those could have run into many millions of dollars."

"Most likely the five-hundred thousand represents the deductible on their liability insurance policy, which they would have to pay in any case. Also, they have probably considered what their legal defense costs might be if we pursue this case to trial and through a series of appeals. The hospital has two pots of money, if you will. First, they are self-insured for the first half-million dollars, which means they would have to pay that much out of their own resources before their insurance kicks in. Then their insurance would take over, but there are limits to the total amount their insurance will pay."

"And the other terms?" Henry Hinkel resumed control of the Hinkel side of the discussion.

"They will not admit any guilt, any wrongdoing, on the part of Dr. McDonald or the hospital itself."

"*Bastards!*"

The word shrieked through the room almost before Stephanie Sorano had finished, accompanied by an equally startling thud of a man's fist on the conference table. Once again a shrill outburst had come from Jeffrey Hinkel. The three of them gasped in unison as they turned toward him, momentarily speechless, waiting to hear what would follow.

"They killed her, they can't get away with just throwing a few dollars at us. It's not right, it's not fair, they have to be punished, someone has to take responsibility for what they did." He paused as suddenly as he had begun, then broke the silence again, his voice quaking as he said, "And they damn near killed Jorge Edmond."

A satisfied thought flashed through Roger's mind: when it came to anything involving their mother, Jeffrey would man up, he would get pissed off instead of breaking down, just like when he heard about that exhumation thing.

Nearly the identical thought occurred to Henry Hinkel, who was equally delighted at the show of angry strength from Jeffrey.

Stephanie Sorano regained her thoughts. "Yes, Mr. Jeffrey Hinkel, you have a very important point. But, Gentlemen, there's more that I need to tell you."

To their utter astonishment Stephanie Sorano recounted the scope of the drug and medical device scandal and cover up. Then, speaking calmly, dispassionately, she added, "One of the defective devices was the suture material that failed during your mother's surgery."

All three of the Hinkel men gasped, thunderstruck by this disclosure. She waited to see if any of them would start talking, asking questions, but they remained silent. She continued, "There will be numerous large suits from the other victims. No one knows as yet how many victims, how many lawsuits, but it's likely to go far beyond the hospital's total insurance coverage. Of course the other patients and families will also sue the company, *Marquis-Herrant*. But it's a shell corporation, a front for the Russian mob, so there's no hope of capturing any resources from it."

Jeffrey Hinkel stood and paced behind the table, but this time his words were spoken with grim determination, not shouted. "Goddamn them, they have to suffer like they made Mother suffer, like they've made all those families suffer."

"Mr. Hinkel, I know how you feel."

"I don't think so, Dr. Sorano."

"I'm sorry, I didn't speak properly, forgive me. You are certainly correct, yes. I do not know how you feel, of course not. I haven't lost a loved one as you have, Mr. Hinkel. But from my experience over the years I do have some idea of what you are going through. The one thing I would like you to keep in mind, though, is that just as I cannot ever fully appreciate how much grief this has caused all of you, the people who are responsible for these horrors will never feel the same pain as you do, either. There is nothing we can do that will hurt them the way all of you have been hurt."

"No, there isn't, you are right, Dr. Sorano," he said in a conciliatory voice. "But there must be something we can do to them, something more than just let them pay a few dollars and go on with business as usual."

"I believe there is, Mr. Hinkel, even though I am quite sure the hospital would never agree to acknowledge their responsibility, notwithstanding their change of leadership. An admission of guilt as part of a settlement would be most unusual. So, if you all decide that you want to insist on some kind of public pronouncement along those lines, you would need to be prepared to pursue going through a trial."

Roger Hinkel weighed in, agreeing with his classmate and onetime object of unrequited affection.

"Stephanie's right. I've never seen a corporate entity willing to admit wrongdoing under these circumstances – they see too many consequences down the road. They could compromise their defense of the other lawsuits, lose their license, there are too many risks. If we want full allocation of blame it would have to go to trial – and we might not win."

"So, let's discuss what we can do short of taking this to trial. We can start with the situation of Dr. Matthew McDonald," Stephanie Sorano said, turning a page in their discussion. "The DNA findings confirm that Mrs. Hinkel's appendix was not ruptured before the operation took place. There was a serious complication during surgery that drained bowel contents into her abdomen and led to her original peritonitis."

She paused to survey her audience, to see whether her stark description was overwhelming the Hinkel men or if they were able to focus on the facts, on their options.

"Is this too much, or may I continue?" she asked.

"We appreciate your concern for our feelings, Dr. Sorano. Please continue, we're all doing fine." The words came from Jeffrey Hinkel calmly, thoughtfully, as his brother and father nodded in agreement.

"Thank you, Mr. Hinkel. Dr. McDonald not only caused the problem that made Mrs. Hinkel so sick, but he lied. He fabricated the surgical report. As far as Dr. McDonald is concerned, we have achieved a degree of reckoning. He has been arrested and faces numerous civil and criminal charges for encouraging Cavendish to purchase the counterfeit drugs and products such as the substandard sutures that ultimately led to Mrs. Hinkel's demise. He is out on bail but has been suspended from the hospital and will very likely lose his medical license as well."

Roger Hinkel spoke up, feeling that he should make sure his father and brother understood the situation as well as he did. "Stephanie is right – that bastard McDonald is done for."

"Molly Cavendish and the pathologist, Dr. Pappelbaugh, are also facing civil and criminal charges for their role in the fraud." Sorano continued. "So the people responsible for this horrible situation will never be able to inflict tragedy on other families."

"That's all reassuring, Counselor," said Henry Hinkel. "In some small way we can take a bit of consolation that our dear Eleanore did not suffer and die in vain. But she is still gone."

"Yes, Mr. Hinkel, we cannot undo the harm that they wrought. The law speaks of '*make whole*' relief – getting enough money damages or protective court orders to make a person who has been injured whole. What you all are feeling, what you know all too well, is that the law cannot make anyone whole in a tragic situation like this, no matter how great the financial compensation. As you and Mr. Jeffrey Hinkel have reminded us, money, punishment, none of that really gives you what you would need to be made whole, which of course is that Eleanore Hinkel would still be alive with you. The law's remedies are always a distant second-best."

The Hinkel men nodded agreement, each of them reflecting on how empty the satisfaction would be from any settlement or judgment, no matter how large the sum.

"So let's consider what we can accomplish. We have to separate the money from the other relief we are seeking. Money first. We will get whatever we can out of the hospital, probably well above the $500,000 they have offered. But the Board of Trustees will know that if they were to approve a very large sum in our case they could set a target for the other suits that would risk putting the hospital out of business. That may well happen in any case. I know many of the people on that Board and they will demand a clear accounting of what took place here. Lester Williamsburg has been pressured to retire. Whether the hospital even survives is an open question at this point. So we need to push hard on the money and be aggressive with McDonald's insurer. The target will have to be well into the millions of dollars."

Henry Hinkel responded, a note of caution in his voice. "I fully appreciate what you are saying, Dr. Sorano, and I do not oppose that course of action, not at all. But it feels as though it would cheapen Eleanore's legacy if we seem only to be after some large amount of money. People in this community would not understand, they would see us as cashing in on her death, as harming their hospital and Dr. McDonald just to make a fortune."

Henry Hinkel was projecting from the ramifications he had seen following a high-dollar lawsuit in his hometown some years earlier. A number of families had endured horrific tragedies from the collapse of a balcony in a downtown hotel. When they later received large settlements, the once sympathetic local chit-chat turned vicious against them. They were vilified in countless conversations at the country club, the Rotary, even in their church groups. No matter that people might accept that the hospital and McDonald had done something awful, there would be a cloud of resentment and jealously. Henry was concerned that an enormous financial settlement would be viewed as a tainted windfall that would not bring honor to his wife, it would only turn her death into grist for common gossip about how the Hinkels had profited from her death.

"I have a suggestion."

Attention once again turned to Jeffrey Hinkel. This time he was speaking deliberately, thoughtfully, with a look in his eyes that signaled confidence in what he was about to say.

"I don't think any of us want this money for ourselves. I certainly don't, and I don't believe Dad, Roger or Sue Anne do either."

Henry and Roger Hinkel nodded in agreement.

"Let's establish a foundation in her name, the Eleanore Hinkel Foundation. It can be dedicated to things that were important to her, her volunteer work with the church or the homeless shelters or the Garden Society. We will announce that not one penny will go to us. We will not profit personally at all."

"Jeffrey – that's brilliant!" Roger Hinkel exploded in admiration for his brother. "What a great idea. The hospital will impose a nondisclosure provision on us as part of the settlement, so we won't be able to say what we think really happened, but that won't matter if we can speak about the good works that will come from her needless death. We can couch what we say in a way that will get the point across without violating any protective order. Brilliant, little brother, brilliant!"

Henry Hinkel joined in.

"I agree, Jeffrey. And I know your sister has no desire to profit from your mother's death. Good thinking, son."

"That is an outstanding suggestion, Mr. Hinkel," said Stephanie Sorano. "Roger is quite correct – I was just about to mention that we would likely be subject to a nondisclosure agreement, but there are always ways to make a point if you have the public's attention."

"Thank you, Dr. Sorano. Dad. Roger. Thank you all."

"That leads me quite nicely to my second point," Stephanie Sorano continued. "Even though the hospital is extremely unlikely to admit wrongdoing, we can pressure them to take corrective actions. It's a common part of such settlements to say something I can paraphrase as: *'We didn't do anything wrong, but we promise to stop doing it.'* We can force them to abide by a long list of measures to assure the safety of people in the hospital. Changes to prevent adverse events from happening in the first place and to catch them early and own up to them when they do occur. I am sure Mike Simkowitz would work with me to draft such a set of actions that we can insist on, and they will go along with them. That much we can do. We will also demand that there be ongoing monitoring by an independent entity of the hospital's compliance with the requirements we impose. So we will get rid of the scurrilous gang that is responsible for what happened, we will impose a wide range of patient safety measures, and we will honor Eleanore Hinkel's memory with a foundation in her name."

"One more thing, everyone, please," said Jeffrey Hinkel, his voice on the verge of breaking. "We should seek formal public recognition of Jorge Edmond's innocence and courage. Jorge is the hero here, his actions saved lives and ended a terrible crime. All at a dreadful cost. He deserves to be recognized for what he has done. He was brave, very brave. We must insist that the hospital honor him in some way and hold him harmless for any medical bills. The doctors say there is still a possibility he might recover and he deserves every chance. And, we should also obtain compensation for his family as well. Everyone agree?"

"Yes, of course," said Henry Hinkel, as Roger nodded his assent. "Thank you for thinking of Mr. Edmond, Jeffrey. You are absolutely right. We would never have known what really happened without him. Good for you, Son." Turning to Stephanie Sorano he continued, "Dr. Sorano, please do as Jeffrey suggested, include arrangements with respect to Jorge Edmond in our settlement demands."

"My pleasure, Mr. Hinkel. I completely agree."

"And thank you so much. You have been terrific to deal with – not that this has been pleasant for anyone, of course, but you have made it as tolerable as possible. I think you know I was not anxious to pursue a legal case, but now I am quite appreciative that you have brought this about. On behalf of all of us, and our dear Eleanore, we thank you."

"You are most welcome, Mr. Hinkel. All of you Misters Hinkel."

Stephanie Sorano had her own reasons to be grateful to the Hinkel family. Yes, there would be substantial legal fees that would further enhance her prominence at Vagram & Marin. But much more important, she had also achieved her own vindication. She was savoring her total victory over Matthew McDonald and Molly Cavendish. This felt good, so very good. Not enough to compensate for being forced to give up the medical profession she loved, never. Just as she had said to the Hinkels, "The law cannot make anyone whole, no matter how great the compensation." The damage was still there, it would never disappear. But the law can do a lot, and it felt good, damn good.

And, Stephanie Sorano wasn't quite finished.

"Roger," she said as the Hinkel family was leaving, "have you got a minute?"

"For you, Stephanie, of course. What's up?"

"It's been great getting back in touch. Maybe we won't go so many years between visits from now on."

Roger Hinkel wasn't quite sure just how to take Stephanie's overture – or even whether it was an overture or just a few random musical notes.

She reached into her soft leather case and pulled out an envelope.

"Stephan wanted me to be sure to say hello to you for him. He sent these for you, thought you might like to see them. These are from last summer."

She handed him several recent photos of herself and her twin brother in bathing suits on a beach somewhere. Roger immediately saw that Stephanie and Stephan Sorano no longer resembled one another in the way they had when they were younger, certainly not in the disconcerting way that had flummoxed him so long ago. Stephanie was still a beautiful, trim athletic woman, while her brother showed clear signs of wear and tear. He was also trim but not as athletic as his sister, his face criss-crossed with lines of aging, his hair still full but entirely gray and receding slightly. Stephanie and her twin brother were very different people now. Roger had a new picture of Stephan in his mind, a welcome image he would treasure. The disturbing old specter was forever expunged, there would be no more gender confusion when he looked at Stephanie.

"That was very thoughtful of Stephan," he said, his words carrying more meaning than Stephanie could understand. "Are you free for a drink? Dinner?"

***

Jeffrey Hinkel packed up his Jeep Wagoneer for his return trip to New Hampshire. He would be alone in his cabin with his memories of his mother, but that was his home now and he felt the urge to go back to the solitary life he had built there. Maybe his father would come to visit sometime, maybe he'd bring Sue Anne and the kids. Maybe even Roger.

This was it, time to leave. He'd come back twice each year to visit his mother, but for now he needed to go home. But he had one last stop to make.

The darkened hospital room was illuminated only by the greenish glow of the bedside monitors tracking Jorge's vital signs. Jeffrey entered and sat next to the big man and took his hand. Tears welled up in his eyes and cascaded down his cheeks as he thought how grateful he was to Jorge for having sacrificed so much to shed light on the atrocities that had been committed against his mother and so many other patients. Just before he was about to leave, he whispered, "Thank you, Jorge, thank you so much. God be with you, my dear friend."

In the dim light, Jeffrey could not be sure, but he thought he saw a faint smile appear on Jorge's face.

Chapter 35. Self-inflicted Wounds

In the ensuing months it turned out that cracking the case at Northeast Suburban did set the stage for dismantling the *Marquis-Herrant* shell company and its network of Russian detail reps. Bringing down the deadly scheme was gratifying to Will Manningham, but he was haunted by unfinished business: once again he had failed to capture the big bosses. He was convinced that the kingpins behind the *Marquis-Herrant* scheme were the same Russians who had profited from the earlier scam that had destroyed his mother and wreaked horrors on countless others with savage cruelty. The same mob leaders who had ordered his assassination and murdered his twin brother, Barry, by mistake. The crime lords behind the gang that had kidnapped, beaten and nearly killed Sally. Will took limited solace in knowing that the Americans who had conspired with the Russians were serving long prison sentences and the Russian minions were all dead, executed by the bosses or brought down by FBI gunfire. What gnawed at him was knowing that the troika that ran the mob had still eluded him. He could not rest until he had tracked them down and set the wheels in motion to punish them.

Will knew full well that the corrupt Russian regime would never prosecute or even extradite three wealthy oligarchs to face trial in the U.S. no matter how evil their crimes. But he hoped that maybe our government or other countries could break up their financial networks, cut off their access to markets and capital, isolate them with travel restrictions. And maybe if they were stripped of their power to infiltrate legitimate businesses and bring home hard currency they would fall out of favor with the Kremlin, be scapegoated and punished in some face-saving charade to placate the international business community. Maybe. It was worth a shot. He owed it to Barry, to Sally, to his mother, to all the innocent victims who had suffered at their hands.

An idea was brewing inside Will: maybe he could track down the elusive ringleaders through the *Marquis-Herrant* operation. Alexandra Parushnikova and the other detail reps had to be their agents. If he could unravel the right information on *Marquis-Herrant* perhaps the trail would lead back to Moscow. He had to delve deeper, explore everything he could find on *Marquis-Herrant*, follow the money all the way to the big bosses.

Will's first thought was to figure out how all the deadly devices from *Marquis-Herrant* had passed inspection and gotten onto the market in the U.S. The scheme had the foul stench of Russian incursion into the U.S. government. He suspected that the detail reps weren't the only Russians working for the mob in the U.S. Maybe the Russians had infiltrated the FDA just like they had planted agents in the Centers for Medicare and Medicaid Services to carry out the scheme that got Barry killed. He didn't know how the government's review process for medical devices worked but he assumed that a new company like *Marquis-Herrant* would have to submit their products for review by the FDA before it could start selling sutures, pacemakers, heart valves or any other devices. After all, he assured himself, the Food and Drug Administration was there to protect the public from defective devices and deadly drugs like the ones that company had been selling, wasn't it? He decided to look for Russian fingerprints in the U.S. government.

But where should he look? He more or less understood that prescription drugs went through extensive testing but he had no idea what happened with medical devices. This would be a fishing expedition without a clue as to what creatures were swimming in the FDA waters. But he was sure there had to be extensive information on the company and their products somewhere inside the Agency. He figured that the FDA must have collected samples of the devices and tested them in their laboratories. Those records would give him a clue as to how the fake ones slipped through and would lead him to the Russian operatives he suspected were hiding in the Agency.

Excited by the prospect of tracking back through the records of the FDA to the people responsible for the *Marquis-Herrant* scam, Will felt a burst of creative energy. His fingers flew across his keyboard as he constructed a computer program to search for information on counterfeit medical devices in the FDA archives. He created a list of search terms like "counterfeit," "phony," "fraudulent," and "fake," not at all sure if anything would come up. Then he added words such as "deadly," "dangerous," "toxic," "hazardous," and "unsafe." Finally, he had one more thought: he would also look for any medical devices that had been recalled by the Agency. With his FBI credentials he had no problem logging into the FDA computers. Soon his program was churning through the Agency's files on tens of thousands of medical devices dating back to 1976.

Will passed a few tense minutes in stony silence as the electronic brains connected their artificial synapses. He grew anxious wondering whether he would find anything useful or just random garbage. After all, the Russian kingpins were no dummies, they had escaped from him before, why did he think they would leave a trail for him to follow this time? And since he knew nothing about the records the FDA had on medical devices this could easily end up being a dead end.

Just as he began to think that his latest brainstorm was really a dud, his monitor lit up as his computer program started spitting out line after line of defective medical devices. All the ones that Fran Pappelbaugh had described and many more. Simple ones like stethoscopes, sphygmomanometers to measure blood pressure, digital thermometers, bandages and gauze pads, medical stockings. Pregnancy test kits. Contact lenses. Syringes, needles, and pumps. Diabetic test strips. More sophisticated devices that burned and disfigured patients or even killed them when they failed. Blood glucose monitors, intra-aortic pumps, spinal implants, lasers. Implantable defibrillators that randomly shocked people into grand mal seizures. Surgical mesh, plates and screws that cut tissues and caused infections. Artificial joints that caused heavy metal poisoning.

Amid the clutter of information, one item caught his eyes: the deadly sutures from *Marquis-Herrant* that were too shoddy to hold tissues together and had killed Eleanore Hinkel. Will's stomach went queasy, as though someone had kicked him in the belly. Bile surged up into his mouth, starbursts exploded in front of his eyes. He could feel his heart pounding, his face flushing as red as his hair. He leaned back, twisted open a bottle of water and swallowed hard, then took several deep breaths.

Will rubbed his right hand over his eyes and wiped his fingers up and down his face. He was stunned. File after file of dangerous medical equipment and supplies that had been allowed to get into people's bodies. How was this possible? Discovering that a handful of counterfeit products from *Marquis-Herrant* had slipped past the FDA and onto the market, OK, maybe that he could understand. A few Russians in key positions could have gotten away with sneaking through a trickle of fake devices. But what he was seeing told him that *Marquis-Herrant* was not alone – defective devices had come from a wide range of manufacturers, big and small, foreign and domestic. But how could they all manage to bypass the FDA's controls on such a massive scale? Why hadn't the FDA spotted them before they got approved? What was going on in the FDA's testing labs? Weren't the FDA's scientists running the right tests? Russian agents couldn't occupy every key position in the Agency, could they? Was everyone in the FDA corrupt or asleep at the wheel?

When he finally regained his bearings, Will realized he needed to understand how the FDA regulated medical devices far better than he did. He had assumed all along that the controls on devices would be similar to those for drugs, that devices would have to go through years of extensive testing to convince the FDA that they were safe and effective before they could be prescribed and sold. Russian agents could have short-circuited the legitimate testing process and gotten their devices approved by fabricating successful test results or concealing negative ones. But not to this extent, that couldn't be possible. Something else had to be going on inside the FDA that let so many dangerous devices onto the market. *Marquis-Herrant* and other companies must have figured out how to manipulate the system.

Staggered by the sheer number of defective devices being sold in this country Will did something he realized he should have done far sooner: he went back to square one and searched for basic information on how the FDA system was designed to work.

Will didn't have to create a new computer program – a simple internet search led him directly to the information he needed. And what he found was as stunning as the endless list of counterfeit devices he had just discovered: the internet was filled with years and years of complaints from scientists and consumer groups that, unlike its rigorous controls on prescription drugs, the FDA exercised very limited authority overseeing medical devices.

The story was clear: no matter how sophisticated or potentially deadly, the vast majority of devices never went through a formal review to determine whether they were safe and effective. Lobbyists for the medical device industry had gotten the Congress to create a gigantic loophole in the law: all the manufacturer had to do was notify the FDA that they were going to sell a device and assert that their product was substantially equivalent to something that was already being used. Most of the time the new devices were being compared to old ones that had never been shown to be safe and effective. Unproven old devices begat unproven new devices. That was all it took for most of the new products to appear on the market, where the detail reps would push them on doctors and hospitals. Only a handful of medical items were subjected to pre-market testing and review. But even then the FDA did none of the testing itself, it relied entirely on information from the manufacturer. Even more disconcerting to Will, the reviews were entirely on paper. FDA scientists and analysts never got their hands on the devices – all they saw were written descriptions and diagrams and summaries of the tests. No mock-ups, no prototypes, nothing.

Will was dispirited, defeated at the very moment he had hoped would lead him to the mob bosses. His search was at a dead end practically before it had begun. He would find nothing useful in the FDA to trace back to Moscow. The wound was self-inflicted by our own government. The U.S. had made it painfully simple for dangerous counterfeit devices to find their way into people's bodies. The Russians didn't need to plant agents in the FDA, all they had to do to get their fake devices on the market was to exploit the loophole in the law. Then, once the products were for sale in this country, the only thing that mattered was marketing them to doctors, a simple task for clever detail reps like Alexandra Parushnikova.

Will slunk down in his chair, crestfallen at having been stymied yet again. His mind went blank for several minutes. At last he sat up and pounded his fist on his desktop. He could not stop, he could not let this setback keep him from fulfilling his vow to avenge his mother, his brother, his wife. Someday he would track down the big kahunas, roust them out of their dachas on the Black

Sea or wherever they were indulging themselves with their ill-gotten fortunes, make them pay for their crimes.

Someday.

Acknowledgements

I am continually inspired by and filled with gratitude and affection for those of my fellow physicians who remain steadfast in their dedication to safeguarding the health of their patients even as the medical corporate enterprise engulfs them and corrupt elements seek to infiltrate and despoil the medical profession.

I deeply appreciate the assistance and encouragement generously provided by so many of my friends and colleagues. I am particularly grateful to my wife, Ta, for her careful proof-reading and creative suggestions.

All shortcomings in this novel are my sole responsibility.

Thank you all.

About the author

Physician, lawyer, scholar, and longtime Washington insider Dr. Peter Budetti was recruited by President Obama's Administration to modernize the government's antifraud efforts in the Centers for Medicare and Medicaid Services. As he oversaw the development of innovative systems using advanced technology to detect and prevent fraud, Dr. Budetti became known as the *Healthcare Antifraud Czar*.

Since leaving CMS, Dr. Budetti is *Of Counsel* to Phillips and Cohen, LLP, the nation's most successful law firm representing whistleblowers. Prior to his years at CMS, Dr. Budetti held senior positions in government and academe. He is the author of numerous articles published in medical and public health journals as well as three novels: *Deadly Bargain, Hemorrhage,* and *Resuscitated.*

Dr. Budetti received his undergraduate degree from the University of Notre Dame, his medical degree from Columbia University College of Physicians and Surgeons and his law degree from the University of California Berkeley Law (Boalt Hall). He trained and was board-certified in pediatrics and is a member of the California and District of Columbia Bars. He is married, has two grown children, seven grandchildren, and a Pekingese-mix doggy. Dr. Budetti and his wife live in Kansas City, Missouri, and spend as much time as possible at their lakehouse in Arkansas.